THE ZOMBIES OF
LAKE WOEBEGOTTEN

THE ZOMBIES OF
LAKE WOEBEGOTTEN

HARRISON GEILLOR

NIGHT SHADE BOOKS
SAN FRANCISCO

Certified Chain of Custody
Promoting Sustainable
Forest Management
www.sfiprogram.org
PwC-SFICOC-272

SUSTAINABLE
FORESTRY
INITIATIVE

First Edition

ISBN: 978-1-59780-196-6

Printed in Canada

Night Shade Books
http://www.nightshadebooks.com

Let us beware of saying that death is the opposite of life. The living being is only a species of the dead, and a very rare species.

—Friedrich Nietzsche, author and philosopher

I think the most un-American thing you can say is, "You can't say that."

—Garrison Keillor, author, philosopher, and radio personality

A NOTE TO VISITORS

Lake Woebegotten, Minnesota has changed a bit since the end of the world, of course, but in matters historical and geographical, and to some extent cultural, things are pretty much as they've always been. The town is situated near Gahan Hill on the eastern shore of the lake that lends the town its name, a lake that amounts to about 700 acres of water—depending on how you count some of the slushy marshy parts that are half land and half liquid around the southern side—and if you're not from farm country and don't know how much an acre is, 770 acres is a little over one square mile (though the lake is more blobby oval than square), and if you don't know how much a square mile is, I'm not sure how much we can help you here, you might want to start with some other book instead.

The name of the town (altitude 1420, population 1,056 as of the 2000 census, though that's not too accurate anymore, as you might imagine) comes from the mispronunciation and subsequent Anglicization of an Ojibwe phrase that means either "Well who would have thought?" or "Some weather we're having, huh?" though the name as it stands now isn't entirely inappropriate for most of the residents, even if "woebegotten" is a little too highfalutin' and overdramatic a word for the descendants of Norwegian Lutherans and German Catholics, each group mostly a stoic and occasionally dour bunch in different ways.

("Woebegotten" is a pretty woebegotten word itself, being a not-entirely-real word that people come out with when they mean to say "woebegone" or "misbegotten" or something similar instead. Still, like "irregardless" and "ain't" and other such linguistic volunteers, the word seems to fill a niche, and most of the dictionaries in the schools hereabouts have the word scribbled in between "woebegone" and "woeful" just as a show of civic pride.)

Lake Woebegotten was first settled in the 1840s by members of a Utopian society that believed, among other things, that physical discomfort due to temperature, hunger, or sickness were indicative of spiritual shortcomings and best treated by fasting and contemplation of the infinite, so they were pretty much all dead by the middle of the first winter. They'd dug a few wells and tilled a few fields, though, which as existing infrastructure made the spot attractive to a couple of groups of weary settlers who found themselves daunted by the prospect of traversing all the vast prairie that started at the edge of town. The soil was stony but the fishing was good, and there was a lot of timber in the form of birch, alder, red oak, and miscellaneous scrub, so they mostly shrugged, said "Good enough," and put down their roots, pastured out the cows, slopped the hogs, and started growing oats, alfalfa, corn, and wheat. White clapboard houses popped up, and shops on Main Street, and a couple of churches, and eventually a stoplight. A sand and gravel pit or two appeared, as did grain silos, a bandshell in the park, and a baseball field. Progress progressed, but only to a certain point, nothing to get too worked up about.

It's still a one-stoplight town, and most of the kids who grew up here and moved away as soon as they were able agree that Lake Woebegotten is a nice enough place to be from.

Given what happened here, but happened even worse everywhere else, some of them probably wish they'd stayed.

DAY ONE:
NOT TOO GOOD A DAY, REALLY, OVERALL

1. FISH ICING

The winter the zombies came to Lake Woebegotten (and everywhere else on the planet, too, of course, but let's not overreach here, knowing your limitations is one of the first steps towards having a life that's not as miserable as it might be otherwise), Gunther Montcrief woke up in the deepest darkest coldest part of the night with a powerful need to urinate, and sat up in his old fish shack with the cracks in the walls stuffed with the crumpled pages from phone books while the wind whistled through the holes he'd missed and his little stove radiated weak heat and the cot springs creaked under him, and he thought about how terrible it was to get old, except being old and alive was better than all the alternatives, which were pretty grim if you dwelled on them, so better if you didn't. Could be worse, after all, could be worse. Still, the time was he could drink like a fish or a sailor and go to bed and sleep straight through the night and get up in the morning and let loose with a stream that sounded like a roaring river as it hit the toilet bowl and then go out to the bar and do it all over again, but since he hit sixty or so he'd developed what the fellas down at the Backtrack Bar called a girlie bladder and it seemed like he had to pee about fifteen minutes after every time he took in a tablespoon of liquid. He thought about just picking a corner of the shack to let fly, but since he barely had room to turn around in here, it didn't seem like a good idea to make it any smellier than it already was, and the smell of piss had a way of cutting right through the smells of wood smoke and fish and old sweaty boots and moist coats and making its presence known. He also considered taking a slug from the nice big bottle of bourbon he had tucked in cozy next to his cot, but the thought of pouring even another drop into his bursting bladder was too horrible to contemplate, maybe even as bad as facing down a plate of lutefisk or trying to repair a foreign car where everything was in metric. So he pulled on his boots over his thick socks and wrapped his big blanket around his long underwear and opened the door to the shack and, yup, that was winter out there, the ice on the lake shining under the moon and starlight, but even though the end of his nose went numb right away it wasn't as cold as the first time he went fishing with his father as a boy, the coldest winter on record hereabouts, when your ears would pretty much just turn to ice and snap right off as soon as you poked your head outside.

Gunther crunched a couple of steps away from the door, the top layer of snow turned into a hard shell of ice, and pulled open the flap of his long underwear, an ice wind taking that opportunity to swoop in and freeze his nethers. He went ahead and did his business, steam rising up from the snow, and thought about the story his father used to tell about his old friend Johnny who went outside to pee one night and got caught in a sudden cold snap, and they found him the next morning frozen through-and-through like an ice cube, his urine frozen too in mid-stream still attached to him, so he looked like a statue or maybe more like an obscene kind of sculptural fountain like they might have in San Francisco, which Gunther's father always without fail called SanSodom FranciscoGomorrah, though he got a wistful faraway look too when he talked about the times he'd been on leave there during the war, as if for a den of relentless iniquity it hadn't been so bad.

It wasn't that cold tonight, not even so cold that your piss froze partway down and hit the ice at your feet with a tinkle, but it was cold enough. Gunther started to put himself away and hotfoot it back to the relative coziness of his little wooden shack on the shore when the sky overhead lit up brighter than noontime, and he shaded his eyes and tilted back his head and there in the great black sky was the biggest fireball he'd ever seen, and he'd seen the every-hundred-fifty-years return of the Whimsy-McKennit comet. This was a streaking meteor that was either the size of a house and up very close or the size of a Midwestern state and very far away, and Gunther felt a dark thrill of satisfaction that the world wouldn't survive him after all, that it didn't much matter if he was the last of the Montcriefs, since this was the dinosaur-killer-sized space rock Hollywood had been trying to scare people with for the last bunch of years. Gunther wondered if it would be earthquakes or tsunamis or volcanoes and then wondered if the people in Lake Woebegotten, deep in central Minnesota away from the dangerous coastlines, would even notice the end of the world, apart from the ones who'd lose their satellite TV reception and their ability to order shoes off the internet. Maybe there'd be killer tornadoes as tall as skyscrapers. It was a thought—

But then the meteor exploded silently into dust, pretty much, tiny cinders no bigger than fireflies drifting down, and off on the distant horizon he could see faint glows, and he wondered if this was only one of a bunch of falling meteors, like the giant flaming rock he'd seen above him was just itself a tiny fragment of something much larger, chopped into seemingly infinite pieces like slivers of a holiday fruitcake when you finally couldn't put off eating it anymore and had to go ahead and be polite. With that big light gone Gunther couldn't see much of anything, his night vision blown, so he stood there in the snow and thought about the end of the world, which maybe wasn't tonight after all, but which anybody with any sense had to realize was long overdue. He went shuffling back toward his shack and heard a strange thumping, and paused in the doorway, but it was too cold for caution and he was letting all the heat out. He pulled the door to behind him and waited a minute for his eyes to get adjusted to the dim and saw his big red-and-white cooler shaking and shuddering and twitching like one of those Mexican jumping beans that had a worm inside and that you really shouldn't eat, as he'd learned as a boy to his dismay.

He went over to the cooler, wondering if maybe a raccoon had somehow gotten in to go after his walleye catch and then been trapped inside, which seemed unlikely, but then most everything did when you thought about it. Gunther popped open the latch and lifted the lid and a dead walleye flopped up over the edge of the cooler and Gunther sat down on his ass hard and it hurt and he started laughing and then just as suddenly he stopped. Turning on his little battery-powered lantern he could see the four good-sized walleye he'd caught, but hadn't yet cleaned, jumping and flapping and jerking around, their ugly mouths full of little sharp teeth working furiously. Looked like they were trying to eat each other and making some good progress, with chunks of scale and flesh missing out of most of them. Gunther had never known fish to come back to life several hours after death and turn to cannibalism but then he wasn't some kind of expert, was he, and since it was happening, that meant it was just something that sometimes happened. Probably had to do with pollution. He grabbed one walleye by the tail and flopped it down on the floor of the shack, where it twitched and twisted and snapped at him until he put his boot down on its side and held it still. After some awkward rummaging around and leaning as far as he could without letting his foot up he found his hatchet and squatted down and aimed a chop just behind the fish's head, but the angle was awkward and it took a few blows before the head was entirely separated. Head removal stopped most things from doing much of anything, in his experience, but it didn't seem to make much difference to this walleye. The body stopped twitching but the mouth kept opening and closing even though anything it ate now would just fall right out the back of its head. Gunther grunted and thought about how chickens run around with their heads cut off and how cockroaches can get by just fine without their heads and thought this must be something similar, and even though he'd never seen the like before, well so what, there was nothing new under the sun and he wasn't so full of himself that he thought he'd seen everything.

He took off the heads of the rest of the fish until all four heads were on the floor together snapping at each other, then he sighed and scooped them up in the blade of his shovel and kicked open the door and ran with the shovel full of heads out in front him like he was in a spoon-and-egg race with a shovel instead of a spoon and fish heads instead of an egg until he reached the hole he'd dug for fishing earlier, which was slushed-over and on its way to being frozen again. He dumped the fish heads in the depression and banged down the shovel a few times until he made a hole and then pushed the heads in and watched them sink.

Back in his shack, warmed up with a big gulp of bourbon even though he knew it would send him back to pee again before first light, he curled up in his blanket and thought about falling stars and when he dreamed, he dreamed of fish heads sinking forever down in dark water, mouths opening and closing, opening and closing, chewing up everything they passed, which it seemed to him in his dream was pretty much everything there was in the world.

2. ZOMBIE WALK

Ingvar Knudsen and Otto Tofte were sipping coffee at the counter in Cafe Lo (the sign out front read Cafe Loquacious, but if you went ahead and said all that you were just putting on airs, and might as well go around wearing Italian leather shoes and driving a red convertible car and thinking you were better than everybody else). They were both looking up at the new flat-screen TV above the counter, which was a controversial addition to the diner. There was a television mounted on the wall in Backtrack Bar where you could watch Twins games and the like, and that seemed right and proper, and even if it was an old screen that gave an orange tint to everything, well who cared, baseball was still baseball even if the ball was orange. Baseball belonged in a bar just as much as beer and whiskey and pickled eggs and holding your nose when you went into the bathroom. But at a diner it seemed like you ought to be alone with your thoughts along with your coffee and maybe a newspaper spread out on the counter, so there was a bit of grumbling when the owner's granddaughter Julie Olafson put in a new shiny flat-screen TV when she moved back home after years away and took over after the old man had a stroke, poor fella, and him so hale and hearty up until then. Julie compromised by keeping the sound turned down, but the picture on, and just now the TV was showing a shaky handheld camera view of lurching bloody men and women staggering slowly down a city street, arms outstretched. One passed close by the camera and he had one eye hanging out of his head like a yo-yo at the end of a string.

Otto grunted. "What's all that then."

"That's something," Ingvar said. "Could be for Hallowe'en, you think."

"Could be," Otto allowed. "Closer to Christmas now, though."

"You bet."

"What it is, I bet," Otto said. "Is one of those zombie walks."

"Oh yeah?"

"Oh yeah."

Ingvar looked into his coffee cup for a long time. "What's that all about then?"

"My nephew Rufus, you know Glenda's boy?"

"Used to play first base for the Martens at the high school, had a good arm. Got himself a scholarship, that right?"

"Up to a college in the cities," Otto said. "Fell in with a wrong crowd. Got a tattoo of a spiderweb on his neck."

Ingvar grunted. "Not something you see every day."

"Broke his mother's heart. He did one of those zombie walks. Everybody dresses up like they're dead, with make-up and all, and go in a big crowd down the street, talking about brains and such. Like a parade."

"So that's fun then. Never see something like that in a parade here."

"I guess," Otto said. "Except for the Pretty Good Brotherhood of Cnut. They lurch along pretty slow in the fourth of July parade."

"They have those swords though. And the Viking helmets with the horns."

"They say it takes all kinds, but I don't know." Otto took a sip of coffee and glanced back at the screen. The zombies were gone, and a couple of shiny-haired newspeople were talking with serious looks on their faces, and there was some kind of text crawling across the bottom of the screen, but Otto couldn't make it out because he'd left his glasses in the truck. He was only forty-two and never needed glasses before and while he'd let Barbara convince him to wear them for driving after he nearly ran down the Munck boy he wasn't about to go around in public, not with those frames Barbara picked out. They were blue and kinda square-looking. Who did she think he was, some kind of rock and roll star?

The screen switched to some kind of star map and Otto figured they were talking about the big meteor shower last night. The sky lit up enough to wake him but not Barbara, who could probably sleep through the end times and the Rapture and a four-piece swing band set up right in her nightstand, because who could hear anything over her snoring anyway? Otto had gone to the window but by then the big light was gone and it was just a bunch of shooting stars, pretty enough but what it came down to was rocks falling out the sky and that wasn't much good to anybody so he went back to bed.

Julie came in from the back and topped up their coffee. She was a pretty girl in her early thirties with ice-blue eyes and an aggressive chest that she pointed at you to make you tip more than was healthy or necessary, and Otto tried not to notice how tight her waitress uniform was, though he half-thought it was on purpose. "Heard on the radio this morning about some kind of riot in the Cities," she said.

"Ish," Ingvar said. He was seventy and looked a hundred, and even though he wore patched bib overalls everybody knew he was sitting pretty, having turned his already-successful family farm into an even more lucrative sand and gravel quarry. Otto didn't think it was right shipping off so much of the town's land, since land wasn't something you could get back, but Ingvar'd bought a new scoreboard for the high school baseball team so you couldn't say he wasn't generous, though he could've tried a little harder to be anonymous about it. Just asking for the gift to be anonymous wasn't enough. Word got around. Made people uncomfortable to be around him, since you were afraid he might be afraid you might ask him for money, as if you would, that'd be the day.

"Everybody's always upset about something." Otto sipped the coffee, which wasn't as good as in the days when Julie's grandfather did the brewing, but it was hot, and since winter was just getting underway hot was the important thing. "Probably too many people trying to get a talking muppet doll for their kids, that kind of thing, people forget the true meaning of the holidays."

"It'll blow over soon, whatever it is," Julie said. "Too cold to be out on the street making a fuss anyway."

"Yep." Ingvar hunched a little more over his coffee as if to warm himself, probably thinking of that big, cold, empty farm-house of his out on the edge of the prairie, his children moved away, wife dead these fifteen years, and all his farmland trans-formed into pretty much a great big hole in the ground where there used to be gravel and where there was, now, just empty space and some iced-up black water. Otto was a farm equipment salesman, not a farmer himself, but he knew it took a special kind of used-up old and tired to turn your back on the land that had sustained your family for generations and let a company come in and rip the land up to spread on driveways and road projects. Ingvar might have gotten a little richer out of the deal but Otto wondered what he did with himself all day now.

The bell over the door jingled, and Otto hunched instinctively against the blast of winter cold that came bursting into the diner. He wasn't about to spin around on his stool to see who'd come in, but the look on Julie's face was enough to make him twist a little and glance back, casually, as if just checking to see what the weather was doing.

His nephew Rufus stood in the doorway, winter coat unzipped and spilling feathers from a long tear in the sleeve, shirt torn half off, hair and eyes wild. Nobody said anything, until finally Julie said, "Get you something?"

"I can't believe you're just sitting here," Rufus said in that tone he had, the one that broke his poor mother's heart, like everybody around him was dumb as a bunch of chickens and he couldn't bear their company. "Haven't you—haven't you watched the news?"

"Heard there was a commotion in the cities," Otto said. "Some kinda riot." He paused. "You get caught up in that?"

Rufus laughed, shook his head, and took a stool on the other side of Ingvar, who was still contemplating his coffee. "You mean you don't know? I guess the media's trying to cover it up, or else they don't believe it…" He shook his head. "I drove here as fast as I could once I got away, to make sure you and mom and everybody was okay, but I should have known, in this town, who would even notice if the dead started walking? You saw a zombie you'd probably just ask him what kind of gas mileage he got in his hearse."

Ingvar turned his head slowly to Rufus. "Zombies, huh? Your uncle was telling us about them. People dress up funny and act dead."

"I'm talking about people who are *dead* acting like they're *alive*," Rufus said. "My girl—" He shot a glance at Otto. "A friend of mine, she's a junior, studying social work, she's been volunteering at the hospital in the hospice unit, and she told me it started down in the morgues, the—you know, the cadavers—they started getting up off the tables and…" He shook his head. "Attacking people. Killing people. And then the people they killed got up and started killing other people. My friend went into the hospital first thing this morning and said it was all screaming and craziness, and she saw a man she knew, who'd died of cancer just the day before, come running down the hallway as fast as a dog chasing a car. Tried to take a bite out of her, but he didn't have any teeth." Rufus covered his eyes and started laughing. "A zombie with no teeth, can you believe that? Like he might gum you to death? So she ran away and there were police running around and shooting and yelling and…"

He uncovered his eyes. "So she came to see me. Campus was normal, no dead people, I guess the skeletons in biology lab don't count, maybe you have to have some muscles left to get up again, I don't know. I told her I'd bring her here, where it was safe, but we had to stop for gas right off the interstate, and she went to pee, and she didn't come back, and when I went looking for her there was blood coming out from under the bathroom door and something inside that sounded like chewing. I thought maybe I could save her, so I pulled the door open, and there was a mechanic in greasy overalls with a big dent in his head and blood all over him and Winnie, she—my friend—she was trying to stand up on a leg that looked like a shark took a bite out of it and her eyes were all glassy and they were both reaching for me." He plucked at his coat. "Almost got me. But I made it to my car, and drove here as fast as I could, and…" Another laugh. "You're just sitting here drinking coffee. The dead have risen from their graves to kill the living, just like in the movies, and you're just sitting here drinking coffee."

"Well," Ingvar said after a moment's contemplation. "That sure is different. A guy could get pretty worked up about something like that."

3. RAPTURE READY

Pastor Daniel Inkfist sat at his desk with his feet up on a pulled-out drawer saying "Hmm" and "You don't say" and "Don't that beat all" and other sorts of things to fill the gasps when his friend Pastor Cantor had to take a breath in the midst of yelling. Eddie Cantor had always been excitable, ever since seminary, but "excitable" usually meant getting worked up about the Twin's chances at the pennant or the sorry state of the offering plate these days or how short skirts were getting every summer, wasn't it shameful, like to make a man lose his mind.

Only now Eddie was yelling about the End Times and the Rapture and other things that, generally speaking, Lutherans didn't put much stock in, since if you actually sat down and looked at the Scripture there wasn't much to support the idea of a time of tribulation and the Antichrist becoming president and legalizing gay marriage and marrying the Pope and carving 666s and swastikas and bar codes into people's foreheads. Eddie had a Southern wife and Daniel supposed she'd been gradually filling him up with Pentecostal hellfire and brimstone over the years and, for whatever reason, it all came bubbling up today. Eddie usually called to talk sports and complain about the challenges of ministering to a flock in St. Paul and to wax nostalgic about their time in the seminary when they'd talked more about theology and the calling and wrestling with matters of faith and less about bake sales and choir robes and Christmas pageants. Now he was talking about the dead rising to smite the unbelievers.

"Now when you say the dead are rising," Daniel finally said, "am I to take that as some kind of metaphor?"

"No, Daniel, you're to take it as me saying that dead people are wandering the streets and attacking anyone they can reach and when people run away and slip on the ice and fall the dead people fall *on* them and start trying to *eat* them. And it's not just people. I saw a run-over dog start dragging itself around even though it had a tire tread mark right across its belly, snapping at people. It's the end times, Daniel! But there's no Christ taking us into heaven! The Lord swore he'd never destroy the Earth with a flood again, and most people assumed that meant next time it would be fire, but it's not fire, it's just *teeth*!"

"Okay then," Daniel said. "So you give Pearl my love then."

"You think I'm crazy, don't you." Eddie's voice had gone hoarse and quiet. "I'm locked in my office, afraid to come out, because we were having a memorial service here and the corpse *sat up* in the coffin and took a bite out of his great-granddaughter's throat. I'm calling you up to warn you. For gosh, Daniel, don't you have any dead people in Lake Woebegotten? Step on a cockroach or something and watch it come back to life if you don't believe me!"

"A lotta guys in a situation like that might call the police," Daniel said.

"You think I haven't tried? The lines are jammed. You call 911 and you don't even get a busy signal, you just get a *drone*. It started last night, did you see it, the shooting stars? I thought I might talk about it in my Christmas sermon in a couple of weeks, about how it reminded me of the star that heralded the birth of Christ, but I think it heralded the coming of the *Anti-christ*, it… you… no time to… before it's…"

"Eddie?" Daniel said, but the connection turned to fuzz and squeals and static. He sighed and dialed Eddie's home number, hoping to catch Pearl and let her know her husband could use a visit right about now, and was maybe a mite under the weather, but he just got a recording saying all lines were busy.

After thinking for a while, Daniel went down to the church basement/rec room/storage area, checked to see that no one else was around, and slid aside the eye-wrenchingly painted backdrop from a never-to-be-repeated vacation bible school performance of *Joseph and the Amazing Technicolor Dreamcoat*. That revealed a concealed door that led to a corridor cut into the living rock, though he'd never really understood the term "living rock," since rock was neither alive nor dead, and saying "living rock" seemed kind of animistic or even pagan, like something Big-Horn Jim who lived in the woods and worshipped Odin might say, except he mostly said "By Thor's Mighty Beard!" and similar exclamations. Daniel picked up the lantern from the floor of the corridor and lit it with a kitchen match, then slid the door shut behind him. He reached up and tugged the cord running along the low ceiling overhead, and though he couldn't hear anything, he knew a bell would be ringing elsewhere.

Daniel walked down the corridor, marveling as always at the steady temperature of about 55 degrees, whether it was muggy summer or bleak winter up above. The floor was rough but mostly even, and though the walls got awfully close together at a few points, it was never so tight he had to turn sideways. No one knew when or why this tunnel had been carved, though there were plenty of theories bandied about by the few who knew of its existence, notably: secret interdenominational love affairs; ill-fated attempts at smuggling liquor; a guy getting bored halfway through digging out a basement and wandering off; and a well-meaning but unworldly minister deciding to take part in the Underground Railroad for runaway slaves despite Lake Woebegotten being too far north to be much use, but it was the thought that counted, anyway.

These days it was mostly just used as a shortcut to avoid going outside in the winter, though it had been useful for negotiating the peace during the Great Lutheran-Catholic Bake Sale War of 1979.

When Daniel reached the other end of the corridor, which opened out into a little stone room with a scrounged couch, a wobbly desk, and a couple of folding chairs, Father Edsel was already waiting for him. The priest was wearing four sweaters and an earflap hat. He'd been assigned to Lake Woebegotten from Galveston, Texas, twenty years before and had never gotten used to the weather. He was known to wear mittens well into spring, and if the parishioners hadn't complained, he would have kept

Our Lady of Eventual Tranquility "a balmy 85 degrees" year-round, and expected the flock to pay his heating bill.

"I suppose you've heard then," Edsel said in that grizzled old-timey prospector voice of his.

"Heard what?"

Edsel sat at the desk, pulled open the drawer, and began laboriously laying out his preferred accoutrements of sin: a pipe, pouch of tobacco, and several small pipe-cleaning implements. "The dead are coming back to life. Hell unleashed on Earth. You didn't hear? It's all over the radio."

By "the radio" Daniel assumed Edsel meant the online radio stations on his computer, because normal radio stations you could hear in Lake Woebegotten didn't carry the kind of conspiracy theories Edsel thrived on: tales of reptilian overlords, the secret machinations of the Batrachian Illuminati (a branch of the Bavarian Illuminati populated solely by the immortal survivors of the lost city of Atlantis), consensual alien abductions, brainwashed sleeper agent Congressmen, and secret military units devoted to exploding the heads of mountain goats by will alone. If pressed, Edsel would admit that he didn't believe in aliens or Atlanteans or reptoids, but he *did* believe in Satan, the Adversary, the Prince of the Morning, Big Red, Lucifer, Shaytan, the Lord of the Flies, the Father of Lies, Old Nick, Mr. Scratch, the Tempter, the Old Serpent, the Lord of this World, Old Hob, the Prince of the Powers of the Air and Darkness, Mephistopheles, the First of the Fallen, Mister Dis, Old Gooseberry, the Angel of the Pit, and the Author of Evil, AKA the Devil. All the workings of various conspiracies could be traced back to Satan, and everyone who saw aliens or reptile-men or Sasquatches or Mothmen was really seeing Satan and his minions.

The rumor was Edsel had even taken part in an exorcism, a real pea-souper, back in the days before the church frowned on such things.

Daniel was less sure about the existence of the devil, though Martin Luther, the namesake of the Lutheran church, had been unequivocal on the subject—he'd encountered the Devil frequently, often while sleeping or having a bowel movement, and found arguing with Satan no more remarkable than bickering with his wife, once going so far as to tell Satan to suck the shit out of his anus. (Early Lutherans were an earthy bunch.) Nevertheless, most Lutherans Daniel knew tended to be more worried about the price of seed corn and diesel fuel than the perils of direct Satanic influence, which, all in all, was the sensible position.

"I had a strange phone call from a colleague," Daniel admitted. "Saying the dead were rising and attacking people. I thought I'd come to see if you'd heard anything odd from your contacts in the cities."

"The archdiocese doesn't even remember I'm out here. This parish doesn't show up on any of the maps because the bishop from back when the organizational charts were drawn up hated the priest here. Ever since then Lake Woebegotten has been a kind of Siberia for priests. Though I fought for the placement, myself. I had too much meddling down in Texas, and it's nice to be left alone." Edsel filled his pipe. "As for the dead coming back to life, that's easy enough to test. Come with me to see Mrs. Mormont. She's not long for this world. The doctor just called and said I should come over when I have a moment to administer last rites, if it's not too much trouble, maybe if her house is on my way to someplace I'm going already. I was just on my way out when you rang the bell." The bell system had been installed during the Bake Sale War when the Catholic and Lutheran ministers had been unable to contact one another directly for fear of reprisal, and so they'd worked out a way to hold clandestine meetings in the tunnel that connected the two church basements. "If she wakes up with a hankering for brains, we'll know the stories are true."

"I'm not sure it's appropriate for me to be at the deathbed of a woman of another faith. It might be seen as an attempt at... poaching, I guess."

Father Edsel grunted and puffed his pipe, clouds of sweet-smelling smoke rising. Daniel had never smelled tobacco like Edsel smoked anywhere else, and he wondered sometimes if it *was* tobacco, but wasn't prepared to address the question. "Widow Mormont hasn't been conscious for days. I don't think anyone's too worried about a deathbed conversion. What do you say?"

"Well, I suppose I could ride along. I don't think there's anything to all this about the living dead, mind you, but if it would help set your mind at rest, I'll come."

"It'll do you good to grapple with Satan," Edsel said. "The soul's like a muscle. You have to make it work to make it strong."

4. THE SIXTH COMMANDMENT

Dolph, proprietor of Dolph's Half Good Grocery (so called for its slogan, "It Isn't Half Bad!"), stood out back on the loading dock and made cryptic hand gestures meant to guide the delivery truck driver in. Though the driver had done this every week for years, he still came in at a slant or scraped his bumper on the railing by the steps half the time, and today he was even unsteadier than usual. "Running late today!" Dolph called when the driver emerged with his clipboard, keeping his voice cheerful, though he was actually mad enough about the delay to eat lead and spit bullets.

"Sorry," the driver said, handing over the clipboard and raising up the sliding door at the back of the truck. "Traffic like you wouldn't believe on the freeway past the warehouse, some kind of pile-up, biggest I've ever seen."

"Hope nobody was hurt." Dolph ran his eyes across the inventory sheet on the clipboard while the driver began hauling boxes out and setting them on the loading dock, willing the man to move faster, faster, faster.

Instead the driver paused, looked Dolph in the eye, and shook his head once. "I saw at least five cars. Three of 'em upside down. There's not a lot of traffic out there in the middle of the day, and the roads were fresh plowed, so I don't know what happened. There were a couple of wreckers and an ambulance and three police cars off on the side, and somebody'd moved the cars out of the way, but there wasn't a soul in sight."

"Probably just inside the ambulance trying to get out of this cold," Dolph said meaningfully, glancing up at the sky, which was the steel-gray of a dignified old patriarch's hair.

"Could be," the driver said, and went back to work double-time, passing boxes over to Dolph, who heaped them haphazardly on the dock. "I heard some funny stuff on the radio, though, apparently all heck's breaking loose over in St. Paul, some kind of epidemic—"

"Yep, I heard something was going around," Dolph said. "That's winter for you. Cold and wet makes you sick."

The driver paused again. "Well, I don't know. Some folks say it's viruses and bacteria and such that make you sick, not getting cold." He put his hands up by his temples and waggled his gloved forefingers like antenna. "You know. Little bugs."

"So that's about all the boxes then."

The driver looked into the empty back of the truck for a long time, as if maybe a box had eluded him, then nodded. "Yep."

"Looks good to me," Dolph said, handing back the clipboard with the signed delivery sheet. "Drive safe now. Stay warm."

"You bet," the driver said.

Dolph looked at the boxes piled there on the dock, thought about the time it would take to get them loaded on the dolly and the pallet jack and take them into the storeroom at the back of the grocery, looked at his watch, and raced for the front of the store. A quick glance up and down the aisles showed no customers—typical in this weather—and Clem, the high-school dropout stockboy/cashier/all-around-dogsbody with the lazy eye, was arranging cans of beans on the shelf according to some arcane system of his own devising, possibly relating to label color.

"You might wanna go over to the bank for some quarters," Dolph said. "No big rush. I think you might be running low." He hoped so. He'd taken just about all the change out of the register and hidden it in his office that morning.

"Oh, I guess so." Clem nodded slowly. "You okay here by yourself?"

"I can manage. Why don't you take a break and get a little lunch over at the Cafe while you're out? Take your time, have a cup of coffee, maybe bring me back a ham and cheese if you think about it, no big deal though."

"Sure thing." Clem went about the painstaking business of finding his coat and scarf and gloves—one glove was over in the freezer section for some reason—and then paused at the door with a little wave before walking out.

Dolph loitered by the front door, and a moment later, Eileen Munson came in carrying a purse as big as a mail bag, looking shapeless in her oversized brown coat, though he knew the shape underneath pretty well by this time.

"Some guys wouldn't keep a gal waiting like that," she said, and Dolph grunted, shut the door, turned the lock, and hung up the little sign that said "Back in fifteen minutes." Eileen was already gone, vanished into his office, and Dolph went in after her, excitement rising as it always did on Eileen's shopping day. A lot of the town's women drove half an hour to the super Wal-Mart over in Dodgewood to do their shopping lately, but Eileen was his most reliable customer.

When Dolph stepped into his cluttered office, Eileen was leaning on the edge of his desk, her clothes in a neat pile on top of the battered filing cabinet, dressed only in some of the most complicated underwear Dolph had ever seen—there were stockings and garters and a sort of bustier thing that didn't quite cover her bosoms and a little lace choker thing around her neck and black high-heeled shoes with little feathery puffs on top and lacy ribboned skimpy underwear that didn't leave much to the imagination, which was okay though, because Dolph had never had much of an imagination anyway.

"You like it?" Eileen said, with that little half-smile she always had when she was showing off something new. "Got it off the internet."

"It's a heckuva deal if you ask me," Dolph said, sweeping the files off his couch while simultaneously dropping his pants.

"You old sweet talker," she said, and he pulled her over to him.

Fifteen minutes wasn't ever long enough, but then again, it did get the job done.

After they were finished and dressed again and sitting on the couch instead of doing other things, Dolph poured her a cup of coffee from the thermos on his desk and had one for himself, and looked at her silently for a while. Eileen was just a hair past forty, both the kids she'd had recently off to college, husband obsessed with restoring the vintage Mustang in his garage (though you'd think he'd get sick of cars, what with running a dealership all day), and she'd been visiting Dolph for the past six months or so, every week, usually wearing something new. She might not be one of those magazine fashion models or Girls Gone Wild like you saw on the late night TV, but she had a sweet pretty face and nice full hips and a good set of curves on her. He said, "How your husband can spend all his time tinkering in the garage when he's got you in the house, I don't know."

She sipped her coffee demurely, which always impressed him, since she wasn't so demure, other times. "He hasn't touched me in months, and when he does, he doesn't like the lights on. He's ashamed of his belly, I think, like I expect him to look the same as he did when he was playing high school football, like time doesn't march on over all of us." She shrugged. "This is more fun. Like playing dress up. Sure gives me something to look forward to every week, better than the Lutheran Women's Circle. But how do you feel about it? You know—adultery?"

"Technically speaking I don't believe it's adultery for me. I'm not married, after all. I'm committing some other kind of sin, no doubt, but not that one."

Eileen shook her head. "I like to know what I'm up to. I looked it up. Minnesota law says, 'when a married woman has sexual intercourse with a man other than her husband, whether married or not, both are guilty of adultery.' Both. That's you too. Burns me up that it doesn't say anything about a husband doing it though. So as long at Brent sleeps with some unmarried girl, that's okay?" She paused. "Not that I think he would. He's only got eyes for that Mustang he's been rebuilding."

Dolph shifted a little on the couch. He was an adulterer? He'd always figured, since he wasn't actually breaking any vows, he was in the clear, and the bulk of the burden of sin was sitting squarely on Eileen. "You should probably do your shopping," he said. "Clem'll be back soon, don't want him to suspect anything."

Eileen rolled her eyes. "That boy's dim, just like his whole family. We could do the naked watusi in the produce section and he wouldn't figure anything out. But I do need to pick up a few things." She leaned over, pecked his cheek, and gave his crotch a friendly squeeze, making him jump. He waited a few moments for things in his loin area to subside before rising himself, and found her filling a basket from his tiny fancy-food half-shelf, with the stuffed grape leaves and truffle-infused olive oil and Belgian chocolates and other such things that he'd finally started carrying at the insistence of some of the summer people. Eileen was the only local who ever bought them, and she didn't buy them, exactly, since their arrangement had evolved to the point where she got to walk out the door with two big free grocery sacks full of whatever she could carry after one of their rendezvous (which he pronounced "randy-voos" for the comical value), something that struck Dolph as a little too close to paying for a lady's affection, though Eileen saw it differently: "Most guys would buy a gal dinner first. You just buy dinner after. It's like you get to eat your dessert first. Isn't that every little boy's dream?"

Dolph went to the door to take down the "Back in fifteen minutes sign," and that's when he saw the dog trying to eat Clem.

Clem didn't look that worried yet—the dog was trying to bite his ankle, and Clem was shaking his leg like he was trying to fling a glob of manure off his heel, trying not to spill the paper cups or diner to-go sack he held in his hand, the result looking like a peculiar sort of spastic modern dance, or else a dance not modern at all, but old: like a dance by St. Vitus, maybe, or else the tarantella. It wasn't a very big dog, looked like old man Levitt's miniature pinscher, though something had gone funny with its back legs, and they were all twisted up.

"That poor dog," Eileen said, standing with him by the doorway. "What's wrong with it?"

Dolph shrugged, pushed open the door, cleared his throat, and said, "Need a hand there?"

"No, I wouldn't put you to any trouble." Clem was dragging his leg now, with the dog's jaws fastened firmly around his pants and, judging by the pained expression on Clem's face, maybe some of the meat underneath.

"No trouble. I could at least take that bag from you."

"That's okay, I've got it."

"I'm happy to," Dolph said. "I'm already outside." He didn't want to stay out here much longer without his coat, either, but Clem was a good Lake Woebegotten Lutheran boy, which meant he'd refuse any offer to help at least twice, maybe three times, though since he had a dog biting him, Dolph was hoping he'd settle for the bare minimum of two.

"I suppose if you've got a hand free," Clem said, and Dolph strode over and took the lunch bag and the beverages from him, and then they both stood looking down at the dog, which looked like its back half had been run over by a car, which might explain why it was so cantankerous, but didn't explain why it wasn't in a ditch licking its wounds and gradually freezing to death. Its jaws were working methodically, though it was trying to chew through a layer of denim and a chunk of boot leather and probably thick socks under that. Dolph didn't speculate on the possibility of long underwear. That was Clem's business.

"Guess I should just reach down and pull it off me." Clem didn't sound excited about the prospect. He bent, grasped the dog's upper and lower jaws, and grunted. "He's on there good." With much prying he got the jaws open and flung the min-pin, whose name was Alta for some reason, toward a convenient snowbank. Alta landed on his ruined back legs, but didn't howl or growl or make a sound, just came crawling forward again, relentless, jaws working, eyes oddly fogged-over.

"Reckon it's rabid?" Clem asked.

"I don't know. Usually you see some frothing and such with rabies." Dolph shook his head.

"Fella at the diner was talking about zombies," Clem said. "Could be a zombie dog."

Dolph didn't say anything for a long moment. Zombies. He was willing to bet Clem still believed in the tooth fairy, but zombies were a stretch even for him. "It could be rabies I guess," Dolph said. "If it weighed more than eight or nine pounds it'd be scary. We should call old man Levitt, let him know."

"You should just put it out of its misery." Eileen joined them on the sidewalk, and with her cheeks rosy from the cold, Dolph thought she looked as pretty as Helen of Troy, and judging from the bulging grocery sacks in her arms, she was fresh from looting Sparta.

"Hate to put down another man's dog. But maybe…" Dolph went inside for a moment and came back with a red plastic grocery basket and a 16-pound frozen turkey. He plopped the basket upside-down over Alta and then put the turkey on top. The basket thumped and rattled a bit, but didn't shift too much under the dog's attempts to escape. "There. All secure. Go on in and call Mr. Levitt, Clem."

Clem nodded and limped toward the door. Probably oughta get that ankle of his checked out, at least splash some alcohol on it. Dolph would have to remind him. It was entirely possible that Clem might be careless and get an infection and lose his foot from something as simple as a dog bite. His daddy had lost three toes and an ear the time he fell asleep on the porch when he was supposed to be repairing a loose board and got frostbite instead, and Clem wasn't anywhere near as bright as his father.

"I'll see you next time." Eileen took a step toward him, and for a moment Dolph had a little thrill that she might touch him in *public*, something he was pretty sure she'd never even done with her husband, but she just said, "Thanks for the groceries," in his ear and then sauntered off to her brown station wagon with the fake wood paneling on the sides.

"Life could be worse," Dolph said, and the dog under the basket under the turkey thumped loudly, as if it wanted to agree, or maybe disagree. It was hard to tell with dogs, especially rabid half-run-over zombie dogs.

5. UNDEATHBED

Pastor Inkfist and Father Edsel trudged from the ice-crusted dirt driveway to the sagging front porch of the Mormont farm. The steps were slippery and the boards creaked ominously as Edsel rapped smartly on the front door. After a moment the inner door opened and the doctor appeared, mustache droopy, face long and tired.

"Doctor Holliday," Edsel said, and Daniel nodded. You never, ever called Doctor Henry Holliday "Doc Holliday," no matter how tempted you might be—the doctor hated the coincidence of sharing a name with a famous gunfighting gambling tubercular dentist, and had said on more than one occasion that he'd almost gone into the civil service instead of medical school just to avoid the jokes. Now he combated any such attempt at levity by being utterly humorless and dour at all times, which meant maybe civil service would have been a good fit for him, after all.

"Come on in," the doctor said. "She doesn't have much longer." They trooped into the dim foyer and started stripping off their layers of coats and stomping the snow off their boots.

"She still unconscious?" Father Edsel asked. "Deathbed confessions are always the juiciest."

Daniel grimaced, but Doctor Holliday just shrugged. "We've been keeping her pretty full of painkillers. I sent the nurse home. Won't be much longer now. Cancer's just about eaten her up."

"Any of the family here?"

"Daughter was supposed to fly in from Orlando, but she

called and said her flight was canceled, some kind of trouble at the airport, all the planes were grounded, I didn't catch all the details. Bad connection. She didn't sound too broken up about it though."

"Let's give the old girl her send-off, then." Edsel carried a little black bag into the bedroom/sickroom, and Daniel followed, curious despite himself. He'd never seen Catholic last rites performed—Lutherans sometimes anointed the sick, but they didn't go around calling it a sacrament or anything.

The widow Mormont was thin as a bundle of sticks, barely taking up any space at all in the narrow hospital bed. Medical devices beeped and booped and flickered mysteriously, and a big crucifix with an intricately carved bleeding Jesus hung on the wall. Daniel, who found even the simple cross of his faith a little creepy when he really thought about it, could never get over the grotesquerie of some Catholic crucifixes. Jesus had suffered, and that was certainly to be remembered, but did you really need a fella with blood all over his feet and side and forehead and wrists looking down at you while you slept?

The three of them stood around the bed, looking at the widow's lined face in its slack repose. "If you can, you should give your last confession," Father Edsel said, laying his hand on her shoulder.

Her eyes fluttered open. "Father," she croaked, then flicked her eyes at Daniel. "And the Pastor, too. You must think I'm some kind of world-class sinner, for both of you to come here."

"Nice to see you again, Maggie," Edsel said, glancing at the doctor. "I didn't expect we'd have a chance to chat."

"What, old Doctor Holliday told you I wasn't going to wake up again?" Her voice was gaining strength now. "I was just pretending to be asleep while he was here. He's depressing. Got the bedside manner of an undertaker. No, I'm awake, and I'll give my confession, though don't expect anything too exciting." She cackled. "I confessed all that stuff a long time ago. Doctor, thanks for keeping the morphine flowing. I can see why my cousin Harold got so addicted to the stuff—he stole his mama's goat and my tricycle to sell for drugs when I was a girl. Good thing I never discovered this stuff when I was a younger woman, or I might have a lot more to confess. Now shoo." She flapped her hands weakly. "This last part's between me and my God and my God's man on the scene here."

Daniel nodded and went with the doctor into the kitchen, where they drank old coffee and made awkward small talk. They were both in the business of salvation, but the divide between spiritual and secular salvation respectively was a tricky one to bridge. They settled on talking about memorial services they'd attended and jello salads and hotdishes they'd eaten in the homes of grieving relatives. After a while Father Edsel came in and said, "She's gone."

He didn't add anything about her rising from the dead and trying to take a big bite out of his face, so Daniel figured the reports of zombies were exaggerated.

The doctor nodded, put down his coffee cup, and took a pen from his breast pocket. "Let me just take a look so I can fill in the death certificate, then we'll call the funeral home."

"I remember in the old days," Daniel said, "If someone died in winter like this, they'd keep the body at the funeral home until spring, when the ground at the cemetery was soft enough to dig into again. It was a mess. Somebody would die and you couldn't have the funeral until four or five months later, made the whole grieving process get dragged out. I know it was hard on a lot of the little cemeteries when they passed that law about allowing winter burials, they had to buy that expensive equipment so they could dig in the frozen dirt like that, but I think it's better this way."

"Cremation's the way to go," Father Edsel said. "No muss, no fuss, no headstone, nice little urn, maybe one of those metal plates like you see on a trophy with the name and dates, no need to get in the car and take a trip out to the cemetery, you can just lean on the mantelpiece and have a chat with the dearly departed."

"I thought you folks frowned on cremation." Lutherans weren't so hot on the idea themselves, mostly. Heck, most of the Lutherans in Lake Woebegotten wouldn't even turn on the furnace in their houses until the temperature got down into the teens—any warmer and you could just put on another sweater or bring out another quilt, couldn't you? Cremation seemed like an overindulgent use of good heat.

Edsel shrugged. "We like to have the body present for the funeral mass, but after that, we don't fuss if they want to take 'ashes to ashes' literally. It's not like it used to—"

The doctor screamed from the other room, and Edsel ran toward the deathbed. Daniel followed and almost crashed into Edsel, who in the doorway saying, "God, dear God." He took a hesitant step into the room, and Daniel saw past him.

The widow Mormont was sitting up in bed, grasping the doctor's head in both hands like a kid holding a basketball and trying to decide whether to pass or shoot, and she looked to be giving him a passionate kiss. She dragged the doctor half-up on the bed, his feet drumming a little on the floorboard—just random drumming, not any sort of beat you'd recognize, or any kind of Morse code message either—making small bubbling moaning noises, except suddenly they stopped.

Widow Mormont looked up at them, her face smeared with blood, something that looked suspiciously like a nose gripped in her teeth, which she chewed and swallowed. Her eyes were foggy and unfocused but it sure seemed like she could see them, all right.

The widow was a zombie. Not any kind of metaphorical zombie, or philosophical zombie, or anything else but a plain old reanimated flesh-eater like you saw in the movies, if you watched those kind of movies, which of course Daniel didn't.

She dropped Doctor Holliday, who slid to the floor—his throat was pretty much gone, as well as his nose, a bit of cheek, and both eyes. The widow started to climb out of the bed, but her legs were bound up in the sheet, and getting herself loose was apparently beyond her. She tore wildly at the hospital corners, but they were tucked in tight. She bent herself forward completely double and started tearing at the sheet and blanket holding her legs with her teeth. Her gown had slipped down, revealing one withered breast, and Daniel averted his eyes, even though taking your eyes off a flesh-eating predator was probably a bad idea. He couldn't help it. The whole situation was too undignified. Daniel finally found his voice, and used it to scream, "Do something!"

"Good idea," Father Edsel said, and left the room.

Daniel stared at his departing back, wondering if he should follow, if the priest was about to drive off and abandon him, but they couldn't just leave the widow here, not when she was like *this*, what would people think?

Before he could commit to any particular course of action, Edsel returned carrying a shotgun. "Where did you get that?" Daniel said, but Edsel ignored the question—probably, Daniel had to admit, because it wasn't all that pertinent—and pointed the gun at the widow. "Get thee behind me, Satan," he said, and pulled both triggers.

The boom was huge, and Daniel jumped even though he'd known it was coming. The widow's head and shoulders pretty much disappeared in a sort of red haze, though considerable chunks of gray and red and white sprayed all over the wall and stuck there. "Or if you can't get behind me, at least get spattered all over the wallpaper," Edsel said.

Daniel started to vomit, as discreetly as he could, but Edsel still noticed, and said, "Oh, good, it wasn't messy enough in here, we needed you to contribute some bodily fluids, very good." He came over and clapped his hand on Daniel's shoulder. "It's all right. I can see you've never wrestled with demons before. It takes some getting used to."

"You—you shot her!"

"I shot *it*, Pastor. That's just a monster. The widow's soul was sent to her heavenly home with full honors, and that body there is just a sort of demon-haunted house. Granted, the headless zombie corpse makes the funeral mass a bit tricky, but we'll manage. You want to do the doctor?" He cracked open the gun and loaded two fresh shells into it.

"Do the—what?" Daniel wiped his mouth on the back of his sleeve. He shouldn't have eaten that tuna noodle hotdish for lunch. It smelled pretty awful coming back out of his stomach like that.

"Doctor Holliday. He's dead." Edsel was using a patient Sunday School sort of voice. "Which means, in a minute, he's going to come back to life and try to eat us."

"You can't know that. Just because the widow came back—"

"I told you, I heard it on the radio. This is happening all over."

"Just because some crackpot talk show host says there are zombies doesn't mean it's true—"

"I never said it was a crackpot talk show host," Edsel said, still patiently. "I was listening to National Public Radio, and the BBC World Service, and I switched around to a couple of other news stations, and they had a lot of conflicting stories, but whenever they had a clip of somebody who'd actually been on the scene talking, they said the same thing: dead people got up and tried to make living people dead too."

"Oh," Daniel said weakly. "But the doctor, he can't…"

"He is," Edsel said, and thrust the shotgun into Daniel's hands. "Funny, the original Doc Holliday died in bed, even though everybody thought he'd die in a gunfight. And this Doc Holliday probably expected to die in bed, and, well…" He shrugged. "We'll see how that turns out."

"The doctor did die in bed." Daniel stared as the doctor's corpse began to stir, moving less like a person and more like some kind of meatskin full of rodents or bugs, all strange ripples and convulsions and twitches. "Like you said, this thing, it's just…" Could he say it? His sermons were about honoring your father and mother and the parable of the talents and turning the other cheek and the prodigal son and the Sermon on the Mount, not about devils and hellfire and damnation, but… "It's just a demon."

Doctor Holliday's body stood up, awkwardly, and though it had no eyes or nose it seemed to sense their presence anyway, and began to lurch toward them, arms outstretched, mouth moving as if chewing its way through the air.

Daniel closed his eyes and fired the gun.

6. THE TELL-TALE PARTS

O tto offered his nephew Rufus a ride home from the diner because the boy's engine was running ragged and the brakes were mushy and it was burning oil, and it was a foreign car besides, which only served to compound the shame of such poor maintenance, but that was college kids for you, and what did you expect from a boy who'd get a spiderweb tattooed on his neck? Rufus rode sullen in the passenger seat of Otto's pickup, fiddling with the radio a little, but not picking up much of anything except static. "I hope your radio's busted," Rufus said, twisting the knob to off. "Otherwise it means the entire communications infrastructure is collapsing under an onslaught of the undead."

"Must be one or the other," Otto said.

Rufus grunted and started poking at one of those cell phones that looked like an oversize throat lozenge, all plasticky-shiny and rounded corners, didn't even flip open. "Can't get any service out here."

Otto didn't figure that deserved any response. Cell phones worked in Lake Woebegotten, after a fashion, but there were more dead zones than live ones. He'd heard you got the best reception if you went all the way to the top of the Borg Co-Op Grain Elevator, where they had the town's highest flagpole but only flew the flag on national (and some Norwegian and German) holidays because it was such a pain to get up there, but if you were going to that kind of trouble to make a phone call, you might as well drive over and say your piece in person, and if you

35

wanted to talk to someone who lived far away, why not just send a letter?

"Have to stop at the store." Otto pulled into one of the diagonal spaces in front of Dolph's Half Good Grocery and Rufus heaved a sigh and climbed out after him. Otto paused to look at the red plastic handbasket sitting upside down on the sidewalk with a frozen turkey on top of it, shuddering a little, then shrugged and walked on into the store.

Dolph, a big bluff man with the look of an ex-football player (though Otto knew he'd never played, owing to a peculiar spinal cord condition that made him fall unconscious if he tilted his head all the way back), was in the process of yelling at Clem, latest in a long line of pig farmers who found themselves perennially outsmarted by their livestock. (No shame in that. Pigs are smart, smarter than most dogs, though their table manners aren't as good, maybe even smarter than goats, though not as fiendishly clever.) "What do you mean you didn't call old man Levitt? That dog's about to chew through the plastic!"

"Uh. Forgot." Clem stood behind the checkstand, and he didn't look so good, sweat pouring down his face and plastering his bowl-cut brown hair to his forehead, eyes deeply shadowed. "Sorry."

"Want something done," Dolph grumbled, and reached over to pick up the phone. Otto went to the freezer section, because if he forgot to pick up the milk again, Barbara wouldn't even say anything, she'd just fix him with that stare of hers, and sigh, and put on her coat, and make a special trip out to the store herself. Rufus looked morosely in at the beer, which was mostly Bud or, if you were feeling fancy, Michelob. Probably got used to drinking things with fruit juice and little paper umbrellas up at college.

Otto went to the check stand, and Dolph hung up the phone, frowning. "Something bad's happening at old man Levitt's place," Dolph said. "I called to tell him to pick up his dog, and he sounded all concerned at first, and then there was this crashing noise, and he started cussing and carrying on and dropped the phone on the floor. All kinds of yelling going on when I hung up." He looked at Clem, nodded to himself sort of decisive-like, and said, "Clem, mind the store, I'm going to run over to his house and see if everything's all right. He's an old fella, might have broken a hip."

"We'll go with you," Otto said. Old man Levitt had been the principal over at the combined high school before becoming superintendent, and he'd looked the other way when Otto's son was caught smoking wacky tobacco out behind the gym, so Otto figured he owed him.

"Are you serious?" Rufus said.

"Are you in a big hurry to get home and see your mother?" Otto said.

"Right," Rufus said. "We'd better go check on him. It's the neighborly thing to do."

"I'm telling you, that dog is a zombie," Rufus said, and Otto nodded, again.

"You're telling me, and you've told me, three times already." The dog was in the back of the truck in a cooler, trying hard to get out. "So I guess everything's a zombie now. I'd better watch out before the frozen turkey I got for Christmas dinner starts flapping around the kitchen, dripping everywhere."

"I think they need a head to reanimate." Rufus had his thinking-hard expression on, which always made him look like he was working out an impacted bowel movement. "It seems to me we're dealing with the classic George Romero *Night of the Living Dead* sort of zombies, just straight-up reanimated corpses hungry for human flesh, probably brought to life by some kind of cosmic radiation. You heard about the meteor shower last night, right? Who knows what came flying down from space? We're obviously not dealing with a *Serpent and the Rainbow* style Haitian zombie, those are just living people who get drugged and mindfucked—"

"Language," Otto said, though he spent most of his time with unmarried agrarian Norwegians, who cursed worse than that, if not always in English.

"Brainwashed, then. Those are the true zombies, the ones we get the word from—'zombi' was originally another name for the snake god Iwa Damballah Wedo—but vodoun zombies don't attack people or eat flesh or brains, they mostly just toil in the sugar cane fields, you know? This is too large-scale to be something like that anyway. And we're lucky because, based on what I've seen, these guys are slow shamblers, so we're not talking about the modern zombie apocalypse you mostly see in movies these days, where some kind of crazy viral prion pandemic disease turns people into mindless, violent, fast-moving rage zombies. I don't even think it's right to call things like that zombies, though, they're not dead, they don't even *think* they're dead, so—"

He just keeps talking, Otto marveled, and said, "Why do you know so much about this nonsense?" Or about movies about this nonsense, anyway. Nobody depended on direct experience anymore. Everything was secondhand, viewed through a screen lit by electricity instead of sunlight. Not that there were many opportunities for the direct study of things like zombies, but the point still stood. Kids today spent too much time inside their own heads, or spewing out the contents of their heads all over the internet, instead of going out in the world and getting things done.

"I took an American Studies pop culture class this past semester," Rufus said, "called 'The Zombie as Metaphor.'"

"So that's what they call a liberal arts education then. Sounds about right." Otto tapped the brakes. "There's the Levitt place." He pulled in behind Dolph's pickup and climbed out in time to see Dolph unlocking the toolbox mounted behind the cab. He removed a deer rifle and checked to see if it was loaded.

"See you got a gun there," Otto said.

"Seemed like the thing to do," Dolph said.

"Aim for the head." Rufus climbed out, holding a tire tool in his hand.

Otto sighed. "We have a flat tire I didn't know about?"

"I'd rather have an assault shotgun, but—"

They heard the unmistakable sound of a chainsaw being started up inside the house, exchanged the sort of looks that carry a great deal of information—mostly information about bewilderment, worry, and curiosity about the make, model, and merits of the particular chainsaw that was being used in there—and then they all headed for the side door (the front door was for Bible salesmen and visits from the military telling you a family member had been killed by friendly fire and the like). Otto wished he'd thought to pick up a jack handle or something from the pickup, keenly aware that the closest thing he had to a weapon was his multi-tool, and the knife blades on that were sufficient for cutting the strapping tape off a pallet of fertilizer but not much else. Not that he expected to find zombies in there, but something was going on. There was no good reason to run a chainsaw inside your house except if a tree fell through your roof, and there was no sign of such arboreal invasion here.

Dolph actually knocked on the door, though the noise of a chainsaw cutting into *something* inside made it impossible to hear, so he knocked a little harder, then shrugged and tried the doorknob. Most people didn't bother to lock their doors in Lake Woebegotten when they were home, but Mr. Levitt was an exception.

"This is ridiculous." Rufus shouldered Dolph aside, jammed the flattened end of the tire iron between the door and the frame, leaned all his scrawny college-boy weight into it, and popped the door open.

In the cozily-furnished living room, old man Levitt was chainsawing a zombie in the neck while kicking another zombie in the face. He was wearing pajamas and worn green slippers—Mr. Levitt that is, not the zombies, which were dressed in filthy rags and tatters—and he was laughing, not hysterically but like he'd just heard a real gut-buster of a joke, as another three or four zombies shambled in from what was probably the kitchen. Levitt glanced over his shoulder, noticed the newcomers, stopped laughing, then knelt down and commenced decapitating the zombie he'd kicked in the face. Otto stood in the doorway staring, feeling like most of his brain was still back in the truck a few miles down the road—it certainly wasn't *here*, where ridiculous things were happening. These couldn't be zombies. Except they couldn't be anything else. They had skull bone showing through flaps of gray skin, and bones poking out of decomposed skin, and they were grayish, and they shambled, and there were three more coming out of the kitchen, kind of slow, mostly because they were all trying to pass through the narrow doorway at once and were getting tangled up in each other.

Despite being understandably a little distracted, Otto did notice that Mr. Levitt was chopping off the zombie's head with a Craftsman 18-inch electric chainsaw, about a fourteen-, maybe fifteen-pounder, looked like the four horsepower kind with the tool-less chain tensioner and the automatic oiler, a damn good tool for an electric saw, though Otto always preferred gas-powered, for one thing you didn't have to worry about the darn cord, though on the other hand with gas-powered you had to pour in fuel and half the time you poured too much and overflowed a little and went around smelling like gas all day and worrying somebody'd flick a cigarette behind them and accidentally set you on fire, so he supposed it could be argued—

Dolph raised his rifle and shot one of the other zombies in the head—it exploded like a jack o' lantern kicked by a kid two weeks after Halloween—while Rufus took a deep breath and went in swinging the tire iron at another zombie, raining blows upon its head. The zombie sat down hard like a little kid shoved down by a bigger kid at the playground and looked up at Rufus with an expression that was half ravenous and half Why Me? until Rufus bashed a good-sized hole in its face. That left one zombie still shambling forward unattended. Not wanting to look like he wasn't trying, Otto took his multi-tool out of his pocket, unfolded the short serrated knife blade, sighed, and hoped the zombie would hold still long enough for Otto to saw its head off, which didn't seem likely, but wasn't that always the way.

Fortunately Mr. Levitt finished with his zombie, stepped around the one Rufus was still hammering on, and shoved the chainsaw into the chest of the final zombie, which was the biggest and freshest-looking of the bunch, once a broad-shouldered man with a horribly-scarred face and lank black hair. There wasn't much blood, and what there was, was more a sort of reddish-brown powder. The zombie grunted and stumbled back, and Levitt kept the saw moving, taking off both its arms just above the elbow, then crouching—he was spry for a fella who had to be pushing eighty—and took off both its legs above the knee. The torso lay on the carpet, head lashing back and forth, mouth opening and closing, stumps wiggling, and Otto stepped over behind the couch and threw up everything he'd eaten at the diner, which was unfortunately chicken and mushroom hotdish, never a meal improved by regurgitation.

Levitt flicked a switch and the chainsaw went silent. What with the gunshot and the yelling—they'd all been yelling, Otto realized, except Levitt, who'd been silent since he stopped laughing—the sudden silence made his ears tingle and everything feel too airless and big.

"What do you think, boys?" Levitt said. "Should we keep this one alive to interrogate? See what he knows?" And he laughed, but this was a wheezy little old man's haw-haw-haw, not the big belly laughs he'd come out with before.

"I told you there were zombies," Rufus said, staring down at the mess he'd made of the zombie at his feet.

"Wish somebody'd told me. I would have put a lock on the cellar door. Maybe finally invested in that acid bath I've been thinking about all those years." Levitt sat down on his couch beside his chainsaw, fished around in the drawer of the end table, and came out with a pack of cigarettes. "I only ever smoke after I kill somebody," he said, as if by way of apology. "I figure this counts. Sure got the same thrill, anyway."

Rufus lifted his head, frowned, and said, "I knew the dead were rising, but how'd they get into your house? So many?"

"Maybe the place is built on an old Indian burial ground," Levitt said. "Happens all the time."

"That guy's not an Indian," Rufus said, pointing at the stumped zombie. "And he doesn't look like he's been dead that long."

"Darn it. Was hoping you'd buy the Indian burial ground thing. Oh well. Better come clean. These all came out of my basement." Levitt puffed on his cigarette and blew out a halo of smoke. They all observed the ring in silence. A good smoke ring was worth appreciating. "That's the problem with shallow graves. I've never been a good housekeeper. One fella I buried and dissolved with lye, now *he's* not going to stand up again and cause any trouble. Turned him into human lutefisk." Levitt grinned. "I've been waiting to make that joke forever. This is very liberating."

Otto didn't understand what was going on, so he was alarmed when Dolph raised the rifle again and pointed it at Mr. Levitt. "You're saying you killed these people?"

"Killed, and then *re*-killed tonight. Though tonight it was self-defense." Levitt looked up at the ceiling, squinting, in thought. "Couldn't try me twice for the same murder anyway, though, could they? Something about double jeopardy maybe? Well, I was never a lawyer, and didn't worry too much about how I'd defend myself. Figured I'd never get caught. Didn't expect to become a footnote in the books until after I fell over from a heart attack or blew a blood vessel in my brain and some grand-nephew or something came and tried to clean out the house and found what I'd been up to all these years. Doesn't much matter now though. The dead are rising, which makes me think I'm going to be pretty far down on the list of priorities for law enforcement."

"Mr. Levitt. You're a serial killer. Holy fuck," Rufus said.

"Language," Otto said.

7. MUSTANG SALLY

Eileen picked pretty much the worse possible day to finally kill her husband, but there was no way she could have known, and really, there's probably no ideal day to kill your spouse, and at least she didn't do it on Valentine's Day or his birthday or their anniversary or any of the other holiday minefields that litter the average longtime married couple's year.

When Eileen got home from her assignation with Dolph she saw her husband Brent Munson's truck, a brand new shiny black Ford Behemoth, parked in the driveway, which meant he'd stopped off at home for a long lunchtime quickie. She'd done the same at the grocery store, but even though she was just as unfaithful as her husband, at least she didn't commit adultery in her own home, and at least Dolph was human. Eileen lugged her free groceries in through the front door and set down her burdens on the kitchen counter, then stepped to the door that led to the garage and put her ear to the wood.

From the other side of the door came the gentle squeak of a car rocking on its shocks, which meant she was right. Brent was at it again. He could at least have the decency to take his dirty business elsewhere. Today was as good a day as any to go ahead with her plans, she figured. Brent was here now. He hadn't even started the radio yet, which meant he was still into the foreplay stage. She had some time, probably about an hour, before he came inside, and that was assuming he skipped the afterglow.

Eileen took her big sun tea jar down from the cupboard and

43

rummaged around in the cabinets under the sink, removing a jug of bleach and the bottle of pure acetone she'd bought last week from the hardware store. She poured almost a gallon of the bleach into the tea jar—clear glass with a few pretty little flowers painted on—then went to the freezer for a big bag of crushed ice, pouring that into the jar too. It would be nice to just give Brent a big tall glass of iced bleach to drink when he came in all sweaty and spent, but he'd probably notice the smell, and there'd be questions after. Her original plan was better.

She measured five tablespoons of acetone and poured that over the ice, then leaned down to look into the jar. The internet said it could take anywhere from ten minutes to twenty minutes for the reaction to start, but in the meantime, she had to keep an eye on it in case the ice started to melt. Boring, but this was what you might call the calm before the storm, so she was trying to be mindful and live in the moment like her meditation books said. Before deciding on murder she'd tried meditation, which hadn't worked out ultimately, but she'd gotten some useful things out of it, including more flexible leg muscles from all the sitting lotus position, and that stretchiness had come in handy with Dolph. Making love in the cramped office of a grocery store required a certain degree of physical fitness.

The ice started melting, so she topped off the jar a few times, keeping it full. Meanwhile the car radio in the garage started playing some power ballad by an '80s hair band, Eileen wasn't sure which one, but it was the usual, and that meant things were well underway with Brent's ritual. He'd be nearing the climax—and his own climax, of course—before too much longer, but you couldn't hurry chemistry.

Even if Brent came in and saw her and asked what she was doing and she said "Making ridiculously dangerous homemade chloroform from a recipe I found on the internet," he'd probably just grunt and make a sandwich, since he never really listened to her anyway. He had no idea she was cheating on him with Dolph, that she had been for months, and she wasn't entirely sure he'd care, though maybe he would—men were funny. Even with his own true love in the garage there, he might still have some possessive feelings about Eileen.

The liquid in the jar was getting good and cloudy, and the green tint from the bleach was gone, so now all she had to do was wait some more, half an hour or so. She put the groceries away, and loaded the dishwasher, and cleaned underneath the burners on the stove, and put a bowl of vinegar in the microwave and ran it for a minute, which was practically magic, it loosened all the nasty hardened gunk that stuck inside on the walls, she'd learned that on the internet, too, and took a soft sponge and cleaned out the inside and rearranged the cans in the pantry alphabetically and then let herself look at the jar again.

The ice was gone, and the liquid was settled and pretty clear again, and down at the bottom there was a good-size clear bubble that was, she knew, the denser liquid blob of chloroform. She skimmed off most of the top liquid with a spoon, and then carefully poured the remainder down the sink, holding her breath while she did it, because if she accidentally tilted too far and sent the chloroform down the sink, she'd have to start all over again. No wonder people shot each other. Trying to kill somebody less obviously was a lot of work.

Finally there was nothing left in the jar but the bubble of chloroform, assuming the internet had given her the right instructions, which was always a question. It would be funny if she'd just made oven cleaner or something, wouldn't it?

Eileen opened up the big flour container and fished around inside until she found the plastic bag she'd hidden in there, and gently removed it. The bag contained a separation funnel, a funny looking piece of glassware she'd had to send away for special, and it was the only part of her plan that worried her, because what did a housewife in Lake Woebegotten need with a piece of special chemistry equipment? If anybody got suspicious... but she knew the town police, Harry and Stevie Ray, and they knew her. They'd never peg her for a killer, so she didn't think they'd dig around too deep. Still, she wished she could have used an eyedropper or something, but apparently chloroform liked to eat plastic.

She was poised to try to use the separation funnel to slurp up the chloroform, though she wasn't exactly sure how that worked, when she stopped. What was she doing? Why did she need to carefully slurp the stuff up anyway? She wasn't going to store it. The recipe online said she needed a separation funnel, so she'd bought one from a chemical supply house, but for her purposes, what good was it?

Eileen remembered the old joke about the woman who always cut the ends off her roast before putting it in the oven, until her husband asked why she did that. "I don't know," she said, "that's how my mother taught me. Let me ask her." So she called her mother, who said, "I don't know, that's just how your grandmother taught me to do it. Let's ask her why." So they called up the grandmother, who said, "I always cut the end off the roast because my roasting pan was too small to hold the whole thing!" Eileen had made the same mistake, doing something because it's how she was *told* to, without thinking about why.

She tossed the separation funnel in the trash can, and stuck a dishtowel down in the bottom of the jar, soaking up the chloroform.

Holding the cloth out at arm's length, because even from here she could smell it, and knocking herself out wasn't part of the plan, she opened the door to the garage.

Brent was in there, and as she'd assumed, he was screwing his car again.

The bitch was a cherry red vintage muscle car that Brent called Mustang Sally, and he'd lavished her with attention from the moment a desperate fella with a gambling problem brought her to Brent's car lot for a quick handful of cash. He'd spent countless hours tinkering with her, buffing her, scavenging pick-and-pulls for slightly-shinier versions of her already perfectly acceptable fixtures and doodads, and at first Eileen hadn't minded—anything that kept him busy and occupied and out from underfoot during the inevitable hours he was at home instead of at the dealership was fine with her. She first got suspicious the day she found him cleaning the leather upholstery in the back seat while buck naked, but he said it was hot in the garage, and it was, so she'd let it go, and anyway, what was she supposed to think?

She'd only realized what was really going on because Brent was so hopelessly non-tech-savvy, and he didn't know how to clear his browser history or delete his cookies or otherwise cover his tracks online, so she'd gotten bored one evening while he was out caressing Sally's undercarriage and started poking around through the history to see what kind of porn he was looking at; she didn't doubt for a minute that he *was* looking, she only hoped he didn't make a mess while doing so, but she didn't skimp on the hand sanitizer after touching the keyboard just in case.

It hadn't even looked like porn, at first, just support groups for people who called themselves objectophiles, which apparently meant people who liked to have sex with objects, and not even necessarily woman- or man- or even animal-shaped objects. There was a woman in love with a fire hydrant, and a guy who liked having sex with his specially modified juicer (which just seemed dangerous to Eileen, though maybe the danger made it hotter, that was certainly her experience with Dolph) and links to a whole separate site about people who were in love with their cars, called "AutoErotic Connection," which was some kind of joke, she gathered. There were pictures, mostly crude drawings, fortunately, but some photographs, too.

Including one of Brent, wearing a cheap plastic Lone Ranger Mask, otherwise buck naked, with his nether regions displayed on Sally's gleaming hood.

Never one to shrink from a fight, she'd confronted Brent about it, expecting denial, shame, tears, and begging in that approximate order, but instead he'd simply shrugged and said, "I'm a man, Eileen. I masturbate. Been doing it pretty regular since I was thirteen."

"This isn't playing with yourself, Brent. There's another woman, and just because she's a car doesn't make any difference to me."

"The heart knows what it wants, Eileen. If you feel like you need to leave me over this, go with my blessing. The kids are grown and it's not like we're spending Saturday nights slow dancing anyway. I like having you here, like how we can lean on each other, but I don't have a lot of happiness in my life, and I'm not letting you take this away." And he'd turned his back on her and gone out to the garage and they'd never spoken of it again.

That was back in September, and she'd been plotting his

murder ever since. Killing him so soon before Christmas seemed a little cold, but it would spare them false attempts at holiday cheer, and it wasn't like the twins were coming home, they were too busy going on ski trips with their college friends. In a way, the timing was good. Lots of people got depressed and did themselves in during the holidays, she'd read.

Brent had the trunk open and he was thrusting, having made some modifications to the trunk's interior to accommodate such peculiar habits, and he was so deep into his groove that he never noticed when she put the chloroform rag over his face. He slumped and fell to the concrete, and she looked down at his naked unconscious body, expecting some twinge of remorse or regret, but all she felt was disgust. Brent spent all his time sitting behind a desk at the dealership, not like Dolph, who had to stay active moving boxes around in the storeroom and such. The difference showed.

She wrapped up the chloroform rag in a bunch of plastic bags to dispose of later, then started the car. Brent never ran the engine inside the garage for more than a few minutes at a time—though she knew he liked to put his privates on the hood while it was vibrating—because he said it was a vintage car with no catalytic converter, which meant the exhaust was about a quarter carbon monoxide, and that stuff could kill you. Apparently modern cars were a lot harder to commit suicide with. Sometimes old things were better.

Eileen got the car running good, purring away—the slut— stuffed some towels along the bottom of the garage door to seal any cracks, then went inside the house and shut the door. Maybe it would look better to put Brent inside the car, but dragging his body across the concrete would have been nearly impossible—he had about 80 pounds on her—and would have scraped him up enough to make even the town policemen suspicious if she'd managed it. No, the towels under the door would make it clear enough the death was intentional, though probably everyone would be polite and rule it an accident. She'd considered faking a suicide note, but Brent wasn't one to pour out his feelings to anything that didn't have an engine, so she figured the silent treatment would be more plausible. Everyone knew the dealership wasn't doing well. Ford got a bailout from the government, but that didn't really trickle down to the people who sold the cars, and even the Cash for Clunkers program everybody liked so much was a big hassle for the dealers, with the government taking forever to pay up and the paperwork was a nightmare. People might be surprised Brent had taken the coward's way out, but not *too* surprised.

Eileen bundled up and went out to run some errands, including a visit to the Post Office to mail some last-minute Christmas gifts and a stop at the library to return some books, making a point of talking to people so she'd stick in their memory if the police asked later, not that she expected them to. She stayed gone about two hours—way longer than the internet said it took to die of carbon monoxide poisoning—then returned home, making a point of pausing by the garage and looking concerned about the sound of a car running inside, just in case one of the neighbors should be watching.

But then the fake look of concern became a real one, because there was a sound other than the engine running. There was a steady rhythmic thumping, like someone pounding on the inside of the garage door. Had a raccoon gotten trapped in there or something? But surely it would have died from the fumes, too...

She went to her car and dug around in the console for the garage door opener—why Brent had even given it to her she'd never know, like he'd let her park in there, ever—and pressed the button.

The door rose, and Brent lurched out, naked, into the icy driveway. He didn't look good, in fact he looked dead, but he was unaccountably lively for a dead man, and the worst thing about it was, he still had an erection, and that was a sight she could have lived quite contentedly without seeing again.

When he came stumbling toward her, arms out, gray face slack, drool running down his chin, teeth gnashing, little soldier standing at attention, she screamed.

Then she put her car in gear and ran him over.

8. THE PRETTY MUCH AVERAGE-LENGTH ARM OF THE LAW

"**H**ow long do I have to sit on him?" Otto asked.

"Until Harry and Stevie Ray get here." Dolph shifted a little on the couch, but kept the nose of the gun pointed at Mr. Levitt, who was lying face-down on the floor, apparently unbothered by having his face mere inches from a pool of leaky zombie gore, with Otto sitting on top of him, butt planted between his shoulder blades, legs on either side.

"What if he tries something?" Otto asked. "I'm not able to defend myself too well like this."

"You outweigh him by forty pounds, Otto. He's an old man. I wouldn't worry."

Otto nodded toward the limbless zombie, which still grunted and did its best to turn over, stuck on its back like a turtle. "That guy there's got forty pounds on *me*, and Mr. Levitt didn't have any trouble taking him out."

"I had my tools with me then," Mr. Levitt offered, tone perfectly reasonable, if a bit muffled from having his face pressed most of the way into the carpet. "And he didn't see it coming. He was a real victim of opportunity. I was never much of a stalker, couldn't be bothered, but I happened upon him broken down out on old route 15, cell phone getting no reception, and offered to bring him here to use the phone, told him I'd talk to the mechanic for him, make sure he got the local's price instead of being charged an arm and a leg. He was grateful right up until the point I put the needle in his neck. Heh." Levitt's laugh was nasty, and his whole body shook with it, sending unpleasant vibrations up through Otto's bottom parts.

"This is sick." Rufus came in from the hallway, holding an old-fashioned bag of the sort country doctors once used, when the world was a better place and people made house calls and nobody knew what HMO stood for and you could pay your medical bill with a bushel of corn or maybe a couple of chickens. Of course they didn't have polio vaccine or chemotherapy back then, so maybe the changing times weren't all bad. "It's all full of finger bones."

"That's a good boy, get those fingerprints all over everything." Levitt cackled again. "Not that it much matters, but in case the civil authorities do get things under control and avert the apocalypse and take me to trial, I appreciate any crime-scene contamination you want to do."

Rufus dropped the bag and moaned, wiping his hands on his shirt. "I went down in the cellar, the dirt's all soft, and there are gaping holes where I guess these zombies came climbing out."

"I always meant to pour concrete down there, cover them all over, I figured, I'm an old man, I'm retired, why do I need my own little personal burial ground anymore? But I just couldn't do it. What if somebody came to the door all alone one afternoon with a petition, nobody else on the street, where would I put him when I was done?"

"Just shut up, please." Otto pressed down on the back of Mr. Levitt's head with the palm of his hand.

A hard rap came at the door. "Come on in!" Dolph said, and the town policemen, Harry and Stevie Ray, entered. Both wore beige uniforms, but the similarities ended there. Harry was in his early fifties, and his big beer gut preceded him wherever he went, and he had enormous muttonchop sideburns as if hoping to disguise the fact that he was going bald on top. Stevie Ray was one of Lake Woebegotten's few black residents, in his late twenties, and he'd done a stint in the Marines and still kept up a good exercise regime, so he didn't have a gut so much, and he had a shaved head, which always made Otto feel cold in sympathy, especially in winter like this. He was a part-time police officer, and also worked as a bartender (and, when the need arose, drunk-remover) at the Backtrack Bar.

When Stevie Ray saw Dolph's gun, he unholstered his pistol and pointed it at him.

"Don't point that at me!" Dolph yelled, setting the rifle down by the couch, barrel pointed up and away. "Point it at old man Levitt! I told you on the phone, he's a serial killer! He's dangerous!"

"He doesn't look like much of a threat right now." Stevie Ray's eyes did a quick scan of the room, taking in the various dead bodies, the signs of struggle, the bloody chainsaw, and all the rest without any obvious reaction. "We got a mess in here," he said at last. "Otto, get up, let me put handcuffs on Mr. Levitt, that's a little better than you sitting on him."

Otto rose, and Stevie Ray slid right in, pressing a knee on Mr. Levitt's back. "If this is a mistake, you have my apologies in advance," Stevie Ray said. "But for the time being it seems like everybody'd feel better if you didn't have your hands free." He snapped the bracelets onto Mr. Levitt's bony wrists.

The elderly killer lifted his head from the carpet and said, "I never did a black one. None ever came wandering by, and there are so few of you in town I knew any of you'd be missed. Oh well. Hope springs eternal."

"I've got you on threatening a peace officer if nothing else," Stevie Ray said, rising. "Why don't you just stay there on the carpet?"

"How can you be so calm?" Dolph said, outraged. "There are chainsaw murder victims in here! Undead monsters! Lake Woebegotten's answer to a geriatric John Wayne Gacy—"

"Gacy!" Levitt was outraged. "A clown, and worse, a buffoon! The only thing we have in common is where we bury the bodies, and—"

"Everybody calm down." Harry's voice was slow and deliberate, and his oxlike expression and measured tones made people assume he was the stupid one and Stevie Ray was the smart one, but in fact they were both pretty smart. "Stevie Ray, you want to make sure the area's secure? I'll see what I can ascertain about the, ah..."

"Zombies?" Rufus offered.

Harry sighed like an inflatable couch sagging under the weight of one too many fat relatives at Christmas. "Yep. I guess that's it. Who here knows the most about them?"

"Me," Rufus said. "I've seen lots of them today. They were all over the cities this morning. I drove here to warn people, you know."

Harry nodded. He strolled over to the limbless zombie and said, "You ever play that zombie game Left 4 Dead?"

Rufus, sounding surprised, said, "Sure, man, all the time, but mostly the sequel lately, it's harder, but so much scarier."

Harry nodded. "Thing I never understood about that game is, it's the zombie apocalypse, and everything's gone to heck, and there's those piles of guns and ammunition and painkillers and gas cans and stuff just sitting there all over the place for people to pick up."

"The game wouldn't be much fun without guns and explosions though."

"You got me there. Not much fun at all."

"How can you be talking about games?" Otto said. He'd played Pong a few times when Rufus was a kid but couldn't see the point. You might as well go out and just hit a real ball around, why not? And now there was some kind of zombie killing game? Well, so what? How was that supposed to be any help to anybody? Playing Pong wasn't going to make you a good tennis player, so killing zombies in some video game probably wasn't too effective as training for killing zombies in the real world.

Harry didn't pay him any attention, just went on talking about the game. "The thing that really gets me, though, is the syringes of adrenaline, you know, you inject them in the game and you can run faster and fight harder? If it was me, and I saw a full syringe laying on the ground in some burned-out grocery store surrounded by the hungry dead, I'm not so sure I'd just up and stick it into the first vein in my arm I came across."

"I might," Rufus said. "But I'd probably be hoping it was something other than adrenaline. Something that would put me out of my misery."

"That's a thought," Harry said. "Why don't we put this one out of his misery?" He nudged the limbless zombie with his boot.

"First, I don't think he's miserable," Rufus said. "I don't think he's feeling anything, other than hungry. And second... he's proof. Of what's happening. A real live... well, you know... a real zombie."

"Guess there might be some value there," Harry agreed. "Shouldn't be any harm in it as long as you stay clear of his teeth. So you've seen these fellas in action. What can you tell me?"

"They're slow. They don't feel pain. They don't stop until you mess up their brains. Even if you take a head off, it keeps moving, though the body stops."

"They contagious? Like, they bite you, you catch it?"

"I don't think it's a disease," Rufus said. "It's just... the dead rising. These bodies were already dead, nobody bit them, they just woke up. So it's contagious, but only because a zombie can kill you, and when you're dead, you become one too."

"Well all right, then." He hitched up his belt, though it slid back down under the weight of his gut. "Seems like we've got a fighting chance then."

"Against the end of the world?" Mr. Levitt said. "How do you figure that?"

"There's about 1,000 people in this town or in the farms just outside," Harry said. "Some of them went down to Florida for the winter, or they're off visiting family for the holidays, so it's not quite all of them, but it's enough. And if it's just the dead waking up and walking around, not like a real plague, well... How many corpses do we have laying around here on any given day, do you think? If you hadn't been keeping dead folks in shallow graves in your basement, Mr. Levitt, we might not have even noticed the zombie situation until one of the old folks passed on and tried to eat their relatives. Now maybe in the cities there's hospitals and morgues full of dead folks and people getting shot dead for their tennis shoes by gangbangers and people overdosing on marijuana and guys jumping off roofs because they can't stand the pressure of their CEO jobs anymore, but around here things are different. Most winters we only lose a handful of folks, and one of those is usually an unmarried agrarian Norwegian who puts a gun in his mouth, and not to be insensitive, but somebody who blows his brains out is solving any future personal zombie problem right then and there. I'd say it's definitely a manageable situation here. We'll call a town meeting, warn everybody to be on the lookout, and we'll just be careful until this whole mess blows over."

"It's not just people turning into zombies," Dolph said. "I think, anyway. We saw this dog, half run over, and it was still trying to bite…"

"What dog?" Mr. Levitt said. "Alta? Here, Alta, come to Daddy!"

"Your dog's a zombie dog now," Otto said. No point trying to pretend something else was happening here now. Hard to admit Rufus had been right all along, but there it was, and he was man enough to admit it.

Mr. Levitt began weeping quietly into the carpet.

"Can I see this zombie dog?" Harry asked.

"It's in a cooler in the truck, I'll go get it." Rufus hurried outside, but he returned a moment later, shaking his head. "The cooler was tipped over, and the lid was open. Alta got away. There was a trail in the snow, going around the house, but, ah…" He looked a little sheepish, but then, Otto thought he always looked a little bit like a sheep, it ran on that side of the family.

"You didn't want to chase a zombie dog unarmed and there were no handguns and ammo just laying around in the driveway." Harry's voice was bland and non-judgmental. "Can't say I blame you. Sounds like a job for animal control anyway." He sighed. "Which, of course, is me."

A great crashing and shouting came from deeper in the house, followed by a scream and a gunshot. Harry had his pistol out in no time, and Dolph lifted his rifle, but Otto just considered reaching for the chainsaw and then changed his mind. He'd be just as likely to cut off his own leg as to do any good. Better to just stand behind the people holding guns.

Old man Levitt lifted his head from the carpet, and smiled despite the tears running down his face. "Sounds like the other officer decided to see what I had hidden up in the attic. Guess he found out. That's where I keep the ladies' auxiliary. Seemed wrong to keep the men and women together. Heh heh heh."

9. FREEZER BURNED

"**W**e should have called the police," Pastor Inkfist said, and Father Edsel just grunted, driving too fast, tapping his fingers on the steering wheel, and humming something that sounded sort of Wagnerian, only more bombastic.

The priest stopped humming, said, "The days of worldly authority are at an end, my boy. Listen." He flicked the radio on and twisted through the channels the old-fashioned way, turning a knob, no "seek" or "scan" to light the way, but even though he turned slowly there was never anything but the hiss of static. "You see? Nothing but empty air. The dead have risen. I don't truck with that Protestant business about the Rapture, but I believe in the end of days, the revelation of St. John the Divine—"

"Now, I don't know, I think that was all metaphor," Daniel said, a bit weakly at first, but gaining strength as he went on, feeling on solid ground. "The Great Beast 666 was a Roman emperor, John was writing about the evils of his own time, not giving us a glimpse of something terrible to come." He paused. "Plus, of course, he was probably eating the wrong sort of mushrooms. I hear those can give you all sorts of ideas."

"There's evil afoot, Inkfist—Hell itself disgorging the dead, demons possessing the corpses, I don't claim to know all the *details*, but surely you admit Satan had a hand in this?"

"I guess, I suppose you'd say, as for Satan, I think for myself I've always seen the church as more practical, ministering the sick, offering spiritual guidance, sure, but mostly—"

"You doubt the existence of demons?" Edsel's eyes were fiery. "There's biblical precedent for this situation *exactly*. Do you recall when Jesus found men emerging from tombs possessed by a demon, and the demon said his name was Legion? And our Lord cast the devils out of the bodies of the men and into a herd of pigs, and those pigs drowned themselves in the sea of Galilee? We have that very same thing here—demons in the bodies of men!"

"I always took the story of Jesus facing Legion to be a parable for the anti-Roman resistance of the time," Daniel said. "That would explain the inconsistency in the way various apostles—"

"We must be warriors for Christ," Edsel interrupted. "Armed with our faith, but also armed with shotguns and baseball bats and flamethrowers, if we can get them."

"Ah. But we can't, of course."

"Nonsense," Edsel said. "Of course we can. And I know just the place. But first, we need to gather the people of the town, and tell them what's happened. The sooner the better, before we're overrun by the dead."

"How do you propose we notify everyone? Go door to door?"

Edsel glanced away from the snow-spattered road to give Daniel a look of complete contempt. "Are you serious? Go forth and harness the mighty power of the Lutheran organization, man. Call up the Women's Circle and get them to unleash the awful majesty of their phone trees!"

"I was thinking to myself, in a horror movie, the black guy *always* dies first," Stevie Ray said. Otto and Rufus and Harry were all jammed in the hallway, with Stevie Ray looking down on them from the attic opening in the ceiling. Dolph and his rifle were out in the living room watching over old man Levitt. "So I was thinking, *Not me*, and I had my gun out. Still scared the crap just about right out of me when the girl-zombie started moving. She's wrapped up in about fifteen layers of heavy-duty plastic, though, so she was mostly just rolling a little bit. I probably could've saved the bullet, but I put one in her head anyway.

Couple other girls up here in plastic, too, but they look like they're pretty much just bones, so they're not moving."

"Good to know," Harry said.

Rufus coughed. "The black guy doesn't always die first in horror movies."

Otto rolled his eyes, but he figured Rufus felt compelled to weigh in, as this was an area in which he had some expertise.

"In the original *Night of the Living Dead* movie, a black guy's even the hero."

"Does he make it out alive in the end?" Stevie Ray asked.

"Well. No."

"Mmm hmm."

"Back to the matter at hand." Harry sniffed. "I thought most serial killers liked just one kind of victim. You know, they like to specialize."

Stevie Ray grunted. "I figure old man Levitt decided he needed to kill a couple of girls now and then just to convince himself he wasn't a homosexual. You know how it is for people of his generation. They have a hard time admitting things like that about themselves."

"Yup," Harry said. "I could see how you may be right."

As always when the subject came up, Otto wondered in a rush of worry if maybe he wasn't secretly gay. He'd never been attracted to men, really, but what did that prove? He wasn't attracted to most women, either. Then Stevie Ray said, "Shit, something else is moving up here," and a moment later he shouted, "Good GOD it's a zombie raccoon, look out below!" and Otto was thankful to have something else to worry about for a couple of minutes.

Dolph wanted to go by Eileen's house and make sure she was okay, that she hadn't fallen victim to a rampaging zombie min-pin or anything else, but was afraid it would look suspicious, so he'd better wait until nightfall, when he'd be less likely to attract notice. The thing about a town as small as Lake Woebegotten was that everybody knew your business, no matter how much you might wish it was otherwise. Still, they'd been discreet, and as far as anybody else knew, Eileen was just one of his customers, nothing special to him, and it was important to maintain the fiction.

Unless, of course, Harry was wrong, and the zombie apocalypse really was going to forever change the very basic structure of life and society, in which case, all the old rules about infidelity might just cease to apply. Probably the few remaining survivors would need to get started repopulating the Earth. Possibly Dolph would have to inseminate a great many women in order to do his part to restore the species to ascendancy. Now wasn't that a pretty thought?

The zombie in the bed of his truck thumped, which was nerve-wracking. They'd weighed the thing down with chains and thrown a tarp over it, and it didn't have any arms or legs, but Dolph could imagine it wriggling its way toward the cab of the truck, silently sliding open the window with its teeth, and sinking fangs into his neck...

Dolph shuddered and stepped on the gas a bit, though he was following Harry and Stevie Ray's squad car, so he couldn't go any faster than they were. They finally reached the police station, which was really just a wing of the town hall, though it did have a jail cell, and Dolph watched as Stevie Ray frog-marched Mr. Levitt in through the side door. Harry came over, as did Otto and Rufus, to peer into the bed of the truck where the zombie struggled. "What do we do with him?" Dolph said.

"You got that big walk-in freezer, right?" Harry said. "You mind tucking him in there until tonight's meeting?"

Dolph stared at him. "You want me to put an undead monster in my *store*?"

"Just for a few hours." Harry's face was totally bland and vaguely pleasant, and Dolph's outrage melted under his calm gaze. "It's just I'm going to be a little busy trying to contact the county sheriff and the state police and booking a multiple murderer and trying to organize a town meeting, so I'm stretched a little thin. You don't mind helping out?"

"Of course not," Dolph said, and muttered something about civic duty that made Harry slap him on the shoulder and say "Good man!" Some people at the last town meeting had been agitating to fire Harry and disband the local police department, like a lot of little towns all over the country were doing—you could subcontract out to the county sheriff for less than the cost of Harry's salary and whatever they paid Stevie Ray, but enough people liked having the personal touch and the familiar face in the town cruiser, and nobody much liked the idea of outsiders coming in and sniffing around the town's crimes. Much better to have Harry there, who'd known everybody for years and could be counted on for a certain level of discretion, even if he could get a little too liberal with the traffic tickets as the end of the fiscal year loomed.

"We can help you with him," Rufus offered, and Otto looked at his nephew sharply. Otto was a lazy son of a gun, Dolph mused, and how he managed to make a living selling things to farmers was a mystery—he must have quite a store of dirty jokes in Norwegian, or else people just bought things from him to make him go away. Dolph had never had another customer besides Otto who *haggled* over the price of a tin of chewing tobacco, and Dolph had quit carrying Otto's brand in self-defense. His nephew was a little odd—with that wispy sad mustache-fuzz, and was that a tattoo of a spiderweb peeking out of the collar of his coat?—but at least he hadn't puked when faced with zombies like his uncle had. Given his choice, Dolph would have preferred to have Rufus by his side in a fight over Otto, but thought he might ultimately be better off facing whatever came at him alone.

"No, I need the pair of you to come in and give Stevie Ray your statement about what you saw at Mr. Levitt's house," Harry said. "We'll have you come in later, Dolph. I have to get the state police on the horn, see if they can send a crime scene tech…"

Rufus shook his head. "Good luck. I bet the state police are pretty busy trying to stop St. Paul from being eaten by the living dead. You didn't see it. It's bad over there."

Harry shrugged. "We'll see. Come on inside. You take care, Dolph." He grinned. "And don't leave town."

Where would I go? Dolph thought. He got back in the truck and drove up around the town square to his store, parking in the loading zone around back. After checking to make sure the zombie was secure, he went in through the back door and called, "Clem! Clem, I need your help unloading something."

Clem the boy wonder didn't answer, so Dolph went into the

front of the store and found him slumped on the stool behind the register with his face on the counter, drool puddling by his cheek. Dolph smacked him on the back of the head, and Clem groaned and lifted his head like it was full of concrete. His eyes were glassy and his skin was pale, and though neither was a difference in kind from his usual appearance, there was definitely a difference of degree, and he was pale and glassy *enough* that Dolph said, "Are you all right, son?"

Clem looked up at him and said, "Dun fill suh gud," voice all mushy and sleepy.

Dolph put the back of his hand against Clem's forehead, and it was hot as a woodstove. "Did you clean out that bite on your leg like I told you?"

"Uhhhh… Uh fuhgoht."

"Let me see it." Dolph came around the counter, and Clem obligingly lifted his pants leg and revealed several ugly red holes in his ankle and calf, most oozing blood mixed with something repulsively yellow-green. "That doesn't look too good," Dolph said, and then Clem's eyes rolled back in his head and he fell off the stool and hit his head on the edge of the counter and landed in a big ugly mess with his bony butt sticking up in the air.

"Clem!" Dolph rolled him over and slapped his face a couple of times and peeled back his eyelids, though he wasn't sure why he did that part, it was just something you saw people do on TV when somebody threw a faint, and in any event it didn't appear to help much. He could call 911 but they were probably swamped with calls, so he went to the phone book and looked up Doctor Holliday's number. He'd probably get here faster, and besides he knew Clem, so if the boy woke up and started answering questions but didn't know who the president was or how much four plus four amounted to, Doctor Holliday would know that was just Clem's normal baseline level of intelligence, not evidence of head trauma.

Dolph dialed, and the line rang and rang and rang without answer, and he was about to hang up when Clem rose from behind the counter, and Dolph just dropped the phone instead, because Clem's head was canted at a funny angle, and now that he was standing up it was obvious his neck was broken, must've landed wrong when he fell, and wasn't that just the luck? Not bad enough to get infected from a zombie dog bite, he had to go and die, and right in the store, too, which would probably play heck with Dolph's insurance.

Clem was still drooling, which he didn't usually do except when sleeping or staring really hard at a packing list, and his eyes were still rolled up, but his mouth was opening and closing ceaselessly as he tried to come for Dolph.

Fortunately death hadn't made him any smarter, and Clem kept trying to walk right through the counter instead of just walking around it, which meant Dolph had a free minute to…

What? Kill him? Re-kill him? But he was Clem! Dumb as a box of elbow macaroni, sure, but loyal, and sweet-natured, and good tempered, and Dolph had known him since he was just a little kid, and he couldn't very well pick up a frozen turkey and smack Clem over the head with it, could he? Shooting those zombies at Mr. Levitt's house had been one thing, they'd been *strangers*, but even if this wasn't really Clem anymore, it sure looked like him. Dolph didn't have his gun now, either, it was still in the truck, and that also made it more difficult, because looking at somebody over the barrel of a rifle had a way of creating some distance between you, the way bludgeoning somebody to death with the contents of a small-town grocery store did not.

So it would have to be containment, then. Dolph danced over toward the back of the store, waving his arms to keep zombie-Clem's eyes on him, not that Clem appeared to be using his only-showing-whites eyes, and for that matter one of the zombies at Mr. Levitt's house didn't have any eyes at all, so how did they get around anyway? Maybe they could smell people, or sense them somehow. Clem eventually figured out how to walk out from behind the register and came lurching down the aisle, knocking into a nice endcap display of pie fillings and sending cans of pumpkin puree and cherries in heavy syrup spilling and rolling every which way. Dolph stayed just out of Clem's reach, backing up carefully toward the rear of the store, knowing that if he lost his balance and tumbled Clem would fall upon him and snap those teeth—and what horrible teeth, the boy never did get the hang of brushing regularly, let alone flossing—and take a big old bite out of whatever part of Dolph's anatomy presented itself.

Dolph got the freezer door open a moment before Clem lurched into the storeroom, and then Dolph did the hardest thing he'd ever done in his life: he just stood there in front of the open freezer until Clem was almost within grasping distance.

He sprang off to the left, nipped quickly around behind Clem, put both hands on the zombie's back, and shoved him into the freezer as hard as he could. Clem stumbled but didn't fall, and Dolph slammed the freezer door just as the zombie was trying to emerge. The door had a latch on the inside—about fifteen years ago one employee, smarter than Clem but only by a whisker, had gotten herself locked inside for hours, so Dolph had a handle put inside—and maybe Clem was too dumb to use it now, but to be safe Dolph dragged a bunch of heavy boxes of pop and soup and such over in front of the door, making a nice solid wall.

He sagged against the door, panting hard, and then remembered the limbless zombie in the truck, the one he was originally supposed to put in the freezer, and he said a profanity so obscene it might have even made Eileen blush, if she'd heard it.

10. WOMEN'S CIRCLE
OF HELL

Eileen backed up her little car, got out, and looked at the motionless corpse of her husband. She hadn't run him over so much as run *into* him, hitting him with the front bumper and sending him flying back to crash against the front of his still-running Mustang. He was definitely dead, though, no motion at all in his chest, and—

The fumes pouring out of the garage were too much for her, so she ran into the house and locked all the doors. So much for making his death look like a suicide. She paced up and down in the living room, gnawing on her thumbnail, trying to decide what to do. It was getting on past lunchtime, but at least it was cold, so not too many people were out and about, but eventually somebody would see Brent's body, and then she'd be in the soup. She couldn't bury him, the ground was frozen solid down for inches, it'd take a backhoe to break the crust, but she could at least get him out of the driveway, maybe put him in the trunk, though it'd have to be the Mustang's trunk since she could hardly have a body sitting out in the back of Brent's pickup truck and her car barely had room in back for a couple bags of groceries, and later after night fell she could drive around to the lake, cut a hole in the ice—Brent had ice fishing gear though he hadn't gone out in recent years, and how hard could it be to use if idiots like her husband managed it?—and slide his body down into the wet darkness where it would go unnoticed until the spring thaw. That would work. It was a plan. She'd have to come up with a believable story about where he'd gone, or maybe she could just claim bewilderment, let people think he'd gotten bored and run out on her—

Her phone rang, startling her near about out of her skin. She considered letting it ring, but what if it was somebody calling about Brent's body, she'd have to pretend to know nothing about it, to be surprised to hear he was all crumpled up half out of the garage, and oh Lord what if there was blood on the front of her car…

"Munson residence, this is Eileen."

"Eileen! This is Pastor Inkfist. How are things with you to-day?"

"Oh, hello Pastor. I'm afraid this isn't the best time—"

"It's a bad time for all of us, Eileen, but I need some of your famous organizational prowess now. Can you get on the phone to all the other members of the Women's Circle? We're holding a meeting in the community center this evening, at six o'clock on the dot."

"At six? People don't like having their supper interrupted, Pastor."

"I know, but we need everyone there, so we have to wait until folks get off work, but no later—it's an emergency."

"What kind of emergency?" She knew from experience that Pastor Inkfist considered things like deciding which child got to play the angel in the Christmas Pageant an emergency, and she had her own actual emergencies to tend to.

"I don't suppose you've noticed anything, ah, odd, lately?"

Besides her gassed husband lying dead in her driveway in front of God and the neighbors and everybody? "Like what?"

"Ah, it… it might be better if it waits for the meeting. But it's vitally important that you get *everyone*, all right? Not just the women, but the men, the children, the families, everyone."

"I can try, Pastor, but—"

"It's a matter of life and death."

"Do you mean the deciding on whether to have a pancake supper or a spaghetti supper kind of life and death, or the actual life-and-death kind of life and death?"

"The latter." He cleared his throat. "And if you could make sure there are chairs set up, and maybe some kind of refreshments, and, ah… whatever a meeting like this might need…"

Helpless. Like all men. "All right, Pastor. I'll do what I can." After another minute of farewells, she hung up and called her right-hand woman in the Women's Circle, Glenda Dreier, and put her on the job.

"You can count on me, Eileen!" Glenda chirped. She was usually perky, and didn't ask any questions, just did what you asked. Made a good hot dog and Velveeta hotdish, too. Generally dependable. Eileen hated her more than she hated just about anybody except her husband, and since he was dead, Glenda just eased into first place. "I'll see you there!"

"Oh. Of course." Eileen would have to go. Presumably with Brent's body in her trunk. That was awkward. Better go tend to that. She was about to go looking for a pair of gloves when the phone rang again.

"Hello, Munson—"

"Eileen, this is Harry, how are you doing today?" He sounded rushed, pushing out the polite greeting like too much toothpaste squirting out of the tube.

The police chief. Calling her. He was the one person she had to make absolutely not at all suspicious. "Oh, I can't complain, I—"

"That's good to hear, listen, is the mayor around?"

Her blood was already chilled from being outside in the winter without a proper coat, but it got a little colder. "No, Brent isn't here, maybe he's at the dealership?"

"They said they thought he went home for lunch," Harry said. "Dang it, I need to talk to him, we've got a serious situation here. Have him call me on my mobile just as soon as he's able. We need to organize a meeting for—"

"Oh, the Pastor called to tell me about that already. An emergency meeting at six tonight at the community center, right?"

There was a long silence. "Huh. Maybe I should talk to the Pastor. Could be he knows some things I should find out about. He's got you calling folks?"

"He does."

"I think I can do him one better than that. When you see

Brent, tell him to get in touch with me as soon as he can. And Eileen? Do me a favor. Keep your doors locked, and don't go out until it's time for the meeting, all right?"

"Whatever you say, Harry. Is everything okay?"

"It will be." He hung up without saying goodbye, which was pretty rude, but she certainly had enough other things to occupy her, so she didn't mind too much. What was all this meeting talk about? Whatever it was, maybe it would distract everyone from Brent's disappearance, though on the other hand if there were a genuine emergency, people would wonder why the mayor of Lake Woebegotten wasn't on hand to deal with it. Mayor. Ha. Time was she'd been proud to be the mayor's wife, except there wasn't much to the job except helping plan the 4th of July parade and riding herd on the town council, that bunch of busybodies who could spend hours debating noise ordinances but had an inordinate amount of trouble getting that big pothole on Main Street filled in. Brent liked to boast that he was in "politics" but he was no more a politician than a spider monkey was King Kong.

And now Brent wasn't anything at all, which was a blessing, but also a problem, and one she'd better deal with, just like she had to deal with all the problems that cropped up in her little corner of the world.

Eileen went outside with her rubber gloves and a bunch of heavy-duty black trash bags and her winter coat with the furry hood up. She'd get Brent back into the garage, and into the Mustang's trunk where he could go unnoticed until after the meeting tonight, whatever that was about, and, hmm, should she drive the Mustang to the meeting even though she never ever drove it and even Brent hardly ever drove it anywhere, or should she go to the meeting in her car and then come back and get the Mustang and oh, Lord, she'd told Harry that Brent hadn't come home for lunch but there was his big black Ford Behemoth sitting in the driveway big as life and what if someone saw it and told Harry and—

Brent's body was gone. There was a little bit of blood, though not much really, on the concrete, with a few strands of Brent's dyed-black hair stuck to it, but of her dead husband himself there was no sign. She walked cautiously around the house, following the peculiar footprints, looked like he was dragging his leg a bit, maybe she could track him, but the trail led through the backyard and into the woods, and the thought of going in there unarmed after him was too terrifying.

That meant she'd better go ahead and get armed. She couldn't let him run loose. If he told someone she'd tried to murder him, she'd never live it down. Good for her he'd gone off into the trees instead of knocking on the neighbor's doors. The carbon monoxide must have addled his brain a bit. So she had that going for her. And she'd always been smarter than him anyway, even at his best.

She stopped briefly in the garage to turn off the Mustang, holding her coat sleeve over her nose even though the fumes had pretty well dissipated by then. Then inside to the bedroom, to the locked gun box in the closet on a high shelf, and inside was an old Army-issue Colt pistol that had belonged to Brent's father, God rest his soul. She loaded it, tucked it into the pocket of her winter coat with the safety firmly on, and then paused, thought a moment, and picked up the knobbly-headed walking stick their son Gerald had brought home during his hippie hiker walkabout phase. It would help her navigate the woods, and in a pinch, it was a good blunt object.

Eileen was nearly out the door when the phone rang, and she considered just walking out, but a cold sort of rage came over her, settling down over her shoulders like a comfortable shawl, so she picked up the phone and said, in a pleasant and even tone, "You motherhumpers need to stop calling me to solve all your problems and learn how to deal with this kind of trivial bullshit yourselves, because I'm tired of being everybody's mother and—"

But before she could really work up a good head of steam Harry's obviously pre-recorded voice harrumphed and said, "This is your chief of police Harry Cusack, calling with an important emergency announcement. All citizens of Lake Woebegotten should assemble at the community center by the town square at 6 p.m. sharp tonight for a vital emergency meeting. Attendance is mandatory. Uh, and refreshments will be served."

Click.

It was that emergency call system that got set up with the money from Homeland Security a few years back, Eileen remembered Brent talking about it—a way to call every single number in town all at once with a single message, helpful in the event of a terrorist attack (unlikely) or industrial catastrophe (somewhat more plausible). Sounded like a truly epic prank call waiting to happen, she'd told him, and he'd shrugged and said only him and the policemen knew how to use it anyway. She checked her watch. Going on 2 p.m. Which meant she had only a few hours to track down Brent, kill him, get him out of sight, and make it to the meeting on time. Her absence would definitely be noted if she didn't arrive, ideally early to help set up. "Refreshments." She shuddered to think what a lifelong bachelor like Harry might consider suitable for such an event. Half-chewed cigars and candy bars?

Patting the pistol in her pocket, she went off into the snow.

11. GUN RUNNING

"All right, the wheels are in motion." Pastor Inkfist turned from the phone to Father Edsel, who paced impatiently around the tiny front room of the parsonage. "How about you?"

He waved a hand impatiently. "I told Sister Klingenberg to make sure everyone's gathered. She'll see it's done."

Daniel nodded, thinking about the fact that both these men of God depended on the women in their respective churches to actually get things like this done, wondering if maybe there was a sermon in this somewhere, or if it was one of those quiet little truths best left ignored lest people started thinking overmuch about the implications. His musings were derailed when Edsel said, "All right, then, let's go get some guns."

"Guns? Are you sure that's a good idea?"

"You can't pray the head off a zombie, Daniel. Let's be practical here. We've seen the abominations. And as Jesus said: I come not to bring peace, but to bring a sword. The only reason he said 'sword' was because assault rifles hadn't been invented yet."

Daniel coughed. "Ah, but the sword of which Jesus spoke was not a literal weapon, but a reference to the ideological upheaval inherent in his message, the divisions that would inevitably come between those who accepted his message and those who rejected it."

"Sometimes a sword is just a sword, Daniel. Are you coming, or not?"

Daniel sighed. "Where are you *going*?"

71

"To the largest stockpile of weapons available in Lake Woebegotten. We're going to Cy's Rustic Comfort Cabins and Bait Shop."

Cyrus Bell was widely considered to be the single most insane person in town, outranking even BigHorn Jim the pagan and that squirrelly fella on the outskirts who talked to himself all the time, called The Narrator by those locals who called him anything at all, and Cyrus shared with Father Edsel a love for and vast and abiding knowledge of conspiracy theories. As such, his motel was not as popular as it might have been, though most of the drop-off in business was down to the internet, really. Before the internet, people might arrive with no idea what to expect from the proprietor and sole employee of the establishment, and find themselves reasonably quite alarmed at the whole experience. Now with all the travel and review websites, though, people who'd experienced Cyrus's admittedly warm hospitality had a way to share their thoughts and feelings with anyone who happened to be clicking around looking for a place to stay in central Minnesota, preferably near a nice lake for fishing.

The locale was good, Daniel thought as Edsel parked in front of the wooden cabin that Cy used for an office. Right on the lake, surrounded by big trees, half a dozen cabins set at peculiar angles to create a sense of privacy, the two largest with their own fishing piers, and Cy even rented rowboats in the summer.

It would have been a suitably modest sort of paradise, if not for the fact that Cy was so friendly. Aggressively friendly. He'd knock on a guest's door before dawn and ask if they wanted to take a boat out, and by the way, did they know the moon was a hollow spaceship full of alien biologists studying Earthlings like ants under a microscope? Or you might come back from a morning looking at the Interesting Historical Landmarks in the area—the site of the first drowning of a white man, the field that would have been a battlefield from the French and Indian War if the French soldiers hadn't gotten lost and ended up back in Canada, the place where the old one-room schoolhouse had been before it burned down, and the like—only to find Cy sitting in your room on your bed sorting through your luggage, and he'd politely explain that he was looking for the CIA tracking devices, which could look like anything, really, even lacy red underwear with those little ribbons, and boy, he'd sure never seen anything like that before, least of all in a married lady's bag. Then he'd put his arm around you and confide how he'd stopped wearing underwear entirely because underpants were an Illuminati conspiracy designed to lower the sperm counts of working-class men. If you called him about getting some fresh towels it could take two or three hours to get off the phone, and if you hung up on him, he'd just come to your door and offer to fix the phone because there must be a problem with the connection.

Edsel got along with him beautifully, of course.

Daniel followed the priest up the line of lopsided ice-rimed paving stones to the office. Edsel pushed open the door, making the bell above jangle, and Cy stood up smiling from his spot behind the counter. The wall in back of him was plastered with bumper stickers, many with questionable grammar and spelling, extolling the virtues of personal weaponry, acknowledging the existence of extraterrestrials, and supporting fringe political candidates from the past thirty years of local, state, and national elections, some of whom had gone on to be successful or notorious cult leaders. "Father! Pastor! What can I do for you today? Want a bite of my tuna fish sandwich?"

"We've come to tell you the end is here," Father Edsel said. "The dead have risen from their graves to devour the living."

Cy tipped his feed cap back on his head, revealing a vast expanse of forehead and making his wide-open face seem even more surprised and alarmed. He wore a camouflage vest with the pockets stuffed with shotgun shells, and he massaged his ammunition in an absent-minded way. "You're saying we've got zombies?"

"Exactly."

"Explains a few things," Cy allowed. "My satellite just up and quit working, so I can't get the internet either, and there's been nothing on the radio or the network TV stations for a few hours. This related to that big light in the sky last night?"

"It could have been a celestial sign," Edsel said solemnly. "Not unlike the star of Bethlehem, which appeared to alert mankind to the coming of the Lord. Only that shattered star last night foretold the coming of the Antichrist."

"And here I just thought it was an orbital weapons platform test by the UN. You never can tell. Well, all right then, zombies. Eating brains, that whole thing?"

"They seem inclined to eat any kind of living flesh they can get their jaws around, Cy."

"Fair enough. What are the rules of engagement?"

"The pastor and I are starting an Interfaith Anti-Zombie Task Force—"

"We're starting a what?" Daniel said.

"—and we'll need weaponry. Zombies are vulnerable chiefly to having their heads blown off. Can you help us out?"

Cy frowned. "Are you sure Pastor Inkfist can be trusted? No offense, Pastor, it's just, you've always struck me as someone more concerned with the laws of man than the laws of God, unlike Father Edsel here. I'd hate for you to turn me in to the state police just because I maybe have a couple of unregistered handguns, not saying I do, mind you."

"In this situation, I think I have to err on the side of expediency, Cyrus. I'm sure if you have any unregistered weapons you simply forgot to fill out the paperwork."

"That must be it," Cy said. "All right, come on to cabin seven."

"I thought you only had six cabins?" Daniel said.

"Cabin seven is what he calls his bunker," Edsel explained, and Cy grinned and led them into the back.

"My daddy built this bomb shelter back in the '50s, before he figured out the Communists were just the dupes of the Trilateral Commission, and that nuclear bombs don't actually work. The Trinity tests were faked, you know, and the bombings in Japan were just conventional TNT bombs and a lot of special effects to make it seem like we had an unstoppable superweapon." Cy spoke the words without heat or inflection, as if he'd said it all many times before and repeated himself now out of habit, but Daniel didn't pay him much attention anyway, as he was gazing around the long, low concrete underground room at the truly awesome quantities of weaponry present there.

There were guns, and not just handguns: also shotguns, assault rifles, sniper rifles, and bristling, black, oily-looking weapons that looked as if they belonged in a science fiction movie about space marines. The guns were mounted on wall racks, interspersed with assorted knives, a machete, and even several ninja throwing stars. Long, low crates lined the walls, and Daniel suspected they were filled with ammunition. He hoped they weren't full of anything else, though he wouldn't have ruled out rocket launchers and stacks of C-4. "Where did you get all this?"

Cy shrugged. "Gun shows. Estate sales. Ads in the backs of magazines. Out of a truck behind a flea market in Minneapolis. Here and there. Been collecting for a long time. Glad they'll finally get some use. I was figuring they'd come in handy when the government decided to declare martial law and socialized medicine and the people had no choice but to openly revolt, but they'll kill zombies too."

"This is wonderful, Cy." Edsel clapped him on the back, then took an Uzi down from the wall and opened a crate to take out a few full clips of ammunition. Didn't even have to hunt around, which told Daniel that Edsel had been down here more than once or twice before. "We'll assemble our warriors for God and bring them back here for arming. How would you like to be ordnance officer for the Interfaith Anti-Zombie league?"

"I'd be honored to serve," Cy said. "Here, Pastor, let me set you up with a Heckler & Koch G36." Daniel accepted the rifle, which didn't weigh much more than a couple of gallons of milk, though it obviously had far less nutritional value. "For myself, I think I'll take this Saiga 12-guage semi-automatic shotgun with a ten-round magazine. I could drop a whole herd of zombies in about three seconds with this baby, but it's got a kick that might trouble you, Pastor."

"Uh," Daniel said, but Cy had joined Edsel before he could come up with anything else to say.

"I don't suppose a knife would be much good against a zombie." Edsel had the Uzi slung over his shoulder on a strap, and he perused the knives arrayed on the wall. "Even a big hunting knife isn't much good for decapitation."

"Well, maybe you'd like this." Cy presented what looked like an ordinary hunting knife, and Edsel's look of disappointment was obvious. "I know it doesn't look like much, but there's a CO_2 cartridge hidden in the hilt, and if you press this button, it releases a big burst of compressed air, about the volume of a basketball, at 850 psi." Daniel looked at him blankly, and Edsel didn't seem much more comprehending, so Cy grinned and said, "Stick this in a zombie's eye and push the button and I'm pretty sure the poor sucker's head will explode. I've only tried it on a pumpkin, but *that* blew up real good."

"Perfect." Edsel plucked the knife from his hand, found a sheath, and slipped it onto his belt.

"Just be sure you don't hit the button by mistake," Cy said, "or you could do yourself a good bit of damage."

And I have to sit next to him in the truck? Daniel thought. Maybe he should assert himself. Why let the priest be the one making all the decisions?

"We're having a full town meeting tonight, Cy," Edsel was saying. "Six o'clock at the community center. You might want to come, sort of hang around in back, gauge peoples' reactions, help us choose the warriors of the faith who most deserve the glorious weapons God has chosen to give us through you, his vessel."

"Sure thing." Cy was always affable, even when he was spilling his crazy all over you. "Should I come armed?"

"Most certainly," Edsel said.

"You know, in a way I've been preparing for this my whole life. Learning survival techniques. Guerilla warfare tactics. Living off the land. I didn't expect zombies, exactly, but I knew something was coming." He shook his head, then grinned his big crazy grin. "Goes to show you just never can tell."

12. PHILOSOPHICAL ZOMBIES

"That's the emergency robo-call done." Harry sat back, feeling like something was finally working halfway right. Maybe it would be the start of a trend. "The meeting's on. Now give me something to tell them, Stevie Ray."

"I wish I could. I can't raise the state police." Stevie Ray leaned back from the desk full of radio equipment and shook his head. "Not the sheriff either, and I'm not getting an answer from the National Guard unit."

"What, you didn't call Homeland Security?" Harry's tone was halfway between mocking and genuinely outraged. No reason to let the civilians, or Stevie Ray either, know how worried that news made him. If they were really cut off...

"No luck there either. I get busy signals, faults on the line, or just plain empty hissing."

"What are we going to do?" Otto said, those big pop-eyes of his bulging, made him look like a walleye. Otto had no more spine than an earthworm, but he could do what he was told, and he wasn't as dumb as some, but Harry would have still sent him home if he hadn't been a witness to the unmasking of a mass murderer.

"We'll keep trying, Otto. That's what we'll do."

"You guys bothered to check the internet?" Rufus pulled out one of those fancy new phones, all shiny and round-edged like some kind of technological chiclet. "That's where the real news is going to break first... Huh. No signal. That's weird. My coverage is usually good in the middle of town."

"Internet's down in here too," Stevie Ray said. "I called over to WoBoCo, but didn't get an answer." WoBoCo was the town's local internet service provider, and pretty much the only game in town unless you wanted to sign up with AOL, which not many people did anymore. At least those initials "AOL" stood for something—"WoBoCo" sounded like an abbreviation, but it wasn't, that was just what the kid who ran the place decided to name it, thought it sounded cool. Harry didn't care what he called it, so long as he kept the service up and running. Harry wasn't a young man, but he liked young men's games, and though he had a big TV and some of the next-gen gaming consoles, he couldn't play his Massively Multiplayer Online Roleplaying Games without the internet, and if the lag got too bad he'd been known to make stern phone calls to WoBoCo personally.

"Of course you didn't get an answer, you idiots." Mr. Levitt was leaning against the bars of the single jail cell with his arms sticking through, like he was hoping to snag a passerby. God, Harry could have done without the reminder of his existence. A serial killer right here under his nose. That was a black eye and no mistake. Never mind that Harry was stretched pretty thin, being 75% of the police department (Stevie Ray was solid but he was only a part-timer), barely able to keep up with making sure drunks stayed off the road, kids stayed out of the quarries, and nobody beat on their spouses too much. But a murderer, that sort of thing he should've noticed. At least Levitt seemed to prey on outsiders. That didn't make Harry feel much better, but it made it a little bit less personal.

"What do you mean, sir?" Harry said, because the old man might have been stone-evil, but he was also self-evidently pretty smart.

Levitt grinned. "Can't figure it out? Need me to lead you to water, you broken-down old horse? Okay. Where is WoBoCo located?"

Harry frowned. "Right here downtown, why?"

"But what *building* is it housed in? I swear, it's no wonder I operated with impunity here for decades if this is the caliber of the local police force."

Harry rose and walked over to the bars, and Stevie Ray said, warningly, "Harry, don't let him get to you." Stevie Ray should have known better than that. Though maybe he was playing along, trying to scare Levitt. He'd have better luck scaring the moon. It was just as far removed from humanity. But the man could be bargained with, maybe.

"If you hit Mr. Levitt, it's going up on YouTube," Rufus said, holding up his phone. "I'll call it a police brutality/elder abuse mash-up." He paused. "I mean, Mr. Levitt probably deserves to go to the gas chamber, but that doesn't mean you have the right to beat him for talking shit about you."

"You're absolutely right, Rufus." Harry said. "Violence is an act of last resort. I'm just coming a little closer to remind Mr. Levitt here that, in the absence of a greater societal framework, I am the whole of the law here, and if this little… crisis… we're in goes on too long, we're going to have no choice but to come up with some sort of homegrown justice system. It'll have a jury of your peers, don't worry about that, but it won't have a complex appeals system, and if a death sentence comes down one night, it'll be carried out by morning. Understand?" Harry didn't think it would come to that—there'd be loss of life, it would be a bad catastrophe, but the National Guard would step in, civilization would carry on, and here, in remote Lake Woebegotten, the impact of the disaster would be minimal. He'd get everyone up to speed at the meeting tonight, and they'd be prepared for a few wandering corpses. Nothing to worry about. Still, if he could worry Mr. Levitt into cooperation, so much the better. "I've never administered a hanging, but I know how to tie a noose."

"So you're saying you'd prefer me to be a *cooperative* monster, then," Levitt said. "All right. I'll tell you what should be *obvious* to you, in exchange for a promise."

"What's that?"

"I want to speak to a priest as soon as possible. I imagine Father Edsel is the only one available. He'll do."

Harry laughed. "What, are you ready to repent?"

"That's between me and the intermediary between me and my god."

"I don't see why you can't have spiritual counsel," Harry said. What could it hurt?

"Very well. WoBoCo is—"

"Holy shit it's in the funeral home!" Rufus sprang up from the bench where he'd been fiddling with his phone, startling all of them, and drawing a low hiss and a flat stare from Mr. Levitt. "WoBoCo! Remember, the guy running the place didn't have enough money for decent office space, so he rented out one of the viewing rooms, the Mathison Brothers said they only really needed two!"

"That's right, there was a stink about it," Otto recalled. "People said it was disrespectful having a high-tech company next to the place where people were grieving, but Will Mathison said unless people in town were willing to start dying a whole lot faster and more regularly, he needed the extra money. It all blew over years ago though. Why—"

"The funeral home." Harry's heart sank. A serial killer, a wily and secretive monster with a rock-solid public persona and sterling reputation, okay, that you could miss. But for Harry to overlook the *funeral home*? Maybe he was getting too old for this job. He picked up his earflap hat and jammed it on his head.

Stevie Ray was on the phone again, and after a moment, shook his head. "No answer at the Mathison Brothers'. There are at least two dead people there now, I know for a fact.'"

"At least two zombies, you mean," Mr. Levitt said, and gave another dry hacking laugh. Harry was really starting to get sick of that sound. "And probably more than that by now. They've been in there all day. You'd better just hope they can't figure out how to work doorknobs. You bunch of morons. I should be running this city, but I'd just end up hunting all of you for sport."

"Stevie Ray, get a couple of the new shotguns, we've got to get over there." Harry looked around as Stevie Ray hurried to the gun locker. He couldn't leave the old man alone, so… "Otto, Rufus, you two are special deputies now. We'll swear a nice oath later."

"Do we get guns?" Rufus said, and Otto just gaped, probably wanting to object, to say he had to get home to Barbara, but now that Rufus was being so manly with the gun talk, Otto didn't feel he could speak up. Good enough for now.

"For now, you just get keys." Harry tossed a ring to Rufus.

"Stay here, keep an eye on Levitt. Don't let him out unless the building catches fire or something. If somebody from the state cops or county police or any damn body in authority calls, let them know our situation here."

"What is our situation here?" Otto said.

"Dire," Mr. Levitt said, and Harry grunted.

Stevie Ray came back holding a pair of guns, and Otto whistled. Harry knew why. He'd heard "shotguns" and expected a double-barrel, maybe a pump-action or even a sawed-off, but the things Stevie Ray carried looked more like exotic insects than shotguns.

"Hot damn," Rufus said. "Is that an Auto Assault-12?"

"It is," Stevie Ray said, giving him a narrow-eyed, thoughtful look. "I tried one out back when I was in the Marines, liked the feel a lot, so when we got some Homeland Security funding to beef up our armaments, I put in for a couple. You… you didn't serve, did you?"

Rufus shook his head. "Call of Duty Modern Warfare 2, dude."

Stevie Ray looked bewildered. "It's a video game," Rufus said, a little sheepishly.

Harry patted Stevie Ray's shoulder. "Only the best damn military shooter ever made. I keep telling you, you need to get yourself a console, me and you could light things up." He sighed. "Come on. Let's get over to the funeral home and see what we're dealing with."

"Why do you want to see a priest?" Rufus asked, cocking his head at Mr. Levitt like the dog in those old stereo ads, with Rufus being the dog and Mr. Levitt being the phonograph horn.

"Don't talk to him," Otto said. "He's a—he's—they didn't say we should *talk* to him."

"People fight for the chance to interview people like me," Mr. Levitt said, still leaning against the bars all casually, like he was chatting at a church supper. "Behavioral psychologists. Psychological profilers. Police detectives. They'd want to study me."

"I think people like you are pretty simple," Rufus said. "You don't think anybody else is real, right? Other people are just playthings. All the other stuff, whether you take trophies or not or whether you were abused as children, all that's just like ornamental details. Not thinking other people are real, thinking you're the one real thing in the universe, that's the main thing."

"Ooh, someone's been reading a lot of *Criminal Minds* fan fiction, hasn't he?" Mr. Levitt said, and Otto didn't know what he was talking about, but it made that smug look disappear from Rufus's face, so Otto was willing to get behind it 100%. His nephew always thought he was smarter than anyone else, but Otto was pretty sure Mr. Levitt had the advantage in brainpower, whatever else was wrong with him.

"I think other people are real, young man," old man Levitt went on. "Killing them would be a lot less *fun* if they weren't. In fact, I have to tell you, while cutting down those zombies in my house had a certain visceral pleasure, it got the adrenaline flowing and the serotonin trickling and I don't mind saying it gave me an erection, which is no trivial thing at my age, it didn't satisfy in the same way killing a *real* person does. I wasn't snuffing out a life tonight. I was just killing bugs. And while I do enjoy killing bugs, it's like junk food, briefly enjoyable, but not really *filling*. Frankly, killing zombies is respectable, it's helpful, it's kind of boring and repetitive. I'd be disappointed if I believed everyone else around me was a p-zombie—"

Otto frowned. Pee zombie? A zombie made of pee? A peeing zombie?

"You know about philosophical zombies?" Rufus said, and Mr. Levitt snorted.

"I have a Ph.D. in pedagogy, young man. I took a philosophy course or two along the way."

Rufus glanced at Otto, and must have read his stony face correctly, because he said, "I was learning about them in this class I took, p-zeds, or p-zombies, or philosophical zombies. They look and act just like ordinary people, but they don't have any kind of real consciousness, they're basically robots—if you poke one with a needle it acts like it experiences pain, but it doesn't *really*, it has no sense of self, it's just a set of behaviors disguised as a human."

"There are people like that?" Otto said. It explained a lot.

Plenty of people just acted and reacted and didn't seem to really have a light going on upstairs.

"No, Mr. Salesman," old man Levitt said. "P-zombies are a construct used in thought experiments to interrogate the philosophy of mind, and to explore issues of behaviorism, materialism, the nature of qualia, and, ah, I can tell from the expression on your face that I might as well be saying 'ooga booga boo' for all you're comprehending. You're no p-zed, at least—you don't demonstrate even the imitation of conscious thought."

"But here I am, the one on the outside of the cage," Otto said, levelly, and was pleased—and surprised to find himself pleased—by the look of admiration Rufus gave him.

"You all really *are* idiots," Mr. Levitt said. "Have you ever heard of a shark cage? They lower divers in a cage into shark-infested waters, and the sharks can't get to the divers inside the bars. Do you know what this is?" He tapped the bars with the ring on his finger, making a metallic *bing*. "This is a *zombie* cage. And you poor fools are all out there in the water with the zombies."

13. A FAIR COP

Gunther Montcrief staggered out of the Backtrack Bar, home of the nightly "It Could Be Worse, All Things Considered, Hour," where he'd been consuming well whiskey for the better part of the morning, until the owner Ace told him if he fell off the stool one more time, he was done. Gunther didn't fall off the stool again, but he did mistake the storage room for the restroom and urinate all over a keg of Krepusky's Red Ribbon Beer, winner of the coveted second prize at four of the past eighteen central Minnesota Beer Festivals. Ace had tossed him out right quick after that, and it was only when the icy December afternoon breeze tickled his pubic hair that Gunther realized he'd not zipped himself up properly, and his willy was hanging out no doubt turning blue with the cold. Frostbite of the manhood. Made him think again of his father's friend Johnny who'd frozen to death peeing, and that made him think of the decapitated-but-still-gnawing fish, and that, damn it, was exactly what he'd been drinking to forget.

He looked up from his futile attempt to operate his zipper and saw the town cops Harry and Stevie Ray come barreling down the street toward him holding guns that belonged in a science fiction movie and he probably would've peed himself again if he hadn't just emptied himself out. They were coming to arrest him for indecent exposure and, who knew, maybe for illegally adulterating alcohol, since peeing all over a keg probably counted as watering beer, but they just went right past him and to the door of the Mathison Brothers Funeral Home,

84

conveniently located right across the street from the Backtrack Bar, so those who found grief a little too much for them could stumble across the street and take refuge in a nice deep highball glass. That's how Gunther had started out drinking so much, as a way to cope with loss, though in recent years the drinking had become heavy enough that he now drank to cope with the fact that he drank too much, a process that was beautiful in its closed-circuit simplicity.

Stevie Ray (who'd cut off Gunther more than once in his capacity as night and weekend bartender at the Backtrack Bar, the man had no regard for a fella's needs) aimed a couple of snap-kicks at the funeral home door while Gunther watched with swaying fascination, wondering what exactly was going on. The door sagged open and Stevie Ray and Harry went in, crouched low, and Gunther walked over after them to see what was going on. He was vaguely aware that following a pair of armed police-men into a building was not the best idea, but he was old, and curious, and he went wherever he damn well pleased unless a burly bartender physically relocated him elsewhere.

Gunther walked into the funeral home and helped himself to a handful of the free mints they kept on the table there in the foyer for grieving relatives with bad breath. The place was appropriately dark and subdued, with a big faintly-patterned carpet and lots of dark wood furniture and cut-glass vases full of faintly droopy flowers. The funeral home was of the old style, with viewing rooms and offices on the main floor (along with some kind of fancy computery business that sublet a chunk of space), family quarters upstairs (rumor said the area above was divided exactly in half, as the Mathison Brothers hadn't spoken to one another voluntarily since the early '90s) and an embalm-ing room in the basement. The thought of dead people under his feet reminded him of those biting fish heads sinking into the water and he shuddered.

Gunther heard the thud of running feet deeper in the build-ing, and then a gunshot so loud it made him jump. The sound was like a switch that turned on his headache, and he groaned as another shot followed, and another. Stevie Ray appeared in one of the viewing room doorways, but backwards, walking in reverse with a gun held out before him, saying "Jesus Christ Jesus Christ Jesus Christ" over and over. Gunther almost hailed him, but deep in his brain he realized that making sudden moves or noises might well result in a startled peace officer/bartender turning a gun on him, so instead he started backing up himself, into a corner by the doorway.

Stevie Ray cleared the door, followed shortly by Harry, who also had his back turned, and a pair of bloody men shambled out. It was the Mathison Brothers, one in a long black plastic apron, the other in his black undertaker's suit, but otherwise identical right down to their piggy little eyes and swept-back gray hair and, now, their incessantly opening-and-closing blood-streaked mouths.

"Well dip me in manure and call me a chocolate caramel," Gunther said. "It's not just the fish."

"Who the heck?" Stevie Ray said, starting to turn, but Harry yelled, "If it's talking a bunch of nonsense, it's not a zombie, so eyes front, soldier! Fire at will!"

Stevie Ray shot Matthew, the brother on the left, and his head pretty much disappeared, replaced by a reddish mist, though bits of bone and brain pattered off the wall, and, more disturbingly, off his own brother. The now-headless body fell straight to the floor like a dropped sail. Gunther spoke, quite conversationally, saying, "Harry said to fire at Will, but you shot Matthew instead. Can't you tell them apart? Will's the one in the plastic apron."

Harry lifted his spaceman gun to his shoulder, sighted on Will Mathison, and pulled his own trigger. He didn't hit Will quite as square-on, so only half of the head disintegrated, leaving the other half standing alone, like the last bit of a wall in a bombed-out building, but apparently half a head was just as useless as none, because that body fell, too. Harry looked behind him now, sighed, and said, "Gunther, get out of here, this is a crime scene."

"They're just like the fish, aren't they?" Gunther said. There was a word for the dead who came back to life. What was it? "Zomboes," he said assertively. "They're zomboes."

Harry appeared to mull that over, shook his head, and turned to Stevie Ray. "We got the two naked corpses, that must have been the original dead ones waiting to get worked on, and the WoBoCo kid, and now the Mathison Brothers—that's all of them, right?"

"I knew there were two bodies here for sure," Stevie Ray said, rubbing the side of his bald head, where he had a gash already crusting up with dried blood. "From that accident over on Big Hole Road. But there could be others. Like—"

"What about the ones on ice?" Gunther said, trying to be helpful. "Don't they keep a bunch of dead bodies down there when the ground's frozen, to bury in the spring?"

Harry didn't tell him to go away again, which was nice, but just shook his head. "There's a statute now, says cemeteries have to allow burial in the winter, too, decided it was cruel to make people wait months to get their loved ones in the ground, so people don't get put on ice like that as much."

Gunther shook his head. Everything changed. Well, what could you do?

"Yeah," Stevie Ray said slowly, "but the law also says the families have to pay the extra costs for winter burial, like propane heaters to warm up the soil and all that, and a lot of people are pretty frugal, so we might want to check down in the funeral home's cooler, just in case somebody decided Uncle Ole or Aunt Lena could wait until springtime to get buried on the cheap."

"All right," Harry said. "You're probably right. Let's go."

"I'm coming too."

"Gunther, go home and dry out," Harry said.

"It was my idea!" Gunther protested. "And you'd send me out there with the zomboes and everything without even a space-man gun?"

"You're drunk. And even if you weren't drunk, you're a civilian. Go home."

Gunther grumbled and went for the door, but he didn't step outside, because it was cold out there, and cold in his fishing shack with the cracks stuffed with old newspaper, and truly the cold bothered him more than the dead headless bodies of the Mathison brothers, since he'd seen his share of bodies back when he was in the service, even if the guns were a lot fancier now. He watched as Harry and Stevie Ray headed through the office toward the stairs that led into the morgue below, and cocked his head for the sound of gunshots, which came along as he'd expected—must have been a couple fellas in the coolers after all, probably pretty annoyed at being laid out in an ice-cold drawer, and he wondered if the cold made the zomboes more sluggish, but no, they were still warm-blooded, and it was cold-blooded things that got sleepy in the cold, except they were probably already embalmed and in embalming didn't they replace your blood with formaldehyde or something? Judging by the third gunshot, being embalmed didn't keep you from coming back as a zombo.

Gunther thought that fact must be significant, and he was staring off into the middle distance trying to figure out *why* that fact tickled his brain when Stevie Ray came running out of the office, wild-eyed, no longer holding his gun, front of his beige uniform shirt all covered in blood. He stumbled to the table and grabbed onto it as if to steady himself, and since feeling unstable on your feet was something Gunther could sympathize with, he said, "You all right?"

"No," Stevie Ray said, and puked.

Harry led the way into the morgue, where Will Mathison had probably been working on embalming a body when the body sat up and took a bite out of him. The room was all tan-colored tile, with big metal sinks and metal tables and weird hoses and cupboards and harsh bright lights overhead. Harry'd been down here before, of course, but it never failed to give him a shiver. For one thing it was *cold*. For another, it looked like the setting from one of his survival horror games, the kind where you crept around the hallways of an abandoned mental hospital with nothing but a rusty pipe for a weapon and the loudest noise on the soundtrack was your avatar's own ragged breath. And now there really *were* zombies.

At least I've logged all those hours playing zombie-killing games, he thought, though he knew it didn't really work that way. Still, while spending time on a firing range was probably nothing like actually shooting a person, people said the practice made the actual act easier, more automatic, so he hoped maybe some similar principle would apply here.

The morgue cooler was a big, shiny, four-drawer affair bolted to one of the walls. "All right, Stevie Ray. You want to open, or you want to shoot?"

"Shoot," he said without hesitation.

Harry considered challenging him to rock-paper-scissors, but what did it matter? His shoulder hurt from the recoil on that automatic shotgun anyway. "All right, but use your pistol, that shotgun makes too big a splash." He went to the first drawer, opened the door, and pulled out the sliding tray, looking at the cold blue feet wiggling and twisting. As soon as the zombie—Lord, it was Missy Hohlt, the first one would have to be someone he knew, and her so young, but she'd always had those seizures, she was bound to hit a big one eventually—saw the light or smelled the air or who knows what, it started twisting and trying to sit up, and Stevie Ray was there, putting a bullet right into her head, dropping her dead. After a moment's thought, Harry slid the drawer closed again. Why not?

He opened the next drawer, saw more bluish feet, this one an old man's he didn't know, and once again the zombie started to get up, and once again, Stevie Ray made it lie down again.

"This isn't so bad," Harry said, opening the next drawer and grinning at Stevie Ray. "I've had more trouble killing rats—"

"HARRY!" Stevie Ray shouted, and Harry felt a searing pain on his arm, and looked over to see that, in defiance of all consistency, this corpse had been slid into the drawer *feet* first, so its head was right there, and in fact its teeth were sunk in Harry's arm, and now it was reaching for him, and Harry tried to get his pistol but his right arm was in agony and his left was his stupid hand and the zombie had his throat, and Lord, it was strong, an old lady with wispy grey hairs and a face wrinkly like a desert canyon seen from an airplane but a grip like a circus strongman.

The zombie pulled him down, and its jaws unclamped from his arm, and Harry said "Oh thank you sweet Jesus" in the sudden lessening of pain, but then the zombie's teeth found his neck, and he felt his hot warm life pumping out of him, and he thought, *No save point, I lose.*

"It jumped up out of the drawer like a flea off a dead dog," Stevie Ray said, swaying. "We put down the first one, and the second one, too, without much trouble, but the third one reached out and grabbed Harry and pulled him off balance, and Harry started screaming, but he was between me and the body in the drawer so I couldn't get off a shot, and then Harry fell on the ground and his throat was all red and torn-up and when I tried to help him the zombie in the cooler came at me, knocked my gun away, and I wound up fighting it hand-to-hand, managed to twist it off my hip and smash its head into the big industrial sink, just kept smashing it and smashing it until it was just in pieces, and then this terrible hammering started up, it was a four-drawer cooler and all four drawers must have been full and the last dead body was *excited*, I guess it heard the commotion, I couldn't stand the noise, and I—I just *ran*." He lifted his gaze to Gunther, and his eyes were as bleak as the sky at the end of the shortest day of winter. "I've been a soldier. I've killed men in combat. But these *things*, and seeing what they did to Harry, I just couldn't, I had to get away…"

"No shame in it," Gunther said. "We all get to a breaking point if we live long enough. What matters is what you do next." What Gunther had done next was get stinking drunk and arrange to stay that way for the foreseeable, but no use mentioning that. "But what about—"

Harry, he was going to say, but then Harry came out of the office, dragging one leg, big bite taken out of his throat, face all gray, eyes blank, and he was a zombo, sure enough, killed and come back. Poor guy. He'd always done right by Gunther, just stuck him in a cell if he needed drying out, never gave him an ass-kicking, just a talking-to.

Stevie Ray was in no shape to cope, and he didn't have his weapon anyway, so Gunther reached into his big old overcoat and took out his pistol, thumbed back the hammer, looked past Stevie Ray's astonished face, took a two-handed target shooter's stance, and put one right in the middle of old Harry's face.

The revolver didn't make heads disappear like those spaceman guns did, but it appeared to get the job done, because Harry died for the second time.

Stevie Ray looked at his dead boss, then back at Gunther, and said, "You told us you didn't have a gun!"

"Said I didn't have a fancy spaceman gun like yours." Gunther put his pistol away. "Just my lousy old sidearm from when I was in the service. Hadn't fired it in years."

"You always carry that thing around?"

"I'm an old man. I live alone. I sometimes black out. Gotta protect myself."

Stevie Ray stood up from the table and looked down at his dead boss. "Oh, shit, Harry, what am I supposed to do now?"

"Guess this makes you the chief," Gunther said. He paused. "Want to buy me and you a drink to celebrate your promotion?"

14. SNOW CREAMED

As Eileen trooped through the snow on the trail of her insufficiently dead husband, she thought about when the twins were little and how they used to make snow cream right after the second snowfall. Never the first snowfall, because she'd always felt the first snow was dirty, no matter how clean and white and fresh it looked—snowflakes were like little lint brushes falling through the air, attracting all the particulates and pollutants and nasty things that normally floated around over your head, so by the time the flakes started piling up on the ground they were steeped in invisible grime, and who would want to eat that?

But after the second snowfall, Brent would go out with a big metal mixing bowl and come back with it full of fresh fluffy snow, and Eileen would mix in the milk and sugar and vanilla until they had a big old batch, and the twins would sit on the barstools at the counter bouncing up and down they were so excited, and they'd all eat the snow cream pretty fast, before it could melt, but not so fast they got ice cream headaches, so it was a delicate balancing act that required a fair bit of attention. One time Todd, the younger of the twins by a whole two minutes, had looked at them in big-eyed alarm, holding his spoon, and said, "Little kids in Africa don't ever get to eat snow cream, do they?" and Brent had said, "Never mind the African kids, think about the little kids in Florida! It doesn't snow there either. They have to make do with *alligator* cream!" And the twins had laughed, the way little kids do at absurd things, and Brent had laughed, as he always amused himself, and Eileen had laughed, too, and that memory was like a warm coal she carried around with her in the snow, a moment of loveliness in the past rescued and revived here in the icy present. They hadn't made snow cream this year, or the year before, or the year before that, not since the kids were much younger, and they hadn't even missed it, none of them; just a little tradition that withered away from lack of attention.

Pretty much like the rest of her marriage.

Walking along with the gun in her coat pocket, a weight that bumped against her side with every step through the ankle- and sometimes knee-deep snow, unseen underbrush branches scraping at her legs, she thought maybe she'd done the wrong thing, deciding to kill Brent. It wasn't remorse, exactly, unless it was like buyer's remorse; she wasn't appalled by the fact of the choice she'd made, she just thought maybe she could have made a better choice. She could have walked out on him. Or even divorced him. Surely his intimate relations with a car were sufficient cause. But killing him had seemed so much better. Planning the murder had given her something to do. It was her hobby. The fantasy she retreated to when things were bad. Of course it hadn't worked out, but that was life, wasn't it? Her father used to say "plan" was a four-letter word, which she hadn't understood for the longest time, it was like saying "dog is a four-legged animal," just a factual statement, but eventually someone had explained it to her, how four-letter words were swear words, and she felt dumb, but started using the expression herself a lot in dark secret hopes that she might make someone else feel dumb and get to explain it. Hadn't happened yet, but time went on.

Sleeping with Dolph and buying fancy underwear was a fantasy too, but it wasn't as satisfying as planning Brent's murder. Probably she shouldn't have gone through with it, but all that planning without follow-through had seemed like a waste of time, and she hated wasting time. And now here she was tromping through the woods looking for her husband so she could finish him off and bury him in the snow where nobody would notice him until spring, probably. In the old days before dumps and garbage pickups, people used to just throw their trash and chicken bones and broken plates and such in their front yards in the winter, and forget about it until springtime came. The snow hid everything. Snow was good that way. If she could have kept a nice snowfall over the top of her marriage, hiding the nasty parts, things might have continued indefinitely, but spring always came eventually, and screwed everything up. But that would end soon. Eileen was no wild woman of the wood, but she could follow a trail as obvious as the one her dying husband had left her.

She paused underneath a tall tree, not unlike all the other tall trees surrounding her, and emerged on the shore of Lake Woebegotten. The ice was thick and solid, that bluish-white of good hard ice, and out of the trees the wind was whipping, blowing snow in little spirals and spins across the surface of the lake, and there were no footprints to be found, and no sign of her husband anywhere. A brain-damaged half-run-over man who'd never been too cunning to begin with had escaped and outsmarted her.

"Shitbiscuits!" she shouted, and took out her gun and fired off three shots right into the lake, punching holes in the ice, and, she hoped, killing some passing sleepy fish. Eileen wanted to kill *something*, by God.

She tromped back home, which took just about forever, and the snow was seeping into her boots, and her foul temper got fouler and fouler, and then, sitting on her back steps, was Dolph, looking much worse than he had this morning. Eileen stopped a few feet away and stared at him. "What are you doing here? What if someone sees you?"

"I was just so worried about you." He rose and came toward her, arms outstretched, which reminded her uncomfortably of the way Brent had looked when he came out of the garage. "I thought Brent was here, I saw his truck, so I went and knocked on the door, I was going to tell him some story, I just had to know you were okay, but Brent's not here and neither are you and so I figured I'd just hang around and see if you came back and—"

"Why are you worried about me? What are you talking about?" Eileen didn't like Dolph in this context, in her yard. When she'd decided to get rid of her husband, it wasn't with any intention of having Dolph hanging around her house instead. It was to have her house to *herself*.

"I know it's going to sound hard to believe, but… There are zombies, Eileen. The dead have risen. There's a town meeting about it tonight, but—"

"Zombies?" Thinking of Brent stumbling out of the garage, looking dead but walking around, and if there were zombies, that made a lot more sense, didn't it? Though it was disappointing that killing him didn't mean getting rid of him after all, it was also heartening to know that she hadn't flubbed the job. She'd murdered Brent just fine. His continued mobility was due to circumstances beyond her control.

Suddenly the sight of Dolph's concerned face made her think of the fact that she'd broken two commandments already today, the fifth and the sixth. Would she break any more before the day was out? Could be. It was barely past four-thirty, though it was already getting dark. The day was young.

"I know it sounds crazy," Dolph said, "but I've seen it with my own eyes."

She started to say of course, she'd seen it with her own eyes, too, in the form of her lurching husband, but admitting she'd seen zombies would mean admitting she'd seen a dead person and she wasn't about to do that. So she just said, "Well, if you say so, I guess I have to believe you," but in a doubtful tone.

Dolph's mouth tightened and his eyes got steely and she felt the barest little flutter of desire. In truth she'd been sleeping with him mostly for the free groceries and the illicit thrill than for the actual fact of *him*, lately, but seeing him get all serious and tough reminded her why she'd been initially attracted to him. He was a smart, hardworking entrepreneur who didn't have shit on his boots or engine oil on his overalls at the end of the workday, and that was a rare thing in these parts.

"There'll be proof at the meeting tonight." He took a deep breath and let it out. "Proof that's waiting in my freezer. And Eileen… Clem got turned."

She frowned. "What do you mean?"

"The dog that bit him—the *zombie* dog—the bite got infected, I guess maybe the mouths of the dead are nastier than the mouths of the living, who knows, but Clem had a fever, and he fainted, and, ah, when he fell, he hit his head… He died. And then he came back."

Eileen stepped toward him, even though they were right in the yard where anyone sufficiently nosy could conceivably see. "Dolph, did you… did you have to…"

Dolph looked away. "I couldn't bring myself to do it, Eileen. He still looks like *Clem*. I just shut him up in the freezer."

Weak, then. Well, no man was perfect. "I understand. Have you told Harry?"

"No. I guess I should."

She looped her arm through his. "Let's do it together."

He frowned, looking down at her hand. "But what about Brent?"

"He wouldn't want me walking around in a zombie apocalypse without a man to keep me safe, Dolph. Don't worry. Now let's go."

"What do you mean Harry's *dead*?" Dolph sat down in one of the hard visitor's chairs in the tiny police station, unsure his legs would hold him up.

"Like I said." Stevie Ray's voice was grim. "We went to clear out the funeral home, and one of the deaders got his hands on Harry. Nothing I could do. He had to be put down."

"You shot Harry?" Eileen asked, and Dolph couldn't decide if she sounded appalled or… excited? It couldn't be excited, could it?

"Probably killed him so he could become chief of police." Mr. Levitt's voice was calm and reasonable and made Dolph's skin crawl.

"Like I'd want the job," Stevie Ray snapped. "No. Gunther Montcrief was the one who shot Harry, actually."

"Gunther?" Dolph couldn't believe it. "That old drunk who lives in a shack out by the lake? He comes into the store and doesn't buy anything but beef jerky, and I think the only thing he drinks is whiskey." Dolph wasn't one to speculate over another man's probable bowel movements, but he imagined Gunther Montcrief hadn't taken a dump in years, making him quite literally full of shit. "He put down *Harry*?"

"Zombie Harry," Stevie Ray reminded. "Gunther used to be a good target shooter, and I guess he'd drunk just enough today to make his hands steady, not enough to make them shaky again. Hell, I might have to make him a special deputy, like these two." He nodded his head toward Rufus and Otto, both sitting miserable and dejected on a bench.

"Why do they get to be special deputies? I've done as much as they did!" Dolph regretted it as soon as he opened his mouth. Like he needed more responsibilities?

"Fine, you're a special deputy, too, then." Stevie Ray laid his head down on the desk. "Everybody's a special deputy. Welcome to law enforcement. Who wants to be chief?"

"Who's going to speak at the meeting Harry called?" Eileen asked.

Stevie Ray lifted his head. "Oh, for damn. It's only, what, an hour from now?"

"It has to be you, Stevie Ray," Dolph said. "You're the face of law enforcement in this town now."

"And what am I supposed to say? 'Harry can't be here tonight, he was eaten by a zombie, but I know he was *planning* to tell you everything's going to be fine, because there aren't so many dead people in town, and they can't eat all of us.' That's going to go over real well. What about the mayor?"

"I haven't seen Brent all day," Eileen said, shrugging. "Don't know what's become of him. I hope he's okay."

Stevie Ray put his head in his hands, and Dolph figured he'd be pulling his hair out in clumps, if he had any hair. "The town council?"

"Will Mathison's dead," Otto said. "Petey Storm's visiting his daughter in Florida. That leaves Mr. Olafson, and he had that stroke a while back, he's just at home in heaven's waiting room, his granddaughter's taken over the Cafe even. I think you're the only kind of authority we've got, Stevie Ray, apart from the pastor and," he grimaced, "Father Edsel."

"I guess—" Dolph began, but then the power went out, plunging them all into the dark.

"Boo," Mr. Levitt said, and cackled. "I hope you all like the dark. I love the dark myself. Do most of my best work there."

The backup generator kicked in—most of the businesses and all the town buildings and as many of the residences that could afford them had generators, because the power usually went out two or three days at least every winter, and other times too if a big wind came blowing across the prairie—restoring the veneer of normalcy, an illusion that would last, Dolph knew, just as long as the propane did. He did a little mental inventory of the propane in his store, and decided he might do well to move it to a more secure location. Not that the people of Lake Woebegotten were apt to riot or steal, but why give them the temptation?

"Guess I'd better try to call the power company," Stevie Ray said.

"Make calls while you can." Mr. Levitt scratched at his wattly neck. "Pretty soon you'll realize we're all alone here. In the cold. With the dead." He grinned. "It's how I lived for years. It's not so bad. You get used to it."

15. A MEETING OF THE MINDS

Pastor Inkfist rubbed at the back of his neck with a handkerchief. Speaking at church didn't bother him a bit, but he was assured a fairly friendly audience there, all things considered. Here in the community center, faced with what looked like the entire population of the town, though, he found himself nervous, and nerves made him sweat, and sweating made him self-conscious, and self-consciousness made him more nervous, and thus a vicious cycle was born.

Eileen Munson had done a great job, as always, though he didn't see her anywhere—instead Glenda Dreier was scooting around the room adjusting chairs and rearranging the muffins and brownies and bars and coffee urn on the refreshment table. Glenda was pious, and (Daniel thought guiltily) brainless, and (Daniel thought even more guiltily) completely oblivious to her own sexiness, which was considerable for a woman with a son old enough to go to college. She had shiny hair and shiny eyes and Daniel always got the impression that she had probably the best over-age-40 breasts in Lake Woebegotten, though he did his best to never let his eyes stray below her neckline. It was inappropriate to think of a parishioner in a sexual way, even though unlike Father Edsel he wasn't bound by a vow of chastity, and indeed he had a wife, Trudy, who'd gone off to visit her recently-divorced sister in Amsterdam of all places about six weeks ago and kept calling with good reasons why she needed to stay a little longer, ranging from ill nieces to moral support, and who gave equally good reasons why Daniel didn't need to join her. He had the sneaking suspicion she didn't even miss him, and he'd grown awfully tired of frozen dinners, but what could he do? Family was family. He'd tried calling her a couple of times in between Edsel's harangues and the zombie attack and the gun acquisition, to no avail. He wanted to check the internet to get an idea if this dead-rising thing was a local problem or if it was happening all over, but hadn't had the chance yet, and anyway he was a little afraid of what he might find out.

The pistol Edsel had forced him to conceal in his waistband was uncomfortable, too, digging into the kidney on the right of his spine. "Why do I need a gun?" Daniel had asked.

"What if the dead storm the meeting, drawn to the presence of all that life like sinful moths to a hellish flame?" Edsel had replied, and Daniel had spent so long wondering how exactly moths could even sin that he'd lost the argument by default.

Edsel was seated next to Daniel on the stage, scowling ferociously at the crowd that was still filing in, hundreds of worried-looking faces, most familiar, if some hadn't been seen in a while. There was BigHorn Jim in the back, wearing his big fur-lined Viking helmet with the curving horns, not because authentic Vikings actually wore helmets like that (they almost certainly didn't) but just because he didn't want to have to explain to everyone he met that he was a Norse pagan who worshipped Odin the All-Father, and the Viking helmet was a sort of visual shorthand, though to most people it just said "crazy" or possibly "devoted Minnesota Vikings fan." There was Cyrus, and Daniel shuddered to think of the weaponry he surely had on his person. There was Julie Olafson (bless her grandfather, he wasn't long for this world, and now his death would bring with it a whole host of problems), and Eileen Munson (no sign of her husband, though it would surely be good to have the mayor here, even if his official duties were usually minimal), and that drunken old goat Gunther Montcrief, and that odd fellow people called The Narrator, sitting in back with his red bow tie and suspenders and darting eyes, muttering to himself in his continual narration, and the rich widowed farmer-turned-quarry-magnate Ingvar Knudsen, and Ace Nybo who ran the

Backtrack Bar, and a scattering of kids home from college, and a few younger kids who were excited by the unexpected spectacle, and a goodly cross-section of Daniel's congregation.

Not everyone called had answered their phones, and not everyone who'd answered had come, but most of the town was present, and the rest would get word soon enough about the... situation... through the infallible information-transmission mechanism that was a small town. Still, there were some faces he'd expected to see, but didn't—the police chief, the funeral director and town councilman, the former school superintendent Mr. Levitt, Dolph from the grocery—and Daniel worried naturally enough that they'd encountered their own dead, and been press-ganged into the unliving ranks. It was dark outside already, and anything could be walking up and down in the darkness.

"I'd like to call this meeting to order."

Edsel rose instantly to his feet, but Daniel just blinked in surprise at Stevie Ray, the part-time bartender, part-time cop, who'd taken the microphone at the lectern in the center of the stage. "Thank you all for coming," Stevie Ray said.

"Yes, thank you." Edsel tried to shoulder Stevie Ray aside, but the cop turned and said, "You'll get your turn to speak, Father, but first I need to make some public safety announcements, and that's my job, not yours."

"I think it's Harry's job," Edsel said.

"Harry's dead." Stevie Ray nodded into the wind generated by the collective gasp in the room. "Which is part of what I'm here to talk about. Take a seat, Father?"

Edsel frowned, but he was clearly smart enough to know the crowd wouldn't respond well if he tried to steamroll Stevie Ray before they got to hear details about that particular bombshell, so he sat down with all the grace of an embarrassed cat.

Stevie Ray rattled a sheet of papers that looked to Daniel like printouts from websites, complete with little banner ads frozen in grayscale and margins running off the page. The officer cleared his throat. "At approximately 3:45 Eastern time this morning an astronomical event of an undetermined nature was observed over the skies in most of the continental United

States. Some of you may have seen it—a great burst of light, like the biggest falling star you've ever seen. Scientists…" He moved a page around, and cleared his throat again. "Scientists are unsure of the…" Stevie Ray looked around the room, sweat running down his forehead, and the crowd looked back at him. Maybe in New York City people would have been on their feet shouting, demanding answers, asking about Harry—Daniel was pretty darn curious about that himself—but here in Lake Woebegotten you let a man have his say, even if it took him a little while to get around to it.

"I'm sorry, folks," Stevie Ray said, putting the pages down. "The situation is this. The dead have come back to life, and they're dangerous. Just like in some kind of horror movie or video game. When the corpses rise, there's nothing human left in them, as far as I can tell, just a terrible hunger. Harry and I went to the funeral home to deal with the living dead there, and Harry… he wasn't fast enough… one of them got him. I've been trying to get in touch with the sheriff, the state police, even the National Guard, the military, anybody, but I'm not having much luck. Some of you may have noticed communications are breaking down, the internet's not too reliable, it goes in and out even though we plugged everything back in at WoBoCo, and cell phones don't seem to be working at all really, maybe because of something in the atmosphere, something related to that explosion in the sky last night, I don't know, and I don't even know if that has anything to do with the dead coming back to life, but…"

There was a rumble in the room now, people talking to their neighbors, in low voices, not exactly impolite, but it might as well have been open insurrection as far as portent goes. Edsel was just smiling all self-satisfied, happy to see Stevie Ray floundering, but Daniel set his eyes on the greater good and got to his feet. The room went silent. "It's true. What he says about the dead. I saw the widow Mormont myself, on her deathbed, and after she passed, her eyes opened, she stood up, and she killed Doctor Holliday."

Another group gasp.

"I sort of thought people might have their doubts," Stevie

Ray said, nodding at Daniel gratefully. "So I arranged a, ah, demonstration, but... maybe it's better if parents with children take the children outside, I don't think they need to see this..."

Reluctantly, parents argued over who had to take the children out into the freezing cold, and it took a few minutes, but eventually the broods were rounded up and led out of the room, and Stevie Ray looked off to the left and beckoned, and Daniel followed his eyes, and there was Dolph the grocer, pushing a wheelbarrow, and in the wheelbarrow was—was—

"An abomination." Father Edsel pointed at the armless, legless, endlessly mouthing thing that Dolph wheeled to center stage and tipped up so everyone could see. The crowd moved forward, everyone staring, and finally old Ingvar Knudsen said, "Yep, that's the living dead," and he was such an old and staid and established voice that nobody else in the audience seemed to question it after that.

Edsel had gone from zero to wild-eyed prophetic preaching mode in seconds, striding up and down the stage, shouting, "This is a thing thrown back up from the depths of Hell!"

"More like the depths of old man Levitt's basement," Dolph said, but under his breath, so only those on stage heard it. Stevie Ray shot him a deadly look, and Daniel wondered what *that* was about. He'd find out. It was hard to keep secrets from a community's spiritual leaders.

"This is what we face, my children." Edsel gripped the lectern with both hands like a shipwrecked man clinging to the only available piece of flotsam. "The great night star was the Star Wormwood, and these are the end times. These walking dead are the shocktroops of Hell, and Armageddon will follow on their heels."

"I don't know about all that," Stevie Ray said, plucking the microphone from in front of the priest. "Harry—before he succumbed to zombie bite—was of the opinion that this was a temporary problem, and something we could weather, if we pull together as a community. You see, there just aren't that many fresh corpses in Lake Woebegotten, if you see what I mean. The ones in the funeral home have been taken care of, at some cost, I know, but they're gone now. And the widow Mormont, I trust, was handled too?"

He looked at Daniel, who nodded queasily, and said, "Doctor Holliday, as well."

"So that's probably about the extent of them." Stevie Ray was loosening up now, warming to his subject. He gestured to Dolph, who wheeled the limbless corpse back offstage. "The town's been through tragedies before. Blizzards, and floods, and fires, and even lion attacks after that circus train wreck back in the '70s. We've always endured, and we'll get through this, too. It looks like we might lose power, but we've got generators, and there's plenty of fuel in town, and when that runs out we've got fireplaces and woodstoves and candles, and those that are running low on supplies can reach out to their neighbors, and we'll all help each other. Apart from the walking dead and all, it's just apt to be another pretty bad winter. Right?" He coughed. "I guess, I'll take questions?" He looked very much like he hoped there wouldn't be any questions.

And there weren't, not right then, because the doors at the back swung open with a creak, and everyone turned to look, expecting to see some children sneaking in to get a peek at the forbidden goings-on, but instead it was all the children running in and screaming, which made people get to their feet, and if not for his elevated position on the stage Daniel wouldn't have seen what they were running from, which was: the lurching form of Brent Munson, car dealer, Lutheran deacon, duly elected mayor, and limping zombie. He just paused in the doorway, his blood-crusted head swinging from side to side at all the people backing away from him, like a starving man at a buffet who can't decide whether to start with the popcorn shrimp or the chicken wings.

"Everyone stay calm, they're slow, just keep a safe distance!" Stevie Ray shouted, but then one of the women at the back—Daniel didn't know her, she must have been a Catholic—tripped and went sprawling, and zombie Brent saw his chance, and advanced upon her, reaching out with clawed hands, jaws opening and shutting, great ropes of drool spilling over his lips, bending down to grab her ankle, and Daniel could pretty much see the future, Brent picking up the woman by her leg—he knew the dead were hellishly strong—and taking a bite out of her calf like a man chowing down on a drumstick.

But suddenly Eileen Munson, Brent's wife, head of the Lutheran Women's Circle, walked against the flow of panicking pig farmers and forty-year-old grandmothers and former factory workers and rest home attendants and unemployed snow machine enthusiasts and mechanics who refused on principle to work on foreign cars and professional dishwashers and relatively honest contractors and gas pump jockeys and fry cooks and roadside fruit stand proprietors and truck drivers, and everyone parted before her, like she was Moses parting the Red Sea (only this was the redneck sea, Daniel thought, with an uncharacteristic lack of charity toward his parishioners, and Father Edsel's too), and Eileen even outstretched her hand like she should have a staff twined with serpents in her grasp, but instead she had a pistol, and she stepped right up to her undead monster husband before he could take a bite out of that poor woman's flesh, and pressed the barrel of the gun against the side of Brent's head soft and deliberate as a kiss, and pulled the trigger.

The noise was less startling than the other gunshots Daniel had heard today—he must be getting used to them—and it had the odd effect of calming the panicked crowd down. A gunshot in a still room makes people panic, he thought, but a gunshot in a panicked room might just be the sound of order being restored by force.

Eileen lowered her pistol and turned to face the crowd, and the new center of the room's attention bowed her head for a moment, then lifted her face, her eyes shining, and said, "I love this town. I'd do anything to save it. I'd even shoot my own husband—the thing that used to be my husband—in the head. I trust everyone else in this room would do the same. Because you are good people, and you are my neighbors, and you are my family, and you are my friends." Then her eyes rolled back and she fell to the floor, though Daniel thought she landed awfully well for a woman in a dead faint, sort of gently crumpling instead of falling and banging her head on a chair or something. But she was probably just lucky, and the good Lord knew she could use some luck after what happened to her husband, though exactly how he'd gotten killed in the first place was something of a mystery. Still, why would you fake a faint in a situation like this?

16. AN ODYSSEY
OF THEODICY

Nobody had much of an appetite for the lemon bars and chocolate squares after Eileen killed her husband, not even once they got the remains of Brent cleaned up, but everyone in the room certainly understood the gravity of the situation, and Dolph the grocer got Eileen up and took her off to grieve—Daniel would have to counsel her later—and after a while everyone went home with promises to keep their eyes open, to check up on each other regularly, and to use the buddy system if they had to go out.

Afterward, Stevie Ray and Father Edsel and Daniel were the only ones left in the community center, Glenda Dreier having cleaned everything up with impressive efficiency, all things considered.

"That could have been better, but if could have been worse," Edsel said, standing with his hands clasped behind his back, looking out over the sea of empty chairs. "I'm afraid your Pollyanna vision of normalcy returning will prove false, but maybe it's better to let people ease into the facts of life in the time of tribulations. No need to panic them all at once."

"I hope you're wrong, Father," Stevie Ray said. "I don't much want to be the only cop in a town abandoned by God."

"God does not abandon us," Daniel said. "Never that. He only tests us."

"We're pretty much the town government now, I suppose," Edsel mused. "Wouldn't you say so, Stevie Ray? Or are you planning on instituting a more secular form of rule?"

"Father, I'll take all the help I can get, and give you all the weight you can carry." He yawned hugely. "I guess we've got a lot to talk about, but I need to get some food and some rest. Can we have a meeting tomorrow morning?"

"Of course," Edsel said, and then turned, and smiled. "I just have one small question. Who was the dead man in the wheelbarrow?"

Daniel gaped. He hadn't even thought about that—the object lesson, the demonstration of truth, the *evidence*... He'd been a person. A stranger. They certainly hadn't ordered him from the Zombie Proof Catalogue.

"I was hoping to save that for tomorrow. But you might as well come over now, Father. He asked to speak to you anyway."

"The zombie?" Daniel blurted. "They can talk?"

"No, sir. Not the zombie. The man who killed the innocent boy who became the zombie. Lake Woebegotten's very own serial killer, former school superintendent Martin Levitt. He's the reason I found out about the zombie uprising. All the victims in his basement got up and decided to come upstairs."

"I see," Edsel said. "Well, well. The Lord does indeed work in mysterious ways, his wonders to perform. Shall we go stare into the face of Evil, Daniel?"

"I don't believe in evil," Daniel said, trying to process. Old man Levitt? The man who had the best Halloween decorations every year, tasteful, very harvest-y, not at all Satanic, who gave the boys and girls apples and toothbrushes? That old man Levitt, a killer? "Not the way you mean, not capital-E-evil, there are just misdirected appetites and misguided people who—"

"Yes, yes," Edsel said, as if soothing a fussy child. His condescension might have enraged Daniel if he'd had the emotional resiliency to feel rage after this long day. "I'm sure you're right. How can we go wrong with moral relativism, after all? Zombies just have misguided appetites, that's all."

"If you two plan to have a theological debate, I'll leave you to it," Stevie Ray said. "Or do you want to come minister to a diseased mind? I promised him a priest to talk to, Father, in exchange for some information he gave us. Not that it would hurt my heart to break a promise to that man, after seeing what he's capable of, but it doesn't cost me anything, if you're willing."

"Everyone deserves the opportunity to receive counsel from a man of the cloth," Edsel said. "Besides, a human murderer makes a nice change from zombies. At least people have *motives*. Zombies are no more spiritually interesting than typhoid fever or exploding gas lines."

"I'd rather have a zombie." Stevie Ray rose and beckoned them to follow him. "At least with zombies, I know it's not personal."

"Hello, Martin," Father Edsel said, pulling a chair over closer to the cell and easing himself down. He laced his fingers over his belly. "I hear you've asked for spiritual counsel."

"I asked for a priest. I suppose you'll do." Levitt sat on the thin bunk. "Might be nice if the new boss brought me something to eat in the meantime, or do you intend to starve your prisoners now that civilization has collapsed?"

Stevie Ray didn't look up from his desk. "Rufus, you want to run over to the Cafe and get our prisoner a sandwich?"

"Alone?" the boy said. "Aren't we supposed to be doing the buddy system?"

"I'll go," Daniel said, happy for the chance to escape what was likely to be an uncomfortable situation.

"No, I'll take him in my truck." Otto stood and stretched, his spine making unpleasant snapping sounds. "I've spent enough time with Mr. Levitt for one day." They bundled up in their coats and scarves and tromped out, and Daniel reluctantly settled back down on the hard wooden bench against the wall. If he had some excuse, he could go… but where? And why? His wife was gone. His flock was scattered. Edsel would think less of him if he departed now, too.

"So, Martin." Edsel appeared to consider an invisible piece of lint on the leg of his pants for a moment before looking in at the prisoner. "Have you come to make a confession? Shall I send these men away to give us some privacy?"

"No, no," Levitt said. "No privacy necessary. These idiots never Mirandized me, so I could take credit for the assassination of the Archduke Ferdinand and none of it would be admissible in court."

"Oh, for heck," Stevie Ray said, swiveling in his chair. "You're under arrest for the murder of… several unidentified persons. You have the right to remain silent. Anything you say can and will be used against you in a court of law. You have the right to an attorney. If you cannot afford an attorney, one will be provided for you. Do you understand these rights?"

Daniel looked on wide-eyed. Reading him his rights! Just like in the movies!

Levitt laughed, a sound that was no more human than the sound of a vacuum cleaner or the click of a gun being cocked. "I do. Shame my attorney is in Minneapolis, being eaten by the dead, so I guess I'll have to go with the public defender. I still don't need any privacy though. I doubt this will be going to trial."

"So you do want to confess?" Edsel seemed only mildly interested.

"Not in the sacramental sense. Not yet. That can wait. I just wanted to talk to you, Father, about *why* I did all the terrible things I did."

"What terrible things were those?"

"Murder. Violating the fifth commandment. Though it's the sixth commandment for the other Christian denominations, it's just you oddball Catholics and Lutherans who number things differently."

"Given that Catholicism was here first, I'd say everyone else is violating precedent." Edsel sniffed. "So, murder? You think you're interesting, Levitt? Murder isn't interesting. It's *old*, as old as Cain and Abel at least."

"Ah, but here's the interesting part." Levitt rose from his cell and leaned against the bars, close enough that he could have reached through and grabbed the toe of Edsel's shoe, though Daniel couldn't imagine a way he could do much damage with that. "The only reason I'm a murderer is because I'm a Catholic."

"Diddled by a priest, were you? Made you into the monster you are today? Also a familiar story, I'm sorry to say. I knew a young priest in Texas, and when I found out he was known to take the occasional liberty with an altar boy, I waited for him in a parking lot one night, hit him over the back of the head, and broke most of his teeth out with a pipe. So believe me. I sympathize. It's no excuse for murder, though, and it's still not interesting."

Levitt's eyes widened, just a bit, and Daniel shivered. He hoped Edsel was lying, but who knew?

"Sounds like you committed the sin of wrath, Father."

"Mmm," Edsel said. "I did indeed. Fortunately, I confessed. Do you know who heard my confession?" Edsel leaned forward. "The priest who'd benefited from my impromptu oral surgery. He told me to say two Our Fathers, and he stepped carefully around me after that, and never touched another person, young or old, inappropriately again. Simple behavioral modification. And the cynics and secular humanists say people don't change. Maybe *you* would have been a good man if there'd been somebody to punch you in the mouth every minute of your life."

"You're misquoting Flannery O'Connor at me now? And quoting a character who was a serial killer at that?"

"O'Connor was a devout and learned Catholic. One of my favorites."

Levitt waved his hand dismissively. "We've wandered off course. I wasn't 'diddled' as you say. No priest ever touched me. But they *taught* me. They taught me that any sin could be forgiven, save one. Do you know the one?"

"Was it being boring? That seems your worst sin at the moment." Edsel yawned, pointedly.

Levitt slammed his hand against the bars hard enough to make the cell door—which hadn't been hung entirely right when it was first installed and tended to rattle and scrape a bit anyway—give a loud metal-on-metal clang. "You *will* listen to me."

"If you start saying something interesting I will," Edsel said mildly.

Levitt ground his teeth together. "The one unforgivable sin is suicide, because the sinner isn't alive to repent. When I began having my… urges… I prayed for relief, and for release, and for guidance. I only saw one way out: killing myself. But I knew, if I killed myself, I would burn forever in the fires of perdition.

Whereas if I gave into my urges—my God-given urges, certainly—and did the terrible things I so desperately wanted to do, and committed those sins, why, as long as I eventually repented, I could yet enter the kingdom of heaven. The choice was perfectly simple. I decided not to kill myself, and I started killing others instead. I would have been a sixteen-year-old suicide instead of a seventy-seven-year-old multiple murderer if I'd been raised outside the Holy Mother Church, Father. What do you think of that?"

Edsel shrugged. "Sounds like the sort of theology I'd expect from a sixteen-year-old. Bit sad and pathetic to hear it emerging from the mouth of a man your age. You'll burn in Hell anyway. You can't be forgiven if you don't repent, and you have to repent in your heart—it's not enough to say the words. Don't you agree, Pastor?"

Daniel, who'd been mesmerized by the back-and-forth between the men, amazed by the almost palpable force of will each displayed, sat up a little straighter. "Ah, God is forgiving, but murder is a very serious sin, and…" He paused, considered prattling on with platitudes, then decided to speak his mind, for once. After all, the only people here to hear him were two Catholics and Stevie Ray, who didn't seem to be listening. "Actually, I don't think Mr. Levitt will go to Hell."

Edsel sighed. "Really. Because Hell's a metaphor, is that it?"

"Not at all. But it's clear Mr. Levitt is a sociopath. He has no conscience or capacity for empathy, and acts only to gratify his own desires. It's my own theory—this isn't church doctrine, it's just something I've come to believe myself—that such people lack immortal souls. They are human in body only, but empty inside, lacking the Divine spark. Mr. Levitt is no more human than a dog, and has no more soul than a dog, either. When dogs die, they don't go to heaven, or Hell. They simply cease to exist. I think that's what will happen to Mr. Levitt. There will be no immortality for him."

They both looked at him in silence for a moment, as did Stevie Ray, which was a bit embarrassing, but Daniel met all their gazes, or at least directed his own gaze to an eye-level point that could conceivably have included all of them.

"You surprise me, Daniel." Edsel's voice had some humor in it. "I can't say I agree with you, and I rather like the image of Martin here turning on a spit over a brimstone barbecue forever, but it shows a livelier mind than I would have credited you with. I think you've got a point, though, about bodies that are human in form only, lacking any soul—that's a rather apt description of the zombies we're contending with lately, don't you think?"

Before Daniel could answer, Edsel turned back to Mr. Levitt. "Is that all? Are you finished with your blistering high school-sophomore-level philosophical devastation of Catholicism?"

"You're as useless as every other priest in the world." Levitt went back to his bunk. "Go on, then. I'll call for you again when I'm sure I'm done killing, to take my confession, and hear me repent."

"You aren't done killing now?" Daniel said. "You've been caught! You're locked in a cell! You'll be in prison soon."

Levitt laughed his coffee-grinder laugh again. "Lots of opportunities to kill in prison. But I don't expect to see the inside of one of those. The dead have come back to life. It's the end of the world. I think the due process of law is a thing of the past."

"In that, we're agreed," Edsel said. "It's the end times. But just because the laws of man have fallen—"

"Hey, I'm sitting right here," Stevie Ray said.

"—doesn't mean the laws of *God* have fallen," Edsel finished. "Justice will be served." He leaned forward. "Because you see, Martin, I'm the only priest left hereabouts, and I have no intention whatever of *hearing* your confession when the time comes. Nor will I administer the last rites. I will simply let you die, unredeemed."

"Father Edsel!" Daniel said. "I know we have our differences, but we both believe in the teachings of Jesus Christ, and above all he taught *forgiveness!*"

"I know," Edsel said, voice heavy with regret. "I've never quite been able to elevate my personal behavior to match that of our Lord and Savior's. It's a failing in myself."

"Vaya con dios, Padre," Levitt said, and laughed again, but Daniel thought the laugh lacked some of the knowingness and relish it had held before.

17. SIMULATIONS AND SHELLFISH

C afe Lo was pretty much deserted, which was unusual so close to the vicinity of dinnertime, but Otto supposed folks had other things on their minds than meatloaf and mashed potatoes. Julie Olafson was still behind the counter, sitting on a wooden stool, reading a paperback book. The only other customer was ancient old Emperor Torvald, who was apparently asleep at the counter, his head resting on his crossed arms, a cup of coffee untouched next to him.

Julie looked up when the door opened. "There's the dinner rush, then. What'll it be, fellas?"

"Just need a sandwich for, ah, police business," Rufus said.

Otto glanced up at the TV, which was still turned on, but just showing a blank blue screen now. He hated those blue screens. In his day, a dead TV showed you gray and white static. You knew where you were when it came to static. That damn blue was just altogether too tranquil.

"You're police now?"

"Special deputies," Rufus said. "You know. During the, uh, emergency."

"What emergency's that? Tuna fish okay? Got lots of tuna fish."

"Sure, that's fine," Rufus said. "What do you mean, what emergency? The, you know. Zombies." He did a little lurching dance-step sort of thing with his arms outstretched and his jaw sagging down. "There was a meeting at the community center about it, you didn't go?"

"Didn't want to close the Cafe. Not that anybody came in. Zombies, is it? Otto, do you hear what your nephew's saying over here? All zombies and secret policemen?"

Otto tore his eyes away from the mesmerizing field of blue. "All true. Call over to the police if you don't believe it. Saw it with my own eyes, anyway—dead people getting up and walking around."

"I'd never call you a liar…" Julie's ice-blue eyes were cold and contemplative, and there was a distance about her that made her very alluring, like something beautiful and mysterious glittering off in the distance.

If I were a younger man, he thought, then looked over at the younger man, Rufus, who was looking at Julie with an interest Otto was pretty sure he could identify. "Maybe we'd better fill you in." He slid onto his usual stool.

"Shouldn't we get back to the station?" Rufus said. "With the food?"

"I need a bite myself, and old man Levitt can by-God wait to eat."

Rufus winced, and Otto frowned. "What?"

"I think he wishes you hadn't mentioned Mr. Levitt." Julie sounded only a tenth of a percent interested, but maybe a full percentage point amused.

"Oh, heck, it won't be any kind of secret for long anyway," Otto grumbled, though he was embarrassed for blabbing police business. He hadn't wanted to be any kind of a special deputy anyway.

"Not if you keep telling people." Rufus slid onto a stool, though, and locked eyes with Julie, and said, "Let me tell you what happened after we left here this morning." He filled her in, telling the story in a pretty disorganized fashion, jumping back and forth all over the place and filling things in as they occurred to him. Rufus was the same way with telling jokes, which always annoyed Otto. As an expert joke teller, he found his nephew's ineptness offensive—Otto was a salesman, and having a story of jokes at varying levels of cleanliness from off-white to downright blue was practically a job requirement—whereas Rufus always gave away the punch line early or forgot some crucial part of the set-up until the joke was done. He could even screw up a knock-knock joke.

She seemed to follow it all right, though, sipping a cup of coffee, nodding here and there, asking the occasional intelligent question, not that she got much in the way of intelligent answers out of Rufus. Otto made a decision not to contribute, and he stuck to it, sticking by the old adage that it was better to be thought a fool than to open your mouth and prove it. Rufus was proving it plenty for the whole family.

When Rufus finally finished—or not so much finished but ran down like an old-timey watch that needed winding and didn't get it—Julie began methodically refilling sugar containers, speaking almost as if to herself. "Old man Levitt. Huh. They say it's always the quiet ones, but he *loves* to talk. Never expect something like that to happen around here though. Serial killers I mean."

"The Midwest is full of them," Rufus said, and why was Otto not surprised his nephew, who didn't know anything about repairing carburetors, replacing water heaters, snaking drains, or pretty much any other manly art, would nonetheless know about serial killers. "There's John Wayne Gacy, and Ed Gein, and that guy in Cleveland, the Butcher, and—"

"But the thing about the zombies is more interesting," Julie said, as if Rufus hadn't spoken at all, which was a response to the boy that Otto would have to give a try himself. Then she reached out and brushed a lock of Rufus's stupid hair out of his eyes, making him freeze, and giving Otto a sudden starburst of jealousy right in the middle of his chest. "Who do you think is right? Harry, who says we'll make it through fine, or old man Levitt, who says we're doomed?" She turned her head toward Otto, including him in the question too, and since Rufus was still apparently paralyzed at being touched halfway tenderly by an attractive young woman—though she was in her thirties so from Rufus's point of view she'd be an older woman, and wasn't getting older just a bitch all around?—Otto jumped into the breach.

"Hard to say. It's tough to get your mind around. Can't really imagine the end of the world. Sort of thing you see in the kind of movies I don't much like to watch. Doesn't seem like something that could happen here."

"There were some scientists who did a study. Computer models." Rufus was twisting a paper napkin in his hands, and his voice was serious and thoughtful in a way it wasn't, usually. Otto wondered if Julie's quiet seriousness was contagious. It would be nice if something like that was contagious, as opposed to just things like the Ebola virus and, he supposed, zombie-ism. "I read about them in this class I took, a class about zombies, you know how they were so popular a few years back, turning up in books and movies all the time, people doing zombie walks where they dressed up, all that. Well, this epidemiologist named Muntz or Bunz or Munz or something, he figured out that the way zombies work in movies is similar to the way infectious diseases spread—people get bitten by a zombie, turn into a zombie, and start biting other people. Just like spreading, I don't know, an STD or a cold, only instead of sex or coughing, it's biting."

He had the good grace to blush furiously and look down when he mentioned STDs, though Otto still had to quell the urge to smack him upside the head. Talking like that in front of a woman. Talking like that in front of anybody. Talking like that at all. But he listened.

"So Munz decided to sort of put the movies to the test, see if people—not like individual people, but *society*, the human race—could survive a zombie uprising. He got a team together and they made a computer model of a city with a million people, and dropped just one zombie into the simulation. Pretty much the classic zombie rules—you get bitten by a zombie, you turn into a zombie yourself within a day. Then they just let the program run."

"How'd it turn out?" Otto said.

Rufus shook his head. "After seven days, ten at the outside, everybody in the city was either dead or a zombie."

They all pondered this. "Not such a good deal," Otto allowed.

"Munz tried some variations," Rufus said. "Locking the zombies away, quarantining them—that didn't work, either. It just added a few more days until the end of the world. So he worked in a cure for zombies, and that didn't help a bunch, either, it only saved ten or fifteen percent of the living, but it wasn't a permanent cure, since after you got cured you could get bitten again and turned back into a zombie."

"Doesn't sound like there's going to be a cure for this one anyway," Julie said. "It's not so much a disease as just getting up out of the grave, right? Unless you figure out a way to cure death, and in that case, we've got a whole bunch of other problems."

"Right." Rufus nodded. "The researchers only found one winning strategy: all-out war. As soon as you see a zombie, you kill it. Systematically wipe them out. Bring in the army. Show no mercy. Burn 'em out. Which happens in the movies, too. Hell, in some of the George Romero movies, the military just nukes the center of the outbreak, killing the zombies and survivors and everybody else."

"Lake Woebegotten isn't a city of a million people though," Julie said. "We're a lot smaller, and I think that works in our favor. And it sounds like we have been killing every zombie we see, right?"

Otto thought of the armless, limbless zombie, but what harm could *that* thing do? They still oughta put it out of its misery. And then there was that zombie dog… "Right," he said.

"And you don't become a zombie just by getting bitten. You become one when you die, so as long as the zombie doesn't kill you, you'll be fine. I'm inclined to be hopeful." Hearing the calm and certainty in Julie's voice made Otto feel better for the first time all day.

"I think you're wrong." Rufus sounded grim. "If a zombie's biting you, there's a good chance you'll die. I saw it happen a few times this morning—God, was it only this morning?—and they take you down hard and quick. And another thing—if you just drop dead of a heart attack, you come back as a zombie. Get in a car wreck? Zombie. Take a too-big bite of Frito pie and choke to death? Zombie. The only thing that seems to stop them is destroying their brains."

"That is a nasty little wrinkle," Julie agreed.

"And there's another thing." Rufus sighed. "I hate to mention it, and I can't know for sure if I'm right, but… We're not talking about a city of a million people with one zombie dropped in the middle. We're probably talking about all the dead people on the entire planet getting up and trying to pull down the living. All of them. Everywhere. Before the internet went down, I was seeing reports from all over the place—Iran, China, India, Australia, Europe, Mexico… I think it's all over. The human civilization thing. I think it's just a matter of time. We can't live like this. Not for long."

Julie took a pack of cigarettes from under the counter, put one in her mouth, and held the pack out toward Otto. He hadn't had a smoke for fifteen years, Barbara had hounded him into quitting, but he took one anyway, a little surprised his hand wasn't shaking. Rufus took one, too, even though Otto knew he liked to smoke those nasty all-natural tobacco cigarettes, like sucking smoke into your lungs was healthier if there was a picture of an Indian chief on the package. Julie flicked open a Zippo—it had some kind of military insignia on it, which meant it had belonged to her grandpa, Otto assumed—and lit them up. "Well, just because the world's ending doesn't mean Lake Woebegotten's going anywhere," she said, after blowing a column of smoke toward the ceiling. "Everybody living here's got a gun, pretty much. We can keep the zombies down. Maybe the cities are burning down, and maybe there won't be satellite TV and Amazon.com and TiVo anymore, but this town was founded by a bunch of people terrified in the middle of marshy nowhere. Half of them didn't survive the winter, but half of them *did*, and they made something here. We can do it, too. Even if we lose power, and the outside world. Lots of us have got no use for the outside world anyway. We've got the town. That's enough."

"But what's the point?" Rufus said. "If the world's ending, if humanity is doomed, then why bother holding on? Why not just get drunk every day until we run out of booze and then blow our brains out so we can die a zombie-free life?"

"Because suicide's a sin," Otto said promptly, and then gritted his teeth when Rufus rolled his eyes.

"There's always hope, Rufus," Julie said. "There was a bottle-neck in human history, did you know that? I read about it. I used to read a lot when I was... traveling. There was a time, maybe 150,000 years ago or more, when the climate changed, and the total population of humans got squeezed down to a few thousand, only a thousand of them capable of breeding. They hunkered down on the shore and ate shellfish because all the animals they used to eat instead were gone, and they managed to survive until things improved. Every single human being on this planet is descended from that group of a thousand breeders. Maybe this zombie thing is temporary. Maybe that star just let off some strange radiation, and when the radiation dies down, things will get better. And won't you be glad we didn't all blow our brains out when that happens?"

"So you're saying we'll have an, ah, responsibility to repopulate the human race?" Rufus said.

"You might better stick with gathering shellfish for the rest of us to eat," Julie said, and ruffled his hair in a distinctly big-sisterly way, which gave Otto's heart a little boost. "There's another thing you see a lot in those zombie movies of yours. You know what that is?"

"What?" Otto said.

"A green zone." Julie's eyes had a strange light to them, and Otto wondered about her past, who she was, really, where she'd gone when she left town, why she'd come back, besides her grandfather getting sick, if there was anything besides that. "A place where the living are protected from zombies, and where civilization continues." She took another drag on her cigarette, let the smoke out, and smiled. "We'd better get started making Lake Woebegotten into a green zone, don't you think?"

Emperor Torvald lifted his head. "If we can make it through the winter," he said. "There won't be a lot of green here until spring, and there's a lot of winter between here and there." He paused, then said, "Maybe you could give a guy one of those cigarettes, Julie?" and then they all sat and smoked a while until Julie gave them all free sandwiches to go, including a tuna fish for Mr. Levitt that she opened up and spat in right in front of all of them, and then she closed up shop and kicked them out into the cold.

"I think I'm in love," Rufus said as they got into the truck.

Otto grunted in a fairly disapproving way, but he was thinking, *Maybe me too.*

TWENTY-SOME-ODD
SCENES FROM THE WINTER,
IN NO PARTICULAR ORDER,
CERTAINLY NOT CHRONOLOGICAL

1

The day after the murder, Stevie Ray called another town meeting, and this time he advised people to institute a basic call-and-response test for finding out if someone was a zombie before shooting them in the head. "I recommend you just say something like, 'Are you a zombie?'"

"And what are you supposed to say back if you're not a zombie?" called a voice from the front row.

Stevie Ray sighed. He was so tired; he'd never signed up to be the only law east of the prairie. "I imagine you can say pretty much anything at all, because zombies can't talk. So even if they say 'Yes, I'm a zombie,' don't shoot. If they say 'Ungh' and lunge at you, then you can shoot them."

"But it's probably best if you don't say 'Yes, I'm a zombie,'" Pastor Inkfist said. "People are a little bit jumpy."

"Funeral services are tomorrow," Father Edsel rumbled. "It'll be closed-casket. Obviously."

2

After her latest pointless visit, Eileen Munson slammed her hands down on Stevie Ray's desk. "How long are you planning to keep Dolph locked up?" she demanded. "For a simple mistake?"

"He killed a man, Eileen," Stevie Ray said, in the weary tone of one who's answered this question before. "He thought he was killing a zombie, so I'm not saying it's necessarily murder, but it's still voluntary manslaughter, or negligent homicide." He cleared his throat. "That's for a judge to decide." Actually he wasn't even sure what negligent homicide was, but it sounded official.

"Judge," Eileen said, sneering. "Like there's going to be a judge coming through here any time soon. Dolph could be stuck in that jail forever!"

"It's not such a bad jail," Mr. Levitt said, leaning on a stool near the door, his eyes half-closed. "Quite cozy, in fact. He's safer in there than the rest of us are out here." That dry old lizard voice still made Stevie Ray's hindbrain want to crawl down his spine and out his butt and run away. *Levitt* belonged in jail, and Stevie Ray wanted to tell everyone what a monster he was, but for the time being, he was more valuable to the town roaming free.

"Nobody asked your opinion, old man," Eileen said.

Levitt grinned at her, then looked ostentatiously at his watch. "I should get another patrol in before dark, Stevie Ray. There are enough seats on that bus to fit thirty-six people, not counting the driver's seat, and we don't know how many of them were occupied. Could be thirty more zombies out there for all we know."

Stevie Ray ground his teeth. "There were only fifteen bags on the bus, so at most there are a dozen zombies left, and they're probably stuck buried in a snowdrift somewhere."

"Snow will be melting soon," Levitt said. "It's almost March already. Spring's only a month away by calendar time. We always find the damndest things when the snow melts, don't we?"

"Just go." Stevie Ray flapped his hands at Mr. Levitt, who smiled his skull smile, gave a salute, put on his coat, and strolled out into the cold.

"Somebody should kill that man," Eileen said.

"I keep hoping a zombie will get him myself," Stevie Ray said. "No such luck so far."

Eileen took that as an opening. "You need to let Dolph out. It's killing him. You can tell."

Stevie Ray swiveled slowly in the big chair and looked into the cell, where Dolph lay on the bunk, facing the wall. Which, with one or two exceptions, was pretty much all he'd done ever since the accident, or murder, or whatever you wanted to call it. "I think killing a man accidentally is what's killing him, Eileen. Not being locked up in here."

"But to lock him up, and let Mr. Levitt go free—"

"Come look at this," Stevie Ray said, rising. He walked across the office, to the big deep-freezer they'd put in the corner. It wasn't plugged in or anything, they weren't going to waste their meager generator power on that, but it was replenished with ice and snow every couple of days. He lifted the lid carefully, just enough for Eileen to look inside, and she gasped.

"How... how many?"

"Seven," Stevie Ray said. "A couple of suicides, a heart attack, the three bus crash zombies he caught, and one fella who died of exposure, a drifter maybe." There were actually eight heads in there. The other was Clem's, the first zombie Levitt had killed without destroying the brain. But Stevie Ray didn't want to tell Eileen that. The severed heads in the freezer began snapping their teeth—they always got more lively when the lid was open. He let the lid drop. "Levitt brought them all. He's protecting the town. Not for good reasons, but… he likes it, and it needs doing, and who else is going to volunteer to walk around in the cold with a machete, looking for monsters?"

"But why keep the heads?" Eileen asked, horrified.

Stevie Ray hesitated. "In case things do get better, the government comes back, all that, we thought, maybe they'd be valuable for scientists, you know, to study." That's what Levitt had told him, and it had the ring of the plausible, but… Levitt liked keeping trophies. Stevie Ray was pretty sure the heads were his trophies now.

"How do you know he's not just finding lost living people in the woods, killing them, waiting for them to rise as zombies, and then beheading them?" Eileen asked. Like Stevie Ray hadn't thought of that.

"He doesn't get a moment when he's not being watched—even if he *thinks* he's not being watched," Stevie Ray said. "Don't worry about it."

"And what if he becomes mayor?" Eileen said. "You've heard the rumors that he's running as a write-in candidate, I'm sure. Should I worry *then*?"

"You have my permission to worry then. Heck, I'll even join you."

3

Rufus sat snoozing in the police station on his first ever solo shift, head resting on the surface of the desk. He'd been reading a graphic novel by the grainy gray light coming in through the windows, but in retrospect *The Walking Dead* hadn't been a great choice—he'd expected it to give him some tips or some insight, but it had only served to depress him, and Mr. Levitt's persistent snoring from the cell in the back of the room had an oddly soporific quality, and Rufus's head had drooped, drooped, drooped. Stevie Ray would get mad if he found Rufus sleeping on duty, but getting fired from a job that included no pay and excessive responsibilities and proximity to a creepy old murderer wasn't the worst thing that could happen. Rufus only agreed to remain a special deputy because the alternative was spending time at home with his mother and her increasingly strained-looking eternal smile.

A thumping, scraping noise at the door woke him, and it took a moment of staring at the pool of drool on the wooden desk before Rufus remembered where he was. "It's open!" he called, but the thump-scrape-thump just continued, like someone wearing oven mitts was trying to work the doorknob while simultaneously attempting to batter the door down in a leisurely fashion.

"Coming!" Rufus called, rising from the desk. Mr. Levitt was awake, too, drifting over to the bars of his cage. Rufus tried to ignore him. The old man treated the world like it was a half-interesting soap opera that he'd watch a little bit, just until something better came on.

Rufus turned the doorknob and the door swung inward and his uncle Otto half-crawled in, eyes wide and red-rimmed, and Rufus struggled to help him up without falling over himself. "Otto, are you okay? What happened?"

"Dog bit me," Otto said, voice slurring. "Fuggin dog bit my fuggin leg."

Rufus eased Otto into the room and helped him sit down on the bench. Otto leaned against the wall, breath coming raggedly, eyes now half-closed, and Rufus bent to look at his leg. The pants and long underwear over Otto's right ankle were shredded and soaked in blood, the flesh a mass of ugly punctures. Rufus whistled. "I think there's some rubbing alcohol here, but you need stitches, Otto. I'll call Morty." Morty was a paramedic and, since Doctor Holliday's unfortunate death by zombie bite (Rufus had joked that, like the historical Doc Holliday, the town's own Doc Holliday had also died of consumption, of a sort, but nobody seemed to think it was funny) and re-death by gunshot, Morty was the town's ranking medical man.

"Fuggin dog," Otto said. "Ugly little bastard. Bit my…" He trailed off, head nodding.

"Was that my dog?" Mr. Levitt demanded. "My Alta?"

"Miniature pissant," Otto muttered.

Mr. Levitt cackled. "Shut up," Rufus said, sorting through the cupboard for the first aid kit. "Why'd you name your dog Alta anyway? What's it supposed to mean?"

"It's a little town in Utah," Mr. Levitt said. "Where I killed my first police officer. I named my dog after the town as a remembrance, because I didn't get to keep a trophy that time. And now Alta's killed a lawman himself. Good dog."

"He's not dead, it's just a bite," Rufus said, frowning. If he'd gone after Alta that night when the dog first escaped from the cooler, Otto wouldn't have gotten bitten.

There was the first aid kit, a white-and-red painted metal box, but the latch was rusted shut, wasn't that always the way, made you thank the good Lord for the invention of plastic. He started hammering the kit on the edge of the counter, bits of oxidized metal flaking off, but the latch stayed pretty much welded closed.

"It's just a bite from a *zombie* dog. You know how they say a dog's mouth is cleaner than a human mouth? I'm guessing that's not true when it's a zombie dog. And when I said your uncle'd been killed, I wasn't being metaphorical or talking about some inevitable future—he's dead, and, oh, looks like you missed that little grace period you get between when they keel over dead and wake up again hungry, because here he comes."

"Very funny, old man—it's sad to see a sadist like you reduced to the old 'Look out behind you!' trick." Rufus tried again to pry up the latch, tearing his thumbnail and sending a bolt of bright white pain through his hand. "Crap in a basket!" he shouted—just a few days back in his mother's house, and his casual college profanity had been replaced by the habitual euphemisms of his youth—and sucked the thumb.

"Murrung," his uncle said, or something similar, and then there was a crash of metal and breaking glass, and Rufus turned.

Otto had gotten his feet tangled up in the desk lamp's cord, and he was jerking one foot over and over trying to get loose, but all he'd done was pull down the gooseneck lamp and break the bulb. Drool poured out of Otto's mouth like a sludgy waterfall, and when he lifted his head, his eyes were bloodshot and blank, his mouth ceaselessly moving. He reached out for Rufus and lunged, managing only to trip and fall face first, landing two feet from his nephew. He reached out his hands and started dragging himself forward. Rufus screamed—like a girl, just a little girl, Mr. Levitt would later say, with some justification—and danced out of the way, chucking the first aid kit at his uncle's head, which didn't seem to be much of a deterrent.

Rufus rushed to the desk and pulled open the drawer with jittering hands, taking out the service revolver Stevie Ray had told him to absolutely not touch except in case of dire emergency, viz., zombies in the cop shop. Meanwhile Otto had untangled his feet and was making his slow implacable way over to Rufus.

"Stop, uncle Otto! Stop right there!"

"That's not your uncle anymore." From his bored tone, Mr. Levitt might as well have been watching a scene on TV. Maybe he was—maybe in his messed-up brain, other people were just objects moving for his amusement, the world nothing more than a picture show populated by imaginary beings. "Bullet in the brain, son, that's the only way."

Rufus lifted the pistol, but—but—it was *Otto*. His uncle. Sure, they'd gotten on each other's nerves in recent years, but when Rufus was a kid, Otto had been his favorite uncle, teaching him to play cards, pulling quarters from his ears by magic, taking him out fishing, showing him how to shoot a gun—how to shoot a gun—how to shoot a gun—

How could Rufus kill the man who'd taught him how to *shoot* a gun *with* a gun? How could he be expected to do this?

In the zombie movies and books Rufus had studied, there was pretty much always a scene where a loved one became a zombie, and the other characters always had a hard time with it, sometimes broke down completely, or killed themselves, and Rufus had always thought: *Nah. Even if it was my own mother, I'd just point and shoot.* But his hands wouldn't stop shaking and he couldn't even get his finger under the trigger guard and Otto was closer, his mouth opening—the mouth that used to tell Rufus dirty jokes when no other adult was around, the mouth that had kissed his forehead when Rufus was just a tiny little thing, the mouth that had whispered, *You're the man of the house now* when his Dad died—Otto's mouth was opening to take a bite out of him, and, well, so be it. Who wanted to live in a world full of zombies anyway? Better to be a zombie yourself. Join the winning side. At least that way, if you had to kill someone you loved, you wouldn't love them anymore.

Rufus closed his eyes, and Otto's outstretched hands touched his chest.

The harsh crack of a gunshot went off, followed by another, and Rufus jumped, eyes popping open, expecting to see Stevie Ray in the doorway—but there was no one new in the room. His uncle Otto writhed on the ground, legs bent funny, knees shredded and white and frothing red.

"Saved your life, son," Mr. Levitt said.

Rufus looked at the prisoner, who still leaned casually against the bars, but now held a pistol in his left hand. "You—where did you get a gun?"

Mr. Levitt nodded at Otto. "You might want to step away from your fellow deputy there. He's still lively, and they don't feel pain."

Rufus stepped away from Otto, and away from Mr. Levitt, too, putting the desk between all of them, for what that was worth. "Where did you get the gun?" he repeated.

"You so-called lawmen did a piss-poor job of booking me, you know that? Didn't remember my Miranda rights, and I never did get searched. I know Harry had a lot on his mind, but still, I expected a *little* better of him. Had the pistol on me the whole time, from when I was killing zombies at my house. Been keeping it under the mattress in here."

"Then why haven't you used it to escape?"

Levitt shrugged. "Seemed like inside a jail cell was a pretty safe place if the zombies were coming. But I've been in here long enough, and safety is boring. I'd like to get out now. What do you say you unlock the door and set me free?"

"And if I don't? You'll kill me?" Rufus still had the pistol, and he didn't think he'd have as much trouble shooting Mr. Levitt as he had shooting Otto… but he knew Mr. Levitt would have absolutely no trouble at all shooting *him*, and the old man was probably a better shot, too.

"No," Mr. Levitt said. "If you don't let me go, I'll *wound* you. Kind of like I did with him." He nodded to Otto, who was trying to get moving again even though his knees were just bulges of shattered bone now. "I'll let the two of you crawl around on the floor together. Since you feel pain, and he doesn't, I'm guessing he'll get to you before you can get away." He lifted the gun.

Stevie Ray will kill me, Rufus thought, but he nodded, and got the keys to the cell, and unlocked the door, and opened it wide.

"Good lad." Mr. Levitt put a bullet in Otto's head in an off-hand sort of way. He sat down at Stevie Ray's desk, grinned, and said, "Why don't you call your boss man, son? I'd like to offer my services to the town. Killing zombies isn't as good as killing ordinary people, but it's a lot better than killing nothing at all. I'd make a good zombie-hunter general. And since I just saved your life, you'll vouch for me, won't you?"

4

"**B**ut what are we supposed to do with him?" Dolph said, in that whiny tone Eileen couldn't stand— she'd had one whiny husband, and a whiny lover didn't much interest her, especially when he was asking stupid questions.

"You shoot him in the head, sweetie." Eileen shifted around, but it was pretty much impossible to get comfortable when sitting on a stack of boxes of frozen fishsticks. Still, there was something reassuring about being in the back of Dolph's grocery, surrounded by supplies. Being close to the man who had more food than anyone else in town was a pretty good position, even if he was a whiner.

Dolph gestured helplessly to the closed freezer door. "But it's *Clem*!"

"It *was* Clem. Now it's a zombie." Eileen contemplated a flat of milk cartons. That stuff would go bad soonest, so maybe they should donate it to the town, get the priest and the minister to distribute it to the townspeople, as a gesture of goodwill, make everybody like them before they learned they'd have to *really* pay for canned goods and everything else once they got good and hungry.

"I don't know how you can do that," Dolph said. "Just… make that distinction. The way you shot Brent tonight…"

"He would have hurt people. Brent didn't want to hurt

people." Except her. But even then, he hadn't so much *wanted* to hurt her, as much as he'd just been *indifferent* to whether he hurt her. "In a way, shooting Brent like that is exactly what Brent would have wanted."

"You aren't… torn up about it?"

She shrugged. "He was my husband. I'm still pretty much in shock, I guess. But you know things haven't been good between us in a long time. That's why I've been spending so much time with you." She sighed. "In a few months I guess we can tell people we've started dating, if you want. Assuming all this blows over." Eileen didn't think it would blow over, and she was making plans for the eventuality of the zombie apocalypse becoming an ongoing thing, but better not to dizzy up poor Dolph's head with all that now. "In the meantime, you should take care of business, and open that freezer door, and kill Clem. What used to be Clem. Or do you want me to do it?" Eileen hadn't exactly developed a taste for blood, like some kind of tiger that eats one little Javanese boy and can't abide the taste of anything but sweet sweet manflesh after that, but she'd discovered she could kill both deliberately and in the heat of the moment if the job needed doing. Killing was just another necessary chore, like cleaning the gutters or scrubbing mildew off the tile in the bathtub. Leave it to a man to bitch and moan about something instead of just going ahead and getting it done.

"No! You shouldn't have to go through something like that, Eileen, after what you've already done tonight. I guess you're right. I should put Clem out of his misery. But… what do I tell his mother?"

"Tell her he died bravely fighting a zombie."

Dolph considered. "I doubt she'd believe *that*. I mean, this is Clem we're talking about. The closest he ever came to brave was stupid. I'd like to kill that *dog* that bit him. It's still out there, and it's only a matter of time until it bites someone else." He sighed. "I think I'll call Stevie Ray, tell him about Clem being locked up in the freezer, make it into *his* problem."

Eileen knew when to push, and when not to, so she just nodded, though she thought, *Weak*. For her purposes, though, Dolph being weak could be okay. "Good idea. Hard to believe

Harry's dead and Stevie Ray's the law in this town now."

"Stevie Ray's all right. He'll do what needs to be done."

"Going to ask him to take care of that zombie in the back of your truck too?"

Dolph grimaced. The limbless zombie—the object lesson for that horrible disaster of a town meeting—was still in his pickup, twitching and moaning. "No. That one, I can shoot. It's not anybody I know."

"I noticed that. Who is it, anyway?"

Dolph cleared his throat. "Harry said we shouldn't tell anybody, before he got killed I mean, he was afraid there'd be a lynch mob—like you could muster up a lynch mob in Lake Woebegotten, it's an uphill battle to whip us into a big enough frenzy to form a bowling league or a pickup softball game, everybody's so damn Norwegian and self-sufficient and inward—but I guess I can tell you if you'll keep it a secret… We found a bunch of dead bodies at Mr. Levitt's place. Dead bodies up and around and attacking people I mean. And Mr. Levitt pretty much admitted he's just… no two ways about it a serial killer, like you'd see on a TV show. Except old. That zombie in the back of my truck, he's one of Mr. Levitt's victims, some drifter I guess."

Eileen whistled. Mr. Levitt didn't enter her orbit very much—he was Catholic, so there was no church connection and he drove a Chevy so there was no car dealership connection—and though he'd been superintendent when her children were in school, she'd never had occasion to talk to anyone up *that* high in the chain of command, but she knew him, a harmless-enough-seeming old man. Just went to show you people had hidden depths. Eileen guessed maybe she was a serial killer herself, in a way, having killed twice in the past day, though maybe it didn't count since she'd killed the same man twice, once with car exhaust, once with a gunshot to the head. Maybe she oughta kill another one just to confirm her status.

"Might as well go out and kill the zombie in your truck now, honey, I don't imagine he's going to start smelling any better. What are we supposed to do with… zombie bodies? Come to think of it, what did they do with Brent?"

"Stevie Ray said they were hauling all the bodies to the funeral home basement until they figure out what to do with them. Did you want Brent, ah, buried?"

"We have to be practical now," Eileen said. "I imagine burning the bodies is the smartest thing." She hopped down off the fishsticks. "Let's go out and kill that poor thing in the bed of your truck, I hate thinking of it out there."

Eileen was wondering how best to go about convincing Dolph to let her be the one to put a bullet in the things's head—he didn't want to do it himself, but he had his manly pride, so she'd have to ease her way up to the suggestion gently—except once they got into their coats and gloves and went out back of the store where Dolph was parked, the zombie was gone. Just stumps for arms and legs, sure, but it had managed to flop and twist and bend its way out of the truck bed and slither off into the darkness and the woods that pressed right up against the town. They could see the trail in the snow, like some kind of horrible giant worm had slithered away, and Dolph cursed. "Should we go in after it?"

Eileen had already tracked one zombie through the trackless wilderness, and had no desire to do so again. "No, honey. Let's make that Stevie Ray's problem, too. What kind of trouble can it get into anyway, with no arms and legs? What's it going to do, bite somebody's ankle?"

"Clem died of a bite to the ankle," Dolph said, tone all dark and broody, and there was no point listening to him anymore when he got like that, so Eileen kissed his cheek and let him escort her home, but didn't let him come inside, looking forward to her first night in the blessedly empty bed of a widow.

5

"I just can't see the point in keeping you here." Stevie Ray pushed the bowl of mixed nuts—all the cashews had been picked out already, of course, that was always the way, it was pretty much nothing but peanuts and miscellaneous nut-dust now—across the desk toward Dolph.

Dolph, who was usually a big bluff man, and one of the loudest voices at any town meeting on any subject that came anywhere close to involving his store in particular or commerce in general (his jeremiad against the installation of a parking meter fifteen years back was still the stuff of local legend), was hunched and quiet tonight, shoulders up halfway to his ears, head down, voice all a-mumble. "Just throw away the key. Lock me up and throw away the key."

"You and me both know I've let a lot worse than you out of this jail because they can do some good in this town." Stevie Ray took a sip from his bottle of snow-cooled beer—he shouldn't be drinking on the job, but given that he was pretty much on the job every waking hour and on call all the sleeping ones, that would entail not drinking at all, and he hadn't gotten a part-time job at a bar where he was paid primarily in free drinks because he didn't like a cold one now and then. He had to keep it under control, yes, and so far he was, and he had a little twinge over what Harry would have said at the sight of him with a bottle of Bud at his desk (probably something like, "I'm ashamed of you—you can't at least drink Krepusky's Red Ribbon Beer, support our local brewmaster?"), but if there was ever a time he needed a drink, it was now, when a criminal he wanted to release was refusing to leave. Stevie Ray made another run at the situation. "It was a terrible thing, but it was an accident—"

"Wasn't any accident. I aimed. I pulled the trigger. I hit what I aimed at. I'm a murderer." Dolph stared at the bowl of mixed nuts—be honest, call it a bowl of peanuts now, and barely that—but didn't eat. He hadn't eaten since what Stevie Ray continued to think of as a terrible tragedy, but not a murder. Not exactly. "You should hold me here until a judge sets bail."

"You and me both know there's no telling when we'll get a judge through here. Nobody's heard from the group we sent to the cities for help. For all we know we're the last town standing."

Dolph shook his head, a stubborn look on his face, which was an improvement at least over looking as blank as a fresh-dead walleye. "With the weather so bad, they could just be holed up somewhere, waiting for a break in the storm to come back. There's going to be a judge. There is. There have to be consequences for what I've done."

"Well, fine, then, in time you'll stand trial and get all the consequences you can eat, you betcha, but you aren't exactly a flight risk, Dolph. I can let you out of here. I know where you live. I know where your store is. I can let you go on your own recognizance. We could use you in this town."

"I can't. I can't face them, anyone, I can't… Just leave me in jail, won't you? I won't cost anything, you can feed me out of my own store, all right?"

Stevie Ray sighed. "What am I supposed to tell Eileen? She's been calling for your release, making like I'm the Gestapo and the KGB and the Spetsnaz all rolled up into one, trampling over your constitutional rights. You want to tell her you refuse to leave the jail?"

"No!" Dolph was truly animated now. "Don't tell her I want to stay, she'll think I'm a coward, tell her it's your idea, that you think it's the best thing, will you do that for me, Stevie Ray? I'll throw in all *your* meals, too, and a case of Michelob, just don't tell her—"

Stevie Ray held up his hands. "Whoa, there, Dolph. It's all

right. We've known each other a long time. You gave my mama credit at the store when she lost her job at the battery factory. I owe you for that still, and I like to think we're friends. I'll tell Eileen whatever you want, but *why?*"

Dolph put his head in his hands, and Stevie Ray figured this was one of those things a man had to say while not looking directly at the man he was saying it too. Sometimes it seemed life was full of those kinds of conversations. "I can't be what she wants me to be, Stevie Ray. Eileen. She's… *ambitious*. I bet Brent never wanted to be mayor, I think it was Eileen who steered him toward it, because she wants me to be mayor now, a big man in the town, king of the hill sitting on a hoard of food, using my supplies to make people do what I want—except I don't want people to do *anything*, and I don't *know* what she wants people to do. I'm sort of scared to find out. I was going to go along with her, too, I'm ashamed to say, it's not very Christian of me, I know, but she has a way of talking about power that makes it sound like a pretty good deal. Then the—accident, no, murder, the thing I did—that happened, and I guess it gave me a new sense of perspective and I don't like her plans anymore. Just leave me here, would you, until the world starts making sense again?"

Well, well. Dolph and Eileen. Stevie Ray had figured they were just good friends, which just goes to show he didn't know everything, and that was a bad quality in a police chief—Harry had sure known everything, and known when to keep it secret, too. Stevie Ray wondered if Eileen and Dolph had been… so close… before Brent got zombified. Better not to think about it. You could stay friends with people better if you *didn't* know all their secrets, probably.

"All right, you can stay here, but I'm only locking you in that cell when Eileen or one of the special deputies is around, you hear? And you're going to help me keep this place clean, too, no freeloading."

"You're a true friend, Stevie Ray." Dolph yawned hugely. "I'd like to sleep now, if I can. Tell the truth I wish I could hibernate, like a bear. When was the last time we had a bear down here? Used to see them from time to time when I was a kid."

"Been a couple years," Stevie Ray said. "Still a lot of black bears farther north and east though. Might be some in the woods around here nobody sees, I guess. I hope not. Just our luck the bear would die and rise back up and come shambling through town, and if there's a sight I don't want to see, it's a zombie bear."

"A zombear. I guess that might make my top ten list of things I don't want to see, too," Dolph agreed.

6

BigHorn Jim tromped through the snow with his Viking battleaxe (which he'd had made special for a pretty penny) over his shoulder, in case he should encounter a *draugr*—the ancient Norse word for the angry spirits of the dead, and the nearest thing in his worldview to match the shambling zombies he'd heard about and so briefly glimpsed at the town meeting. Mainly he was out to hunt firewood, though. His lodge up past the lake got cold when the winter wind came whipping down the prairie, and though he'd laid in a lot of wood, you could never have too much.

He paused by a cleft of rock, leaning toward the snow-heaped opening and sniffing. He couldn't smell anything besides the burning cold insides of his own nostrils, but he liked to imagine he could smell bear. He'd seen a small black bear, a solitary male, in the fall, gorging itself for the winter, and he figured it was denned up here for the winter, sleeping, wouldn't wake up until late March or early April, probably, coming out hungry and pissed-off in springtime. When it did come out, BigHorn Jim would be waiting with his axe to bring the bear down, and would fashion a cape from its skin. (Maybe also some slippers, if there was enough fur left over.) There weren't many chances for valiant battle out here in Central Minnesota, even during the early days of Ragnarok when *draugr* wandered the earth, but he thought killing a bear in single combat might be enough to get him an eternal free ticket to the mead-and-roast-boar hall of Valhalla in his appointed afterlife. The greatest Viking warriors, known as berserkers, had worn bear skins or wolf skins to battle—even the name, berserker, came from *bjorn serkr*, bear shirt. Some said berserkers even transformed into bears on the field of battle. BigHorn Jim needed a bear shirt of his own. He would slay the bear and wear its skin, and be filled with the beast's power then. A grizzly would have been better—Vikings had not fought Minnesota black bears, he was fairly certain—but he knew Odin would appreciate his effort, and Jim would take his place alongside the *einherjar* in this, the doomed battle of the last days.

"See you in the springtime, *bjorn*," he said, and went on his way.

7

Julie sat up in bed—well it wasn't a bed really, but Otto wasn't too comfortable with all the accoutrements and such so he didn't want to dwell on that, it was horizontal and padded and that was close enough—and lit a cigarette. She took a drag, then offered it to Otto, who said, "Erm, no, thanks." He was fairly certain Barbara wouldn't discover he'd been unfaithful to her—she never had before, not that he'd ever had like a regular mistress or anything, but he'd spent a lot of years in motels as a salesman, and sometimes you met a nice lady in a bar, and sometimes she wasn't even a professional—since Otto knew how to talk nice and smile and hide the truth behind a shell of jokes and misdirection, but if his wife smelled cigarette smoke on his breath he'd catch seven kinds of heck, and no amount of smooth talking or sweet nothings would save him then.

"You, uh, always sleep down here?" Otto said, looking around Julie's finished basement, which did not resemble his own finished basement—which contained a ping-pong table and an illuminated beer sign that wasn't illuminated since they were conserving generator power and a refurbished jukebox that unfortunately hadn't worked in about twelve years—in any respect at all

"No, Otto, I just have sex down here. I sleep in a normal bed upstairs."

She slid off the bed—which was, really, a broad platform padded in black leather and fitted with D-rings and O-rings, and which appeared to have various hinged wood and metal

144

appendages folded away underneath. Otto hadn't looked too closely, afraid of what he'd see, and in the light of nothing but hurricane lamps the whole basement was pretty dim. Various wood and metal and leather things loomed around the edges, though, and he was pretty sure that was a cage—big, tall, narrow, with a domed top like a birdcage for a human—over in one corner, and there were definitely various whips hanging on the wall on hooks in pegboard.

Otto gestured to encompass the room. "You didn't want to use any of this... stuff... with me?"

Julie, who was dressed in a couple of bits of leather and not much else, and who was certainly the most in-shape woman Otto had ever seen naked, if not definitely the most beautiful—Barbara when she was 19 on their wedding night was pretty hard to beat, misty as the memories were by now—pulled on a dark silk robe patterned with a Chinese dragon. "No, I just wanted to get laid. If you're interested in the... optional extras... well, my client base has been diminished by recent events, and I'd be willing to consider new applicants."

The light dawned on Otto. "You do this sort of thing professionally?"

"Not sex. I'm not a prostitute, But the whips, the restraints, humiliation, cages, hot wax... my customers can order prix fixe or a la carte." She shrugged. "I developed a certain, I don't know, authoritative bearing while I was in the service, and when I got out and was looking for civilian work, I found out some men would pay pretty well for getting screamed at by a drill sergeant in a leather corset."

Otto thought about that. He'd had the odd thought that combined women and restraints, sure, maybe scarves tying wrists to a headboard or something, but he'd never much thought about getting tied up himself, and even in the fantasies giggling over the absurdity of the whole process seemed as likely as anything else. "Hard to imagine there's much call for this sort of thing in Lake Woebegotten."

"It's not as busy as it was in Minneapolis, it's true." Julie sat on a stool over by a little bar and poured herself a couple fingers of whiskey. Otto was ready to politely decline a drink but she didn't offer. "I took a hit when I came here to take over the diner, but what can you do? It's family. I almost didn't bother to set up the dungeon here, but I found a few local customers, and some of my old clients make the drive to see me. Well. They used to anyway. Before…" She waved her hand vaguely.

Otto nodded. "So you're one of those, what's it called, a dominatrix?"

"Just dom is fine. That's what they call men who do what I do. I don't need a special and sillier-sounding job title just because I happen to be a woman, do I?"

That distinction was a bit too esoteric for Otto, who still called flight attendants stewardesses, female actors actresses, and pretty much all waitresses "sweetheart," so he fell back on reliable flattery: "You happen to be one heck of a woman, Julie." He started looking around for his pants and shirt, feeling a bit self-conscious about his poochy gut—he wasn't fat, had never run to fat, but his middle was getting saggy from too many years eating meals on the road—and his graying chest hair, and the cold air in the basement made his nipples hard, which never failed to make him feel somehow vaguely less masculine.

"You're sweet, Otto. Thanks for coming home with me. I love older men—they're experienced, they take their time, and they know their way around the territory."

That "older" stung a bit, but a very beautiful young woman had just given him the best afternoon he'd had in ages, so he wouldn't hold it against her that she'd told the truth. "I, uh, thank you, ma'am."

She laughed. "You don't need to call me ma'am. Makes me feel like I'm at work. Are you going on patrol today?"

Otto finished buttoning his shirt and nodded. "Yeah, taking a snow machine out with Father Edsel. That's always an adventure."

"Good luck. Or should I say good hunting?"

"I hope we don't have to hunt anything." Otto had gone out patrolling in the brutal cold three days in a row now, and apart from two zombie raccoons and a zombie housecat, he hadn't encountered any of the ravenous dead, certainly no humans. He tended to think Harry was right—there just wasn't going to be much of a zombie problem in Lake Woebegotten. Otto personally hoped that killing zombified wildlife was going to be the full extent of his responsibilities as a member of the Interfaith Anti-Zombie Patrol. Zombie critters didn't worry him overmuch. Half the animals in this world would bite you if they could anyway, so your attitude toward them didn't have to change much just because they were zombies. "You ought to join the patrols, Julie. A person with your military background could do a lot of good." He'd been surprised when she told him about her experience as a soldier, but in retrospect, it made sense—she was tough as nails and old boot leather, even if she could be soft when she wanted.

"Maybe. Though my experience in the military is part of why I don't want to—it looks too much like a bunch of boys playing soldiers without any idea of what they're doing, and I'm afraid someone's going to get hurt. Everybody's so zombie-paranoid, they're jumping at shadows, and I'm sure someone's going to get hurt."

"Oh, I don't know, we've got Gunther Montcrief, he was in the military." He was also drunk most days, but then, Ulysses S. Grant was a famous drunk, too, and it hadn't affected his sense of strategy any. Not that Gunther exhibited much in the way of strategy, but he'd killed some zombie dogs, so he'd pulled his weight. "And Stevie Ray's pretty sharp."

"I'll keep it in mind."

Otto wanted to leave, but didn't want to seem like the kind of guy who'd want to leave, so he cleared his throat and scrabbled desperately for conversation and said, "Do you have any plans for Christmas?" It was just a few days away.

"Why? Inviting me over to your place?" She grinned, or at least showed her teeth, and when Otto stammered, she waved her hand and said, "Joking, joking. I'll just stay here with my grandfather, and do a little reading, and hold a pistol in my hand so I can put him down as soon as he dies and, I hope, a moment before he comes back as a monster. I owe him peace."

Otto hadn't really considered her circumstances, but having a relative on their deathbed in this new world couldn't be comfortable. "It's a shame you have to go through all this, Julie. I'm sorry for it."

"If I hadn't had to move here to take care of him, if there were anyone else left in my family, I'd still be in Minneapolis, and based on what your nephew's told us about events there, I'd almost certainly be dead, or in much more desperate circumstances than I am now. Being in a small town in a cold place is a pretty good strategic position, given the circumstances. Shame over half the population of America lives in cities now." She had a faraway look on her face. "It is hard, though. And lonely. That's why I invited you back here from the diner. I just wanted someone to tell me I was beautiful. To feel like there was still beauty in the world."

"You're beautiful all right. Do you think we'll, ah, do this again?"

"It's the other side of the end of the world, Otto. There's no telling what might happen."

After a few more floundering attempts at chit-chat Otto left—she said goodbye warmly enough, though she didn't go through the ritual Lake Woebegotten insistence that he stay a while longer, have a little lunch, none of that, just went to show she'd lived away for too long—but there was no kiss or anything. Otto tromped through the snow, which wasn't too deep yet, looking around to make sure he wasn't observed, as if Julie's house wasn't at the end of a long driveway some ways away from anyone else, and got in his truck, and got it warmed up, and drove back to town. He needed to stop by the police station to pick up a gun before going to meet Father Edsel for the patrol. It was going to be boring, and the priest sure could talk, but at least he had some warm recent memories to let his mind dwell on.

He parked outside the police station and climbed out of the truck, and something the color of filthy plowed snow streaked toward him from underneath another car, and before he knew what was happening, a sharp pain jolted through his ankle, and just kept getting worse, and he howled and hopped and shook his foot, where some ball of stinking fur had its teeth sunk into him. It was a God, oh Lord Jesus it was *that* dog, Mr. Levitt's dog, the dead dog, and how had it moved so fast with its messed-up back legs, maybe you could get around pretty good if you didn't feel any pain, but Otto sure was feeling pain, and then the dog took off, carrying who knew how many mouthfuls of Otto's flesh. He leaned against his truck, groaning, the whole lower half of his leg wrapped in hot pain that would only get worse, he knew. Otto limp-hopped toward the police station, then slipped on the ice, went down, banged his head good, and dragged himself toward the door. He couldn't quite reach the handle, and he was seeing stars only the stars were made of blackness, and so he banged on the door, hoping Stevie Ray was inside, that someone could help him up, warm him up, bandage him up—

The door opened, and his nephew Rufus was there, and Otto had definitely never been happier to see the boy, stupid tattoo and all, and Rufus made a fuss, and Otto said, "Dog bit me," and Rufus helped him up, and it seemed like everything was going to be all right.

8

Afterward, pillow-talking—if you could call it pillow talk when there was no pillow, and it technically wasn't even a bed—Rufus said, "That was awesome."

"As usual," Julie said. "I love sleeping with young men. So much passion, so much energy, so much stamina—my favorite."

Rufus smiled, despite the melancholy he felt stealing over him, as it did more and more lately. "I'm glad we get together this way. It takes my mind off... well, everything. For a little while. The whole situation. Even with everything I saw in the cities, it didn't really become real for me until Otto died, and changed. He was... He was my *uncle*. It wasn't like living in a movie anymore after that, it was just *living*."

"He was a sweet man." Julie touched Rufus's cheek—pretty much the tenderest gesture she'd ever shown him—then rose from the leather-covered platform Rufus privately thought of as Fuck Station Zero.

"I don't know if I'd call him 'sweet,' but he was family." Julie and Rufus had enjoyed a few conversations on the subject of family since first hooking up, not long after the New Year. "Losing him was sort of a wake-up call, and then Dolph killing that guy because he thought he was a zombie, and now with this bus crash, who knows how many zombies wandering around out in the snow... There's never going to be 'normal' again."

"We'll find a new normal. I still say we can make this place a green zone." She considered. "Let me show you something."

Rufus wondered if she was *finally* going to break out some of the stuff in her basement for their private use—despite the surroundings they had totally vanilla sex, which was in keeping with his limited experience, but he was eager to expand his horizons, something Julie wasn't that interested in, saying if you worked at an ice cream store you got really sick of ice cream, but heck, that didn't mean you wouldn't let your *lovers* have a little ice cream every once in a while, did it?—a hope that swelled as she walked into one of the more cluttered corners of the dungeon and picked up a long rattan cane, okay, not his first choice, but he had an open mind…

Julie used the cane to snag a heavy dropcloth draped over some tall object in the corner, and pulled it down, revealing a rounded iron cage about the size of a phone booth…

…with a drooling male zombie inside, arms and ankles in leather-and-chain restraints, mouth filled with a ball-gag from out of that old classic movie *Pulp Fiction*. The zombie was pretty messed-up, with big black patches of frostbite on its face and half its nose missing and bulging eyes, and it grunted and banged itself against the bars of the cage—sealed with a mighty padlock, Rufus was glad to notice—trying to get at Julie, chewing on its gag.

Unable to come up with anything that seemed like an appropriate response, Rufus fell back on the neutral politeness of his upbringing: "Well, that sure is interesting. What's that all about?" He hoped it wasn't any kind of kinky sex thing, because he wasn't *that* open-minded.

"One of the bus crash zombies. Or so I assume. I found it in my yard. Set a trap for it, caught it, brought it down here." She shrugged.

"Why didn't you call old man Levitt to get rid of it?" Levitt was not technically head of the Interfaith Anti-Zombification League, but he was pretty much their go-to exterminator. "I mean, it's dangerous leaving those things around."

Julie gave him a look of withering scorn that was diminished not at all by the fact that she was still naked and still hot. "I can kill vermin myself, Rufus. I don't want it dead. I want to observe it."

"Observe it doing *what*? They don't do much."

She shook her head. "How do we know? We kill them pretty quickly. How smart *are* they? Can they figure out how to open doors? Climb out of a pit? Can they communicate with each other at all? Are they afraid of anything—fire, loud noises, bright lights? Most importantly, how long do they stay active? If they don't have anything to eat, does it matter? Do they rot more slowly than normal corpses? If we truly live in a world of the living dead, if this is the new normal, then we *need* to know these things, in order to protect ourselves. It's winter now. No one's going too far in Minnesota for a couple more months. But spring will come, and if there are hordes of these things wandering the state looking for live food, what's to keep them from coming for us? If they die—die again, die forever—after a few weeks or months, then we don't have too much to worry about. But if they're tougher than that, we need to know what we're up against, so we can set up defenses." She shook her head. "Just because the world has stopped making sense in this one way, because a fundamental aspect of the rational world has caved in around us, that doesn't mean we should abandon science entirely. So I'm making observations. First rule of strategy: know your enemy. Until we know what we're facing, we can't adequately prepare." She looked at the zombie for a moment longer, then draped the cloth back over it. The thumping inside gradually subsided, and the zombie in the cage was quiet.

"You're pretty badass, Julie," Rufus said.

"There are a couple of badasses already in this town. That part's covered. What we need are some *smart*-asses."

"Just be careful you don't get bitten," Rufus said, in what he thought of as his smooth-lover-man voice. "I'd hate for anything to happen to you, baby."

Another look of scorn. "First thing I did was smash all its teeth out, Rufus. I'm a careful woman. That's the same reason I make you wear condoms even though I'm still on the last dregs of my birth control. I don't like leaving things to chance."

Badass, Rufus thought again.

9

The man called the Narrator said:

"I was at the Lutheran church Christmas pageant, presided over by Pastor Inkfist, who from the determined look on his face might have been running the Chinese Opera or at the very least the Cirque Du Soleil, and at first it didn't look like anything was going to go spectacularly wrong. After the terrible events at the Catholic Christmas Pageant over at Our Lady of Eventual Tranquility the night before, everybody in the audience was prepared for some kind of dreadful tragedy, and some of the people in the audience had even brought along their own popcorn. Father Edsel was right up there in the front row, arms crossed, glaring at everybody, apparently playing the part of the Old Testament God who was about to become a lot less relevant after the upcoming miraculous birth.

"Little ten-year-old Gina Kvalheim was playing the Virgin Mary, and she was pretty cute, everybody said so, with the pillow stuffed up under her dress to make her look pregnant. Marty Throp, also ten but looking about two feet shorter than his holy wife, played the part of Joseph, with the hem of his robe dragging on the floor, and the Innkeeper was Lemmy Holst, who had a big booming voice just like his daddy, who'd been a cattle auctioneer, and while Lemmy projected his lines to the back of the house, the other two pretty much mumbled by comparison, making it sound like a one-sided conversation, but it wasn't like nobody knew the story: no room at the inn, what do you expect when there's a census going on, but hey, there's a barn, help yourself.

"The pageant didn't usually draw that many folks, just the parents of the kids, and pretty much every child who wanted one and a few who didn't want one got a part, even if it meant some years there were seven or eight wise men and a whole host of angels and various children playing the parts of sheep and cows and donkeys with much enthusiastic mooing and bleating and whinnying. But what with all the dark and disturbing events in town lately, and the zombies and whatnot, people felt more of a need than usual to gather together in the winter and push back the dark a little, plus people who hadn't gone to the Catholic Pageant had missed all the shenanigans with the unusually carnivorous baby Jesus so they were here hoping for a repeat performance, if not of the same specific thing than of something equally scandalous and worthy of tut-tutting and discussing over a piece of rhubarb pie, assuming there was any of that good pie left, at the Cafe Lo later on.

"It didn't look like they were going to have much luck, but then right when Gina was lifting up the bundled baby Jesus— gingerly, just in case, but nope, it was still just a little baby doll, that's all—BigHorn Jim stood up from a seat near the back, that big helmet of his askew, his big red beard all braided like cornrows for your chin, and started shouting for everyone's attention. Now the truth was he'd had everyone's attention beforehand, because the town's only neo-pagan didn't spend a lot of time coming into churches, not because people tried to convert him—Lutherans aren't a pushy bunch as a rule—but just because there was a distinct shortage of mead and cursing and loud singing in the holy houses of Lake Woebegotten. BigHorn Jim wasn't too social at all, though he got together with the old fellas from the Pretty Good Brotherhood of Cnut every once in a while to carouse, since they liked all that old Viking stuff, and could sing a song and toast each other and swing around big swords, though theirs were strictly ceremonial and only came out during parades, while it was rumored BigHorn Jim used his sword to cut down timber at the very least.

"Well he got everyone's attention all right, and he started hollering about how all us Christians were in league with the zombies, except he called them *draugr*, because BigHorn Jim is never one to use an English word where a Norse one will do, something we can all respect even as we simultaneously find it... kind of annoying. He said Jesus Christ Our Lord and Savior was the original zombie, rising from the dead and encouraging his followers to eat flesh and drink blood, which shows a certain kind of muddled thinking, because zombies mostly don't go around offering their body and blood to people as sacraments, though I guess if pressed some of us might admit the whole consuming-the-blood-and-body thing sounds a little funny when you put it the way he did. Pastor Inkfist asked the resident Viking warrior—who by all evidence had dipped fairly deeply into his mead supply before coming to the pageant—pretty politely to keep it down and let the kids finish, and a couple of the actors on stage started crying though some of the others took the opportunity to play football with the swaddled body of the baby Jesus for a ball. Father Edsel took a harder line, though, standing up and beckoning to the new police chief Stevie Ray and a couple of other fellas known more for their burliness than their kindness, and they hustled BigHorn Jim out, with him hollering the whole time that Ragnarok was upon us. Myrtle Friberg turned to Sigmund Sigmond and asked what Ragnarok was, and Sigmund said he thought it was one of those wild music festivals, and that something like that wasn't really his idea of a good time, but you know, it takes all kinds, and, of course, he's right.

"After that the pageant settled down to its typical routine, though nobody could find the doll standing in for the baby Jesus and Pastor Inkfist had to wrap one of his shoes in a couple of handkerchiefs as a stand-in. Which is all right, really, because the Christmas story is all about humble origins, and it doesn't get more humble than being born a shoe wrapped in a couple of snotrags."

The people sitting next to the Narrator in the audience were pretty annoyed at his constant stream of talk, especially since he got louder and louder as he tried to talk over BigHorn Jim's speech, but that's what you got for coming in late: you had to sit in the back with the weirdoes.

10

Pastor Daniel Inkfist had to admit the Catholic church had a certain grandeur that his own sacred space lacked, but he wasn't entirely sure that was a good thing; too much grandeur had to be bad for the soul, just like eating too much marshmallow fluff or divinity fudge. It could overwhelm a person. But Edsel had insisted on the home altar advantage, and he had the guns, so here they were.

"Gentlemen," Edsel began, standing at his pulpit, and then Eileen Munson cleared her throat loudly and pointedly and Daniel covered his mouth so none of the dozen people watching raptly from the front pew would see his smile. "And lady, of course," Edsel said, uncharacteristically magnanimous, possibly because he was standing exactly where he wanted to stand. Daniel had never actually heard the man preach, and this probably wasn't the full experience, as Edsel was wearing a red-and-black plaid shirt and jeans instead of his vestments, but there was definitely something of the orator about him, and a touch of the kind of wild-eyed-prophet that was a lot better temperamentally suited to the blazing desert than to the icy winter prairie. Edsel said,

"We live in a fallen world, my children. The end times are upon us, and none can doubt it—the dead that walk among us prove that fact. They are soulless bodies fuelled not by the divine spark of life but by the unholy fire of Hell itself. A little piece of the Devil resides in every one of these ravening bodies, and what is the Devil? What is Evil? Evil is hunger without hesitation. Evil is action without thought of consequences. Evil the gratification of immediate needs at the expense of future happiness. Evil is an unthinking slavering mouth, snapping teeth, hands twisted into claws and eager to rip out guts and tear out throats and—this is the important part—drag you down to their level. These creatures that we, for convenience, call zombies, have only one goal: to make everyone they see as dead as they are themselves. To strike fear into our hearts, to drive our thoughts from God, to make us desperate creatures scrabbling to hold onto… this." He slapped himself in the chest, not unlike a gorilla giving a display of aggression. "This shell. This weak vessel. But the body is only a body. These monsters are only bodies without the benefit of a soul. Don't let them frighten you. Don't let them drag you down, to forget your inner divinity and become obsessed with fear over the integrity of your body."

Daniel had some more complex ideas about mind-body duality than that, but now didn't seem like the time to interrupt. He should have known when Edsel said he wanted to make an opening statement that it was going to be a barn burner.

"But!" Edsel held up a warning forefinger. "God gave us these bodies, and so we should protect them. God wouldn't want us to contribute our flesh to the army of Hell, would he? So to honor God, we must defend ourselves. We will kill the zombies, gentlemen—and lady. You are the brave ones, the ones who've heard the call—" *The ones who aren't known drunks or lunatics, who have some idea how to use a gun, anyway,* Daniel thought. "—and you will be the town's staunch defenders in this time of tribulation. Seven Catholic men. Six Lutheran men and one good Lutheran lady. You, my sons—and daughter—are the Interfaith Anti-Zombie Defense Initiative."

Daniel sighed. Initiative. Sometimes it was League, or Patrol, or Task Force, Edsel couldn't seem to decide, and Daniel's suggestion that they come up with a name that had a snappy memorable acronym—the sort of thing you could paint easily on the side of a pickup truck or snowmobile, say, so people would know not to panic when a passel of armed men appeared in their driveways shouting quasi-military jargon—had been met with outright scorn. "This is the Time of Tribulation, Daniel," Edsel had said. "Not the Tee-oh-Tee. Acronyms belong to another age."

Now Daniel stood up. He didn't get a pulpit, he just got to stand up there next to Edsel as if he were the world's oldest altar boy, and he didn't have the same booming oratorical style, but he'd been in front of a lot of rooms full of sleepy Sunday morning churchgoers, so at least he wasn't noticeably nervous. "You'll work in teams, always two at a time, so you can watch one another's backs. You'll be provided weapons—Cyrus Bell has graciously offered to loan us a few items from his, ah, extensive gun collection—and we'll make sure you have gas for your trucks and snowmobiles for as long as we're able. We'll divide the day into shifts, and, unless the weather's especially bad, you'll all take a turn patrolling a particular part of the town. We've marked your routes on these maps. Now, of course, you should be on the lookout for human zombies—we don't know how many you're likely to encounter, we're trying to make sure nobody in town is left alone so that nobody dies alone—but you also have to watch out for dead *animals*. We've seen a dog zombie, and we've heard of zombie fish—" Daniel didn't know how reliable Gunther Montcrief was, but he was one of the few men who'd actually killed a zombie in this town, so he was inclined to take his word about the fish, even if he was too much of a drinker to serve on this Task Force, or Initiative, or whatever—"and there may be other kinds of zombie animals."

"Zombie pocket gophers," someone said, maybe one of the Brock brothers, and a few others sniggered.

"Their bites are nasty," Daniel said, tone sharp. "You all heard what happened to poor Clem over at the grocery." Clem's zombie was still in the freezer, and he'd been dead for days. Nobody could quite bring themselves to kill him. Even Stevie Ray said he was too busy to go do it himself, but everyone knew it was really because he didn't have the heart. "Bitten on the ankle by a zombie dog and dead just a little bit later. I can only imagine their mouths get nastier the longer they're dead, too. Even a pocket gopher could be lethal." He paused. "Assuming it could bite through your clothes, which is pretty unlikely, I guess."

"How about zombie bugs?" Eileen said, and Daniel was pretty well derailed then.

"Uh," Daniel said. "That is…" Lord, if *bugs* didn't die… it wasn't so bad in winter, but come summer, when the mosquitoes started to breed, there'd be clouds of the things, and they normally died off, but if their little zombie blood-sucking corpses kept flying around…

"Probably not," Otto's nephew Rufus said. "Probably only animals with bigger brains. Bugs barely have any brains at all, at least, not the way bigger animals do. They just have, like… ganglia."

"There you go," Daniel said. "Ganglia, nothing to worry about. So we can—"

"I don't know," Otto said. "Cockroaches can run around without their heads for a while, can't they? That's practically a zombie anyway."

"You make a good point," Daniel said, "but—"

"If the Lord of Flies sees fit to unleash a plague of undead locusts upon us, we'll face that problem when it comes," Edsel rumbled. "In the meantime, watch out for things we're sure might come back from the dead and try to kill us: zombie badgers, bats, beavers, birds, bobcats, chipmunks, cows, coyotes, deer, dogs, foxes, mice, mink, moose, muskrats, otters, porcupines, possums, rabbits, raccoons, shrews, snakes, squirrels, wolverines, wolves, and woodchucks. And, yes, pocket gophers."

Was that list alphabetical? Had Edsel practiced that?

"How about bears?" Eileen Munson said.

"Haven't seen a bear in these parts for a few years," Stevie Ray said. He was in the back of the church—technically he wasn't part of the task force, since he felt it was incompatible with his position as a law enforcement officer to take part in a group of unregulated armed vigilantes, but at the same time he wasn't going to let such a group have its first meeting without his observation, and he'd insisted his special deputies Otto and Rufus be on board, even though Otto was a bit weaselly and Rufus was, to all appearances, the very definition of a surly snotnosed teen punk. "Then again, it'd be just our luck to get a bear this year, so, yeah, keep your eyes open. If you see one, just shoot it in the head. Lots of times—Cyrus Bell has plenty of ammunition, so don't be afraid to use it up. I hate to kill a bear that's minding its own business, but I don't want a zombie bear walking down Main Street."

"Gentlemen," Edsel said. "There's punch and cake over in the reception hall. We'll hand out your patrol assignments there. God bless you all for your service and your courage." He clapped his hands, an applause of one, and the men—and Eileen—made their way out, until it was just Edsel, Daniel, and Stevie Ray.

"Quite a posse you've got there," Stevie Ray said.

"Brave men and true!" Edsel shouted. He pointed at the figure of Christ on the cross, and as always, Daniel winced when he saw it—the blood, the crown of thorns, the droopy hangdog eyes, the jutting ribs, the loincloth, give him a nice clean cross anytime, who wanted to be reminded of all that suffering every time you wanted to think about God? "Satan torments us with a mockery of our Lord and Savior, the one man who's ever *truly* risen from the dead."

"Well," Daniel said. "There was Lazarus. And of course the boy the prophet Elijah brought back to life. Plus the dead son of the Shunammite woman resurrected by the prophet Elisha, and the dead body that came back to life when it touched Elisha's bones in the tomb, and the various dead saints who arose and entered Jerusalem after Jesus' own resurrection, and Dorcas who was returned to life by Peter, and Eutychus who fell from the window… lots of others."

"None of them were *immortal*," Edsel said. "Only Christ was granted physical immortality."

"The zombies aren't too immortal, either," Stevie Ray said. "They die just fine when you take off the head."

"Daniel—ha, not me, the biblical Daniel, of course, said, 'Many of those who sleep in the dust of the ground will awake, these to everlasting life, but the others to disgrace and everlasting contempt.'" Daniel had brooded over that passage lately. It seemed to him that it meant something very different from what he'd always assumed it meant. "Perhaps the zombies are those who are disgraced?"

"They are dead bodies inhabited by demons sent by Satan," Edsel said flatly. "It's as obvious as knowing water is wet, snow is cold, and monkeys—and their antics—are hilarious. We will kill these creatures, all of them we can, and prove ourselves worthy for the eventual return of our Lord."

There was silence for a moment. Then Stevie Ray said, "At least we don't have to worry about zombie monkeys. I'd sure hate to be in the rainforest right about now."

11

Come on, Chief. You know I'm the man this town needs now. I'm finally in my element." Mr. Levitt sat comfortably in the chair behind Stevie Ray's desk. He still had his gun, and Stevie Ray was still holding his service pistol, but neither of them were pointing their weapons at the other anymore. Rufus was sitting in the corner by his dead uncle, holding his head in his hands. At some point this had stopped being a hostage situation, exactly, and had become a negotiation instead.

"You're a confessed murderer," Stevie Ray said, still half-hidden from Levitt's line of sight by the coat tree near the front door. The coat tree wasn't cover, but it was concealment, which was something. If Levitt shot him maybe he wouldn't get the headshot, and Stevie Ray could at least take comfort that he'd return as a zombie and eat the son of a gun. "You think I'm going to let you walk around loose in this town?"

"Who knows about my… colorful history? You, the boy, Dolph. Harry did, but he's dead, and the same with Otto. Why, if I wanted to, I could reduce the number of witnesses to one, right now, and do you think I'd have a hard time hunting a *grocer*? I could slip back into my role as a respected pillar of society like *that*." He snapped his fingers. "So how about we do it without the bloodshed? Don't get me wrong, I like bloodshed, live for it, but I'm taking the long view. I think I'd have more fun as the town's heroic zombie-hunter, adored by all. And if your little fairy tale comes true and civilization is restored, and the judges start coming back to town, why, you can take me back into custody and see justice served."

The fact was, having Levitt in jail was a pain in the ass. Someone always needed to be here with him, to make sure he didn't escape or kill himself, though the former was looking increasingly moot and the latter was never likely, since rattlesnakes, proverbially, didn't commit suicide. "How do I know you won't go on a killing spree?"

"They didn't require an abnormal psychology class or criminology studies for your job as a bartender, Chief? I'm not a disorganized spree killer. I'm *organized*. Methodical. I'm a planner. It's not my inclination to run through town pumping bullets into people. I find the whole idea… distasteful. Worse, boring. And if I wanted to kill people, I would have killed Rufus there. And you, when you walked in the door—an ambush would not have been difficult to set up. I *didn't*—there's all the proof of my sincerity you need. Hear me well: I'm not going back into that cell. I'm *bored* in there. Pushing your psychological buttons is about as challenging as playing tic-tac-toe with a chicken. I need something to engage my mind. So let me be a zombie killer, join the little task force the preachers have set up—I hear they're down a man." He nodded toward the body of Otto.

Stevie Ray considered. Levitt was rational. Crazy, yes, certainly, crazy as the winter nights were long, but not a raving madman. And he certainly wouldn't balk at putting any zombies down, human or otherwise. Most importantly, the *only* way this situation could end was either in a hail of bullets, or in granting Mr. Levitt's request to serve the town. "You'll need to put down the gun. First step."

"I can do that. But you have to let me out of here, Chief. It's not optional. Maybe you see an old man when you look at me, but push me, and you might be surprised."

"Understood. The gun?"

Levitt looked at him—or at the coat rack, though he sure seemed to be looking *through* the coat rack—and laid his pistol on the desk.

"Rufus," Stevie Ray barked. "Get the gun."

Rufus looked up blankly, then nodded, walked over about as

slow as a fella with gout and bunions and plantar fascitis, and picked up the gun. He plodded back to the spot by his dead uncle and sat back down.

"All right," Stevie Ray said. "I have conditions. One: you will wear a tracking bracelet. Harry got a couple of them with the Homeland Security money, those house arrest things, go around your ankle, tamperproof, we always know exactly where you are."

"Fine with me," Levitt said. "Still a lot more privacy than I had in that box."

"Two: you *will* be brought to justice. Either some higher authority will set things right and the world will go back to normal, or this town will elect a new mayor and get its organizational eggs in a row, and when that happens, I'll tell whoever takes charge what you are, who you are, and how ironclad the proof is. I'm also going to leave some of that evidence in a location known only to me, to be opened if I die, *or* Rufus dies, *or* Dolph dies—you won't be picking off the witnesses."

"You're living in the past, Chief—the days of swift and fair trials are over, so what do I care if there are witnesses? But, of course, if those measures console you, I have no objection." Levitt was grinning, hands laced behind his head, stocking feet up on the desk, happy as a pig in poop.

"The last condition," Stevie Ray said, "is your first target: that zombie dog that killed Clem and Otto."

The smile froze on Levitt's face, then melted and drained away. "My Alta? No, don't be ridiculous, I'm not going to—"

Stevie Ray came around the coat tree, gun extended. "It's the price you pay for your freedom, Mr. Levitt. Come on. You're supposed to be a hard man. Can't kill one little dog?"

Levitt smiled again, but there was no joy in it now, more one primate showing his teeth to another in aggression. "I can kill *anything*, Chief. Be good for you to remember that."

"I'm the one with the gun now."

"Never liked guns anyway. Give me a boning knife anytime."

Stevie Ray pushed the safety off.

Levitt sighed. "Fine, fine, I'll kill Alta, I suppose he's not my little precious anymore anyway."

"Okay," Stevie Ray said. "Let's get you hooked up with that bracelet. Rufus, you want to keep that gun on our guest until he's got his nice new jewelry on?"

Rufus nodded, though he still didn't speak, and rose to his feet.

"This will be fun," Mr. Levitt said. "Do you think I can get a badge? I'd love to have my own badge."

12

The Catholic Christmas Pageant went beautifully at first, with kids dressed in choir robes as angels, holy singing—the Catholics do beautiful hymns, you can say what you like but you can't deny that, something about hearing words sung in Latin speaks to the heart, maybe because you can imagine they're saying anything at all, anything that speaks to your own heart and sense of the sacred—and, of course, the Nativity story, because no small-town pageant is complete without a ten-year-old playing the Virgin Mary and two young wise men who are slowly coming to realize they never even asked what frankincense and myrrh *are*, and why does that other kid get to be the one who hands out the gold, never mind asking what a baby would do with gold, anyway.

The pageant took place in the hall attached to the Catholic church, where a stage had been set up and a bunch of folding chairs brought in. The children blundered through their lines with customary aplomb, and turnout hadn't been affected too adversely by the appearance last week of zombies. None of the kids had really seen any zombies, and though the power had stopped working most everybody had fuel for their generators and oil for their furnaces and their pantries were stocked, so the ongoing disaster was largely abstract for the children—and only slightly less so for their parents. It was in almost all ways a typical Christmas pageant.

Until the boy playing Joseph pulled the blanket away from the wooden cradle as prelude to lifting up the traditional baby Jesus, veteran of countless pageants—the baby was a doll, and in fact a *girl* doll judging by the eyelashes, but that doll had served as the infant Jesus for a long time and issues of potentially transgender religious icons were generally ignored.

Except that doll was gone, and in its place barely fitting into a cradle that had in fact always rather dwarfed the doll, there was a zombie: one with no arms or legs, true, but that was even more grotesque if somewhat less dangerous than a whole zombie, and young Joseph screamed and jumped back (fortunately retaining his full complement of fingers), and all the other children screamed too, and then a general exodus began from the stage—Exodus not usually being a component of a Catholic Christmas pageant, or really Christmas stories in general, but the ad-lib seemed justified by the circumstances—with children in angel robes and shepherd robes (basically the same robes, if you wanted to get picky) leaping into the laps of their parents, screaming "Zombie zombie zombie Jesus!" and similar cries, except for those who took the more elemental route of just sobbing. General bedlam threatened to take hold, until Father Edsel strode onto the stage from the wings, holding a big long knife.

Without hesitation he stepped to the cradle, looked down at the zombie—which no one in the audience had really seen, except maybe the ones on their feet in the front row, owing to its literally low profile—and then drove the knife into the zombie's eye. The force of his blow was too much for the cradle—which was wooden, and not too well-made to begin with, and also a veteran of countless pageants—and it simply splintered into a few big pieces right there on the stage, with the dead torso of a murder victim, transformed by energies or causes unknown (if much speculated-upon) into a ravenous monster, and then transformed again by causes generally mysterious (though a few people in town knew about Levitt's chainsaw) into the limbless parody of a monster it was now.

Then Edsel pressed a button on the hilt of the knife and the zombie's head exploded like a grapefruit stuffed with firecrackers. The patter of exploded headmeat did nothing to calm the crowd.

Edsel kicked the body once or twice, a ferociously concentrated look on his face (though whether it was concentrated rage, hate, disgust, or some other emotion no one could quite agree), then, satisfied it was dead, turned to face the now largely silent but still highly keyed-up crowd. "People of Lake Woebegotten!" he boomed. "This creature is an agent of the devil, but it did not slip into this cradle to torment us on its own. It was placed here by hands—*human hands*! We face not only unholy creatures risen from Hell, but human collaborators as well, perhaps Satanists, perhaps mere agents of chaos, perhaps pranksters unaware of how their latest prank endangers their very immortal *souls*! Be vigilant!"

He paused, then stooped, picked up the cradle blanket, and draped it over the limbless corpse. "The pageant is over. Give the children a round of applause."

The crowd complied with subdued clapping, though it wasn't entirely clear what, or who, they were clapping for.

13

Ingvar Knudsen had a big house full of not much but emptiness, ancient wooden furniture, his dead wife's vast collection of antique teapots, including teapots shaped like chickens, pumpkins (and other melons, including a few summer squash), the heads of Indian chiefs, basketballs, boots, penguins, pilgrims, sailing ships, bears, gazelles, gargoyles, pandas, and the Roman Coliseum. She'd never intended to be a teapot collector—she'd had a couple of nice antique Fiesta teapots she liked, and a silver tea service she'd inherited and kept out for display—but some relative noticed her three teapots in the kitchen and decided she must be a collector, and so it began. Anyone unfortunate to be deemed a collector by their relatives can share this tale of woe, because every Christmas and birthday sees the same thing: a procession of variations on whatever it is you're supposed to be collecting, whether it's teapots, snow globes, unicorn statuettes, novelty socks, candlestick holders, or salt shakers, with relatives smiling widely at their finds and the collector outwardly grateful but increasingly thinking *where am I going to put all these* and *who's going to dust them*? But the teapots reminded Ingvar of his late wife, so he kept them all, arrayed on the shelves he'd built for her in their big old farmhouse kitchen, and he kept them dusted, too, though otherwise he was an indifferent housekeeper and considered it a job well done if he didn't track pig manure in on the rug. Since he'd sold all his land to the quarrymen, rock dust was more likely than pig manure, and that made him sad, but he'd wanted to be sure to provide a nice inheritance for his grandchildren, all of whom lived away, and none of whom had been much interested in continuing the family farm; no wonder, since their parents, Ingvar's own children, hadn't wanted to, either.

Now of course he hadn't heard from his children or grandchildren in some time, most of them having chosen new homes in typical former-Minnesotan fashion: by going someplace where it didn't snow. He hoped they were all right. He hoped they were surviving the very new year, the Year of the Zombie maybe it should be called, someplace safe and warm, but who knew? He didn't much expect to survive long enough to hear from any of them. He was now the second-oldest-man in town, outranked only by Emperor Torvald, who was much younger in spirit and mind, having reverted in his nineties back to somewhere around his early teens, complete with undisguised lusting over women a considerably large fraction of his age. Even without the town's only doctor dying he wasn't a prospect for longer life, speaking strictly by statistics, though he still got around all right so long as he didn't hurry, and had never smoked a day in his life, and didn't drink much, and didn't even eat much meat, having grown up in times when meat was a luxury. Still, even without extraordinary abuse, normal wear and tear would get him soon enough. He was just sad he was going to die alone. His wife had passed the year before, and this had been his first Christmas a widower, and his children had actually pulled together and planned to return to the frozen north of their youths—their own kids, not knowing any better, were excited by the prospect of a white Christmas—so Ingvar wouldn't have to spend it alone. He'd laid in an epic quantity of supplies, from food to extra fuel for the generators to lots of extra heating oil because his children, after so long in warmer climes, were apt to be overly sensitive to the sort of cold which would merely make Ingvar himself shrug and put on another sweater. He'd always been a thrifty man, but he'd intended to throw caution and parsimony to the wind in order to host a great family fete… And now he was alone in his big farmhouse with an undecorated Christmas tree waiting for the worst to happen.

Then one day not long after the New Year pastor Daniel

Inkfist knocked on his door. "Hello, Ingvar, how are you holding up?" he asked. The college boy, what was his name, Randy? Something silly and modern like Rumpus? was there too, holding a rifle and looking around, which was probably prudent but still made Ingvar uncomfortable. He'd been in a war—two of them, actually—and didn't like the sight of an armed vigilant man—or boy—in his front yard. It brought back unpleasant associations.

"Oh, not too bad, can't complain," Ingvar said, which was exactly the same response he would have given if he'd been in the jaws of a mountain lion or actually on fire or being tortured in an Iron Maiden at the time, though it was also the answer he would have given while bathing in the fountain of youth just prior to reclining on a pile of fluffy thousand-dollar bills while being waited on hand-and-foot by doe-eyed maidens in gold bikinis.

"You mind if we come in?"

Ingvar ushered them in, got them seated on the couch—still covered in plastic, as his wife would've wanted—and offered them coffee, which they accepted, because as cold as it was, who wouldn't want something hot to sip?

After fifteen or twenty minutes of conversation about the weather, the state of the town, the upcoming mayoral election, and confirmation that no one had heard anything from the outside world at all, Daniel said, "Let me get right to the point, Ingvar. Since we lost contact with the outside world, some of our townspeople have been struggling. They don't have enough oil for heat or enough wood laid by, and we've had one house fire—"

"I heard about that," Ingvar said. There was no 911 to call now. No fire engines came screaming in. Lucky it was winter or the woods around the house might have caught too.

"Well. Things are rough for some of our people. And then there are all the ones who live alone, we're trying to get people to move in together, share resources, but—"

"I've got plenty of room here," Ingvar said, shrugging. "Enough fuel to get me through the winter even if I make it 68 degrees night and day." Next winter was a different story, but he could gather wood next fall, assuming he lived that long. "Enough food to feed a battalion, assuming you've got somebody who can cook—I'm not much good if it gets beyond making a hamburger or some eggs. Enough gas to keep the gennie running for a good long while if I'm careful."

Pastor Inkfist's eyes went wide. "Oh, Ingvar, we were just coming by to see if you maybe had some canned food or fuel or old blankets you could donate, we've been going door-to-door and—"

"No need. Got a lot of room here. Could use the company. Send anyone who needs a place over. We'll work it out."

Rufus spoke up: "You sure you can handle it? I mean, we could send ten, fifteen people today, are you really up to dealing with them, getting them settled, working out the, uh, bathroom situation? I mean, that's a lot to do for… for anyone."

For someone so old, Ingvar thought, with more amusement than anger. To be so young that you thought being young and inexperienced somehow made you *more* qualified to deal with life's problems; it was a kind of stupid that pretty much everyone suffered from at one point or another. "I raised eight children in this house, son. And ran the biggest family farm in Drizzle County while I did it. I imagine I can handle having a few of my neighbors visit."

And that's how what came to be known as Ingvar's House of a Thousand Orphans got started. In truth there were only two orphans, the six- and eight-year-old kids who lost their parents in the fire, but the name seemed to fit anyway, since Ingvar opened his door to pretty much anybody in need, putting rollaway beds in hallways and cots in the basement, with whole families sleeping in double beds in his guestrooms. The bathroom was a bit of an issue, but with severely limited hot water nobody much wanted to shower, and when everybody kind of smelled equally bad you got used to it.

The townsfolk of Lake Woebegotten didn't like to impose or take charity, so pretty soon every little minor repair he hadn't gotten around to yet was done, and far from making more work for him, Ingvar's open-door policy meant he pretty much didn't have to lift a finger—coffee was made in the morning, supper was set before him at the long (and very crowded) big table every night, and the only chore he held onto (and even that took some effort to retain) was dusting his wife's teapots. The bustle had a restorative effect on Ingvar, too. A house full of jostling people made the long winter seem a lot shorter, and it was always easy to get a game of euchre going, and having kids around gave him hope for the future. He felt like he might not die so soon after all, that he could live a good long while, that in a way letting all these people into his house and—though he'd never say so out loud—his heart had given him new life, and better yet, a reason for life. The kids all started calling him Grandpa Ingvar. Life was good.

Of course, all that was before the bus crash, and what came after.

14

BigHorn Jim found the squirming limbless zombie in the woods north of the lake, humping along at great speed—considering its relative lack of arms and legs—in pursuit of a ground squirrel that really should have been snug in a hollow tree for winter by now. The snow had iced over, creating a sort of armored snow that didn't want to break unless you really hammered your boot down, and the limbless zombie was sort of sledding on its belly, head lifted, jaws snapping, propelling itself by undulations of its abdominal muscles and flailings of its leg stumps.

BigHorn Jim was pretty sure the little beast was taunting the zombie, or else the cold had made it stupid, because the squirrel could have easily shot up any of the nearby trees and been completely free. Jim's religion included tales of Ratatoskr, the squirrel that ran up and down the trunk of the world tree Yggdrasil, carrying messages from the nameless eagle at the top of the great ash to the dragon who dwells beneath the roots, telling lies and spreading gossip and gnawing at the tree's bark as he goes. The squirrel was not quite a trickster figure, more of a low troublemaker, but in a battle between old rat-tooth and a *draugr*, BigHorn Jim knew which side he'd take. He took the throwing axe from his belt, hefted it in his hand, and judged the angle. Throwing the axe and hitting a rapidly-moving prone object would be difficult, and only severing the head or damaging the brain would stop a *draugr*, so he reluctantly put the axe away. He was a fearsome enough warrior, he knew, but some feats were beyond him.

Thinking of Ratatoskr made him think of spreading trouble and sowing discord, though, and how such things could be used to achieve good ends—like shaking the townspeople out of their complacency. None of them seemed to want to face the new facts of their existence: that Ragnarok was upon them, and the world soon to burn. They were still going to the store, going to the cafe, going to the bar, getting haircuts—they were even going to have their Christmas pageants, as usual.

Jim, who'd been a Lutheran himself once not so many years ago, and was a lifelong Minnesotan, knew that a certain dogged perseverance was a defining trait of many of his fellow residents, for better or worse, but in this case, it was worse, because if they didn't realize the monsters were *here*, and that they had to *fight*, they'd all be stoically standing their ground while the *draugr* ate their guts, saying, "Well that's not too good a deal" as the teeth sank into their throats, and that was no way to die. They were all going to die *anyway* of course—Lutheranism and Norse Paganism shared few beliefs, but predestination was one point of intersection, and what was going to happen was going to happen—but the *way* you died mattered, and if BigHorn Jim could shake them from their stupor, he'd be doing them all a service, and making new warriors for the feasting hall in Valhalla, maybe.

He uncoiled the length of rope from around his waist, crept up on the zombie, slipped the rope up under its thighs and around its belly, braced the rope over his shoulder, and began dragging the wriggling protesting zombie behind him. Jim wasn't sure what exactly he was going to *do* with the zombie, but he was sure he'd come up with something suitably shocking.

The squirrel chittered at Jim angrily as he departed, but that was squirrels for you.

15

"I thought you had a tracking bracelet on him?" Rufus said, fidgeting with his pistol—Stevie Ray *really* wished he wouldn't do that, but the kid was unteachable, he thought weapons in real life worked like they did in video games, never going off by accident, and if they did, it was no big deal, and infinite ammo was just a cheat code away.

"Put the gun away!" he snapped. "It's not a toy!"

Rufus looked startled, then sheepish, then tucked the weapon into the holster at his belt, closing the snap over it. "Sorry, boss." The "boss" was only a little bit sarcastic, which, by Rufus's standards, meant it was damn near sincere.

"It's all right. I just don't want you shooting yourself, or me, or anybody else. As for the bracelet—yes, Mr. Levitt has a bracelet on his ankle. It has pretty lights on it, and he comes over here regularly to plug it in and charge it up again off the gennie. As far as he knows, it works, and we can track his every move… but it doesn't work. We never even got the tracking software installed, and now I can't find it. Harry bought a bunch of stuff when we got a big bunch of Homeland Security anti-terrorist money, fancy guns and good vests and those house-arrest bracelets, but we never *used* the bracelets before. It's a shame. I hear they're pretty much impossible to tamper with."

"So we've got a serial killer, just wandering around unsupervised?"

"Two things." Stevie Ray held up a forefinger. "He *thinks* he's being monitored, which is almost as good. And I've got someone following him and keeping watch pretty much every minute he's awake. The perfect guy for the job: the most paranoid person in Lake Woebegotten."

"Father Edsel's watching him?" Rufus said, frowning.

"Okay," Stevie Ray said. "Point. I should've said, the second most paranoid person in Lake Woebegotten."

16

"**A**ll right!" Stevie Ray shouted. "Everyone settle down. Thank you all for coming tonight. We're going to hear speeches from our two mayoral candidates. First up we've got Eileen Munson, and then we'll hear from Julie Olafson. They've both got some real good ideas about what we should do, as a town, going forward, so I'm sure we'll—"

"We want to hear from Mr. Levitt!" Cyrus Bell shouted from the back of the hall, and, if the temperature inside the town meeting hall hadn't already been so cold as to make the distinction entirely academic, Stevie Ray's blood would've run cold. Cyrus was supposed to be on *their* side—but a man who thought the zombies were part of a conspiracy perpetrated by aliens who lived inside a hollow spaceship moon was, by definition, apt to be unreliable. "He's our man!"

A few scattered shouts of "Yeah!" rang out in the crowd, and someone shouted, "Bring out the hero of the bus crash battle!" and "Let him run!" and other similar exhortations.

"Listen," Stevie Ray said, "It's nice to see you all so excited about the political process, it means we're a healthy community, but we had a process, and people interested in being mayor had to put their names in last month and get their platforms written up for those flyers we handed out, and Mr. Levitt just didn't get his name into the ring in time, so I'm afraid—"

"Levitt!" shouted Cyrus Bell, and the survivors from the Knudsen farm—the ones who hadn't seen *everything* that happened that day, of course, but who'd seen the bits that looked heroic, from a distance, at least—took up the call too. "Leh-vitt! Leh-vitt! Leh-vitt!"

Cyrus. He'd been assigned to look after Levitt, to partner with him on patrols most days and watch him from afar with some of his assorted spy equipment on other days, and now he was supporting the man's bid for mayor? Stevie Ray would have to sit down and have a talk with Cyrus, even if that did entail exposing himself to the man's high-octane crazy.

Stevie Ray looked around for ideas on how to stop this train wreck from happening, but Father Edsel and Pastor Inkfist seemed equally at a loss—Inkfist merely befuddled, Edsel pissed-off. They'd backed themselves into a corner. They'd wanted to use Levitt, like some kind of attack dog—or trained viper—and so they'd kept his terrible secret… a secret. They could tell the people here, now, that their hero was a murderer, but who would believe them? And if they *did* believe, they'd realize Stevie Ray and the others who knew about Levitt had voluntarily released him, allowed him to walk freely—relatively freely—about the town. That wouldn't go over well. The idea of putting a bullet in Mr. Levitt's brain was more and more appealing with every passing day, but Stevie Ray could barely bring himself to gun down a zombie, much less a man, even one as monstrous as Mr. Levitt, unless he had no choice.

Levitt himself stood up from the front row, turned to the crowd, raised his arms over his head, and—though his back was to the stage, so Stevie Ray couldn't be sure, he was pretty sure anyway—gave them his big pie-eating grin. "Thank you!" he shouted. "I'm honored to have your support! I didn't go looking for the job, but if you want me to be the mayor, I'll certainly serve, and I'd be happy to say a few words about my vision for the town's future just as soon as these little ladies up on the stage have their say."

Julie and Eileen—who were normally about as friendly with each other as boiling oil and barbarian invaders—exchanged what Stevie Ray could only think of as a very *womanly* look at Levitt's crack about "little ladies." Eileen looked pissed, and Stevie Ray thought maybe she *would* say something about Levitt's true character—did the old man even know she *knew*? But before it could become an issue, Dolph stood up and cleared his throat. "Uh, everyone, sorry to interrupt, but there's something you should know. I wasn't going to say anything, but…"

This is it, Stevie Ray thought. *He's going to tell them where Mr. Levitt's bodies are buried. Or were buried, before they woke up.* Edsel and Inkfist had twin looks of terror, and Eileen's expression was pleasantly surprised. Well, why not. She wouldn't get any of the blowback from the deception. If Minnesotans were a tar-and-feathering type of people, he'd be worried for his skin, but they were more of a cold-shoulder-and-shun bunch of punishers. Unfortunately, in a zombie apocalypse, being shunned by the community could be as deadly as firing squad.

"Something to say, Dolph?" Mr. Levitt drawled. "Had a lot of time to think while you were in jail, did you?" He grinned at the crowd, but he misjudged them—the townspeople mostly felt bad for Dolph, and no one laughed. Levitt didn't really understand people, after all, not any more than a rattlesnake did.

"I did, but this is… something else. You all know I took in little Mary Cooper." Mary was ten, one of the orphans who'd needed to be relocated after the battle of the bus crash burned down the Knudsen Farm. Dolph had offered to foster her as part of his decision to stop moping in his cell and start trying to redeem himself and make up for his mistakes instead. Mary was with him, staring at her shoes, blushing bright red. "Mary was there, at the farm, when our brave boys—and Eileen, of course—fought off the zombies. She was in the kitchen when… Well, Mary, do you want to tell them what you told me?"

The little girl mumbled something, and Dolph put a hand on her shoulder, gently. "Speak up, darling."

Everyone was silent, the only noise the hum of the space heaters, when Mary pointed at Mr. Levitt and said, "That man killed Grandpa Ingvar."

The crowd didn't exactly explode—this wasn't Los Angeles or something after all—but there was a definite murmur.

"Honey," Mr. Levitt said, in his sour old-man voice, "I know it's confusing, but Mr. Knudsen was a zombie, and I had no choice—"

"I was hidin' under the kitchen table," she said. "Grandpa

Ingvar said, you stay right there and be quiet, don't you worry 'bout a thing, and he patted my hand, and I saw when you came in the door and he stood up and said oh thank goodness you're here and you had that big ol' knife thing and you—and you—" The little girl began to sob and clutched Dolph's leg, and he patted her head.

"He was a zombie!" Levitt said, voice a little too high, a little too shrill. "He'd turned!"

Stevie Ray had lain awake nights and wondered if all the "zombies" Levitt had killed in the battle really were undead, or if he'd just taken the opportunity to murder some living souls for his own amusement—some of the bite marks on some of the bodies could have been postmortem, like they'd been bitten *after* getting shot or cut up, though he wasn't any kind of doctor, so he couldn't be sure. He'd even wondered if maybe Levitt had bitten those people *himself* to make it look like they'd been attacked by zombies. In the chaos, anything was possible, and Levitt had certainly been all-over-blood by the time it was over, so who knows what he'd been up to?

Should I take him into custody? Stevie Ray thought. *On the say-so of a ten-year-old girl who might even have been coached to say this by Dolph?*

But Dolph surprised him by taking a more nuanced and direct approach to sabotage: "Nobody's saying you did it on purpose, Mr. Levitt. That would be crazy. I know it was an accident, that it was a scary time, you were probably disoriented—I mean, the things you did that day, it would have taken a lot out of somebody half your age—and Ingvar must have surprised you, and you just struck him without even thinking about it, maybe never even realized your mistake. But it *was* a mistake, a terrible mistake—and you all know I know what I'm talking about when I talk about terrible mistakes. I've made them myself, and…" He shook his head. "I'm not qualified to be mayor, either. You're a hero, Mr. Levitt, no denying that, but it's time you take a break. You've done enough for the people in this town. You don't want to be mayor. A job that important, you wouldn't want to make any more mistakes." Dolph coughed. "Uh, that's all. I'm going to take Mary home to bed now. Someone want to walk me?"

Rufus escorted them out, and Mr. Levitt leapt up on stage—he was still a nimble old goat—and shouldered Stevie Ray aside to stand at the lectern. "I'd be a fine mayor, and I have no intention of withdrawing my name from the race! I'm not confused, that little *girl's* confused, and Dolph, he just wants to believe he's not the only one damn fool enough to kill an innocent man for no reason, so he's trying to drag *my* name down with him! I know you're all too smart for that!"

The only response was a strained silence and a few coughs, and Stevie Ray laid his hand on Mr. Levitt's shoulder. "We're running behind, and Julie and Eileen need to make their speeches. We've heard what you have to say. Now let them have their turn."

Mr. Levitt raised his arms and made V-for-Victory signs with his fingers, another gesture that showed his complete failure to read this crowd, and then he left the stage, walking all cocky, like he was the cat who got the cream *and* the canary.

After Eileen and Julie's speeches, people lined up to vote then and there, shuffling through the line of curtained voting booths they'd set up, though they just wrote down their choices on slips of paper. Stevie Ray and Rufus counted the votes, and any momentum Mr. Levitt had gained was pretty well derailed by Dolph's speech, though he still did better than Julie, who, having lived too long off and away in the cities, never really had a chance. Stevie Ray went to the podium and said, "Ladies and gentlemen, may I present your new mayor: Eileen Munson!"

Eileen took the stage beaming and smiling and waving at the cheering townsfolk, and Stevie Ray thought, *Whatever reservations I have about that woman's leadership, she's a damn sight better than Mr. Levitt would have been.* Was there even a name for rule by serial killer? Murderarchy? Killocracy?

The runner-up himself was nowhere to be seen.

17

"So that's the deal, then," Cyrus Bell said, looking around him nervously, even though they were sitting in one of his cabins, and no one could possibly be watching or listening—though Cyrus's paranoid worldview allowed for the possibility of miniature cameras in the light fixtures, mechanical teleoperated houseflies, and psychic warriors lurking insubstantially in the closets via astral projection. "I've been watching you for Stevie Ray, who says I have to make sure you don't do anything crazy—I hate that word crazy, what's that even mean?—and at first I went along with it, Father Edsel said it was a good idea, but me, I'm not a—I'm not a—I'm not a snitch, you know? Spying on people? Informing on people? When so many people spy on *me*? I admit it felt good being on the other side of the conspiracy for once, but what if I'm a dupe, a patsy, what if they're using me, setting me up for a fall, or if it's a test, if they're doing a psychological experiment on me, or—"

"That's good, Cy," Mr. Levitt said soothingly, patting him on the back. "You did well. I'm glad you told me. And you're going to stop watching me, right?"

Cy nodded. "But keep telling Father and Stevie Ray that I *am* watching you, that you aren't doing anything at all but looking for zombies and killing them when you find them, that's all. A man deserves his privacy, and…" Cy licked his lips. "And that other little thing. The thing you promised."

"Of course." Mr. Levitt handed over a bundle of dirty rags, and Cyrus opened them reverently, revealing a very old but well-preserved pistol with a squarish body and a round barrel. Mr. Levitt had taken it off one of his victims back in the early '70s and held onto it, because you never knew when you might need a dead man's gun.

"Is it... is it really his? It's really Hitler's gun?" Cyrus wasn't a Nazi sympathizer, just an obsessed history—and history of weaponry—buff, but he couldn't keep the excitement out of his voice."

"It is," Mr. Levitt said, thinking, *moron.* "My father brought it back with him from the war."

Cyrus stared at the gun. "Is there any, you know, provenance, or..."

"Oh, those kinds of papers, Cy, they can be faked, you know that. You can't trust a paper trail."

"That's true," Cy said doubtfully.

"But you can feel the psychic emanations, can't you? Whenever I hold that pistol I feel the temperature drop by a degree or two, all that evil, that charisma, that power, lingering on the grip of the gun where the Führer's hand touched it. Do you feel the presence?"

Cy shivered. "I do. I do. It's colder now."

Mr. Levitt patted him on the shoulder. "You keep that pistol—I never had a son to pass it on to, and you deserve it, for the kind and honorable treatment you've given me. Just keep giving those reports to Stevie Ray and Father Edsel. I'm going to leave now. Happy New Year, Cy."

Cyrus didn't look up from the gun, but Levitt felt his attention shift and focus on him. "Why do they want me to watch you, anyway, Mr. Levitt?"

"Why do the people who watch you want to watch *you,* Cy?"

"I don't know," he whispered.

"I don't either," Mr. Levitt said. "But I bet it's because we're free and honorable men who won't do what we're told."

"God bless you, Mr. Levitt."

"He already has by giving me a friend like you, Cy."

18

Lake Woebegotten had always been a pretty quiet place, apart from the cry of the loons over the lake, the Sunday church bells, the occasional plane passing overhead, the old air raid siren at unpredictable and incomprehensible intervals, and, on still days, the rumble of trucks drifting over from the nearest state highway. Since the zombie apocalypse it had grown even quieter, and as a result everyone tended to speak a little quieter, too, as if they were at a funeral, and they almost were: the world's funeral, you could say.

So the noise of grinding, crunching metal was audible to Rufus and Joe Brock that day, driving in Joe's four-wheel-drive pickup with the snow chains doing a perimeter sweep and looking for zombies. The old Andersen Road pretty much looped around the town on its way to nowhere in particular, and they were doing a leisurely—but vigilant—drive on a morning when there was actually some sunshine for once, peeking out occasionally from the gray cloud armor the sky'd been wearing for months. You couldn't really see the road, since the town snowplow was being used mostly for the downtown area and to keep the road to Ingvar's House of a Thousand Orphans clear, but you could sorta tell where the road was if you'd been on it a few hundred or thousand times before, and it was flat and curved around only gently, so the truck handled the ice fine. They went past trees, and fences, and fields, and more trees, and hadn't seen much in the way of life, or, more importantly, unlife, except for a rabbit that went haring off across the road. Joe ran the rabbit over just to be on the safe side, and he and Rufus—who were not destined to be best of friends regardless, Joe being a sledneck who liked beer, crushing beer cans on his head, and hunting, and Rufus being, well, you know what Rufus is like by now—had been arguing about that decision for the past fifteen minutes, with Rufus taking the position that since the rabbit had been going fast it was obviously not a zombie, and Joe asking when was the last time you saw a rabbit running around in the dead frigid heart of February, and Rufus saying they couldn't just go around killing indiscriminately and Joe saying he'd been known to run down a rabbit just for fun now and then even before the zombie apocalypse, and from there it was pretty clear they just had fundamental differences of worldview vis-à-vis animal rights, basic morality, and the edibility of intentionally-created roadkill.

Then the big crash, metal-on-metal, made itself heard over their bickering and the big truck's engine. "All right," Joe said. "Finally some real action."

"We should call Stevie Ray," Rufus said.

Joe sniffed and looked like he wanted to spit, but he wasn't about to spit in his own truck, and it was too damn cold and gray outside—though it wasn't actually snowing at the moment, too cold for that—to roll down the window or open the door to spit, so he swallowed it instead and said, "This is Interfaith Anti-Zombie Et Cetera business."

Rufus occasionally felt torn between his status as the town's only surviving special deputy—which made him second-in-command in the town police if you wanted to be grandiose about it—and his membership in a quasi-legal vigilante pest removal hunting club-type organization, but this wasn't one of those times. "Unless zombies have started driving heavy machinery and holding demolition derbies, that wasn't a zombie. Sounds more like a car accident, which means we need the police, and Morty. Let me see the radio."

Joe, who hadn't yet had the opportunity to shoot at something human-shaped even once, scowled and handed over the radio. There were only a handful of police radios available, nowhere near enough for everyone to have them, and only Stevie Ray and

Father Edsel—as head of the Anti-Zombie League—had radios full-time. "Stevie Ray, you there, think we got a car accident out near Andersen Road, right by the highway turn-off. Maybe get Morty and come check it out?"

"On my way," Stevie Ray crackled back.

"He didn't even say 'over and out,'" Joe said. "How're you supposed to know if he's done talking?"

"When he doesn't say anything else, it's probably a safe bet. That must be it up there." Rufus pointed at the flash of sunlight off a windshield in the distance. "Something off in the ditch there."

"Funny time to be driving," Joe said. "Don't see a lot of that anymore." Gas was precious, as the town had only one gas station and its tanks hadn't even been full when the outside world stopped communicating, and Stevie Ray had strictly rationed gas—even the Interfaith Anti-Zombie Coalition had to depend mostly on their own stores, but fortunately they were mostly farmers, and had a decent supply of fuel put aside amongst themselves.

"It looks like they came off the highway off-ramp and took the curve wrong and went into the ditch," Rufus said, shading his eyes. Looked like two vehicles in the ditch now, one big, one smaller, and that was just mind-boggling—the chance of there being two vehicles out here at the same time, and them actually managing to collide, had to be smaller than the chance of finding intelligent alien life on the surface of the sun.

"If the driver died, we could be looking at a zombie-type situation," Joe said. He pulled off the side of the road about fifty yards back, on the same side as the accident, but he managed to stay out of the ditch. By now the shape of the vehicles was clear: a big truck that was probably black before it got coated in twenty kinds of ice and road grime, and a yellow school bus, the short-bus kind, both tipped over on their sides in the ditch. Joe opened the door, letting in a blast of cold air, and said, "I've been waiting for this. Wish I had a couple of pistols, but my deer rifle will do." He climbed out of the truck, reached toward the rifle hanging on the gun rack behind the seat, then screamed and fell. From where Rufus sat, it looked like Joe's feet had slipped, and there was a loud crack as Joe's head hit some part of the truck as he went down.

"Joe!" Rufus scooted across the seat... and saw the zombie, a slender girl in her twenties maybe dressed in a puffy gray coat, with her neck bent at a funny angle, down in the ditch, from where she'd reached to grab Joe's ankles and drag him down. She climbed up his body and bit down on his neck, and Joe screamed, a sound even louder than the noise of the crash had been.

Rufus thought *Gun, gun*, and started fumbling in the glove compartment where he'd stashed his sidearm. He got the pistol in his hand and aimed it with a wavering hand at the zombie eating Joe, pulled the trigger, and nothing happened, oh God, he was doomed, oh wait, the safety was on, there, take that off. Rufus fired, the crash of the gunshot the loudest thing yet in an uncharacteristically loud morning, but he missed completely, just gouging a hole in some snow a good two feet to the left of the zombie, which paid no attention to the sound. The zombie lost interest in Joe, who shivered all over, then pushed himself up to his knees, eyes glassy and blank, mouth working.

"Crap!" Rufus shouted, firing another shot that didn't hit anything—Stevie Ray had been on him to practice shooting more, but Rufus had honestly believed all his hours of dual-wielding pistols in video games had given him a pretty good understanding of the rudiments of shootistry. Guess not. Joe and the zombie who'd killed him were taking an interest in Rufus now, and three other zombies were coming down the ditch from the direction of the crash, all with big chunks of flesh missing from their necks like they'd been bitten to death, and so he slammed the truck door shut and locked it and stepped on the gas and drove past the crash, trying to decide if he was cowardly or smart or some heretofore unexperienced combination of the two, and the back of the truck fishtailed around because he'd accelerated too fast on the ice and if he went off into the ditch he'd be just another bus crash zombie in minutes, so he eased off on his panic and the accelerator and pumped the brakes and got things under control.

Rolling so slowly past the crash was terrifying, but it gave him time to see the situation, if not to entirely understand it: The truck was hitched up to the short bus, and had been towing it, and when one of them—who knew which—went off into the ditch, the other one went with it. They'd probably been driving on the highway, coming from who knows where, and for whatever reason this was the exit they'd decided to try, maybe in a search of more food or fuel. They could have been refugees, but Rufus didn't figure they were a rescue party, not in such a ramshackle vehicular arrangement as that.

He finally remembered his radio as the zombies became dots in his rearview. "Stevie Ray! It's a bus crash, and there are zombies, at least four, and they got Joe, so make that five, I—I don't know what to do!"

The radio crackled. "On my way. I'll call Mr. Levitt and the rest of the League."

"Should I, ah… Try to take some of them out?"

"Wait for backup. We don't need you being a zombie too."

Rufus closed his eyes and thanked the Lord, and never mind he'd been an atheist since about five minutes after starting college. "Yes, sir." He twisted around to look out the back window. The zombies were wandering away from the crash, off across the field beside the ditch. He counted five, six, ten, fifteen, maybe, black spots against the snow. Lurching into the woods, spreading out, not staying together. He could take a rifle, climb up on the roof of the truck, and pick them off one at a time… if he were playing a video game, and had a sniper rifle. He knew he'd just make a lot of noise and probably hit nothing if he did it, here, and might even attract their attention.

"We'll round them up," he said. "They won't get far." So he just sat there, and watched the zombies disappear into the woods.

19

"He's in here," Dolph said, gesturing at the freezer door.

"Haul it open then." Mr. Levitt held a machete in one hand and a pistol in the other.

Dolph took a deep breath, grabbed the handle of the walk-in, and pulled. Mr. Levitt stepped forward, there was a meaty *thunk*, and then silence.

"Are you all right?" Dolph stood behind the door, trying not to think of it as a shield.

"Mmm hmm," Mr. Levitt said. "Clem's not even bleeding much, probably because he's been dead so long. Whoo-ee, he tore up a lot of the meat in here. Ah, here's some that's not gnawed on." Mr. Levitt came out, pistol holstered, machete at his belt, holding a few steaks tucked under one arm, and Clem's severed head, held by the hair, in his other hand. Clem's eyes rolled and his teeth snapped. "I'll take these."

"What?" Dolph said, staring at Clem's head.

"The steaks. Much obliged."

Dolph didn't say anything, not even, "Who do you think you are?" or "That's shoplifting," just watched until Mr. Levitt was gone, then looked at the headless, motionless body of his former employee laying in the middle of the walk-in among the wreckage of frozen food. Dolph tried not to think—to become a sort of zombie himself, in fact—as he went about the grim business of cleaning up.

20

"You were a good puppy," Mr. Levitt said, stepping on his beloved Alta with his foot, and then shooting him right in the brain. He looked up at Stevie Ray. "Satisfied?"

"I can't believe he came when you called," Stevie Ray said, shivering, and not just from the cold. They were out behind Dolph's store, by the trash bins and the loading dock. "Do you think he just responded to the *noise*, or…"

"He heard his master's voice," Mr. Levitt said. "Now, where do you want to burn the bodies? Because now that I'm on the job, there are going to be a *lot* of bodies to burn."

21

Mr. Levitt surveyed the scene of the bus crash and clucked his tongue. "I could have killed them all when they were bunched up here together. Anyone could have. But your deputy pissed himself and ran away instead."

"He's just a kid," Stevie Ray said mildly.

"Eighteen years old. I was fighting in Korea when I was eighteen. Might say it's where I learned my trade." Mr. Levitt cracked his knuckles. "Still, nice to know there's definitely something to hunt now. I was getting awfully sick of killing zombie dogs and cats and porcupines. You notice there aren't any bird zombies? I wonder if it's a mammal thing. Hunting zombie birds... that would at least pose an interesting challenge. Anyway, I'll round up the boys, we'll go out hunting, bring in a few more heads for the collection. Rufus said there were at least fifteen?"

"He wasn't sure, but he thinks so."

"Not a big bus, but even a small bus can hold a lot of people." Mr. Levitt walked around the wreckage. "Probably only one or two died in the crash, but then they woke up and attacked the other ones, judging by all the blood splashed around in there. I'm not inclined to believe anything Deputy Pisspants says, so until I know otherwise, I'm going to assume there's a zombie for every seat on that bus. It's the only way to be safe."

"You're the zombie killer," Stevie Ray said. The evil old man had a knack for the job, that was for sure, and according to Cyrus, Mr. Levitt hadn't yet killed anyone who *wasn't* a zombie, so the fragile arrangement was still working. "So go do your job."

"It's good to have a purpose," Mr. Levitt said. "See you tonight with my bounty."

That night, Mr. Levitt returned with only three heads. "The rest are who knows where, off in two dozen different directions for all I know. We'll find them in time, I'm sure. Let's hope it's me who finds them and not one of the patrols—they're apt to end up a bunch of Interfaith Zombie Chow if they're not careful." He tossed the heads into the freezer one by one, and Stevie Ray winced at every *thunk*.

22

"**O**h, heck, it's on fire," Stevie Ray said, staring at the flames in the lower windows of Ingvar's House of a Thousand Orphans. People—mostly kids, none dressed warmly enough—were streaming out into the late February cold. They'd gotten the call from Rufus, whose patrol had encountered a terrified child a quarter mile from Ingvar's farm, talking about how a big pack of zombies came wandering up to the house and started breaking windows and biting people. It had to be the bus crash zombies—even by conservative estimates there were a dozen unaccounted for—and Stevie Ray had no idea how many people were staying in the big rambling farmhouse... and no way to know how many of them had already fallen to zombie attacks, only to join the ranks of their attackers themselves.

"You and Deputy Diapers round up the survivors." Mr. Levitt climbed out of the truck, holding his machete. "I'll go in and kill the dead ones."

"By yourself? Are you crazy—" But the old man was already loping toward the front door, distressingly spry, as always. There were probably survivors inside, and what would stop Mr. Levitt from just killing them for fun and saying they were zombies when he found them? With luck, he'd have his hands full with *actual* zombies. And with a little more luck, Mr. Levitt would be overpowered, or get trapped inside and die in the fire, or in some other way cease to be the problem that plagued Stevie Ray all night and most of every day.

And then Stevie Ray saw a zombie come lurching around the house, chasing a woman clutching a baby to her chest, and he got out of the car with his service revolver and started shooting as the members of the Interfaith Anti-Zombie Cavalry pulled up in the driveway behind him.

23

Dolph carried a rifle with him as he walked down Main Street at twilight, head full of sound and fury and shame and self-loathing and disappointment. That filthy murdering old man Mr. Levitt had more guts than Dolph did, and Mr. Levitt was *scum*. Clem had cooled his heels—and the rest of him—in Dolph's freezer for days, with Dolph unable to get up the nerve to do what was necessary, and finally Stevie Ray sent over their new resident zombie killer, who did the job as easily as Dolph would unload a box of cheese crackers. What would Eileen say? She already thought he wasn't much of a man, since he was hesitant to put himself forward as mayor—but why would he want to be mayor? He had a store to run! The town's only stockpile of supplies! It was a big important responsibility! Which, he thought glumly, he'd probably find a way to screw up too.

And now he had to go tell Clem's family that their boy had been laid to rest... and hope they didn't ask to see the body, since Mr. Levitt had kept the head. Stevie Ray was setting up a place outside town for bodies to be burned, so maybe he could just tell them the body was already ashes... a lie, a cowardly lie, but Dolph was a coward, wasn't he?

Dolph sensed someone ahead of him, and looked up, and saw a zombie lurching unsteadily down the middle of the street, stumbling and staggering but making his way inexorably toward Dolph, who froze, and then remembered his gun.

I won't be a coward this time, he thought. The zombie reached out one arm toward Dolph, who lifted the rifle to his shoulder, took aim at its head, and fired. The zombie spun, dropped to the pavement, and lay unmoving, and people began to emerge from the Backtrack Bar in response to the gunshot as Dolph lifted his own arms in victory and shouted "It's okay, I got him!"

For no reason Dolph could comprehend, as the danger was now over, a couple of the people who'd emerged from the bar began to scream and carry on, and Stevie Ray was there pointing a gun at him and telling him to put down the rifle *right now* and put his hands behind his head, and that was Dolph's first real inkling that he might have made the worst mistake in a lifetime that already included some pretty bad ones.

24

"**Y**ou're cut off," Ace said, taking the glass from in front of Gunther Montcrief's spot at the bar. "There's only so much whiskey in the world now until I can convince Stevie Ray over there to let me set up a still, so I'm keeping you to a five-drink maximum."

"Sumbitch," Gunther said.

"You know I won't be sworn at in my own bar. Now get on out of here." Gunther stared at the bar for a long moment, sniffed, and decided against arguing further—it never did any good with Ace. The bar was packed pretty full—everybody wanted a drink, and why not, they were in the time of the zomboes now—and he had to shove his way past a lot of quiet people drinking by candlelight. He stepped out into the cold air, and it was bracing, but not particularly sobering, and he stumbled on the curb, which seemed to have been moved some distance higher than it usually was, probably part of the zombo plot, make people trip and bust their heads and come back to life as monsters. He regained his footing and set off down the center of the street, trying to remember if he had enough to drink at his fishing shack, and then he saw Dolph from the grocery store coming toward him, and though the store was closed by now and only sold beer anyway, well, beer was better than water, and maybe Dolph could be convinced to nip into the store and open up and sell him a case or two or three.

Gunther lifted his hand in a wave, and then Dolph lifted a rifle to his shoulder, and Gunther thought with uncharacteristic clarity, *Oh, he thinks I'm a zombo the way I'm stumbling around, shouldn't have drank so much,* and then he didn't think anything more ever again at all.

25

Mr. Levitt took off his earflap hat, and his earlobes instantly went numb. Winter was easing up—it was no longer so cold your extremities would turn blue, then black, and then fall off shortly after being exposed unprotected to air—but it was still a long way from the warmth of spring. If you were quiet and you listened—two things Mr. Levitt was pretty good at—you could hear the creak and squeak of trees swaying as the ice on their branches melted, easing their burden of cold.

This was the oldest cemetery in the area, so it wasn't as active as the newer one closer to town, but some of the older families buried their kin here with their illustrious descendants who'd founded the town. The earliest dead white people in the area were the denizens of a fur trading post populated mostly by drunken Frenchmen who'd died in a fire—though some had frozen to death afterward because it was winter and their shelter had burned down—but as far as Mr. Levitt knew none of them were buried here. Then there'd been the Utopian community where it turned out the leader told all the young girls that his flesh physically transformed into the flesh of Christ every night in a sort of full-body transubstantiation, and that by sleeping with him while he was suffused with the holy spirit, they might have the chance to bear the new Messiah. Winter killed most of them before sexually-transmitted diseases could. There were a few of those Utopians buried in a corner of the cemetery, but they were far too old for Mr. Levitt's purposes. This ground held the earliest Lutheran settlers, too, though, and many of the names on the memorials here would be familiar to anyone driving through the area, as those surnames adorned various roads, nature trails, baseball fields, and primary schools. Plenty of them adorned the idiot living descendants of those proud and brave—or, more likely, stubborn and self-effacing—settlers, too. The dead around Lake Woebegotten easily outnumbered the living. As would become apparent in a few more weeks, Mr. Levitt suspected.

The old man scouted out the newest-looking headstone and crouched down on the frozen earth, ignoring the twinge in his back—flesh as a general rule was weak, he'd proven that again and again, but he didn't like to think about the weakness in *his* flesh—and pressed his ear to the soil. The numbness in his ear was replaced by an icy fiery pain that soon vanished into a dull throb. He might lose an ear to frostbite yet if he wasn't careful, but he couldn't help it; the sound was so *wonderful*.

Scratch. Scratch. Scrabble scrabble thump scratch. Scratch. Scratch.

Mr. Levitt grinned, sat up, glanced at the name on the headstone, and said, "Hell-o Erlene Mildred Borgerson, devoted wife and mother. You must be getting pretty hungry down there. I imagine you've smashed through the lid of your casket by now, and you're just clawing at the dirt, aren't you? I bet you even made a little progress, but it's hard as a rock now, isn't it? Those last few feet of soil are a bitch. But don't worry—spring is coming. The ground will thaw. You've probably scraped your fingers to the bone by now, but I have faith in you. You can use your wristbones for spades. And then you can go looking for some food. And I'll make sure you find it."

He put his earflap hat back on, pausing at a few other tombstones, listening for scratching. He didn't hear much, but that was okay. The newer cemeteries were more recently occupied, and sounded a lot livelier.

He kept trying to estimate how many dead might rise from the town's Lutheran and Catholic graveyards, but the math defeated him—there were too many unknown variables. He mulled it over again. He knew the annual death rate in America—pre zombie-apocalypse—was about 0.8%. There were around 2,000 people in Lake Woebegotten and environs, so say 16 people died a year. If they were all embalmed and buried locally—some were cremated and some wound up elsewhere but this was a back-of-the-envelope thing—and if he assumed that any bodies buried within the last ten years could rise from the dead, there were about 160 zombies underground desperately trying to go out for breakfast.

Who knew how accurate that estimate was, though? The number could be half that, or double. Though Mr. Levitt had created a lot of dead bodies in his time, he didn't know very much about the mortuary sciences, as his interest in the bodies ended more or less when they became corpses. Still, he knew embalming techniques had come a long way in the past decades, and had heard stories of embalmed and be-coffined corpses dug up many years after death that looked remarkably lifelike, apart from being yellowish and saggy. On one of his cemetery visits yesterday he'd heard scratching from one grave with a headstone that bore an end date over fifteen years in the past. As long as the bodies had brains in their heads and ligaments and tendons bound to their bones, he suspected, they'd come climbing out of the ground once spring was sprung. There was a pet cemetery, too, but pets weren't embalmed, so they were surely all bones, which was too bad, because the sight of Rover and Snowball and Spot attacking their former owners would have cheered him up, especially after what he'd been forced to do to Alta, but you couldn't have everything.

Levitt had figured out the danger posed by the town's grave-yards months ago, but no one else seemed to have even considered the threat from below. Morons. He'd planned to tell the townspeople about the cemeteries, detail men to surround the areas with guns or some of Cyrus Bell's more exotic weaponry—he had at least two flamethrowers—and become even more of a hero when Rising Day came and the dead were easily defeated thanks to his leadership. Of course, he'd expected to be mayor in that scenario, riding an easy tide of victory after pretty much single-handedly killing all the bus crash zombies who'd attacked Ingvar's house. Sure, a few others had died in the process, but it was a chaotic situation, and as far as anyone knew for *sure* those deaths were accidental. Damn Dolph and his hearsay evidence and heartstring-tugging little girl testimony anyway. He should have checked under the table for witnesses. Still, some little girl's word shouldn't have been enough to turn the people against him. They should have voted him mayor anyway, instead of a *woman*.

But the people of Lake Woebegotten had foolishly decided to go another way. And as far as he was concerned, they could go on all the way to Hell. He wasn't planning to tell anybody about the scrabbling dead below their feet. Quite the opposite. He was going to arrange a feast for them. He just needed to figure out how best to maximize the carnage. If he couldn't get into politics, he had to amuse himself some other way, and the total destruction of the town would definitely be amusing. Afterward, he could light out, find another town, and offer his services. He thought he could play the role of brave, tragic sole survivor beautifully. He patted Erlene Mildred Borgerson's headstone and said, "See you soon, darling. Save the last dance for me."

He walked off, whistling, wondering where he might find a backhoe and the diesel fuel to run it.

THE FIRST DAY
OF SPRING, MORE OR LESS:
NICE WEATHER, SHAME ABOUT
THE ZOMBIES THOUGH

1. EILEEN VS. THE GREAT BEAST

E ileen woke, as she did every morning since becoming mayor and having no choice but to prove herself a woman of the people, to the sound of screaming children. She sat up on the air mattress in her laundry room—which was really just a *room* now that she mostly washed her clothes in the bathtub instead of the washing machine in order to conserve generator power, and she didn't like to think about what she'd do when the propane was entirely gone and she couldn't even run the power long enough to operate the pump to pull up water from the well. The *room* was tiny, with just enough space on the floor for her air mattress (leaky, of course) to fit between the wall and the useless white appliances, and it smelled of ancient fabric softener and drifting molecules of lint and distant mildew. She'd hated this room when she was married, seeing it as a sort of concretized symbol of her domestic servitude and the endless drudgery of being a wife, and she hated it now, though it served at least as a sort of inner sanctum, a space she could claim completely as her own, though largely just because it was too small to squeeze another cot or pallet in here.

Eileen got up, did an impromptu dance to get rid of her by now usual morning leg cramp, splashed her face with some cold water from the big industrial sink where she'd once rinsed out poop stains when her children were babies, and blood stains when her children played hockey, and puke stains when her children were teenagers. She dipped her toothbrush in a dish of baking soda and scrubbed her teeth and gums vigorously, because Lake

Woebegotten didn't have a dentist, and the thought of Morty the paramedic attempting dentistry based on a book from the library was too horrible to contemplate.

She spat into the sink, steeled herself, dressed in the least-smelly clothes from the pile she kept inside the dryer, and went out to greet her constituents.

The kitchen was crammed, but at least it was warm from the woodstove. There were five children on and around the big butcher block table eating instant oatmeal noisily and messily, and seven adults lounging at various points staring dolefully into their strictly rationed half-cups of instant coffee. Eileen knew all their names, had known most of them since she was a girl, but she thought of them all simply as *the great beast.* When she'd decided to run for mayor she'd picked up a few books from the library about politics and read about Alexander Hamilton, who'd responded to his rival Thomas Jefferson's comments about the greatness of the people by saying, "Your people, sir, is nothing but a great beast." Hamilton had never become President but he'd gotten his face on the ten dollar bill, and that was pretty good, though on the other hand he'd been shot and killed in a duel so he was probably a poor figure to model yourself after. He definitely had a point about people being beastly, though. Especially when they were crammed in your house and you had to let them in because they were too dumb to lay in enough fuel in their own houses and you were the mayor now and such largesse was expected and oh, of course the old married couple should get to sleep in the master bedroom while you went to sleep in the laundry room because the kids' old rooms were filled with bunk beds and rollaways and cots to accommodate the who-can-even-remember-how-many-children are living here now in a house that had felt too crowded for her taste with just two inhabitants.

"Morning mayor!" they chorused, and that was some small thrill, though it was smaller every day. Being mayor had never meant a whole heck of a lot in Lake Woebegotten—her husband had managed the job, after all, and he could make a mess out of falling out of bed in the morning—but she'd foolishly expected the public perception of the office to change now that the town was an outpost alone on the frontier of a hostile world, in dire need of leadership. Leading Minnesotans was tricky business. They mostly just wanted to do things on their own, and they'd nod at you and listen and be polite and shrug and then go on doing whatever they thought was best.

Eileen elbowed her way to the stove and poured the last of the hot water into a cup with a pitiful half-spoonful of coffee crystals. There was no peaceful place to sit and sip, no unoccupied chair, so she smiled and nodded and refrained from screaming and throwing elbows and made her way toward the living room and the door that led out to the porch. If she wanted privacy at all in her waking hours she had to go outside into the cold. It would be so easy to poison them all, she mused. Slip some rat poison in with the instant coffee, that would do it in no time. Though then she'd have a house full of zombies, which would be even worse, marginally.

She'd finally gotten the house to herself by killing her husband, and it had been a blissful little while of sleeping diagonal in her bed and not having to pick up anyone's dirty underwear and doing dishes for one, basically a kind of solitary paradise—leaving aside the whole zombie situation and dwindling fuel and lack of electricity and Dolph's cowardice and imprisonment and subsequent release and decision to just plain flat out ignore her from now on—until Ingvar's house burned down and all his dozens of refugees started looking for new homes and, as the leader of the town, Eileen had really had no choice but to open her doors to them. They'd been living with her for nearly six weeks now.

She'd wanted power, and instead, she'd somehow ended up with responsibility.

Eileen stepped out onto the porch, expecting the bracing blast of cold to do the job of waking her up that a half-cup of elderly instant coffee couldn't do... but it wasn't that cold. Brisk, sure, but only brisk. The snow had been gradually disappearing in the past couple of weeks, the town filled with the dripping of melting icicles, patches of white mostly clinging to shadows, the deep frost that turned the soil to stone finally loosening and the first green shoots poking up and reaching for the sun.

By the calendar, spring had already come—the vernal equinox had, anyway—but this was the first day it had really *felt* like spring, and Eileen took a deep breath of air that didn't burn her nostrils. Despite the hordes of people in her house and the responsibilities she'd only vaguely understood when she began campaigning for this job, she felt kind of hopeful. On a morning like this, with winter finally giving up its grip, the future seemed possible again.

The odd fellow folks called the Narrator wandered into the yard, squinting up at the sky, a low murmur coming from his mouth, sounding sort of like distant traffic or the sea or a toilet that wouldn't stop running. He was dressed in suspenders and a bow tie twisted from horizontal to mostly vertical and he only had one shoe on, and the way he sort of slowly wove across the lawn made her wonder if he'd gotten himself zombified. What if he was saying "Brains, brains, brains" over and over?

But as he came closer she could make out his actual words, which were:

"Spring had come at last to Lake Woebegotten, with the snow keeping itself mostly to the shadows, and birds chirping as they flew hither and yonder looking for fat earthworms to have for breakfast, and all the animals of the forests and fields starting to get frisky, and the flowers, of course, just beginning to poke their heads up out of the ground like sleepy teenagers emerging from under their covers at noon. Of course, that spring, flowers weren't the only thing you could expect to see coming up out of the ground, because that was the spring—"

He came a little too close to the front door then, and because Eileen was afraid he'd invite himself in for a half-cup of instant coffee, she interrupted him with a loud "Shoo!" and flapped her hands at him like you would at a stray cat, and the Narrator obligingly wandered off toward the edge of her property. She watched him weave on out of sight, then went inside to take her turn in the bathroom—there was a *chart*, with a *rotation*, and if you overslept or missed your slot then woe betide you because you'd have to make do with sponge baths until tomorrow, even if you were the mayor and this was your house—and get her cold shower and get dressed and ride over to the town hall where she had her "office" in a converted supply closet so she could keep this community from starving to death, drowning in sewage, being overrun by zombies, and generally collapsing. It was a lot of work but she guessed it beat housewifing.

One of the very few perqs of being mayor: she got a second half-cup of instant coffee because Stevie Ray was courteous that way, though he was the one who'd imposed—he'd say "suggested"—the rationing of supplies anyway

"Thanks all of you for coming out this morning," she said, addressing the newly formed town council, which had not been elected so much as simply coalesced, drawing in the people who were interested and dedicated and willing to get some work done. They sat around a long wooden table in the town hall's one conference room, with sunlight streaming in the windows, and it could almost have been a normal day in an undestroyed world, except then, she wouldn't be mayor, would she?

She sipped her coffee, savoring the heat and warmth and the smell, though the flavor had never done much for her, and that powdered creamer substitute was no match for real milk.

Once upon a time she could have prevailed upon her lover Dolph to dip into his store's supplies and give her anything she asked for, as such transactions had been central to their relationship, but things between them had dissolved, and after his accident, and imprisonment, and breakdown, and subsequent total personality shift, their relationship had cooled. It wouldn't do for her to be caught angling for special favors anyway. Minnesotans weren't too willing to tolerate corruption in their elected officials. Power wasn't everything it was cracked up to be, that was for sure.

She looked around the table, smiling and nodding as everyone got settled and took out their notebooks or fussed their coffee into some semblance of acceptability with little packets of artificial sweetener and powdered milk. Being mayor wasn't exactly like being an empress, but Stevie Ray listened to her, and he was the man with the guns, so that was something.

And Pastor Inkfist treated her with a lot more respect than he had when she was head of the Women's Circle—not that he'd disrespected her then, exactly, he'd just treated her like a mop or a microwave or an old reliable car, something that would do its job without complaint, something you didn't have to worry about. Brent had treated her the same way, and look where that had gotten him. Father Edsel didn't treat her with much respect, but he didn't treat anybody with respect, so she didn't let it bother her; he was just a Catholic anyway.

Julie Olafson—who was only on the council as far as Eileen was concerned because of some hereditary sentimentalism over her grandfather, who'd served as a councilman for many years, though officially she was here in her capacity as a diner owner, serving as a representative of the town's business interests, which should have been Dolph's job except he'd become a Communist or whatever and decided to give his store's entire inventory over to the town to be distributed to those in need, which was both disappointing for her as a onetime lover disgusted at his weakness and gratifying for her as a mayor who appreciated the supplies—was staring into her coffee with her eyebrows drawn down, scowling, and while Eileen thought it *should* be nice having another woman on the council, she actually just found it annoying. Julie hadn't come close to Eileen's numbers in the mayoral race, but she'd gotten *some* votes, and that was irksome. Plus she had all sorts of ideas. Maybe even a vision, always talking about making the town into a green zone. Eileen, whose vision didn't extend much beyond the next few days unless she strained herself tremendously, found that quality sort of offensive. Above her station. Uppity. Things like that.

The last member of the council was an unmarried Norwegian farmer named Torkelson who smelled of pig manure and had hands the size of cast-iron skillets, and who represented the interests of unmarried Norwegian farmers who smelled of various kinds of manure. He didn't talk much, was often drunk, and tended to nod gravely at anything anyone said to him, often as a brief precursor to nodding off. But Eileen was scrupulously nice to him, always shaking his hand (though she washed her own thoroughly afterward), because Lake Woebegotten wasn't getting food trucked in anymore, and Dolph's store was pretty well cleaned out, and the town would only survive if the farmers kept farming and shared what they grew and raised with everyone else. It was an annoying situation.

Eileen didn't like situations that couldn't be favorably affected by the judicious application of chloroform or shotgun shells. She was good at thinking in a straight line, and could think in a straight line remarkably hard and far and thoroughly, but being mayor required thinking around corners, and that was kind of a stretch.

"So on the agenda today, we need to talk about sanitation, and about what kind of help the townspeople can give the farmers, and that's about it, right?"

"Defense," Julie said. "It's right here on the agenda. The first item, actually."

"Ah, of course." Eileen picked up the agenda—the copies were handmade since nobody wanted to waste power on the library's copy machine for so few pieces of paper—and made a great show of squinting at it. "Just had a little trouble reading the handwriting, here." Julie went on and on about defense, Eileen heard she'd been in the military though apparently not in the US armed forces, and how did that even work, it sounded sort of disloyal, Eileen didn't know the details and wasn't about to ask but she figured it must involve something like the French Foreign Legion, the service for people who'd been disgraced and lived under assumed names and had syphilis. "Well, then. What do you suggest for defense? Should we dig a moat around the town? Fill it with lake water?" She smiled, but no one else seemed to find it amusing, which just went to show none of them were funny.

Julie stood up. Who did she think she was? "I don't want to talk about practical measures today—I think the InterFaith group is doing a fine job patrolling, and after the events at the Knudsen farm, everyone is being especially diligent."

"Volunteers have quadrupled," Father Edsel rumbled. "We're turning people away because we don't have enough fuel for the vehicles."

"Is Mr. Levitt still… behaving?" Eileen asked, giving the Father a meaningful look. Everyone in this room, excepting Julie and the pig farmer, knew exactly what Levitt was, and why they needed to be concerned about him, especially after Dolph's accusations on election night.

"After moping over the mayoral race for a while, he's going on regular patrols again," the priest said. "Stevie Ray thinks it's best to keep him occupied." Best to keep him where someone armed could keep an eye on him, more like it, Eileen figured. "I understand he's spending most of his free time visiting the local graveyards. He says he has more friends dead than alive these days. He's been keeping things tidy around the graves, things like that."

"He's a credit to the community," Edsel said, not bothering to hide the crushing sarcasm in his voice. Even though he was bossy, Catholic, and crazy, Eileen sometimes found herself liking Edsel. He was as straightforward as a bulldozer.

"We're keeping an eye on him," Stevie Ray said.

Eileen nodded. Stevie Ray had told her that he wanted to lock Mr. Levitt up again, permanently this time, that letting him out had been a terrible mistake even if it had seemed like the only choice at the time, but he didn't want to move against the man too quickly—he thought Levitt was entirely capable of climbing to the top of the grain elevator with a sniper rifle and picking off townspeople, or wiring himself with explosives, or going on a last killing spree, if he felt threatened. Better to lull him into a false sense of security and then strike when he wasn't expecting it. Eileen thought Stevie Ray was just afraid to go toe-to-toe with the man. A little poison, or a well-placed bullet, would have solved the problem, but Eileen wasn't ready to suggest summary executions just yet. She needed to get everyone to accept her as judge as well as mayor first, and that was something she planned to ease up to.

"Back to my point," Julie said. "I want to talk about the zombies—about the *nature* of the zombies. I've been… making some observations, and I've discovered something important. Something all of you should know. I think it will change the way we defend ourselves."

"What's that?" Eileen said.

"Easier if I show you," Julie said, rising. "Would you all come with me to my grandfather's house, after we finish the rest of the meeting?" That was met by a generally uncomfortable silence until she said, "I thought I'd make us all a little lunch." Cafe Lo had never been known for its food, since the owner had been—still was, Eileen corrected herself, he wasn't dead yet, and was technically a town councilman, even—a generally terrible cook. His grand-daughter Julie, on the other hand, could do wondrous things with a few potatoes and cans of tuna fish, and Eileen—who'd always been a more dutiful than inspired cook—found her irritation at Julie's presumption subsiding at the thought of eating a hot meal prepared by someone who knew a saucepan from a casserole dish. "That sounds just fine," she said. "Shall we talk about how the town can help the farmers, Mr. Torkelson?

"Yah, we was thinking, we could use the zombies to pull plows, how about that? Hang a piece of meat on a string in front of their face and they'd pull all day, I betcha." He beamed, delighted at the idea, and it took quite some time for the others to convince him there might be some downsides to the idea.

2. BIOTROPIC, WHATEVER THAT MEANS

Pastor Inkfist froze when, after feeding them all a little lunch of lemon bars, chocolate chip cookies—home-made tasting, not from one of those tubes Dolph's store was handing out—sandwiches with cold slices of lunch meat and cheese (from Wisconsin, though you couldn't hold that against her) and a dab of this and that and the other thing from her re-frigerator, plus pickles and some leftover hotdish warmed up on the stove (which was good since hotdish tasted better the second day, everyone knew that, it gave the flavor of the soup time to soak into the noodles), Julie said, "Shall we go down to the basement then?"

They were all seated around Julie's old wooden kitchen table, and the door to the basement was right *there* just a few feet away, a fact that had made Pastor Inkfist's extremities tingle and cheeks just slightly blush. Everyone else seemed to have forgotten that they'd come over here for any reason other than enjoying Julie's hospitality, as they all blinked around at each other with bits of cream of mushroom soup dabbing their chins. "Your basement?" Eileen said. "Oh, of course, you wanted to show us something."

"You want to go… down there?" Daniel said, trying to sound casual. "In your basement?"

"I do," she said. "It's important."

"But, ah, that is…" Daniel couldn't think of a way out. Julie had obviously decided to confess her sinful lifestyle, which was prob-ably good for the soul though no one really needed to hear a thing like that, it was better left between her and God, but the more pressing problem for Daniel was that confessing her sin might mean mentioning *him*, and that wouldn't do good things for his standing in the community. And he felt, sinfulness aside, he could still do the people of Lake Woebegotten good. If nothing else he was a small moderating influence on Father Edsel's apocalyptic furor. "I'm not so sure…"

"Spit it out, Pastor," Edsel said, mopping up the last of his hot-dish juice with one of those heat-and-serve dinner rolls that in Daniel's opinion tasted better than fresh homemade bread.

"Ah, I seem to recall your grandfather telling me the basement was… flooded. And that there was a rat problem."

"I wouldn't worry about… rats, Pastor," Julie said, giving him one of those maddening half-smiles that could have meant anything at all. "It's quite nice down there. Except for… well. You'll see. Come along." She stood up from the table, lit a lantern, opened the wooden door to the basement, and descended the stairs. Daniel could imagine the glint and gleam of bits of metal and shiny leather in that lantern-light. He squeezed his eyes shut for a moment, then stood and followed the others downstairs. Might as well face his fate like a man then.

The nice thing about having an affair—no, not an affair, he'd never slept with her, it was an *arrangement*—with Julie was that it both satisfied his desire for sexual release (even if it was all technically self-gratification, doing it in front of her made it so much better) and assuaged his guilt over such improper behavior, since beforehand she hit him with switches and called him a dirty little bitch and made him lick her boots and otherwise compelled pre-emptive penance.

He kept his eyes forward as he descended the stairs, not looking down, not wanting to see the reaction of his fellow council members when they saw Julie's dungeon, but he did think they were awfully quiet—Edsel at least should have been shouting about something or other—so he risked a peek. Julie was lighting other lanterns around the room… and none of her, ah, equipment was in sight. There were lots of things pushed to the edges of the walls and covered with heavy painter's dropcloths—including the tall round-topped thing in the far corner that must be some kind of cage or even, shudder to think, an iron maiden—and she'd moved a ratty old orange couch and a coffee table scattered with magazines down here. Daniel's heart started beating normally again, and he felt like he'd just had a narrow escape, sort of like when you successfully pretend you've already tried the lutefisk at Christmas time and manage to avoid being given a second helping, which would really have been the first helping, which would really be one helping too many.

"What's all this?" Eileen said, gesturing at the draped shapes by the walls. "Antique furniture?" Daniel resisted the urge to shout "It's nothing!" because, well, that would probably get him funny looks at best and provoke further inquiries at worst.

"Just grandpa's old junk," Julie said. "This is what I want to show you." She went to the far corner, to that tall drape-covered thing, and Daniel thought, *I'll finally see it*, though he was worried it was going to be something *really* hinky, or kinky, or however you said it.

Julie pulled the dropcloth down, revealing the object beneath.

Everyone was silent, except for Mr. Torkelson, who whistled.

Father Edsel finally spoke, and he said, "Where'd you get the cage?"

It was awfully dim in there, but Daniel though Julie was maybe blushing herself a bit. "You'd have to ask grandpa. It was down here when I moved in."

"Okay, then," Stevie Ray said. "Then where'd you get the *zombie*?"

That interested Daniel a little more, too. The object in the corner was a human-sized cage with a circular base and iron bars curving upward into a domed top like a birdcage, and the cage door was closed with a big padlock. Inside a zombie stood swaying, dressed in rags, bound at the wrists and ankles, gagged, and with a blindfold tied around its eyes.

"Found it wandering in the yard a while back. I figure it's one of the bus crash zombies, must have gotten separated from the pack of them somehow. I've been studying it."

A while back? Daniel thought. He and Julie had been down here, in this basement, doing… all sorts of things… and all the time there'd been a zombie in the corner? He shuddered.

"Probably a law against keeping dead bodies in your basement," Stevie Ray said. "But I guess I can let it slide." He shook his head. "Damn dangerous, though."

"I thought it was important," Julie said.

"Studying it. Interesting." Edsel paced before the cage, arms clasped behind his back. "And when I say 'interesting' I don't mean it in the conventional Minnesotan sense of bad, disturbing, or in poor taste. I mean… interesting. You've brought us here to share your results?"

Julie nodded. "I have. This zombie has been in my care for some months now, and it's just as lively as it was when I first caught it, even though it hasn't had anything to eat. It *is* decomposing, though not as fast as a corpse should, nowhere close, even considering how cold it's been. I'd sort of hoped all the zombies would just rot away if they didn't feed, but whatever they're subsisting on… it's not food. And maybe they will rot away, but not quick enough to do us any good. And by 'us' I mean humanity in general, I guess. The dead outnumber the living—"

"No they don't," Eileen said promptly. "The number of people alive on Earth today are more than all the people who ever lived before. Because of the baby boom. Population growth. Like that. I read it on the internet."

Eileen looked terribly pleased with herself, but Julie just shook her head minutely and said, "No, that's just one of those bits of nonsense that gets spread around because it sounds good, even though there's not a bit of truth in it. The best estimate of the number of people born on Earth, from the time we first became recognizably human to now, is around one hundred and six billion. Since the total population is a bit over six billion—well, a lot less than that now, I'd say, all things considered—the living only equal about six percent of the dead. In other words, the dead outnumber the living about seventeen to one." She shook her head. "Those are pretty bad odds in any war. On the bright side, we're not contending against all the dead who've ever lived. To become a zombie, it looks like you've got to have a brain in your head, and since corpses rot pretty fast, the vast majority of the planet's dead are nothing but dust now. We only have to worry about the freshly dead. What I wonder about… is the dead in their graves."

"I said cremation was the way to go," Edsel said darkly.

"What do you mean?" Daniel asked.

"The embalmed dead, you mean," Eileen said, getting a nod of approval from Julie. "Huh. Were any of the bodies that got up in the Mathison Brothers Funeral Home embalmed?"

"They were," Stevie Ray said. "Huh. Wish one of the brothers was still around to tell me how long the brains stay intact in an embalmed body." He frowned. "And how long people have been embalming bodies. And, oh Lord, and how many embalmed bodies with embalmed brains are buried in the ground in the three, no, four cemeteries in and around town."

"You think the dead will rise from their *graves*?" Edsel said, with that wild-eyed prophet look on his face. "And seek to kill the living?"

"It occurred to me this morning," Julie said. "When I stepped out my front door and my boot squelched down in muddy dirt instead of thumping down on frozen dirt. The ground is thawing. It might be a good idea for us to dig up a couple of graves—from five years ago, ten, fifteen, twenty—and see what we find. Figure out how many graves might be holding things that are hungry. The ground's going soft, and the zombies are *strong*, and tenacious. I don't necessarily expect the lawns to start sprouting zombies like wildflowers, but… it's a concern, wouldn't you think?"

"You did right to bring this to our attention," Stevie Ray said, "but why did you need to bring us down *here*?"

"To show you something else I figured out. About how the zombies hunt. See how he's trying to get at us?" The zombie in the cage was pressed against the bars, thumping its head against them, trying to reach out with manacled hands.

"Sure," Daniel said, wanting to contribute something.

"But it can't see—it's blindfolded. So if it's not hunting by sight…"

"Maybe by sound?" Edsel said, thoughtfully.

"Let's see," Julie said, and unlocked the cage. Everyone else stepped back, Stevie Ray going for his gun, but Julie said, "No, it's okay, he's restrained." The zombie lurched out at her, tripped, and fell—but the chain around its neck caught it short, so it sort of leaned out, legs tangled, in a position that would have strangled something that had to breathe. Julie picked up a pair of bulky earmuff-looking things from one of the covered tables. "Noise-canceling headphones," she said, and slipped them over the zombie's head. "Now it can't hear anything. But watch." She stepped back to the others, and the zombie found its feet—and lurched for them, the chain jerking it up short again.

"Smell?" Edsel said, and something in his tone was utterly abhorrent to Daniel—like he was *enjoying* this.

"Smelling salts," Julie said, taking a caplet from her pocket. "When this hits your nose, you can't smell *anything* else." She cracked one under the zombie's nostrils, releasing a pungent odor that made Daniel's eyes water even a few feet away... and the zombie didn't react at all, but just kept trying to get at Julie, its toothless mouth doing its best to open and close ceaselessly over the rubber gag, but its best wasn't much good, so it was more like a lip quiver, really.

Julie turned to face the others, spreading out her hands. "It's not smell, or sight, or hearing, or even tasting the air like a snake, not with that gag in. So how is it sensing us?"

"Touch? Minute changes in air currents and pressure from our presence?" Edsel said.

"Possible, and hard to test." Julie went to the table and picked up a yardstick with a hunting knife lashed to the end with duct tape. "But it doesn't seem to respond to touch much otherwise—" She suddenly jabbed the zombie in the ribs with the improvised spear, and it didn't react particularly at all. "And they can track us even outside, when changes in the air wouldn't be noticeable. Look, let's move across the basement." Julie herded them to the far side of the big basement, then led them on a slow walk around the perimeter... and the zombie followed their progress, straining at the end of its chain, pointed toward them as unerringly as a magnet drawn to metal.

"It's using some other sense," she said quietly. "I'm almost certain. It can somehow sense *life*. Look, Stevie Ray, Mr. Torkelson, Father Edsel, Eileen, you walk over there—Daniel and I will stay here." She pointed, and the four of them went to the other side of the basement. This time, the zombie followed them, ignoring Daniel and Julie. "It always goes for the bigger life form, or the more numerous lives. I brought my grandfather's cat down here—the cat wasn't happy about that, by the way—and, when I was at the top of the stairs, the zombie tried to get at the cat. But as soon as I came within a couple dozen yards, the zombie immediately tried to come after me instead. I think the zombies are biotropic."

"Whatever that means," Eileen muttered, glaring around at the world in general.

"Drawn to life," Father Edsel said. "So all those people crammed together at Ingvar's…"

"Moths to a flame," Julie said. "Man-eating moths. Or flame-eating moths. And the flames are humans. Sorry. The comparison doesn't really work. But, yes: they seek out life. Knowing that, it seems to me, has certain implications for our security."

"I should post a lookout on top of the granary tower," Stevie Ray said. "Because this town still has several hundred inhabitants, and if there are hordes of zombies roaming the prairie looking for life and destroying it as they go, they're sure to find us eventually."

"I've been thinking about perimeter defenses," Julie said. "Trenches. Walls. Guards. If we're going to make Lake Woebegotten a green zone, we'll need to protect ourselves from the outside. And we need to think long and hard before we have any big all-town meetings in the future, knowing that kind of group is catnip to zombies." She glanced at Eileen. "If that sounds all right with the mayor."

"Stevie Ray's our head of security," Eileen said, voice dripping sugary venom. "If he sees merit in your plans, I'll certainly support them."

Edsel clapped Daniel on the back, almost hard enough to send him sprawling. "Shall we round up the boys?" he said. "We've got bodies to dig up and ditches to dig and lookouts to post." He took a deep breath. "I love springtime. You can finally get out and *do* things again."

3. BEAR SHI(R)T

igHorn Jim grew weary of waiting for the bear to awaken, and didn't find any *draugr* to dispatch—he entirely missed the battle of the bus crash zombies, which was more disappointing than getting to a potluck supper and finding out there was nothing left but a dish of lutefisk and some burned lefse—so he decided to take matters into his own hands. He dressed himself in his best warrior garb, including a good pair of insulated boots, a leather football helmet—no horns, this wasn't for show—and the wolfskin cape he'd bought off the internet back when there was such a thing, even though he had his doubts about the actual wolfiness of the pelt, which seemed more beaverish to him if he was being completely honest. Then he took the genuine reproduction *breið-øx*—a battleaxe with a crescent-shaped blade about 18 inches long and a three-foot-long wooden handle—and strapped it to his back. He'd found the axesmith on the internet, too, a guy who specialized in making weapons for Renaissance Faire melees, though Jim had sharpened the blade into a razor edge himself. The axe hadn't been cheap. It had cost him the last of his settlement money from the accident at the light bulb factory, where he'd worked before his near-death and subsequent conversion to Norse fundamentalism. He'd completely given up light bulbs after leaving the factory. It was all firelight for him after that.

Which brought him to the last of his provisions before he set out from his shack. He took a bucket of sludgy old oil, a heap of dirty rags, and a few lengths of wood too big for kindling but too thin to be properly called logs. Thus armed, he tromped in snowshoes out to the bear's lair. The walk was cold, what with him wearing a wolfskin and not much else, but the snow was reduced to patches on the ground and there was a definite hint of springtime in the air. A good day for killing, Jim thought, though he'd never really encountered a bad day for killing, and indeed one of his favorite things about killing—which was still a pretty abstract subject for him, at least vis-à-vis single combat, though he'd done his share of hunting—was that killing was versatile. On a good day, you killed with joy. On a bad day, you killed to make yourself feel better. After all, however bad things were, whether your wife had left you or a forklift operator had accidentally dropped a crate on your head at work or whatever, you could always go out and kill something and think to yourself, *At least I'm not dead.*

Such happy thoughts kept Jim company as he navigated to the bear's lair. Once upon a time a glacier had crawled across the land here, Jim imagined, tearing up the ground, and when it receded it left the bones of the earth exposed. Like this spot, a jumble of bare rocks—bear rocks, ha ha, they'd love that joke in Valhalla, assuming they spoke English nowadays and could get puns—with a dark hole in the center, mostly clogged with leaves and branches. Jim poked at the opening with one of the pieces of stovewood, clearing it out, and peered into the blackness, but he couldn't see anything except the aforementioned blackness. In storybooks bear lairs were vast, people going deep into caves and finding bears at the back, and maybe sometimes their dens were like that, but in Jim's experience as a woodsboy and -man, bears mostly penned themselves up in spots not much bigger than they could turn around in. If he poked the stick in there, he might even hit the flesh of the black bear inside, and that would probably be enough to wake the beast. But he was going to do something more dramatic, as befitted the beginning of an epic battle.

Jim unstrapped his axe and leaned it against a handy tree. Then he wrapped a bunch of dirty rags around a piece of wood, tying up a nice bundle, and smeared sludgy used oil on the cloth. He took out his Zippo—flint and tinder would've been better, or better yet just a couple of sticks, or better still a coal from a lightning strike carried around in a bucket, but he was in a hurry and couldn't go around waiting for lucky thunder-storms—flicked up the flame, and lit the rags. They whooshed into life with alarming speed, a sudden bright heat in his face that made his eyebrows want to retract into his head, and he held out the torch at arm's length.

"*Bjorn!*" he shouted, and threw the torch into the dark hole of the bear's lair.

Then he waited. He didn't have to wait long.

When a bear awakes in the spring, it tends to be in poor humor. Bears don't truly hibernate the way some animals do, shutting down non-essential functions and going into a dor-mant state, and they're more active than you might think—they tend to wake up a little and move around in their dens from time to time, finding a new position and falling asleep again, pretty much the way restless people do at night, though in this case the night lasts all winter. The females even give birth during hibernation, and as any mother can tell you, having babies is a difficult experience to sleep through. It doesn't take extraordi-nary measures—like being hit with a flaming torch—to wake up a hibernating bear, usually, though they tend to be a little foggy at first, like you or me before our coffee or shower, and at least one bear researcher accidentally fell on top of a sleep-ing bear and lived to tell the story of how she took about eight minutes to wake up entirely. But they don't eat or drink at all or poop and pee much, so when they *do* wake up for good and all, they've got a lot of bodily demands fighting for their attention: they're hungry, really hungry, profoundly hungry, and they've got a lot of body to be hungry with. They're thirsty, too, and that makes anybody foul-tempered. Plus, they have to pee like the dickens. Add to all that some fool human trying to set you on fire—rapidly accelerating the wake-up process—and you have a recipe for definite unpleasantness.

This particular bear—a male, fortunately, or it would have been even worse, as female bears who are new mothers are not renowned for their patience and lack of aggression, though females tend to be smaller, so that's also a factor—burst out of the den in a fury, fur smoking from the torch's impact, rather large and impressive teeth bared. At its fully-fed autumn weight the bear would have run well over 500 pounds, but it was only in the 400s after the long winter, though for a 200-pound human, the difference between being hit by 550 pounds of angry omnivore as opposed to 450 pounds of the same is probably negligible.

Jim had his opening move all planned, and he held his long axe in a good two-handed grip, ready to smash the bear right between the eyes with the butt of the weapon.

Here's how it went in his head: on impact the bear stopped like a sparrow hitting a window, went cross-eyed, and fell stunned to the ground. Then Jim could lop off its head with an axe blow or two and skin it at his leisure. Bear steaks all winter long. A bearskin cloak that would allow him to consign his suspicious wolfskin to throw rug status. Odin would be impressed. Thor would buy him a tankard of mead. He was a little fuzzy on the last bits, but a definite sense of community was involved.

Here's how it went in reality: The axe handle didn't hit the bear smack in the face, that being a relatively small target and Jim being rather more stunned by the emergence of his adversary than he'd expected, making minute adjustments of stance impossible. Instead, the handle hit the bear in the right shoulder, and, having a flaw deep in the wood that Jim didn't know about and the weaponsmith either hadn't known about or hadn't cared about, the handle shattered for its last two feet, leaving him holding an incredibly unwieldy and poorly-balanced hatchet. Barely holding, at that, since the impact of the bear sent a shudder down the axe and through Jim's arms and shoulder and body in general that made the recoil of a double-barreled shotgun seem like a lover's butterfly kiss in comparison. Jim had his feet planted pretty well but when an unstoppable bear hits you, you're unlikely to stay an immovable object for long, and Jim went right back over, legs under him, and subsequently under the bear. Whether the bear connected Jim with the fiery wake-up call or just wanted to vent its anger on whatever living thing it first encountered didn't much matter, practically speaking, because it was all claws and teeth and mauling. To his admittedly temporary shame, Jim's dismayed shout upon realization of his impending death was not *swina bqllr!* (that's "pig penises!" to you and me) or *meyla krafla mikli thur syr!* (son of a stinking sow corpse, loosely) or even the pithy *kamphundr* (corpse-eater, though that had the advantage of being both a nasty insult and a description that was going to be true in a minute or two) but a simple childhood exclamation he'd always favored: "Oh shitballs!"

He'd been living the life of a Norse warrior—as well as he could in central Minnesota where his neighbors were all either Lutheran or Catholic—long enough to know that how you died mattered. He would not die with fear in his heart—with crap in his underpants, yes, but not fear in his heart. And he wouldn't die alone. He still had the axe (well, hatchet) in his hand, and he used the last of his strength to swing his arm and plant the axe right in the bear's neck. Blood gushed in a warm wave over him, and the bear voided its bowels, too—a smell that made an impression even on Jim's fading senses—and slumped its considerable weight on his body. Jim worked the blade out, and crossed his eyes to see where he was aiming, and forced the nearly dead weight of his arm to strike again, this time at the bear's head. He hit his mark, and got the blade right between its eyes, sinking into the bone and sticking there, and that was it for Jim's valiant enemy.

"See you in Valhalla, *bjorn*," Jim said, and closed his eyes, and waited for the Valkyries.

But before Jim died, the bear stirred, and Jim opened his eyes again—his eyelids felt made of cement, but taking a look seemed important—and the bear, dead-eyed and oozing various things from its wounds, opened and closed its mouth on whatever bits of Jim it could fasten onto. That wasn't right. Jim had struck the bear in the head specifically to avoid this outcome. Head strikes were supposed to kill zombies. Though maybe bear skulls were thicker than he'd expected. Or maybe it wasn't enough to nick the front of the brain, maybe you had to destroy more of it. Or maybe animals were different, maybe it was all about the hind-brain for them. Jim could have come up with various theories, if he wasn't being eaten at the moment. Whatever the cause, he knew what he was dealing with:

Draugr bjorn.

Jim was pleased with himself for thinking that entirely in his adopted language, but then it occurred to him that he was likely to become a *draugr* himself too in a minute, which was depressing.

Fortunately the bear took a nice big bite out of the side of his head, making zombie-hood impossible, not that Jim was able to appreciate the accidental mercy, since he was dead.

4. LEVITT OR LEAVE IT

Because Cy had the runs and couldn't leave his cabins without making a fuss and a muss both, Rufus had been assigned to spy on Mr. Levitt for the day, something Stevie Ray took a lot more seriously—and he'd never taken it lightly—since the accusations against Levitt at the town meeting. He was trying to get Eileen and the rest of the council to appoint a judge so they could bring Mr. Levitt to trial, Stevie Ray being uncomfortable with notions of summary execution, which Rufus as a recently-liberal college student could appreciate in theory, though in practice the old guy had never stopped giving him the creeps, even if he *had* saved Rufus from getting eaten by his own uncle.

Except when Rufus knocked on the old guy's door in the morning, Mr. Levitt was not happy to see him. "Where's Cy?" he snapped.

"Probably in the toilet," Rufus said, stepping back. "He's sick. I'm, uh, supposed to go with you on patrol."

"I'm supposed to babysit you as well as kill zombies now?" Levitt scowled, and he looked suddenly so *old* to Rufus, neck all thin and scrawny, like a chicken's. Why couldn't he fall off a snowmobile and snap that chicken neck and save everyone a lot of trouble?

"We haven't even seen a zombie since the day Ingvar's house burned down." Rufus frowned. "And, uh, I don't need babysitting."

Levitt snorted. "The price of liberty is eternal vigilance, boy-oh. Well, come in, I need to finish getting ready." He turned and headed back into his house. Which, last time Rufus had entered it, had led to a scene of destruction and chaos reminiscent of a Hieronymus Bosch painting or a close-out sale at a wholesale footwear outlet, complete with chainsaws and blood.

"I think I'll just wait out in the truck," Rufus said, and took a step back off the porch.

From inside the house, Levitt sighed. "All right," he said after a moment. "I'm coming." He emerged zipping up a fleece jacket and holding a long steel pry bar.

"What's that for? You decided to start beating zombies to death?"

"No, it's for beating *you* to death," Levitt said, and swung the pry bar overhand like he was attempting to split a piece of wood. But he was standing on the top step while Rufus was at the bottom, so Rufus took the quick-thinking action of dropping to his butt, and Mr. Levitt missed him by a mile. The old guy overbalanced, too, the weight of the bar pulling him over, and he fell off the steps with a squawk, landing on top of Rufus, weapon sprawling away.

Please break a hip, Rufus thought, but then the old guy started rabbit-punching him in the side, right below his ribs, and snarling at him, and snapping his teeth not unlike a zombie, only with more profanity. There was a lot of "ruining everything" and "snot-nosed kid" and "have to kill you twice" in there before Rufus realized he'd better start fighting back, or the old man was actually going to kill him *with his bare hands*.

Rufus had some things in his favor. Old man Levitt was formidable, and wiry, and had that kind of stringy muscle that some old men develop, and he'd also had a lot of practice with hitting people and hurting people, and he didn't hesitate. But most of the time he took his victims by surprise, or poisoned them, or drugged them, or he was fighting zombies, who—though they had many terrifying qualities—were not particularly skillful hand-to-hand combatants. Rufus wasn't a karate kung-fu type either, but he was better than a zombie. Moreover, Rufus outweighed the old man by probably thirty pounds, and while he didn't have that psychotic fire in his belly, he *did* have the adrenal system of a healthy young man of not yet twenty, which meant somewhere deep in his reptile brain he knew how to fight back ferociously, and his glands pumped him full of the sort of chemicals that enhance your strength and slow down your subjective time sense and generally give you an edge in battle. Once upon a time Rufus had been somewhat couch-potato-like, but a winter in the zombie apocalypse, with lots of hauling firewood and shoveling snow and going on patrol and even fighting the occasional undead monster, had improved his physical condition considerably.

A psychopathic and relatively healthy seventy-year-old versus a more-or-less ordinary and physically fit nineteen-year-old does not have a completely foreordained outcome. Craziness and experience count for a lot, but so does youth and desperation.

Which is why Rufus just plain dead-lifted old man Levitt off himself, grabbing hold of the man's torso and pushing, lifting that snapping spit-dribbling face a good foot away from his own, and then tossed the guy off to the side—the side *away* from the wrecking bar, too, for good measure. Rufus rolled toward the bar in time to avoid getting kicked by Mr. Levitt—who was up already, he was fast as a greased squirrel with rabies—and rolled over the pry bar and picked it up as he rolled. He managed to block Levitt's next kick with the bar, sending the old man hopping backwards and cursing. "What are you doing!" Rufus shouted, because he was at heart more of a talker and less of a fighter. "We're supposed to be on the same side here!"

"I'm a lot closer to the dead than I am to the living," Levitt said, reaching down to massage the shin he'd banged on the wrecking bar. "I've got different allegiances. You idiots deserve to be zombie food." He shook his head. "Why did Cyrus have to get sick *today* of all days? Yesterday I could have just endured your idiot company, but I'm tired of waiting, this is the day I've decided to *move*."

Rufus stood up, not feeling too bad, a little bruised maybe. He lifted the wrecking bar. "If I killed you now, Stevie Ray would believe it was self-defense."

"So do it then."

Rufus frowned. He wasn't about to beat an old man to death with a piece of steel, not now that he wasn't being actively attacked.

Levitt snorted. "Thought so. I'm taking the truck. Step out of my way and I won't try to kill you again."

"Where do you think you're going to *go*?" Rufus said. "You've got that tracking bracelet thingy on your leg!"

"How right you are. So why don't you just get out of my way, call Stevie Ray, and the two of you can just track me to my lair and bring me to justice. How about that?"

Crap. Did Levitt know the bracelet was useless, or did he just not *care*? "This doesn't make any sense." There was a whine in Rufus's voice, and he hated hearing it, but he hadn't learned to train the whine out of himself yet. "We're supposed to go on patrol! I thought you *liked* killing zombies!"

"Killing zombies." Levitt spat. "It's like jerking off. If you can't find someone to sleep with, sure, you jerk off, because it's better than nothing. But only a fool likes jerking off *better* than sleeping with someone else. I miss the intimacy of killing *real* people. People who can think, and be afraid."

"I'm not just going to let you go on a killing spree."

"Then you'll have to kill me."

Mr. Levitt stood looking at him for a moment. Rufus pulled out his handgun and pointed it at the old man. "Turn around and put your hands behind your head."

"No," Mr. Levitt said. "Wrecking bar, pistol, what do I care? I'm leaving. The only way you can stop me is to kill me. And I'll do my best to kill you if you try." He brushed past Rufus, who kept his gun up.

"I said stop!"

"Shut up, boy." Levitt climbed into the truck and shut the door. Rufus squeezed his eyes shut and pulled the trigger. The report of the handgun was enormous and made his ears ring.

He opened his eyes.

"Don't get down to the firing range much, do you?" Mr. Levitt said, looking at the driver's-side mirror Rufus had shot and pretty well blown apart. "Missing me at this distance, that takes a special kind of incompetence." Mr. Levitt hurled something out the window at Rufus, making him squawk and dance backward before realizing it was just his coffee thermos. "I can't drink caffeine anymore," Levitt said grouchily. "Makes my heart beat too fast and have to pee all the time. Getting old's a bitch, kid." He put the truck in gear and drove away. Rufus thought about firing the gun after him, but if he couldn't hit the old guy from three feet away, how could he hit him in a speeding-off vehicle?

Well, he'd just call Stevie Ray, and they'd track the old guy, and—

The radio was in the truck. With Mr. Levitt. And the phones didn't work any more. And, heck. He went into Levitt's garage to check the old guy's car, but it was out of gas, the tank siphoned dry by Stevie Ray's orders. Well, it was only a couple miles back to town. He'd run the whole way. At least the weather was nice. Rufus just hoped Mr. Levitt wouldn't kill anybody before they could track him down.

"Darn it," Stevie Ray said. "I thought the ankle bracelet would keep him from running off. Like a placebo effect." Stevie Ray stared off into space with a furious expression on his face, tapping his fingers on the top of his neat desk. "Or a deterrent. Whatever. Like those security cameras in stores that aren't even hooked up to anything, they're just supposed to make you *think* you're being watched. I really counted on Cyrus spying on him though."

Rufus nodded. "Levitt was pretty pissed that I was there and Cyrus wasn't. You think Cyrus is working with him?"

"I wondered," Stevie Ray said. "Thought about pulling him off Levitt and getting someone else to watch the old lunatic, but it's not like I've got a lot of manpower here. I sat Cyrus down and had a talk with him after the mayoral election, remember how he spoke up for Levitt? Cyrus told me he was just trying to get Levitt's trust so he wouldn't suspect him of reporting back to me, that he was deep undercover, all that. Maybe it was bullshit." Stevie Ray massaged his temples. "And now the old man says he's going on a killing spree?"

"That was, uh, more or less the gist, yeah."

"Okay then. We need to find him. Think you can get your Anti-Zombie club together to go hunting for him?"

"I can, but… they think he's a hero, Stevie Ray. They look up to him like some kind of badass, even with the rumors about him accidentally killing Ingvar." He put little air-quotes around "accidentally."

"Fair enough. Don't tell them he's a murderer. Tell them he's got a touch of dementia, we were trying to keep it quiet, but now he's having a bad spell and he's confused and he wandered off and we need to find him for his own protection." He paused. "Tell them he might get violent."

"That might work," Rufus said. "Are you coming?"

Stevie Ray shook his head. "I have to take care of something else. I was over at Julie's this morning and… never mind, I'll tell you later."

"Julie's, huh?" Rufus had been there the night before. "She, ah, doing well?"

"As well as any of us are," Stevie Ray said. "I'll go get her once I'm done with my other errand, and get her on the trail, too. Might have to tell her what Mr. Levitt *really* is. Probably better if more people I trust know it anyway."

Rufus coughed. "I, uh, think Julie knows about him. I guess… Otto told her." No harm in blaming the dead for your own in-discretions, he figured.

Stevie Ray actually smiled. "That woman sure can keep a secret."

"If we catch Mr. Levitt… what are we going to do with him?" Rufus wondered if they could even have a trial, really. A lot of people believed Mr. Levitt was a hero. They hadn't seen the bodies buried under his house coming back to life—they'd just heard the stories of him putting zombies back *down*.

Stevie Ray shook his head. "Postpone the problem, probably. Lock him up again. We never should have let him out. I'm sure he saved some lives, of course, being our chief zombie hunter… but not enough to offset the lives he's taken. Or *wants* to take. It'll be all right. Take this radio—it's the last one, so don't lose it or let another murderer run off with it. I thought Harry was crazy for ordering half a dozen of the things with the Homeland

Security money, but now I wish we had more. Remember, Levitt can hear anything we say over the air since he got your radio. Just set up a meeting and give people their instructions in person. And happy hunting."

5. DEATH IN
THE LIVING ROOM

When Dolph decided he wanted to take a larger hand in the town's affairs—to continue his penance for his horrible mistake with Gunther Montcrief, and to get himself out of the house sometimes because, committed as he was to fostering some of the displaced orphans from the battle of the bus crash, he hadn't changed so fundamentally that he'd stopped finding kids basically pretty annoying self-centered creatures. The older ones could watch the younger ones with only occasional course-corrections from him, but being in the cyclone of children—especially children cooped up all winter long, since even playing in the snow out in the yard was worrisome when you thought the little moppets might encounter zombies—was wearing. He needed to get out and do something useful that didn't involve kids.

The problem was, Eileen was in charge of town now, and Eileen didn't have much use for him. He was too ashamed to go talk to Stevie Ray, because the man had cut him so much slack and done him so many favors—Dolph was still officially free on his own recognizance, awaiting some future court date in some hypothetical future where a court existed—that he didn't want to impose any further. That left one other member of the newly formed town council with any actual authority and say-so: Julie Olafson.

As Dolph walked out to her farmhouse (it was only a few miles, and the weather was practically mild, and it wasn't like he had gas to spare), he pondered the stories he'd heard about Julie. Certainly she was a good granddaughter, returning from her life out in the wider world when her grandfather got sick. She was an excellent cook, made an adequate cup of coffee, ran a tight business—Dolph, whose business could at times have been a bit tighter, truth be told, appreciated that quality of competence—and was, by all accounts, a formidable woman. There were other rumors, murmured in the depths of the Backtrack Bar, that were hard to believe: that she was a lady of negotiable virtue, that she was a lesbian, that she liked sleeping with fathers and sons at the same time, that she had assorted "deviant" preferences (without much in the way of elaboration beyond "she likes things like they like out in California and New York City"), that she was a Democrat, and that she'd trained in the CIA as an assassin, though that last came from Cyrus, who also believed she'd traveled in the Orient learning mystical powers, served in the Earth First Battalion, and had personally killed several Al-Qaeda accountants. Since Cyrus got all his information from the people beaming signals to him from inside the hollow spaceship moon, his contributions could be safely ignored, though Julie did have a certain military quality in her bearing, and he'd once heard her offhandedly mention something about "the service." He didn't know what service that was. Maybe it would come up when he talked to her. Dolph was just the right age to have avoided being drafted for any wars, and he had the layperson's fascination with the military.

The Olafson house was a big old white-going-to-gray farmhouse, large enough for a family of ten or more, and once upon a time it had held that many—Julie had aunts and uncles innumerable, pretty much all ancient and/or dead and/or far away by now, though, certainly not up to caring for their even more astonishingly elderly father. Dolph went up the front steps and knocked on the door, honing his pitch, which emphasized heavily his willingness to do just about anything to make the world a better place. He'd voted for Julie in the mayoral election—he might let that slip, too, though it'd be heck to pay if word got back to Eileen, since there was pretty much an unwritten rule that you should vote for someone you've slept with if the issue comes up—because he liked what she had to say about making Lake Woebegotten into a green zone, a place of safety and prosperity. She was forward-looking, willing to engage with the world as it was, and she was a good listener—not like Eileen, who seemed to think running the town was no harder than running a house, and hated to take advice from anyone. Dolph would do whatever he could to be on the front lines of building a better future, even if it meant doing nothing but planting fields or chopping trees or catching fish or digging latrines.

Julie didn't come to the door. It was a big house, though, so he knocked harder and waited longer and, after a moment, saw someone moving inside, just a shape shuffling past a curtained window. "Julie?" he called. "That you?" No answer. He touched the doorknob, and it was unlocked—there was still no crime to speak of in Lake Woebegotten, and zombies were too stupid to work doorknobs, locked or not. He pushed open the door and said, "Julie, I don't mean to intrude, I can come back if it's a bad time, but—"

The zombie in the hospital gown jerked its head toward him and started shuffling forward. The ancient couch between them stymied the monster somewhat, and it grunted, saliva dripping down its front. Freshly dead, then—still had spit to dribble.

Dolph considered just stepping back outside and pulling the door shut and walking off, trusting in the lack of your average zombie's hand-eye coordination to keep Julie's brain-craving grandpa from causing him any trouble, but locking up your troubles—especially troubles in the form of zombies—and hoping for someone else to deal with the problem was something the *old* Dolph would have done, the Dolph who'd enjoyed afternoon delights with a married woman and reveled in the feeling of, well, *naughtiness* it gave him; the Dolph who'd seriously considered Eileen's suggestion that he become some sort of grocery-hoarding kingpin; the Dolph who'd pretty much died forever the same afternoon that Gunther Montcrief did. The new Dolph tried to face his responsibilities head-on. Julie might be in the house, in danger, or she might come home to find danger there, or the zombie might blunder out a window and stroll in just the right direction and end up in town biting some kid. So he had to do something. Well, all right then.

Dolph stepped into the living room and shut the door behind him. "Mr. Olafson, I'm sorry it's come to this. You made the best patty melt I ever had in my life, and you were never stingy with the butter."

Mr. Olafson didn't say anything, just kept trying to lurch through the couch toward him. Dolph looked around the room for something he could use as a weapon, and his eye fell upon one of the traditional implements favored by those who chose to keep and bear arms on the spur of the moment, as it were: a fireplace poker. He stepped carefully around the ottoman and the pile of old magazines and avoided the rucked-up hump of a throw rug, careful not to lose his balance or fall, because zombies could move quick when they thought there was easy meat on the floor. Dolph picked up the fire poker, a comforting iron weight, the end blackened from years of, well, poking at fires, as the name of the tool implied. The end would turn red when he swung it, he knew. Fresh zombies had fresh blood. Dolph didn't much like thinking about that.

Poor Mr. Olafson was totally stymied by the couch, too. He was trying to chew his way through the back of the couch now, unable to understand that he should walk around it, and apparently too uncoordinated to go over it. He'd been sick for a long time, and his body looked like a collection of matchsticks jumbled up in a pillowcase, and there were liver spots on his mostly-bald head, and wisps of white hair sticking up on the fringes like he'd just gotten out of bed. Which he had, pretty much, for the last time. Dolph walked over to him, lifting the poker, and sighed. He was supposed to crack this old man across the face, and then separate his head from his body? Maybe he could drag the old fella out back, look for an axe—the woodpile was back there, surely there was an axe somewhere nearby—and do it halfway cleanly. There'd have to be some initial violence to bring him down, though. One zombie wasn't really all that dangerous, Dolph realized, not if you were ready for it, and knew what you were up against, and paid attention. In fact, it was… kind of pitiful.

"I'm really sorry, Mr. Olafson," he said again, and closed his eyes, and swung the poker.

The sound was so loud that at first Dolph thought he had somehow hit the old man's head hard enough to make it explode, and indeed when he opened his eyes, half the gentleman's head was gone, one eye peering out from under a wispy-hair-framed liver spot, the other eye nowhere to be found. The funny thing was, Dolph hadn't even felt the impact of the poker hitting flesh, and shouldn't his arm be vibrating a little, and why wasn't there anything red—or for that matter gray—on the end of the poker anyway?

"It's all right, Dolph," Julie said from behind him. "He's... well... he was already dead. But he's dead again."

Dolph turned, and Julie was putting away a rather large pistol into a holster on her hip. The thing was, she wasn't wearing much except the pistol, and what appeared to be some strategically-placed bits of leather and chrome. Dolph's own fantasies about female attire leaned more toward women wearing stockings and high heels and things frilly and red, but there was certainly something arresting about her get-up. "Ah," he said, and then fell back on a dependable conversational standby: "That's a pretty nice-looking gun."

"It's an IMI Jericho 941," Julie said, patting the holster, which was also black leather, and matched the rest of her outfit. "Sometimes called a Baby Eagle. Forty-five caliber double action/single action semi-automatic. One of the models favored by the Israeli Army."

"Is that where you served?" Dolph asked, still just trying to keep a lid of normalcy on what was a rather surreal situation: holding a fireplace poker and standing over the dead grandfather of a woman in a fetish outfit.

Julie walked around the couch and looked down at her grandfather and sighed. "He was a good man. I'd hoped to be with him at the end, to make this part easier, but I was... busy." She glanced at Dolph. "Your question. Yes. I was a volunteer in the Israeli army for a few years."

Dolph said, "Oh."

"I'm Jewish, of course," she said. "Not very observant, but in college I took an interest in Israel, and also wanted combat training—self-defense was very important to me, for reasons I won't bore you with—and it's harder for a woman to get substantive combat training in the American services, so…" She shrugged. "The Israeli army has a program for foreign Jewish volunteers."

"I thought Mr. Olafson was Lutheran. Saw him at church a lot."

"He was Lutheran, originally. And he liked the sense of community at church, I think. But grandmother was Jewish, and grandfather converted when they were first married. Not that it mattered much for my mother and aunts and uncles and cousins and me, growing up—grandfather didn't want to give up any of the traditions he'd grown up with, so we just had Passover *and* Easter. Lefse and latkes, matzoh ball soup and beer cheese soup. You never noticed, he decorated the house with blue lights during the holidays, for Hanukkah?"

"I just thought he liked blue lights."

"That too," Julie said. "Well. He may not have been the most observant Jew, but I'd like to cover his body now, and light candles. You'll stay with him while I change clothes? And help me wash his body, and bury him afterward?"

"We're supposed to burn…" he said, but stopped at Julie's ferocious glare. "Whatever you want."

"My grandmother is buried in the family plot behind the house. She was laid to rest in just a shroud, as she wished. My grandfather wished the same. I hope the earth is soft enough to dig, now." She knelt, closed her grandfather's eyes—no magical passing-the-palm-over-the-eyes to close them trick here like they did in the movies, she had to actually touch the lid and pull it down and press it firmly with her thumb to make sure it stayed closed—and then took a woven afghan from the couch and draped it over his body, covering up almost everything but a few bone and brain fragments that had scattered farther away. "While we're digging, you can tell me what you were doing in my living room, hmm?"

6. MINNESOTA PASTORAL

I t occurred to Pastor Inkfist that, if Julie really thought there was an intruder or a zombie or something upstairs, it probably wasn't the most considerate thing for her to leave him tied up like this in the basement. "Julie?" he called, but she didn't answer, which didn't do his heart good. Daniel wasn't entirely naked. Julie had an array of interesting undergarments designed for the discerning male, and he was wearing one of the most uncomfortable of the bunch now, but while the discomfort was rather… enjoyable… under her attentions, at the moment it just chafed. His wrists here tied in front of him with soft red ropes, his ankles similarly restricted, and he figured he was gong to make a nice meal for a zombie.

After the council meeting broke up and the others left, Daniel lingered, and hemmed and hawed and finally asked if Julie had a little time this afternoon to fit him into her schedule, as it was.

"What do you propose to barter?" she'd asked, cool as you please.

"Ah, my wife, she had a lot of beauty products, you know, bath salts and shampoos and make-up and… um… luxury items, you know, like you can't get anymore…" His voice just trailed off as she slowly shook her head. "I guess maybe that's not your sort of thing," he said weakly.

"You might say that," she agreed. "Anything else?"

Daniel hadn't come here with much of anything in mind for trade besides the contents of his wife's medicine cabinet—he'd already given Julie some of his hand tools, a bunch of books, and all his spare pillows and blankets—but he thought hard and said, "Antibiotics! I've got, oh, half a bottle of amoxicillin. Doc Holliday prescribed them over the phone last year when my wife called thinking she had an ear infection, but it turned out she just had swimmer's ear, and she didn't end up using most of them. Are those any good to you?"

"Less than a year old? All right. You'll bring it next time. Are you ready now?"

"Yes."

"Yes, what?"

He'd closed his eyes and answered the way she liked to be answered, and she'd led him to the basement, and put on the outfit he liked, and put *him* in the outfit he liked, and started in with the implements, and then she'd heard a noise upstairs and now here he was in a not very tenuous position.

When he heard the gunshot up above, he closed his eyes and started to pray. *Oh Lord,* he thought, *if it is your will that I die here this day for my weakness, I will understand, but if you let me live another day, I will repent for my—*

Then he remembered Julie's original safety lecture. "What if I have a heart attack?" she'd said, as if there were anyone in town in better physical condition than she was. "While you're… compromised? That's why I'll always leave these where you can reach them."

He looked around, and there were the red-handled paramedic shears, strong enough to cut through leather, vinyl, canvas, and even light metals. Reaching them was easy—they were on the table with some other things that needed to be within reach—but maneuvering them with his wrists bound together was harder. He managed to cut through the ropes tying his ankles, but couldn't twist his hands sufficiently to cut the ropes around his wrists. Daniel ended up propping the shears on the table, holding them in place with some heavier items, slipping the ropes between the blades, and pushing the handle down with his chin. Awkward—especially the way these particular undergarments rode up—but it got the job done, and the ropes parted enough for him to get unwrapped and untangled.

He hopped around a bit getting out of the underwear, then put on his own clothes quickly, looking around for a weapon. If he wanted to *lash* a zombie, that was pretty well-covered, but he didn't think a cat-o'-nine-tails would make much of an impression. Likewise the cattle prod—which Julie said wasn't a *real* cattle prod, but one with a weaker current meant for use on people, no, that he'd wanted to dabble in that, especially. He didn't think zombies would respond much to electricity. At best, he'd make their skin burn, which wouldn't smell too nice.

He hunted around until he found a telescoping, locking metal rod, that happened to have a couple of leather cuffs dangling from the ends—some kind of bar for holding hands or feet apart, apparently. It had a nice heft to it, though, and would work as a club until he could find something better. Daniel crept up the stairs slowly, listening… and heard voices talking. Zombies didn't talk. Ergo, there weren't zombies up there. At least, not anymore. But Julie didn't talk to *herself*—at least, he doubted it, she was pretty self-contained—which meant someone *else* was up there.

Daniel put down the spreader bar, peeked into the kitchen—all clear—and hurried to the back door, out, and around the side. There were no unfamiliar vehicles in the driveway to give away the identity of the visitor. Probably not Edsel—he didn't talk quietly, and his voice carried—but it could have been anyone else. What if it was Eileen? The *mayor*? If *she* found out what he and Julie got up to, what he *paid* Julie to do, if she told…

He considered just running to his car and driving away, but that wasn't very Christian. What if Julie had a problem? Daniel straightened, tried to smooth down his hair by touch alone, went up the steps to the front door, and knocked, not too hard.

Julie answered the door, wearing a t-shirt and jeans now, and gave him just the barest hint of a smile. "Pastor. What can I do for you?"

"Just, ah, going around, checking on… everyone. How are you?"

"Come in," she said, standing aside. Daniel looked past her and saw Dolph standing by the couch, looking sort of shame-faced, and he thought, *another customer*?

"My grandfather passed away," Julie said. "I sent him to his second death. We were going to bury him."

"But we're supposed to burn—of course. Yes. He wanted to be buried? Next to his wife? Certainly. Perhaps you'd like me to say a few words?"

Another ghost of a smile. "Do you know the Kaddish, Pastor?"

Daniel had to admit that he did not, but he was willing to learn, because all paths to God were deserving of respect, even if he privately thought some of them were pretty darned odd.

After about forty minutes of chipping away at the earth—which was pretty pliable for the first five inches and then basically turned to stone—even Julie had to sigh and shake her head and admit they couldn't do the job with shovels. "Grandfather had an electrical post-hole digger," she said, and Daniel had a vision of trying to dig a six-foot-deep, six-foot-long, three-foot-wide hole one post-hole worth of dirt at a time. It was not a pleasant vision. Not as harrowing as the vision that assailed St. John the Divine, certainly, not an *apocalyptic* vision, but a vision of unbearable tedium.

"I, ah, know where we can get a backhoe," Dolph said, standing over by the shrouded corpse of Julie's grandfather.

"Today?" Julie said. "Right now? Jewish rites call for interment as soon as possible."

"Don't see why not," Dolph said. "It's at the construction site, where they tore down the old elementary school because after they pulled out the asbestos and lead and assorted toxins and carcinogens there was barely enough material left to even really consider it a building. They were supposed to be putting a rest home there, apparently that was the booming business, geriatric care, but, well, things have understandably stalled. The crew's from over in St. Elmer, and they didn't come back once the zombies started rising and such. But their backhoe is still there. Probably still gassed up. If the Reverend can drive me over, I can get it."

"Do either of you know how to drive a backhoe loader?" Julie asked.

"I drove a forklift a few times," Dolph said.

"A backhoe is not a forklift," Julie said, shaking her head. "Pastor?"

Daniel could barely drive a stick shift. "I don't think so…"

"Then you stay with grandfather," Julie said. "Dolph and I will take your car, and I will drive the backhoe here, and dig the grave."

"Ah, I could go with you," Daniel said, coughing into his fist. He'd spent his fair share of time with the dead, of course, any minister had, but he'd had his fill of corpses. Besides, he wanted to spend time with Julie, to talk to her, to talk *business* with her, regarding their particular form of business, which was of course a sin, but God couldn't be too upset about it, after all he'd let Daniel out of the basement alive and hadn't sent him into some sort of devoured-by-zombies situation, and he was a forgiving God, anyway, so why not give him a few things to forgive? It was expected.

"No, the body can't be left alone," Julie said. "Someone must attend it at all times. You are a man of God, after all—it should be you."

Before Daniel could protest further, Julie was holding out her hands for his keys. Daniel wanted to ask why they had to take *his* car, why they couldn't just take Julie's truck, but he knew it was because Julie loved her truck, and if she was going to be driving the backhoe, that meant Dolph would have to drive *her* truck, and she didn't let anyone else drive her truck. If he pressed, Julie would just explain that, completely unselfconsciously and unapologetically, and she might take it out on him later by, well, *not* taking it out on him, and he didn't want that. So Daniel handed over the keys and started explaining how sometimes the windshield wipers stick on the intermittent position and how the brakes are a little touchy, and Dolph started telling him about his own truck and how it pulls to the right, always has, you have to put a subtle leftward pressure on the wheel just to keep it straight, which reminded Daniel about his first car, a Pinto, and how the windows got frozen in the rolled-down position one winter and Daniel had to put trash bags over them when he parked to keep the snow out and had to wear earmuffs and a scarf all the time when driving, and then Julie went from tapping her foot and clearing her throat to actually pulling Dolph away in the direction of Daniel's car.

Then the pastor was alone, with the shrouded body of Julie's grandfather, out in the warmer-than-usual but still, objectively, rather cold day, wishing he'd asked if it would be all right to take the body back inside, or if that would be disrespectful. He didn't know a lot about Judaism, but he didn't look down on the faith, especially—if it was good enough for Jesus, it certainly wasn't his place to criticize it. Though the emphasis on burying bodies so quickly did make for a hectic day. Hardly time to organize a get-together after the funeral and get some hotdish and lemon bars for the survivors this way. Seemed kind of uncivilized.

Daniel stood watching the snow melt and thinking about the words he'd say once the body was finally in the ground, maybe something tying into springtime and renewal and things like that, working up some pretty good phrases that he could maybe use in his next service too, nothing wrong with a little recycling, assuming he was allowed to hold services what with the whole biotropic issue of zombies being attracted to large crowds of people, but that was a worry for another time.

Then a zombie bear with what appeared to be a hatchet stuck in its head came ambling around the side of the barn, lurching and stumbling, all crusty with blood and dirt and various oozing things, and Daniel suddenly had a worry that was very much of the moment.

7. BACKHOED

Mr. Levitt had originally planned to do the morning patrol with Cyrus, and then either convince the lunatic to drive him over to the construction site or just dispose of him, but with Rufus running around and sounding the alarm, Levitt had to move up his timetable. He got to the ruins of the old elementary school much earlier than anticipated, which ran the risk of throwing off his timing—he'd planned to lead the zombies into town right around evening mealtime, ringing a dinner bell as he went—but so what if the zombies arrived in town in time for a little lunch instead of their supper? A meal was a meal.

Rufus's continued habit of drawing breath was a trial and a vexation to Mr. Levitt. He didn't usually leave his victims alive—sort of negated the whole point of them being victims—but Rufus had been a bit tougher than Mr. Levitt had expected. Truth was, Levitt's heart was still beating hard and uncertainly, like he'd eaten too many cheese balls and bratwurst and ridden too many spinny rides at the state fair. The kid had managed to hurt him, and Levitt didn't like to think about how close Rufus had come to killing him before Levitt made his escape—an escape fueled by bluff, bluster, bullshit, and good luck. A small part of Levitt's brain thought, *You know, mostly you've killed people who trusted you, sneaking up on them from behind, or else you've killed zombies, which is no harder than chopping the head off a chicken once you get the hang of it, so maybe you're not as tough as you think you are,* but a lifetime of utterly assumed superiority quickly overwhelmed any self-doubt. The little punk Rufus had just gotten lucky. Lousy shot, too. Using a handgun wasn't even interesting, it was too *easy*, and the kid had even flubbed that, from a distance of just a few feet. You had to make an effort to be that terrible at something. Besides, leaving Rufus alive for now meant Levitt could feed him to the zombies later. A little treat. He'd have planned it that way in the first place if he'd given the subject any thought.

Levitt nosed the truck through the gate, busting the chain there, and drove through the fence, which was topped with barbed wire to keep out trespassers and would-be thieves, as if you got many of those in Lake Woebegotten. In the old days, nobody had bothered to lock up. Made it so much easier to get into people's houses back then...

Levitt parked behind the remains of the old school—in his years as school superintendent he'd suppressed the reports about the asbestos and such, not because he gave a damn about the cost to the county to fix it, but because he thought it was funny that the new generation of marching morons under his ultimate care were soaking up poison—and closed the gate again, looping the busted chain around to make it look, at first glance, like it had never been open. Then he did a walk-through around the construction site to see if he had everything he needed to do the job.

The spot was pretty isolated, surrounded by fields that wouldn't get planted this year if Levitt's plan worked, which it would, of course, so he took his time, figuring it was unlikely he'd be spotted. And if he was bothered, well, he'd gotten some goodies from Cyrus, most of which he'd had to leave behind at the house when he fled Rufus's assault, but he had a few things secreted in the pockets of his hunting jacket, including a few ancient but probably still potent fragmentation grenades, a pistol—currently unloaded with the clip in another pocket, which was why he hadn't pulled it out to use on Rufus—and a knife or three, naturally, for any close-in work. He didn't want to think about why he hadn't pulled one of *those* on Rufus. Mr. Levitt couldn't countenance the idea of cowardice in himself; he preferred to think of it as discretion, if he thought of it at all.

Mr. Levitt hummed as he collected materials. Some pieces of sheet metal, a roll of chicken wire, baling wire, tin snips. The big dirty yellow backhoe loader was all well and good, and he knew how to run one—he doubted the controls had been changed noticeably in the decades since he'd worked construction as a young man, burying his first victims in the foundations of buildings in St. Paul—but it wasn't exactly zombie-proof. An hour of snipping, heaving, bending, banging, and binding improved that situation a lot, though: once he was done, the open cab was enclosed on three sides with sheet metal, with slit windows messily cut and covered in chicken wire so he could see where he was going, and for the front opening he just made do with the chicken wire alone, with lengths of rebar woven through the links to provide some reinforcement. He festooned the hood and every other projecting surface with barbed wire to tangle up any would-be zombie boarders. The result was a kind of backhoe/tank that didn't even look half-assed—maybe one-quarter-assed at best—but it didn't need to be pretty, just moderately zombie-proof. In his various encounters with the creatures, Levitt hadn't been able to determine exactly how they sensed their prey, but they certainly seemed able to sniff out the living somehow, and if he was the only breather-in-residence, he figured they'd come at him. In fact, he was counting on it. He just needed to make sure they didn't *get* to him before he had the chance to lead them to a nicer sort of buffet.

Levitt climbed into the cab, pulling the sheet-metal door shut after him and twisting it closed with stiff metal wire. He put his hands on the controls. The keys were still in it, at least. So people hadn't *totally* lost all their trust. Be funny if he'd gone to all this trouble and the thing didn't have any gas, but when he cranked it up, the fuel gauge needle moved to three-quarters full. That would be fine. He wasn't going to be covering ground quickly in this thing, but the nearest graveyard was only a half mile away, and from there he'd work his way in toward the town, hitting the other graveyards, and, he hoped, building quite the little following along the way. Now, unfortunately, he had to sit in the thing for a while to let it warm up, since it hadn't been run all winter, and until some oil got circulating, he'd risk the thing seizing up and dying on him if he tried to make it do too much. He couldn't remember if it was safe to *drive* the thing while it warmed up, if he only had to worry about using the boom arm and dipper stick and bucket, because it had been so long since he'd done this kind of work, but he figured he'd better err on the side of caution. Waiting twenty minutes wouldn't kill him, but it was an unnecessary delay—he should have gotten the machine started while he was doing all his upgrades, but he hadn't thought about it for some reason, and now he had to pay the price by… sitting here, being bored, something he'd never been much good at doing.

That treacherous part deep in his brain said, *Getting harder to think, isn't it? You're getting tired more easily but you aren't sleeping much at night, you have to pee all the time, there are aches you never had before, you need reading glasses, you put things down and forget where you put them, that mind like a steel trap you were always so proud of is starting to go rusty, you're getting* old.

Well, darn it to heck, if he was getting old, he was going to end in a blaze of bloody glory. If he was going to die soon—time moved on, and it wouldn't wait for him, much as he wanted to believe otherwise—he was going to take as much of the world with him as he could. If Mr. Levitt was going to cease to exist, so was the town of Lake Woebegotten.

After ten minutes he couldn't stand it anymore, so he started up the backhoe and began trundling through the site, cursing because he'd forgotten to undo the gate and then just busting through it, because, what the heck, who cared? The bucket on the machine's front—like the scoop on a bulldozer—hung onto a chunk of the fence so he moved it up and down a couple of times to dislodge the metal. There. Free and clear. He turned left on the road and pushed the machine up to its top speed, which was all of about 25 miles per hour. Ah, well. He'd get there in time. The backhoe snorted and rumbled and vibrated fit to make his butt go numb, belching out diesel exhaust as it went.

Mr. Levitt couldn't help it: he whooped. There was something wonderful about piloting a big machine on an errand of devastation.

"Where the heck's the backhoe?" Dolph said, scratching his head.

"Judging by the smashed-open fence, I'd say someone stole it." Julie walked around the side of the road a bit, peering at the ground. The snow was melting, but there was still enough to show tracks, and she pointed. "There, see? It was driven out of here, and turned left. Away from town. Odd." She sniffed. "I can still smell the exhaust in the air, can't you?"

Dolph sniffed, and she was right. The air had been so pure since the zombie apocalypse started, he should have noticed the sweet chemical tang in the air right away. "Yep," he said. "Why would someone steal the backhoe? I mean, I know *we* were going to, ah, borrow it, but, no offense, I doubt there's another family that needs to do a Jewish funeral real quick."

"It does seem improbable," Julie said. "I'm curious. Aren't you?"

"You bet."

"Then let's follow the trail. Even on a snowy road, we can go faster than a backhoe loader, don't you think? If we can still smell the exhaust, it can't be far. If it's someone on a legitimate errand, we'll wait our turn to borrow the machine. And if it's something more nefarious…"

Nefarious, Dolph thought. *What a woman.* "At least we know zombies can't drive tractors," he said.

Julie nodded. "True. But living humans are much more dangerous than zombies. It's just, zombies are *always* dangerous, and the living are only *sometimes* dangerous. It can be confusing." She got back into the car, and Dolph followed.

Mr. Levitt got to the Ebenezer Lutheran Cemetery—the biggest one in town, so the most important one to hit—and got to work right away. He maneuvered the backhoe toward one of the areas that had seemed the most active during his reconnaissance earlier in the winter, worked the levers, and—after a few false starts that knocked over headstones and threatened to tip over the whole loader—he got the backhoe extended out to pretty much its maximum, dipped the bucket into the earth, and started scraping the first few feet of soil off a whole row of graves. He dumped the dirt and moved on to the next section of graveyard, not bothering to see if his work had done any good. He figured the zombies had probably smashed through the tops of their coffins already, and just needed a hand getting through the hard earth above them. If he dug down *too* deep, or went over the same spot more than a couple of times, he'd risk hitting zombies who'd already dragged themselves partway to the surface, and though dismembered undead were highly amusing, they weren't much good for his purposes.

After scraping half a dozen rows of graves, he noticed some movement out of the corner of his eye and turned to look through one of his slit windows.

There. A dirt-streaked hand reaching up from the ground in the iconic rising-from-the-grave zombie style, beloved of movie posters and cheap paperback book covers. A corpse dragged itself out of the earth, looking shriveled but basically whole, wearing a filthy black suit. Looked like it had been an old man, but zombies didn't suffer the aches and pangs of the elderly *living*—one advantage Mr. Levitt had to admit they had over himself. There was other movement in the dirt, so he turned back to his work, running the backhoe a fair distance away. The loader was slow, but he could give a bunch of even slower zombies a pretty good runaround, and do a couple of circuits through the graveyard at the end to attract any stragglers to him. They'd follow him to the next graveyard, and the next, and then to the center of town, and then... buffet time. Even on an ordinary day there were always people in the bar, and the Cafe during the increasingly few hours when it was open, and people lined up taking the last of that idiot Dolph's giveaway supplies, and getting together at the community center, and who knows, on a day like this, spring beginning to peek out its head, there might even be people in the park in the center of town, or on the Larry "Old Hardhead" Munson Memorial Baseball Field, having a slightly snowy pickup game. And, of course: there was the new elementary school, built some years back to replace the old one. Closed all winter, of course, in light of the emergency, but the town council had pushed to get it going again, drafted some teachers—who seemed to like having something to do—and managed to get the little ones out from underfoot. He wondered if zombies liked children better than adults—if they had more life, if they were tastier. Mr. Levitt didn't have any particular interest in children—they were too easy to scare, they didn't pretend to be brave, it was dull—but he knew unleashing zombies on them would thoroughly unhinge any of the townspeople who managed to survive this onslaught.

Waiting until a night with a town meeting would have been better for maximum carnage, but Mr. Levitt's boredom had gotten the best of him, and he couldn't stand waiting any longer. Besides, as the weather got warmer, he would've risked the chance of zombies crawling out of graves on their own, and once the town was alerted to the time bomb in their cemeteries, they would have taken steps to deal with the problem.

Mr. Levitt scraped some more graves, and now there was a goodly horde of fifteen or twenty zombies staggering toward him, men and women, dirty and disheveled, some with just ragged stumps at the ends of their arms, probably having destroyed their hands in the process of smashing out of their coffins. Ah, well. Long as they still had teeth.

Then the horde of zombies swerved away from him, toward the cemetery's front gate, and why would they do *that*, when Mr. Levitt was the only fresh meat for miles?

The answer was simple. Someone else was here. That wouldn't do.

A moment later there was a whine, a crack, and a hole appeared in the sheet metal about a foot to the left of his head. Mr. Levitt stared. Someone was *shooting* at him.

That wasn't very sporting. He'd have to do something about that.

He reached into his coat and took out a grenade.

8. WHAT TO DO WHEN THE WORLD EXPLODES

66 can't hit him at this distance," Julie said, lowering her weapon. She was standing by the driver's side, using the car's roof to steady to her aim, and coincidentally keeping the car between her and the oncoming zombies. "I'm firing blind, since the vehicle is armored, and I didn't bring extra ammunition with me—I can't afford to just shoot at him blind." She shook her head. "I have to loop around, get a clear shot."

"Uh," Dolph said, crouching beside her, wishing he had a gun. "But... zombies."

"Yes. Zombies. And in that backhoe loader, a man, trying to free *more* zombies. If we don't stop him, the situation gets markedly worse, very quickly. Who can it be? Who would do such a thing?"

"Mr. Levitt," Dolph said promptly.

"Ah," Julie said. "I'd heard he was more... sinister... than he seemed. That he was a monster. Monsters do have their place in a conflict. I knew some, in the military, people who channeled their desire to kill into socially acceptable works. But, if this monster was leashed and serving us before, that seems to have changed, doesn't it?"

"I'd say so."

"Then I'll shoot him in the head."

Dolph, who'd accidentally shot another human being in the head not so very long ago, fought a wave of nausea. "Uh, just, like that, in cold, uh, cold..."

"It's self-defense. His weapon is a backhoe. His bullets are *zombies*. You understand that?"

"I do. Yeah, I do."

"Good. You run that way—some of the zombies will pursue you, but you should be able to outrun them. I have a better chance if I don't have to avoid *all* the creatures myself."

Dolph closed his eyes for a moment. He'd wanted to help, to serve the town, and had told Julie as much, he'd come to her to get an assignment, to find out how he could do some good. Apparently by being unarmed zombie bait. Well, heck. Being a man was about doing things you didn't want to do, sometimes. "Yes, ma'am," he said.

"Now," Julie said, and Dolph set off running, wishing there were some big crypts to hide behind, but this was a Lutheran cemetery, so it was mostly modest low headstones. He looked over his shoulder after a few seconds to see how many zombies he was attracting—there had to be thirty of them milling around by now, drifting toward the car—and how far Julie had gotten but instead he saw Mr. Levitt pushing open his improvised sheet-metal door and popping out of the backhoe like an elderly sideways jack-o-lantern. He hurled something overhand toward the car, which was odd, because what was he going to do, throw a *rock* to try to scare them off, or—

The first explosion was eardrum-shatteringly loud, and the second explosion, which he realized later was the car's gas tank catching fire and blowing up, was both loud and *hot*, and a wave of burning air pressed against his back and tossed him, not too gently, toward a nearby headstone, and it was only by terrific twisting in the air that he managed to smash his shoulder into a chunk of good weathered marble instead of smashing open his head. He couldn't hear much, his ears were ringing, but underneath the ringing there was something—laughter. That old bastard Mr. Levitt, *laughing*, big old belly laughs, just like he'd laughed the night Dolph saw him chainsawing zombies to death.

Dolph got to his feet, swaying and unsteady, and promptly discovered the zombies aren't distracted at all by exploding cars. They were dedicated. Focused. One-track minds.

And that track said "lunch," and the special of the day was lightly-toasted Dolph, and there wasn't so much as a tree branch he could use for a weapon.

When the car exploded, Julie thought: *He has grenades. That is bad. He has destroyed our transportation. That is also bad.* Nor could she call for backup. The town council had to share one radio, and Eileen had theirs today, and cell phones had stopped working ages ago.

There was only a single sentient hostile, though. Get a clear shot at him, and she'd be fine—the zombies were manageable. Let him be distracted by the merrily burning car while she crept up on him. Levitt's sightlines—if indeed it was Levitt—had to be hampered by the improvised armor on the backhoe. That would work to her advantage.

As she crept through the churned-up dirt, keeping an eye on the encroaching zombies at her three-o'-clock and another eye on the backhoe, which didn't leave an eye for much of anything else, she dearly hoped Dolph had gotten clear of the explosion. He seemed a nice man, and was attractive—by local standards—and she'd thought of taking him as a lover, since Rufus was enthusiastic but ultimately unsatisfactory in bed due to his tendency to treat the female body like a video game controller, where if he executed the same combination of button-presses and joystick-diddles exactly the same way each time, the result would also be identically successful. Julie had tried to teach him that making love was like fighting a battle: plans were well and good, and having tactics in mind was certainly laudable, but you had to pay attention to the situation on the ground and adapt your approach to rapidly-changing conditions... except whenever Julie began talking to Rufus that way, he started talking about some military video game, and their meager common ground was promptly lost.

Julie liked sex. She'd largely gone without during her time in the Israeli Army, and she'd missed it immensely. Her training had taught her the importance of pragmatism, and she was pragmatic about her love life, too. She didn't lie, except by omission—men could be silly when they found out about other men—and she made no promises. She got what she wanted, and gave good value in return.

The sex was different from the domination stuff. That was just a good way for a healthy woman with a lot of self-confidence and no foolish inhibitions to make money, or, in this new world order, obtain antibiotics and generator fuel.

But this wasn't sex; this was a literal battle, and she couldn't let her worry over Dolph's possibly-exploded condition distract her from the matter at hand.

She squatted behind a headstone and braced her wrists on top, gun extended. The zombies were a good forty yards away, shuffling toward her slowly, and the backhoe was turning in her direction, soon to point its more-exposed front toward her. As long as he kept the front shovel low instead of raising it like a shield—which is what Julie would have done—she could put a bullet through the chicken wire and into Levitt's chest. Turn, turn, turn, almost there—

Something grabbed Julie's legs and pulled. She took one hand off the pistol and steadied herself, looking down to see a horrible worm-eaten face pressing up out of the soil as the occupant of the grave she was crouching over began pulling himself out of the dirt, using Julie's legs for a handhold. She pointed the pistol at its face, then paused, because the gunshot would alert Levitt to her existence. He might think she was dead in the car explosion if she kept quiet, but if she made noise… he had grenades. A pistol was very little good against a grenade.

So Julie rolled away, and kicked at the zombie's face, hearing bone crunch. It was only partially out of the ground, still buried to halfway up its chest, so she got to her feet, reared back her foot, and kicked as hard as she could, as if trying to drive a soccer ball down the length of the field.

The zombie's head, not being attached with a great deal of structural integrity after its time in the grave, separated and went rolling across the grass. Julie crouched back in her position, lifting the pistol… but the backhoe was trundling away, showing her only its backside, and even if she squeezed off a shot at this distance there was no chance she'd actually hit the old man, not with a piece of sheet metal blocking her sight of his precise position. Most of the zombies—more than she could easily count—were following after the backhoe, more attracted to Levitt than herself, presumably because they'd been closer to his position when he left, though three or four zombies were ambling toward her, and there was another knot across the cemetery, possibly in the process of eating Dolph?

Julie took a deep breath. Mr. Levitt was a problem, but she had more immediate problems. She lifted her gun, took aim, and fired seven times, killing four zombies with headshots. Meaning she'd missed three times, hitting chests or limbs. Usually a shot in the mass of the body was good enough, but with zombies, only headshots were relevant. She needed more practice shooting, she was rusty, but even with Cyrus Bell's significant and shocking collection of weapons and ammunition, bullets were not infinite, and wasting them on target practice seemed contraindicated.

After checking hurriedly to confirm the zombies were dead, she ran as best she could over the broken earth, through smoke-filled air, to see if she could save Dolph from relatively certain death.

Dolph didn't have a weapon, and he had zombies, and he needed to reverse those situations as soon as possible. Not usually a particularly quick thinker—sometimes a rash *actor*, yes, of course, but not a particularly swift cogitator—he found that shambling corpses with snapping jaws concentrated his mind pretty well. He stripped off his coat and tore off his flannel shirt, popping the buttons, leaving him in just his undershirt, which reminded him that, spring or not, it was still *cold*. He dodged around the zombies toward a hunk of smoldering wreckage hurled out of the car's engine. At a glance he wasn't sure what it was, a fuel pump or distributor cap or who knows what, but it was heavy, and ouch darn it, *hot*. He spread out his shirt on the ground like a blanket and nudge-kicked the lump of fused smoking metal into the center of the cloth, hoping it wasn't hot enough to get the shirt burning, because that would sorta defeat the purpose. Dolph grabbed the sleeves and shirt tails and tied a couple of knots and turned to face his enemies, new weapon dangling in his hand.

He didn't know if this kind of weapon had a name—over-sized sap? homebrew mace?—but it was the same general idea as wielding a tube sock full of quarters, or a pillowcase with a toaster inside it, or a scarf with one end tied around a can of beans. A rope with a weight at the end. Dolph started the weapon swinging, and it felt pretty good. He swung out and caught one of the three zombies on the side of the head hard enough to make its neck snap, and that zombie crashed into the other ones, but not hard enough to send them off balance. Dolph kept his weapon spinning as he backed up, hoping he wouldn't trip over one of those recessed headstones that sit flat on the ground, just waiting to catch your heel and tip you over backwards.

Julie appeared behind the zombies, and Dolph's heart soared. She lifted her pistol, closed one eye…

And nothing much happened, and Julie looked at her gun in disgust, and Dolph—who'd stopped backing up when he saw Julie because he didn't want to accidentally step or stumble into her line of fire—was suddenly way too close to a pair of zombies, with a weapon that didn't do much good if you were closer in than arm's length. He did his best, swinging at the nearest zombie—who'd been buried, inexplicably, in one of those powder-blue tuxedos, and was missing most of his nose, which didn't help his appearance any—but the blow didn't have any force in it, and the shirt just wrapped around the zombie's neck, not even giving it pause. The other zombie tried to get at him, and the two creatures sort of got tangled up as they attempted to inhabit the same prime biting space at once, giving Dolph another moment to dance back, but then, of course, wasn't that always the way, he *did* encounter one of those flat grave markers and, splat, over on his ass, that's all she wrote, zombie chow, no doubt.

But there was Julie, reaching out and grabbing both zombies by the side of the head and slamming their decaying noggins together with a good loud crunch. Then she did something fancy and spinny that involved her leg sweeping out their legs and the zombies fell. Julie reached down to the one with Dolph's shirt wrapped around its neck—that zombie was face-down—

grabbed both ends of the shirt, planted her foot between the zombie's shoulder blades, and pulled up on the shirt while she pressed down with her foot.

After a moment of terrific strain, the zombie's neck popped. It didn't come clean off the neck, the body was too recently dead for that, Dolph supposed, but the connections between brain and spinal cord were sundered, and that was enough, apparently, because the body stopped moving and the head contented itself with gnawing at the dirt. Meanwhile Dolph got to his feet and aimed a kick at the other zombie.

The kick didn't go so well. The zombie turned its head at the last minute and the toe of Dolph's boot went right into its mouth. Dolph wasn't wearing his steel-capped workboots, either, but his comfier leather hiking boots, since he'd taken that walk out to Julie's house, comfort was important, but as the zombie's unspeakably powerful jaws closed down and he felt the leather pressing against the tops of his toes he regretted choosing comfort over steel. He'd be toeless, and he'd get one of those nasty infected zombie bites, and even if he survived this encounter, it'd mean a slow death, or maybe a foot amputation to stop the infection if Morty the paramedic was up to such a procedure.

"Pull your foot out!" Julie said, and Dolph tried, but the zombie was like a snapping turtle. Dolph knew a fella once who had snapping turtles in his pond, and the way he cleaned it out was, he stuck a broomstick into the pond, and a bunch of snapping turtles bit down on the stick, like they'd bite down on anything, and he pulled the stick out of the water with a bunch of turtles hanging from it, dangling, all their weight hanging from their jaws, but they wouldn't let go, and the fella just took a machete and whack, whack, whack, separated the heads from the bodies, and the shells just thunk, thunk, thunked on the ground. Jaws held onto the stick for a minute after the heads were severed, too, he said, though Dolph was never sure if he believed that part. He wished he had a machete now, though.

"No, pull your *foot* out! Of the boot!" Julie said, and this time Dolph got it, curling his toes away from those grinding teeth—which hadn't parted the leather, quite—and kneeling to untie the laces, his fingers stupid and stumbly and cold, finally getting the laces limber enough that he could pull his foot, clad in a thick wool sock, free.

The zombie chewed on the boot for a moment, lashing its head back and forth like a puppy with a chew toy, before it realized it had lost the chewy center, and it lifted its head. This time Julie stomped down on the back of its neck—Dolph shuddered to think what would've happened if she'd stomped like that with his foot in the zombie's mouth, the impact would have cost him toes for sure—and the thing stopped moving, except for its head. A zombie with a broken spine was still a cranky biting thing, but the lack of mobility made them a lot less dangerous.

"We have to get back to town," Julie said. "We have to warn everyone. Stevie Ray, Eileen, Father Edsel, all of them. Levitt is coming. And he is bringing zombies."

"I'll get the car—" Dolph said, then remembered the car was a smoking wreck. He reached down and tried to pull the boot out of the zombie's mouth. The zombie didn't want to let go. Dolph sighed. "Give me a hand with this? I can't walk back to town with just one boot on."

9. A PASTOR AND A POLITICIAN WALK INTO A BEAR

Not long after the meeting at Julie's house, Eileen decided the other woman had to die.

It was nothing personal. Not that Eileen liked Julie personally, because she didn't, but the need for killing was strictly political, and occasionally secular rulers had to do such things, had to take—what did they call it in thriller novels? extraordinary sanctions?—well, they had to kill people, that's all. Julie had lost the mayoral race but she was still sticking her nose in, researching zombies, babbling about green zones, and making Stevie Ray and Father Edsel dance to her tune. And the worst of it was seeing Pastor Inkfist making those moon eyes at the woman all during lunch. Disgusting. Sure, Eileen often found the pastor exasperating, but she was his right-hand woman, the head of the Women's Circle, the person in his congregation who actually got things *accomplished*. Unlike Julie, who didn't even come to church. Maybe she wasn't Lutheran. She wasn't Catholic, either. Being Catholic wasn't as good as being Lutheran but being neither one was even worse, that was for sure.

Julie was a threat to Eileen's security. Since Eileen didn't have a black-ops team of special forces soldiers at her disposal—though that was one of her fantasies, only in the fantasies the muscular, devoted young men served her in the bedroom and battlefield both, not that she'd ever admit to such imaginings in a hundred million years—she had to take care of business herself. So be it.

Eileen had access to guns, but a gun was no good. A gun

implied a human hand, and Eileen couldn't have that. Not that Stevie Ray was up to doing a complex investigation with ballistics and forensics and such, but why even make him suspicious? You could get away with murder in this town—obviously, look at Mr. Levitt, Eileen was going to have to do something about him soon, couldn't have people like that walking around loose, no matter how much dirty work they were willing to do—but it was better by far if no one suspected you of murder in the first place. So Eileen threaded her way through her house full of noisy guests, going into the garage.

Ah, the garage. With Mustang Sally still sitting there, shiny and red. The other woman who happened to be a car. The garage should have been the site of Eileen's first great triumph, but things had gotten so messy here. She'd learned from her mistakes though. Her next murder would go a lot more smoothly. Eileen went to the workbench and considered the items there, finally choosing a huge red pipe wrench. The weight in her hand was considerable and reassuring. She slipped the wrench into her purse—the handle stuck out, but so what, who was going to see it?—and went out to the driveway, climbing into her little car (she had a gas ration, for town business, which this was) shouting to the woman smoking a cigarette on the front steps to put that thing out, there were kids around, and then reversing out of the driveway and heading for Julie's.

She had plenty of time to think about her plans on the drive over. They were pretty simple. Get into Julie's house. Get Julie to turn her back. Bash Julie over the head with the pipe wrench. Throw her body down the basement stairs, and just shut the door behind her. Zombies were no better at climbing stairs than they were at using doorknobs, probably, so she'd stay down there with the other zombie. Sure, somebody would no doubt come over and check on Julie eventually, and they might encounter the basement zombie and get killed, and yes, Julie's grandfather who'd been a nice old man was sure to die in his sickbed of the neglect and subsequently become zombified himself, but those problems could be dealt with later. Getting rid of the threat to Eileen's power was the important thing.

Eileen pulled into the farmhouse's driveway. Julie's truck

was there, which was promising. Such a big house, and nobody in it except Julie herself, who hadn't taken in even one single boarder, who'd never offered, and, when asked, had simply said she couldn't do it, because she needed her privacy. No explanation, no apologies, and while Minnesotans were deft at applying social pressure, Julie seemed completely immune, even indifferent, to such pressure. It just wasn't fair that Eileen's house was crammed with refugees and Julie's was empty. It made sense now—Julie had a secret zombie R&D lab in the basement—but that was no excuse. Once Julie was dead, Eileen could have the town seize the farmhouse and turn it into a refugee camp. Move everyone out of *her* place. That would be satisfying. Julie would finally do Eileen some good in her death.

Eileen went up to the front door with her pipe wrench in her purse and knocked on the door.

It opened a crack, then all the way—and Pastor Inkfist was there, hair disheveled, eyes wild. He grabbed Eileen by the arm and pulled her through the door, slamming it shut and locking it behind him. "Did you see the bear?" he asked.

"Bear? What bear?"

Pastor Inkfist went to a window across the living room, passing by a—was that a puddle of *blood*? What had happened here after Julie showed them the zombie? Was she already dead? "Where's Julie?" she asked.

"Gone with Dolph." He looked out the window, head turning ceaselessly back and forth, a motion that reminded her uncomfortably of a zombie's automatic movements.

"Ah. Dolph? Pastor, what's going on?" She wanted to slap him, shake him, and make him answer her, but the pastor was easily befuddled. He could be moved the way you wanted him moved with a little patience though. "Please, you're scaring me." Eileen wasn't scared—annoyed, yes—but he *expected* her to be scared, and if she did as he expected, he might do as she wished.

He turned from the window, running a hand through his hair, which didn't make it any less messy. "Of course, Eileen, mayor, that is, I'm sorry." He took a deep breath. "Julie's grandfather died. Became a zombie. Julie killed him. I came over to talk to her about some, ah, town business—"

Eileen ground her teeth at that. *What* town business? Any town business should go through *her*.

"—and I found her and Dolph getting ready to bury the old man. I was going to help dig the grave, but the ground was too frozen—"

"We're supposed to burn bodies," Eileen said. "We agreed." Julie, flouting the rules, as if they didn't apply to her! *That* could get her kicked off the council, at least. Since it didn't look like Eileen would be able to murder her today. At least she could remove the woman from influence.

Pastor Inkfist looked at her as if she were an idiot, and she wanted to smash him across the face with her pipe wrench, but instead she just returned his stare, and he cleared his throat. "Be that as it may. Dolph and Julie went to get a backhoe from the elementary school construction site so they could dig a grave with it, though they've been gone a while now, and anyway, I was staying with the body, it's a Jewish rule, that the body not be left unattended—"

Jewish? Who the heck was Jewish? Eileen supposed she'd probably met Jews, once or twice, though she couldn't have said when exactly.

"—and so I've been hiding in here ever since," the pastor said.

Eileen realized she'd missed something. That Jewish business had thrown her. "Since what?"

"Since I saw the *bear*." The pastor was no good at hiding his exasperation. "The zombie bear with a hatchet in its head. It's still out there somewhere, and if it's biotropic like the human zombies are, it's going to be *twice* as interested in us now that you're here. Though at least it hasn't touched the corpse, Julie would be so angry if that happened, a real bear might be interested in a dead person, but I suppose zombie bears don't stoop to, well, I hate to say 'carrion,' but a body is a body, but then again aren't you supposed to play dead if a bear attacks you, or is that only with grizzly bears?" The pastor shook his head, sharply—had he, wonder of wonders, realized he was babbling? He usually *never* realized that, especially not when he gave his sermons. "Oh, I hope Julie gets back soon," he said. "She can help us, she can take care of all this—"

"We don't need Julie," Eileen snapped. "We can certainly handle this ourselves." If there even *was* a bear, which Eileen would want to see before she believed.

She got her wish.

While it's true that zombies lack the fine motor skill to open doors, bears never had those motor skills anyway, so zombie bears don't feel the lack. This particular zombie bear, which was probably not the only zombie bear in the world but was certainly the only one in Lake Woebegotten at the moment, could sense the life inside the farmhouse. All it wanted was that life, to consume it, to take it into itself. The bear wasn't a bear anymore. It wasn't even a dead bear.

It was total need in the *shape* of a dead bear.

The zombear stopped ranging around the house, came up on the porch, stood upright, put its paws up on the big window there, and pushed in toward the life.

The window shattered, and a few hundred pounds of undead bear crashed through it. The bear had some trouble getting the back half of its body over the sill, lacking the coordination of the living, and Pastor Inkfist—in what might have been bravery, but was more likely panic—snatched up a standing lamp and rushed the bear, swinging the long wooden pole and smashing the bear on the head with the lampshade. The bear had a *hatchet* in its *head*, surely it was pretty close to having its brain destroyed anyway, so if he could slam the lamp down on the hatchet—though the blade was *huge*, it was like the snapped-off top of a battleaxe—maybe he could drive it deeper into the creature's head, like hammering a wedge into a piece of wood. Get it deeper into the brain, destroy enough to make the darn zombie lie down already.

The bear didn't take much notice of the lamp, and managed to clamber over the sill, making Daniel move back. He whacked it across the head with the lamp again, and this time only succeeded in dislodging the hatchet completely. The wound in the bear's head didn't even look that serious, there was a little bit of white skull peeking out, but no gray of brain. The blade clattered to the floor, and Eileen snatched it up. "Amateur," she said, sniffing. "Get out of the way and let a professional do the killing, would you?"

Daniel stared at her, still holding his lamp-club—the shade was totally destroyed, the bulb shattered, he hoped Julie wouldn't be annoyed—and thinking, *Professional what?* Eileen was probably a good housewife and was certainly a ferocious organizer, but neither of those things qualified her as a zombie bear killer of particular note. Though she *had* killed her zombie husband, which indicated a willingness to do the deed, at least, so he stepped aside.

Eileen walked up to the bear, pretty as you please, and raised the hatchet up high. If looks could kill the undead, the bear would have dropped over right away. The contempt on Eileen's face was *scorching*.

But the bear didn't care. It reached out with one giant paw, almost lazily, and swatted Eileen to the floor. Dazed, she said, "What—what—" and the bear lowered its head and took a big bite out of her belly.

Daniel screamed and ran for the front door, snatching Julie's keys off the wall, and climbed into her truck—even though he knew she'd never beat him again, not after such a transgression, no matter how dire his straits, he was leaving her grandfather's body unattended, too, that was even worse—and started driving toward town as fast as he could. If he could get to Stevie Ray, get Father Edsel, they could get the Anti-Zombie Society into action, they could kill the bear, and Eileen, Eileen too, if she rose, oh, what a horrible thought, a zombie *mayor*, the town's *second* zombie mayor, nobody was going to want to run for office next time, no sir.

Being town minister wasn't such a great job, either, though.

10. EYES IN THE SKY

After Stevie Ray sent Rufus on his Levitt-hunting mission, he got in the patrol car and drove through the center of town, kinda slow, in case the old guy was lurking in wait. Didn't seem likely, but Levitt was sort of like a horror movie monster—you halfway expected to see him pop out of just about anywhere.

Stevie Ray drove on out of the center of town, past the park, and the baseball field, and the library, and the lodge of the Pretty Good Brotherhood of Cnut. Some wit had vandalized their sign with red spray-paint in the form of a proofreader's mark indicating the "n" and the "u" should be transposed, but the joke was lost on everyone except maybe the occasional English teacher. Everyone else was merely mystified by the appearance of a sideways 'S' on the sign, though a few assumed it had something to do with Satanism, and had complained to Stevie Ray about it. Cleaning up graffiti was pretty far down on his list of important tasks, though, and anyway, it was the Brotherhood's own fault for not spelling it Knut or Canute or any of the other ten ways the name could be Anglicized.

The brothers were all right, though. Old guys, but many were veterans of foreign wars, and he'd told them to feel free to sharpen up those supposedly Viking swords they marched with in the Fourth of July Parade every year, just in case they needed to act as shock troops and behead an invading zombie army. He'd figured that was unlikely until Julie sprang this whole biotropic thing on him. Now he knew the town glowed like a beacon for any passing zombies looking for a feast. It was time to institute some defensive measures.

After a while Stevie Ray reached the Borg Co-Op Grain Elevator, rising in splendid isolation here near a great confluence of fields. The elevator was the highest point in town, higher even than the water tower, and the daredevil Stevie Ray had sent a message to—asking a town teenager to run it over in person since there weren't enough radios and weren't any phones—was here waiting for him.

Malcolm Madland was a dark-haired moody teenager and something of a troublemaker, but in a fairly harmless way. Mostly he enjoyed climbing things, and was the town's only tagger. He'd put his graffiti on the side of the water tower, on the roofs of most of the businesses, and on pretty much any other place that was inaccessible for the average person. Harry had found him more exasperating than anything else, and mostly made him paint over his own graffiti, which was fine with Malcolm; he just liked climbing high and splashing paint, and painting over his old tags just gave him a blank canvas for the next batch. Eventually Harry told him that he'd be a more successful criminal if he stopped *signing his work*, and from that point on Malcolm stopped using the big loopy overlapping "MM" symbol he favored and started spray painting other incomprehensible designs. Like Harry said, "I still know it's *him*, but at least now he's making an honest effort at covering his tracks."

Malcolm was the obvious culprit for tagging the Brotherhood's sign, but the wit seemed maybe a little beyond him. If it had been a picture of a penis, then Stevie Ray would have been comfortable accusing him, but given the nature of the crime, he had his doubts.

"You call me here to hassle me, copper?" Malcolm said, smoking a cigarette. "You gonna rub me out?"

Copper? *Rub me out*? Malcolm must have gotten his hands on some gangster movies from the forties. Better than "pig" at least. "Pig" as an insult had never made sense to Stevie Ray, really, though. Pigs were smart, smarter than dogs. And they were delicious. They provided livelihood for a lot of the farmers around here too. They could get smelly. There was that.

"I need your help, actually. You ever climb to the top of the grain elevator?"

Malcolm cut his eyes left. "No. Course not."

Of course, yes. "Now's your chance, then," Stevie Ray said. "I need a lookout. Someone to climb up there, and stay up there a while, scanning the horizon in all directions. You can't do it all yourself, but you're the first one I thought of."

Malcolm frowned. "What'd I be looking for?"

"Oh, you know. Military convoys. Cars with survivors. Now that it's spring, people might use the roads again, we might have some visitors." Stevie Ray cleared his throat. "People. On foot. Especially… large groups of them. You can see for miles on a clear day, all the way across the prairie."

"Like a pirate in a crow's nest," Malcolm said thoughtfully. Then he remembered to sneer. "Why should I help you?"

Stevie Ray shrugged. "There's only so much spray paint left in town. I confiscated Dolph's whole supply. Help me out, and I'll make sure a few cans make it your way, and if some tags pop up here and there, well, we're in a zombie situation here. I can't go cracking down on minor crimes like that."

Malcolm began to smile. "It's a deal."

"Take this radio and these binoculars." The binoculars hurt. They were Swarovski 42MM ELs, and had belonged to his mother, an avid birdwatcher. They were the single most expensive thing she'd owned, and she'd passed them on to her son, though Stevie Ray had only ever used them for the times he went bow-hunting for deer. They were beautiful optics, but they were the only binoculars he had, and if this kid dropped them… "Call in if you see anything. And don't fall down from up there, your mother would kill me." He paused. "And don't hurt those binoculars, or I'll kill *you*. They mean more to me than you do."

"Yeah, yeah," Malcolm said, and vanished around the side of the elevator.

Stevie Ray watched him scale up the ladder on the side, then returned to his truck. As he was driving away, he thought he heard something—a distant boom, with another boom immediately afterward—and stopped the truck, listening for a repeat of the sound, but there was nothing. He glanced at the elevator, and Malcolm was coming back *down* at speed. He ran over to the truck, waving his arms. "Chief!" he called. "Chief, something just exploded, out by the new Lutheran cemetery!"

"See, you're earning your spray paint already," Stevie Ray said, and put the truck in gear, and headed to the source of the explosion. What kind of job did he have where he had to race *toward* explosions? What had he been thinking signing up for this?

Stevie Ray was about halfway to the cemetery when he saw Julie and Dolph on the side of the road, walking—Dolph was almost limping—and they waved their arms at him furiously. "What are you doing out here?" he said, and they climbed into the car, Julie in front, Dolph in back, and Dolph started babbling until Julie said, "Stop, I'll tell him," and she did, in clipped, clear, precise language, everything—her dead grandfather, the trip to get the backhoe, the discovery of the theft, and Levitt's shenanigans at the graveyard, grenade and all.

"Well don't that beat all," Stevie Ray said wonderingly. "That man was a junkyard dog, but I thought he was a dog on a chain. I was wrong. I knew he was up to something—" he filled them in about Levitt's attack on Rufus—"but I didn't expect anything like this."

"The dead have been down in those graves like time bombs waiting to go off, but it just never occurred to me," Julie said, shaking her head in frustration. "Not until today at the meeting. If only we'd realized the danger posed by the graveyards, we could have taken steps, but…"

Stevie Ray shrugged. "If ifs and buts were candy and nuts… Sure, I wish we'd thought to post guards at the graveyards too, but if we'd covered that line of attack, Levitt would've done something else instead. Set the town on fire. Climbed the church steeple with a sniper rifle. His crazy just started boiling over, and it was gonna splash out somehow. What do you think his plans are now?"

"Get together as many zombies as possible and head toward town," Dolph said.

"I didn't pass him on the road, and he would've come this way if he was going to town," Stevie Ray said.

"Not if he planned to hit the other cemeteries first," Julie said, and Stevie Ray groaned. He reached for his car radio. "Rufus, pick up."

"Here boss," Rufus crackled.

"Levitt's on a backhoe, probably out on Cheetham Road, probably being trailed by forty or fifty zombies. Check the old Lutheran cemetery, and if he's not there, head on over to the Catholic cemetery."

"Uh… okay, boss," Rufus said. "But you know Mr. Levitt probably heard what you just said, right? I mean, he's got my radio."

"I do," Stevie Ray said. "And if you're listening, Mr. Levitt, you old son of a gun, you should know: we're coming for you."

After a moment of hissing silence, Mr. Levitt's voice spoke, first with that dry heh-heh-heh laugh of his: "Come along. I'm having a dinner party. You're the dinner." That was all.

Stevie Ray turned off the radio and turned to Julie. "So now that Mr. Levitt thinks we're going to the cemeteries to head him off, where do you think he's *actually* going to go instead?"

"The new elementary school," Dolph said. "He was school superintendent, once, so maybe… I don't know. But I think he might try to lead the zombies he already has to the school."

"Then let's make sure that doesn't work." Stevie Ray rubbed his eyes. "We'll have to do it ourselves. Because of the radio, we can't risk coordinating with Edsel or the Anti-Zombie guys, or Levitt will change his plans. So we'll go, evacuate the school, and set up an ambush."

"I believe I can help with the tactical planning," Julie said, and there was a light in her eyes that would have been kind of sexy if it wasn't also kind of scary.

11. THE OMEGA SCENARIO

Because Mr. Levitt had a police radio, Father Edsel didn't bother telling Stevie Ray or the Anti-Zombie fighters what he had in mind. Let them chase Levitt around cemeteries—where, if the old man had any sense, he wouldn't bother going at all—while Father Edsel, as usual, took care of things himself.

He was on his way to visit Cyrus Bell anyway, having heard the man was ill and wanting to check on him—mostly to make sure he didn't die and turn into a zombie, at least, not without a friend there to kill him—so he didn't even have to turn his car around when he heard the chatter on his radio. The Rustic Comfort Cabins were neat and trim as always, though the bait shop, usually an eternally-open institution, was closed. Nobody wanted to do any ice fishing when the dead fish would promptly come back to life and try to eat you, which was the same reason deer hunting and hog butchering had gone out of fashion, and why Mr. Torkelson's farm was rather more filled with hogs than it usually was after the winter slaughter season. Once the last of the frozen meat from Dolph's store was gone, this was going to be a town full of vegetarians, except for chickens, because birds didn't appear to get zombified, just mammals and fish and reptiles, for whatever reason, who knew why, God surely had his plans.

Edsel went to Cy's preferred cabin and pounded on the door. After a moment, Cy came to the door, bags under his eyes, sweat soaking his undershirt, and a putrid smell emerging from behind him. "Father," he said. "I'm sick. I think the CIA has poisoned me." He paused. "Or else that walleye jerky wasn't cured as good as I thought. Been dumping my insides out into the toilet and the garbage can all night."

"I heard about your illness," Edsel said. Normally he'd barge right in, assuming an invitation was implicit, but the cabin wasn't that inviting. "I came planning to see if you needed anything, I did, but circumstances have changed. Now I need something from you." He put a hand on Cy's shoulder—even though said shoulder was frankly kind of damp and sweaty—and said, "I need the remote, Cy."

Cy's eyes shone. "Is it... is it the Omega Scenario?"

Father Edsel, who had no idea what the Omega Scenario was, simply nodded gravely. "I'm afraid so."

"I can't believe it's come to this," Cy said. "I'll come with—" He paused, looked alarmed, and ran to the bathroom, where unspeakable sounds soon emerged. Edsel stood in the doorway, waiting as patiently as he could, though he knew the seventh seal was cracked, the end was near, and so on. There were things on this Earth you could hurry along, and things you couldn't, and a man in the throes of vomiting was one of the things you couldn't. Cy returned, shaking his head. "All right. I can't go. But let this be your fallback location if you can't stop the invasion. How are you going to lure the moon people to ground zero?"

"I have some ideas in mind," Edsel said. "Best I don't elaborate. Someone might be listening." He looked upward, and Cy nodded and held a finger to his lips.

"Let's go get the remote," he whispered, though his whisper was basically the volume of his ordinary speaking voice, only harsher-sounding. "You remember where the packages are placed? You don't want to be in the vicinity when they go, but you need to be within a few hundred yards for the signal to work.

"Of course," Edsel said, calmly enough, all things considered. He'd been quite alarmed when Cyrus had confided the secret of his explosives. The notion of large quantities of C-4 hidden in places often frequented by the people and children of the town was naturally pretty disturbing, and Cy's rambling rationale—if the Chinese invaded, or the townsfolk were transformed into pod people, or whatever, there would be a sort of self-destruct option of last resort—was hardly reassuring, since Cy was apt to assume anybody was Chinese, and as for pod people, well, the whole point with them was you couldn't tell them from everybody else. Cy had explained that plastic explosive was very stable, that you could shoot it with a gun or hit it with a hammer and it would remain utterly inert—you could even set it on fire, and it would just burn slow, like a piece of damp wood, and not explode. Cy was generally pretty reliable when it came to ordnance, at least, so Edsel took his word for it, and accepted that unless the detonators were triggered—remotely, using a device Cy had rigged himself—the explosives wouldn't go off.

Edsel had convinced Cy to put the remote in a lockbox that required two keys, one in Cy's possession, one in Edsel's, so that—Edsel explained—if one of them was Manchurian Candidated or taken over by pod people, they couldn't blow up half the town of their own accord. Cy had seen the sense in that. He led Edsel down to his bunker/armory, where they made a great ritual out of taking out their keys, slotting them into the twin keyholes together, turning them in tandem, and opening the box.

The remote didn't look like much, just a garage door opener that had undergone some impromptu open-compartment surgery, and it was held together mostly with lots of electrical tape. "Just turn it on and you'll see a red light, get within range, press the button, the light turns green, that means it's active, press it again, and kaboom," Cy said.

"You're a warrior for God," Edsel said, and clapped Cy on the back.

"After we stop the invasion, maybe we can smash the moon right out of the sky," Cy said.

"It's good to dream big," Edsel agreed.

Next, Father Edsel raced to Mr. Torkelson's farm and hammered on his screen door. Torkelson ambled out, wearing overalls, with manure on his boots. "See you, Father," he said.

"Springtime, huh? Uff da. Gonna have a lot of piglets here soon. Some guys might say you can't have too many pigs, but me, I'd have to think about it."

"I'd like to take some of those pigs off your hands, Mr. Torkelson," Edsel said.

"Oh yeah? Planning a barbecue then?"

"Something like that," the priest replied.

"They'll trample up the field," Torkelson said, backing the big truck up to the Larry "Old Hardhead" Munson Memorial Baseball Field, which was fenced off pretty good. "It's all muddy and snow melted in there anyway. Some folks might not like so many pigs as this running around on the baseball field."

"They'll like it fine," Edsel said, looking into the field. Four bases, and a pitcher's mound. And under all four bases and the mound were who knew how many pounds of explosives. Molded into blocks and buried. "We'll put some pigs in the bandshell, too," Edsel said. "And over by the statue of the Hypothetical Viking." There was a lot of explosives under those, too, Cy had assured him.

"Good way to get pig shit all over the bandshell, that," Torkelson said.

"That's just an unimportant side effect."

"It's your money," Torkelson said, and Edsel almost laughed. He was giving the man all the money in the church coffers for his pigs. As if money still mattered. Well, whatever made the farmer happy. Edsel suspected he was mostly happy to get rid of some of the pigs.

Stevie Ray came trotting over to the truck from the direction of the police station, with Julie and Dolph in tow. At least Eileen wasn't with them. "My fellow councilpersons!" Edsel boomed. "Mr. Torkelson is here to help us with our little zombie problem."

Stevie Ray just gaped at the horde of pigs streaming onto the community baseball field, and Dolph looked utterly confused, but Julie began to laugh, and slowly clapped her hands.

Mr. Levitt didn't have quite the merry band of zombies he'd

hoped for since he had to abandon his plan to dig up the other cemeteries, but that was okay. The great thing about zombies was, they were self-replicating. Out here on the outskirts of town, there were a few farmhouses, and because people were banding together to share resources and heating oil and just generally crowd together in sheeplike masses, those houses were packed with people, and every one was a beacon to his zombies. All Levitt had to do was lead his merry band of zombies within sight of a farmhouse, and the horde would peel off, bash in windows, and make short work of the occupants. It was a beautiful thing, even from the vantage point of a backhoe loader—the screaming, the breaking glass, the people trying to run away. There were escapees here and there, but who cared? Let word of Levitt's coming spread out before him. Once the zombies finished off a house and the new dead rose, they inevitably came back toward Levitt, following his lead, hoping to eat him, unable to understand that he was their benefactor. Ah, well. Why should zombies be any more grateful than the living?

After hitting three houses, the ranks of Levitt's zombie army had tripled, to well over a hundred shambling, bent-necked, bloody, undead Minnesotans. Enough to do serious damage at the elementary school and the bar and the diner, and once they got a decent foothold in town, they'd multiply exponentially, and that would be that. Maybe Levitt's brood would spread across the whole Earth and devour all the living.

The backhoe rumbled just fine across the frozen fields. Levitt was avoiding the roads, since the radio was full of squawkings from Rufus and the morons in his old coterie, the Anti-Zombie Etc. There was a silence on the part of Stevie Ray and Father Edsel, the only remotely formidable people with power, and he might have construed that as ominous, but he was leading a horde of zombies to the center of town; the only ominous thing around here was *him*.

If they'd made him mayor, he would have gotten to ride in the fourth of July parade. They'd turned on him, though, the ingrates, so he'd been forced to organize his *own* parade.

"Grand Marshal of the Zombies!" he shouted, and then

downtown was in view. The baseball field, the park, and then—
the school. The bar. The diner.

The buffet.

Daniel parked his car near the elementary school and put
his head down on the steering wheel and just let himself shake.
Lord, he prayed, *your poor servant can bear no more. So much
death. So much destruction. So many invitations to sin. Just,
please, can't you grant me a little peace?*

Daniel got out of the car and started walking, planning to
cut across the park and go to the police station so he could tell
Stevie Ray about the zombie bear, and the zombie mayor, and
all his other failures. But there was a strange noise and mill-
ing-about from the baseball field, and he walked over, and saw
hundreds of pigs snuffling and running and rooting around on
the diamond. The pastor leaned over the fence, looking in at
the pigs, trying to understand what was happening. Were they
transforming the park into an old-style town common? Letting
the pigs graze? Did pigs even graze? If so, what were they graz-
ing on a baseball field?

Seeing the pigs reminded him of his conversation with Edsel,
when Edsel had insisted that zombies were demons possessing
the bodies of the dead, as the demon Legion had taken over
the body of the pigs. Was this some plan of Edsel's? Was he, ha,
planning to do an exorcism, as he was rumored to have done at
his old parish in Texas? To drive the demons from the dead into
the bodies of these pigs, and then drive the pigs into the lake, as
the pigs infested by Legion had fled downward to the sea?

Could something like that actually *work*?

A mechanical rumble caught Daniel's attention, because it
was so out-of-the-ordinary, and he looked to see a backhoe
loader coming across the park. Was that Julie driving it? If so,
why was she here, and not digging a grave for her grandfather?
What was—

Then he saw the zombies. Scores of them, hordes of them, a
wall of them, shambling, dropping bits, wearing funeral finery
ground with mud, the relentless opening and closing and gnashing of their jaws audible even over the rumble of the backhoe,

and, what was that, someone shouting? Someone shouting "No! You're going the wrong way! Morons! Stupid dead morons!"

Daniel was frozen, watching the wall of the shambling dead approach, hemming him in from the back and both sides, and he vaulted the wall of the baseball field in a demonstration of athleticism he could never have repeated in the absence of such total fear-fuelled adrenal panic. Daniel ran through the pigs, kicking them out of his way, stumbling, making them squeal, trying to get to the bleachers, trying to get away, but when he looked back, the zombies were climbing over the wall, and then climbing over the *other* zombies who were climbing the wall, and attacking the pigs, and the squealing was unspeakable, and Daniel prayed, *Dear Lord, oh Lord, oh Jesus, take me away from all this.*

Stevie Ray wished for his binoculars, but he had to make do with the scope from his hunting rifle, which was like looking through a porthole onto a stormy sea. They were watching from what Edsel assured them was a safe distance, and they'd done their best to make sure there were no people anywhere near the park or the baseball field, and they'd moved the kids out of the elementary school, but Stevie Ray couldn't help feeling like things were too sloppy, too sudden—not that you necessarily got a lot of time to plan for a zombie invasion. He squinted through the scope. "Levitt's not going for it. He knows something's wrong. Oh heck, he's out of the tractor, he's running the other way, off toward the lake."

"I'll go after him," Julie said. "It's time he was finished."

"I'll go," Dolph said. "Please. Let me. I… need to do this. And Julie, you're needed to help clean up the cemeteries, you're better at organizing people, doing sweeps, all that stuff. But I've been a hunter. I can go after one guy."

"If you're sure," Julie said, but then the radio crackled, and Rufus said, "Guys, I've totally got this. I'm on that side of the lake right now, I thought he might loop around and try to sneak into town from this direction. I'll, uh, you know. Capture him."

"You need to kill him, Rufus," Stevie Ray said, not an ounce of doubt in his voice, or, surprisingly, in his heart. "He's too dangerous. He can't be left alive."

Silence, a crackle of static, then, "You got it, boss."

"I'm going to go anyway," Dolph said. "You know. Just in case."

"Probably for the best," Stevie Ray said. "Father, I think all the zombies are on the baseball field. I don't see any stragglers."

"Then let us call down the fires of heaven," Edsel said, and pushed the buttons on his little remote.

Stevie Ray wasn't thrilled to discover a lunatic had put explosives in the heart of his town, but he had to admit, in this particular instance, it sure came in handy.

The zombies, and the zombie pigs, were nearly upon Daniel when he saw the light. He thought it was heaven opening, the Lord himself sending a golden chariot of fire to bear Daniel to heaven. He went on believing that as the full explosive power of a great many pounds of C-4 was unleashed, vaporizing the dead nearest the bombs, and turning the remainder into smoking gobbets of flying flesh. Daniel's last thought was probably supposed to be "Blessed are the meek," but in the voice he heard inside his head it sounded more like, "Blessed are the meat," and what exactly his brain meant by that, who can say?

Daniel was right near second base. He pretty much became vapor. He would have been glad to know he didn't contribute overmuch to the mess.

"It actually smells kind of good," Stevie Ray said, or rather shouted, since he could barely hear anything over the ringing in his ears. The baseball field and bandshell had become pillars of fire, and now a few trees were burning, and chunks of meat were raining from the sky. Most of the chunks were pig—there'd been a lot of pigs, enough teeming living pigs to exert an unstoppable biotropic pull on the horde of zombies, enough to distract them from all other potential targets—but a not-insignificant portion of the chunks, Stevie Ray knew, were the remnants of the recently reanimated corpses of townspeople who'd been buried by their loved ones in the cemeteries of Lake Woebegotten. "Smells kind of like pulled pork barbecue." Stevie Ray turned his head and vomited. Then he wiped off his mouth, looked at Julie, and said, "Guess we should head over to the cemeteries and kill whatever zombies are left."

"Sure," Father Edsel said. "Leave the cleaning-up here to the man of God. Story of my life."

"I'm pretty sure you'll just call the nuns and tell them to deal with it," Stevie Ray said.

"It's like you read my mind," Father Edsel said.

12. SPRING ICE

As he ran through the forest in pursuit of his quarry, Rufus was thinking about the idea of the Zombie Master. You saw it a lot in zombie movies and video games and collectible card games and roleplaying games and even in books, because the fact was, as his Zombies as Metaphor professor had explained, zombies didn't make the most relatable sort of villain. Any story of man-versus-zombie was, really, a story of man-versus-nature, because zombies were mindless killers—they might as well be hurricanes or volcanoes for all the intentionality they had. Even in a story of man versus man-eating-tiger or man-eating-shark, you could anthropomorphize the animals, make them seem to have comprehensible emotions or motivations, but zombies—despite *being* almost human—were much harder to ascribe human motivations to. So you had the concept of a Zombie Master: a zombie who retained his ability to think and plan, and usually a zombie who could control other zombies—the kind of zombie who could give sadistic speeches and cackle like a supervillain and, generally, add that almost-human touch to a story, creating a villain you could really love to hate, in a way you couldn't love to hate an act of nature like a flash flood or a tornado or a cave-in.

Well, this was real life, and there weren't any Zombie Masters, unless you wanted to count Mr. Levitt, which is what Rufus had decided to do. Because Mr. Levitt was lacking some essential human qualities. Empathy. Sympathy. A conscience.

He just had urges, and he acted on them, however he might rationalize his behavior. He basically *was* a Zombie Master, an engine of need with a brain on top of it, and as if to prove the point, he'd actually led an army of zombies against the living. That was treachery. Collaboration. And Rufus had played enough WWII-era video games to know what you did with collaborators.

He'd spotted the old man running off toward the lake, covering ground pretty good, wearing a camouflage hunting jacket that would work well in the autumn but didn't help too much when there was still a fair bit of snow on the ground and the only green was the needles on the evergreens. Rufus went after him, pistol in hand, trying to be stealthy, hoping the old guy would get winded and pause for a rest and then, bam, Rufus would walk up on him and shoot him in the back of the head. Not very sporting, but if you gave Mr. Levitt a fair chance, the thing was, he'd *win*, and he didn't give a rip about fairness himself.

The trees got thicker as they neared the lake, and he lost sight of the old guy, and Rufus was feeling a little winded himself, so he paused by a tree and looked at the ground for footprints, and that was weird, because there *were* footprints in the patchy snow, but they just stopped at the base of that tree, so where—

A great weight slammed into Rufus's head, driving him to the ground. Rufus tried to roll over, but something was pressing on his back, bolts of pain ripping through him, and suddenly his back felt warm, then cold, and he thought he knew how a leaky pool toy must feel: all the air inside leaking out. But this wasn't air. He was pretty sure it was oh heck it was blood.

Mr. Levitt, who'd jumped out of the tree onto Rufus's back, leaned forward and whispered in his ear: "Don't worry. I won't let you come back as a zombie." He rolled Rufus over onto his back, and Rufus groped for his pistol, but it was somehow no longer in his hand. Mr. Levitt looked down at him with no more interest than Rufus would show an ant scurrying across a picnic table. "Don't fall asleep, now," Mr. Levitt said. "Open those eyes wide. That's my direct route to the brain."

Rufus's final thought as the point of Mr. Levitt's very long, very bloody hunting knife descended toward his eye was, *Game over.*

Mr. Levitt limped away from Rufus's corpse. Jumping out of the tree had certainly been nice and dramatic, but it hadn't done his body any good, and his knee in particular was twinging every tenth step or so in a way that worried him mightily. His plan to assault the town hadn't worked out, though he consoled himself that there was no way he could have prepared himself for *exploding pigs.* There just wasn't a contingency plan for something like that. He decided departure was the better part of valor. Now that the weather was getting warm and travel was less dangerous, he could hole up for a few days, get his strength back, and then escape town, steal a vehicle and see what was happening in St. Elmer or Anoka or someplace, maybe even get down to the cities and see how things were faring there, if some humanity was holding on or if it was pure zombie free-for-all. Lake Woebegotten had been his home for a long time, and it would've been satisfying to destroy it, but Levitt was not a sentimental fellow. He could turn his back and head for less hostile pastures without a backwards glance.

But first he needed a place to rest. The day's activities had taken a toll on him. There were a few fishing shacks around the lake, and Gunther Montcrief's at least would be uninhabited, and might even still have some supplies laid in. Levitt wasn't a hundred percent sure where Gunther's shack was, but the lake was there on his left, still iced over though it would begin breaking up soon, and if he just followed around the shoreline he was sure to find Gunther's place or some other.

The police radio he was still carrying crackled. "I just found Rufus's body," Dolph said. "Mr. Levitt, if you're listening, I'm coming for you, and you won't like it when I find you."

Morons. Wonderful morons. "Why, thank you for warning me," Mr. Levitt said. "Imagine what you could have done if you'd retained the element of surprise. Idiot."

Levitt knew his trail wouldn't be too hard to find—even when he avoided walking in snow, the patches of bare earth were soft and muddy and took footprints, too. So if he couldn't hide, he'd just have to prepare a little surprise for Dolph.

And, ah, right there, that was Gunther's shack, must be, all gray-weathered boards and a tin roof. Maybe there'd be something useful inside. Like chains, or rope.

Dolph had not been especially close to Rufus, but the boy had seemed about as nice as you could expect for a guy who had a tattoo of a spiderweb on his neck and looked like he might wear eyeliner if he thought he could get away with it. Seeing him bled out on the snow, all cut up, had turned Dolph's stomach, but it had also stiffened his resolve.

Of course, telling Levitt he was coming for him maybe hadn't been the smartest thing, but Dolph wasn't a man-hunter by training. He was just blundering along. He'd have to hope that blundering was good enough.

Dolph wasn't an exceptional tracker, either, that was more Stevie Ray's gig, but Stevie Ray and the rest of the town's forces were cleaning up stray zombies and securing the cemeteries, since even the ones Levitt hadn't dug up needed to be sanitized—eventually the zombies would claw their way out of the thawing ground even without help from a backhoe. Really, Levitt was just one guy, a small target, and he was Dolph's responsibility now. Fortunately the trail wasn't at all tricky to follow. Nobody had gone walking in the woods lately, so that one set of footprints leading away from Rufus's body was pretty obvious. Dolph didn't follow right on top of the footprints, ranging off to one side or the other of the track, trying to be quiet, holding his gun—one of Cyrus's ridiculous little machine guns that looked almost like a toy but most certainly wasn't—at the ready.

Then he saw the shack, looking like it was held together by duct tape and superglue. Mr. Levitt was probably in there, judging by the tracks that led right up to the door. Well, Dolph didn't need any heroics. He pointed the gun at about chest height and pulled the trigger, and though it made a noise like a sewing machine it bucked in his hand like a living thing, and stitched a swooping line across the side of the shack. Dolph held the gun with both hands, braced himself, and sprayed another shower of bullets into the shack, back and forth, up and down, trying to cover every possible corner and nook inside. There were no screams, but a headshot or heart shot wouldn't give you time to scream, right? Dolph went cautiously to the shack and pushed at the door with his foot. Having been shot half to pieces, the door didn't so much open as disintegrate when his foot touched it. Inside there was only darkness, but was that a mound of blankets or a body in the back—

Something flashed down past Dolph's eyes and then something tightened around his throat and he was jerked backwards off his feet, gun flying from his grip. He scrabbled at his throat and felt coarse rope. Somebody had lassoed him! He twisted and turned his head and there was Mr. Levitt holding the other end of the rope, whistling, and throwing one end of the rope in the air over a handy tree branch. "Never hung somebody before," he said conversationally. "It's good to expand your repertoire though." He hauled on the rope, and the pressure on Dolph's throat was unbearable. He struggled to his knees, then to his feet, gasping breaths in the brief moments when there was slack in the rope, trying to get the noose off over his head, but Levitt pulled relentlessly, and Dolph went up on tiptoes as the old guy grunted and strained. "Just need to get you an inch or two off the ground, and I can tie this end off and let you strangle," Levitt said. "Darn cheap rope has too much give in it, keeps stretching, should've known that drunk Montcrief wouldn't have any decent rope out here—"

Dolph thought the blood was being cut off to his brain, resulting in hallucinations, because an unlikely pair came out of the trees behind Mr. Levitt then: one of them was Eileen, but a zombified Eileen, not pretty at all, wearing a torn blouse and bloody skirt with gaping eyes.

And walking by her side, big as you please, was an obviously dead and equally bloody black bear.

Mr. Levitt must have heard them—which meant it wasn't a hallucination, and *that* was interesting, although, *Oh, Eileen, you were tough and kind of crazy but I cared about you once*—because he looked back and let go of the rope and stumbled away. Dolph collapsed to his knees, coughing and gasping and pulling the rope off over his head. Then he got to his feet, and ran as hard and as fast as he could away from the zombies and Mr. Levitt. Julie had explained the whole biotropic situation to him. All things being equal, the zombies could come after him *or* Mr. Levitt, they were both equally appealing, but zombies tended toward whatever target was closest, and Dolph wanted to make that choice obvious. He paused by a tree about fifty yards away and looked back to see if he'd managed to escape Eileen and her bear-friend's notice.

Mr. Levitt was running, too, straight away from them, in the direction of the lake, and Eileen and the bear were following him, not very fast—zombies were never very fast—but implacable. And Mr. Levitt wasn't going to break any land speed records himself. In fact, he was limping and favoring one leg and firing a pistol pretty much blindly behind him. Dolph didn't think much of the old murderer's chances. He leaned up against a tree to watch the show.

A bear. A *zombie bear*. How nice it would have been to lead *that* beast to the center of town! But having the bear come after *him* was less satisfying. Mr. Levitt was pleased to see that his mayoral rival Eileen had gotten herself killed at some point, but it was cold comfort when she wanted to eat him. If it was just Eileen he'd have stood his ground and taken aim and shot her in the head… but there was that *bear*. Bears had small heads in relation to the rest of their bulk, making it a trickier shot. Bears were just generally a lot tougher than people, and it seemed faster than human zombies, too. He aimed a few running shots at them, hoping to get lucky, but wasn't surprised when the gun went empty with his pursuers still on his heels.

The bear, frankly, worried him, but he had an idea. Get some distance between them, and then lob a grenade. Tough or not, the bear wouldn't survive *that*. At least he'd stumbled into some kind of clearing, the ground was snowy and slick with ice but there were no trees, and that made it easier to put on a burst of speed despite that twinge in his knee. The prospect of onrushing death did have a way of tapping into your body's hidden resources, he'd found. He looked back, and judged they were far enough away to risk his Hail Mary move.

He took the grenade from his pocket, pulled the pin, and tried to think of something nasty to say, but, heck, they were *zombies*, it wasn't like they'd appreciate his wit. So he just chucked the grenade at them and waited.

What a beautiful throw. Levitt had played a lot of baseball in his youth, and he still had the arm. The grenade actually bounced off the bear's back, Levitt saw it, and then—boom. A flash of white, a lot of smoke, and pieces of bear scattering far and wide. Pieces of Eileen, too, for that matter. "Yes!" Levitt shouted, actually jumping in the air in his excitement, though that wasn't such a good idea, because when he landed his knee twisted, and he went down pretty hard. The ground was uncommonly hard and cold here, and—

Oh, heck.

You're on the lake, idiot, that small treacherous part of his mind whispered. *You thought you were in a clearing, you were just running blind, you ran out on the ice, and it's thin ice, and you just threw a* grenade *onto that thin ice*—

The noise of ice on a lake breaking is unlike any other noise. It doesn't just crack, it squeaks, and sighs, and moans, and it was doing all of that now, a chorus of icy disinterested death. The remains of Eileen and the bear vanished as the ice gave way beneath them, black water splashing, and as black cracks raced through the ice toward him, Mr. Levitt tried to get to his feet and run, to make it to shore, but his knee was too bad off, and the ground gave way beneath him, and there was the water, as cold as his heart, as merciless as himself, as welcoming as only death can be.

Mr. Levitt sank into the freezing water, and he couldn't think of any good last words, not that there was anyone around to hear them anyway.

The voice in his head had a last word, though. That word was *Moron*.

Dolph watched Mr. Levitt fall into the ice, and radioed Stevie Ray to tell him what had happened—including the sudden appearance of Eileen and a bear—and what he planned to do. Stevie Ray told him to be careful, but that it sounded like a good plan. So Dolph picked through the ruins of the fish shack and found, miraculously unshattered, most of a bottle of bourbon, hidden so deep under the little pallet there that even the owner had probably not known of its continued existence. Dolph took a few bits of blanket, chose a spot on the shore of the lake where the ice was all broken up, and sat on the blankets, and sipped the bourbon, just a bit. He didn't want to get drunk. He just wanted to savor being alive.

After about an hour, the water rippled. A head emerged. Then a torso. It was a zombie, walking up out of the water, face nibbled by fish—maybe even zombie fish—skin blue from the cold. A familiar face, though, even blue and fish-gnawed. A hateful face. Mr. Levitt's face.

Dolph stood up, lifted his gun, took careful aim, and put a bullet right into the center of that face.

The twice-dead body fell back into the water and floated there.

Dolph took another sip of his bourbon, smiled at the world in general, and started the walk back to town.

EPILOGUE:
A PRETTY NICE NIGHT

After the town meeting that evening, Stevie Ray, Father Edsel, Julie, and Dolph sat in a booth in Cafe Lo sipping instant coffee by the light of a couple of camping lanterns.

"There's still a lot of work to do," Stevie Ray said. "We need to get lookouts up on the grain elevator night and day. We should probably build some barricades, maybe even a wall around downtown, if we can manage it. Maybe dig some trenches. It shouldn't be hard to keep zombies out, but now that the weather's changed, we might have to worry about other things—gangs of survivors, Road Warrior type stuff, you know?"

"They won't find us easy pickings," Edsel said. "We have Cyrus Bell's stash. Which, ah, you might want to seize. A man who plants explosives on the baseball field shouldn't have ready access to that kind of weaponry."

"*You* explain it to him, then," Stevie Ray said. "Convince him it's a good idea to keep the weapons at the police station. I'm sure not storming up there threatening to trample on his right to bear arms, even if they are illegal arms."

"I'll see what I can do," Edsel said.

"You going to stand for mayor, Julie?" Dolph asked.

"If the town will have me. But even if they don't, I'll help whoever they do elect. This is my home now. I went away, for a while, but this is the place I came back to, and I want to protect it. I don't feel like we've done too good a job so far. I want to do better."

"We're all just learning as we go," Stevie Ray said. "And today could have been a whole lot worse. We've got guards posted at the cemeteries, so there won't be any more surprises from that direction at least. Maybe we're past the worst of it. But even if we're not, at least we're preparing for the worst."

"I propose a toast," Father Edsel said. "Though toasting with coffee instead of wine is an abomination, it will have to do. To Lake Woebegotten."

"To Lake Woebegotten, the Green Zone of central Minnesota," Dolph said. "Where all the women are brave."

"Where all the men are pure of heart," Julie said.

"And where each child is more unique than the last," Stevie Ray said, clinking his coffee mug against the others.

Outside the diner, the Narrator stood on the sidewalk gazing up at the big moon overhead. He'd lost his other shoe somewhere, and his glasses sat askew on the bridge of his nose, giving him even more of an absent-minded-professor air than usual. A nasty bite mark on his left calf—from a raccoon, maybe, or even a pocket gopher—oozed fluids of various hues and consistencies. He said:

"Night fell on the first day of spring in Lake Woebegotten— not the first day by calendar time, but the first day that *felt* like spring, like a day for new beginnings and bold new enterprises and rebirth and renewal and no more long underwear for a while—and the people were peaceful and full of hope, at least, the ones that were still alive. Over on the outskirts of town—"

The Narrator coughed, a messy, wet cough that spilled down the front of his shirt. "Ah, must be allergies, those come right along with the flowers, it's the dark side of spring, everything's got a dark side—"

Another cough, and now the Narrator stumbled and went down on one knee, and his skin was looking a bit grayish, his eyes behind his off-kilter glasses getting a little glassy themselves. "The good people of Lake Woebegotten, they—ah—that is, they all knew—"

The Narrator turned his head, and looked through the windows of the diner, and saw the lantern light there, dimly. And glowing far more brightly than the lanterns, he saw the life of the people inside there, talking and laughing and clinking their mugs together like they were at a fancy cocktail party or some such, and he said, like he'd just discovered the word:

"Brains?"

And got to his feet and headed on inside Cafe Lo to get a bite to eat.

Night Shade Books Is an Independent Publisher of Quality SF, Fantasy and Horror

"*The Loving Dead* is really kind of hot, in a very creepy way. Read it. You know you'd love you some sweet zombie sumpin' sumpin'. Buy it, bitches! Ride this zombie Zeppelin of love like there's no tomorrow."

— **Christopher Moore**, author of *Lamb* and *A Dirty Job*

the loving deAd

ameliabeamer

ISBN: 978-1-59780-194-2, Trade Paperback; $14.95

Girls! Zombies! Zeppelins! If Chuck Palahniuk and Christopher Moore had a zombie love child, it would look like *The Loving Dead*.

Kate and Michael, twenty-something housemates working at the same Trader Joe's supermarket, are thoroughly screwed when people start turning into zombies at their house party in the Oakland hills. The zombie plague is a sexually transmitted disease, turning its victims into shambling, horny, voracious killers. Thrust into extremes by the unfolding tragedy, Kate and Michael are forced to confront the decisions they've made, and their fears of commitment, while trying to stay alive. Michael convinces Kate to meet him in the one place in the Bay Area that's likely to be safe and secure from the zombie hordes: Alcatraz. But can they stay human long enough?

Night Shade Books Is an Independent Publisher of Quality SF, Fantasy and Horror

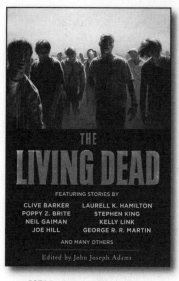

ISBN: 978-1-59780-143-0
Trade Paperback $15.95

Zombies have invaded popular culture, becoming the monsters that best express the fears and anxieties of the modern West. Zombies have been depicted as mind-controlled minions, the disintegrating dead, the ultimate lumpenproletariat, but in all cases, they reflect us, mere mortals afraid of death in a society on the verge of collapse.

Gathering together the best zombie literature of the last three decades from many of today's most renowned authors of fantasy, speculative fiction, and horror, including Stephen King, Harlan Ellison, George R. R. Martin, Clive Barker, Neil Gaiman, and Poppy Z. Brite, *The Living Dead* covers the broad spectrum of zombie fiction.

Two years ago, readers eagerly devoured *The Living Dead*. *Publishers Weekly* named it one of the Best Books of the Year, and BarnesAndNoble.com called it "The best zombie fiction collection ever." Now acclaimed editor John Joseph Adams is back with 43 more of the best, most chilling, most thrilling zombie stories anywhere, including virtuoso performances by zombie fiction legends Max Brooks (*World War Z, The Zombie Survival Guide*), Robert Kirkman (*The Walking Dead*), and David Wellington (*Monster Island*).

ISBN: 978-1-59780-190-4
Trade Paperback $15.99

The Living Dead 2 has more of what zombie fans hunger for — more scares, more action, more... brains.

Find these Night Shade titles and many others online at http://www.nightshadebooks.com or wherever books are sold.

Night Shade Books Is an Independent Publisher of Quality SF, Fantasy and Horror

Night Shade Books Is an Independent Publisher of Quality SF, Fantasy and Horror

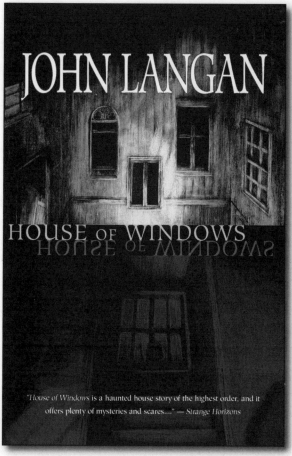

ISBN 978-1-59780-195-9, Trade Paperback; $14.95

When a young writer finds himself cornered by a beautiful widow in the waning hours of a late-night cocktail party, he seeks at first to escape, to return to his wife and infant son. But the tale she weaves, of her missing husband, a renowned English professor, and her lost stepson, a soldier killed on a battlefield on the other side of the world, and of phantasmal visions, a family curse, and a house... the Belvedere House, a striking mansion whose features suggest a face hidden just out of view, draws him in, capturing him.

What follows is a deeply psychological ghost story of memory and malediction, loss and remorse. From John Langan (*Mr. Gaunt and Other Uneasy Encounters*) comes *House of Windows*, a chilling novel in the tradition of Peter Straub, Joe Hill, and Laird Barron.

ABOUT THE AUTHOR

Harrison Geillor was born in a small three-room farm house in central MN, sometime in the middle of the twentieth century. He attended one of Minnesota's prestigious institutions of higher learning, were he obtained a degree in English. Like English majors everywhere, he went on to work in a variety of jobs that had nothing to do with books or literature. At some point in his life he decided that the best way to appreciate Minnesota was to appreciate it from afar. He splits his time between Santa Cruz and San Francisco, only returning to Minnesota for smelt fishing, and the occasional family reunion.